Tom Clancy's
Op-Center™

WAR
OF
EAGLES

Created by
Tom Clancy and Steve Pieczenik

written by
Jeff Rovin

PEN

PENGUIN BOOKS

Published by the Penguin Group
Penguin Books Ltd, 80 Strand, London WC2R 0RL, England
Penguin Group (USA) Inc., 375 Hudson Street, New York, New York 10014, USA
Penguin Group (Canada), 90 Eglinton Avenue East, Suite 700, Toronto,
Ontario, Canada M4P 3YZ (a division of Pearson Penguin Canada Inc.)
Penguin Ireland, 25 St Stephen's Green, Dublin 2, Ireland (a division of Penguin Books Ltd)
Penguin Group (Australia), 250 Camberwell Road, Camberwell, Victoria 3124,
Australia (a division of Pearson Australia Group Pty Ltd)
Penguin Books India Pvt Ltd, 11 Community Centre,
Panchsheel Park, New Delhi – 110 017, India
Penguin Group (NZ), cnr Airborne and Rosedale Roads, Albany,
Auckland 1310, New Zealand (a division of Pearson New Zealand Ltd)
Penguin Books (South Africa) (Pty) Ltd, 24 Sturdee Avenue,
Rosebank 2196, South Africa

Penguin Books Ltd, Registered Offices: 80 Strand, London WC2R 0RL, England

www.penguin.com

First published in the United States of America by The Berkley Publishing Group 2005
First published in Great Britain in Penguin Books 2005

2

OP-CENTER™ is a trademark of Jack Ryan Limited Partnership and S&R Literary, Inc

TOM CLANCY'S OP-CENTER: WAR OF EAGLES

This is a work of fiction. Names, characters, places, and incidents either are the product
of the author's imagination or are used fictitiously, and any resemblances to actual persons,
living or dead, business establishments, events or locales is entirely coincidental.

Printed in England by Clays Ltd, St Ives plc

Acknowledgments

We would like to acknowledge the valuable assistance of Martin H. Greenberg, Ph.D.; Larry Segriff; Denise Little; John Helfers; Brittiany Koren; Victoria Bundonis Rovin; Roberta Pieczenik, Ph.D.; Carl La Greca; and Tom Colgan, our editor. But most important, it is for you, our readers, to determine how successful our collective endeavor has been.

—Tom Clancy and Steve Pieczenik

ONE

Charleston, South Carolina
Monday, 4:57 A.M.

When Jesse Wheedles was a young man stationed at the Charleston Naval Base, he had a very precise and accurate job description. The Athens, Georgia, native was chief mess management specialist. He was proud of that position. Wheedles was more than just a cook, more than just a bagger who put together MREs—meals ready to eat—for consumption by sailors in transit. Wheedles was a craftsman. His job was to make certain that whatever their rating, whatever their taste, when someone sat down in his mess hall, he or she had the best soup, hottest entrée, and finest cookies and coffee in the United States Navy.

He had a paper napkin signed, "Amazing food!" by Undersecretary Sabrina Brighton proving just how well he had succeeded.

Wheedles wondered what life would have been like had he stayed with the navy. After his hitch, he took over the family restaurant, a roadside diner that was struggling to survive in the face of fast food and coffee bars. They hung on ten years, after which his dad sold the property to a developer, divided the profit among his three sons, and called it a day.

Wheedles lost his share of the $90,000 in an Internet start-up.

Now both the former mess chief and the naval base were doing something else. The base had been there for nearly ninety-five years, ever since President Theodore Roosevelt visited Charleston for its bicentennial celebration and decided that it would be a more suitable location for a naval facility than Beaufort. His decision didn't sit well with the citizens of that city, who sent a wreath and their condolences when the base finally closed.

Southerners forgave, but they did not forget.

The military presence here had a long and significant history. During the American Revolution it had been the site of a major British siege. The fall of Charleston resulted in the single greatest loss of troops for the American cause and had effectively left the Southern colonies in the hands of the Crown. The proud port had also been one of the lifelines of the Confederacy, dry dock for the submarine *H. L. Hunley*, and the home base for ironclad blockade runners.

Fort Sumter, the flash point of the Civil War, was located here. The martial history of Charleston, built and shaped by sinew and soul, was too important to end with the cold, blind judgment of a computer.

But so it had.

The facility had been shut down in 1996 as part of the Base Realignment and Closure Program. That was a day of great mourning for the city. There was concern at the time that the loss of the fleet and four thousand support jobs would kill the harbor and drag Charleston with it. But federal agencies and commercial enterprises sailed to the rescue, filling the base with tenants and barely causing a skipped beat in the economic pulse of the city.

The redevelopment project even saved the struggling

career of thirty-seven-year-old Jesse Wheedles. Thanks to his former navy CO who was on the harbor renewal advisory board, Wheedles got a job as the morning manager of Teddy R's, a new waterfront restaurant that catered to freighter and tanker crews arriving or departing on the early morning tide. It was a great position, because he got to do something he enjoyed and was good at, and he loved arriving before sunup to turn on the grill and get the deep fryer bubbling. He loved the feeling of literally firing up his day almost as much as he enjoyed the taste of the night sea air. Unlike the navy, where everyone had been groomed and uniformed in a kind of hive look and personality, the men who came to his restaurant were multicultural. They looked, spoke, and even smelled different. He welcomed the opportunity to experience a little bit of Bulgaria or Hong Kong, of Venezuela or Great Britain right on his doorstep. Wheedles was also delighted by the fact that when he left work at two in the afternoon there was still warm daylight to enjoy with his wife and young twins.

There was just one thing Wheedles had never anticipated: that one day a freighter might explode in the predawn blackness, destroying a significant section of the dock, Teddy R's, and ending his life.

TWO

Charleston, South Carolina
Monday, 5:01 A.M.

Charleston PD Harbor Patrol Sergeant Al Graff had the wheel of his small white patrol boat. His partner, Officer Randy Molina, was in the well. He was scanning the mouth of the Ashley River with night-vision goggles, watching for small vessels. Over the past few months drug dealers from the Caribbean had been making drops along the Southeastern seaboard, meeting local distributors who brought the narcotics to shore in rowboats. Graff and Molina had not had a piece of that action yet. They hoped they would. The snakes who piloted those boats were generally not good swimmers. Especially if one of the oars accidentally struck them on the head.

It was a warm morning with a soft westerly wind. The eight-year veteran was about to turn back toward the mainland when something exploded a half-mile behind them. Both men turned. The blast lit the historic waterfront rooftops and the ornate spire of Saint Phillips. The rolling cloud itself blew much higher, spawning a spray of yellow and magnesium-white tendrils. They tumbled to earth tracing hot, jagged paths in the sky as the smoke roamed outward, thinning and growing darker. Within moments the surface shock wave of the blast had reached the boat, causing ripples that heaved the small vessel violently from side to side.

While Molina simultaneously radioed the Coast Guard and the CPDHP dispatcher for assistance, Graff swung the patrol boat toward the rising crimson cloud. It was obvious that a freighter had exploded. Graff could see the outline of the hull against the flames. The vessel was spilling oil into the harbor, which fueled the fire. There wasn't a lot of it, since the ship had just arrived and not yet been refueled for the return trip, but there was enough to keep the area around it flaming.

A pair of CPDHP helicopters arrived within minutes to drop fire-retardant foam around the outside perimeter of the blaze to form a floating barricade that would keep it from reaching other ships. Big canvas hoses were rushed over by the harbormaster's dock crew to keep embers from igniting buildings or wooden structures on neighboring vessels.

It appeared that only two structures had been damaged on the waterfront: the Southern Bells music shop and Teddy R's. It looked to Graff like the restaurant had taken the bulk of the hit.

Trucks from the Charleston Fire Department, North Battalion, arrived just a few minutes later to help hose down the remaining structures and to mount an immediate search and rescue for survivors in the freighter or in the two burning buildings. The joint CPD/CFD antiterrorist task force was next on the scene, arriving moments after the main firefighting unit. While specialists from Fire Station 3 used their mobile hazmat lab to test for signs of radiological, bacteriological, or chemical agents, their CPD counterparts rushed to secure and search other vessels. The highway patrol blocked roads around the sector to keep perpetrators from escaping, while spotters directed patrolmen to buildings that had a direct line of sight with the afflicted vessel. If this was a rocket-propelled grenade, they might be in time to stop the attacker from leaving.

It was a slick, tightly coordinated operation that had been rehearsed numerous times. There were no rivalries, no competition between the departments. Everyone knew exactly what to do, and they did it with unflinching courage.

Graff and Molina had two jobs: to watch the coast to make sure this wasn't a distraction created by smugglers, and to search for anyone who may have survived the explosion.

A quick circuit of the blast perimeter did not produce any survivors. It did produce body parts, however, limbs with charred skin and remarkably clean, unblemished white bone bobbing on the choppy river. There were pieces of clothing that did not sink with the rest of the ship and tangled mats of hair and fresh blood. Graff was not equipped to retrieve the evidence, but he did photograph it, along with the target itself.

The pictures, taken with a sat-link digital camera, were automatically sent to the CHP and to the FBI field division in Columbia and to Bureau headquarters in Washington, D.C. There, the images would be compared to a database of shipyard attacks to look for similarities. The remains and clothing would be studied to try to isolate distinctive national, cultural, or obvious blast characteristics. If this were a deliberate event, laboratory examination would determine the nature of the explosive used. If they found a fragment of the container used to house the explosive, scientists might be able to locate and read skin cells shed by the individual who had placed it. That would not tell them his identity, but it would tell them his ethnicity.

Graff documented the scene unemotionally. He did not know who these people were or what they were doing on the vessel or dock. He did not know which of them had families. Since terrorism had become a daily possibility on every American calendar, Graff's default setting was to protect the harbor, the city, and the nation. He was emotionless about his work but passionate about his responsibility. He was also thinking back as he took pictures, running through the first two hours of his shift to make sure there was nothing he might have seen that did not seem suspicious at the time: a light on the water, an unusual sound from the hull of the freighter, movement somewhere along the dark wharf.

Molina informed him that the "scoop sloop" would be there within a quarter hour. That was the patrol boat with the nets and freezers required for evidence recovery. Graff acknowledged the update as he stood on the prow and continued to take pictures. He took each one twice, one through a night-vision lens and another with a flash. Comparing the two would help forensics experts construct a true-color image of the remains, something that would help them to pinpoint skin tone.

As they neared the hole in the vessel, Graff saw something that punched through the professional detachment. Something that put the nature of the vessel, if not the explosion, in context.

He saw a little bead bracelet floating on the choppy waters.

With a little girl's hand still attached.

THREE

Washington, D.C.
Monday, 7:33 A.M.

The call came as a surprise to Paul Hood. He was just sitting down with a cup of coffee and a power bar when his assistant put through Lorraine Sanders, chief of staff to President Dan Debenport. The forty-six-year-old director of Op-Center was being asked to breakfast in the Oval Office at the White House.

He ate the power bar anyway. The china at the White House was Jacksonian—old and delicate—and the less he used the happier he was.

This was obviously not a crisis. That was not something a new president discussed over bran muffins. Also, an official car usually arrived within moments of the call. It was also not a social visit, since those invitations typically came with more than ninety minutes' advance notice. It was certainly not a get-to-know-you meeting, because Hood knew Debenport well. The senator had been chairman of the Congressional Intelligence Oversight Committee, the group that controlled the budget of Op-Center. The fact that it was being held in the Oval Office indicated that it was to be a working breakfast. Moreover, the timing could hardly be coincidental. The White House knew what was happening this morning.

As an intelligence officer, Hood knew when he was in what analysts called "the twilight zone." He had enough information to stay engaged but not enough to tell him why or with what. Op-Center's FBI liaison once described it as working on a crossword puzzle where you have scattered answers but not enough connective tissue to help solve the damn thing.

Which is pretty much the state of American intelligence, Hood thought. Traditionally reactive, using the military fist to squash an enemy instead of surgical subterfuge to cut him out. Destroy the entire puzzle, and you don't need to worry about this one across or that one down.

Maybe it was just as well Hood did not know what was going on. He would find out soon enough and, besides, he was too exhausted to think. Hood was not just sleepy but sapped of energy, of imagination. It had been a long and difficult nine months since an electromagnetic pulse explosion had all but destroyed the National Crisis Management Center. Hood and his staff had not only been working around the clock to repair the facility and protect national interests, they had been looking for ways to streamline and economize, to reinvent Op-Center in the wake of severe budget cuts.

Hood also had a personal mission. He needed to find a way to fall in love with his job again. Op-Center was not just a place but the beating heart of American crisis management. Hood had been present for its birth, when the mission was uncorrupted and clear, and opportunity was boundless. He was also there for death and loss in Korea, Russia, Spain. It was odd. Triumphs, of which there were many, were short-lived. That was what professionals were supposed to achieve. Failures, of which there were fewer, hit harder. These included the deaths in the disbanded military unit Striker and the assassination of political liaison Martha Mackall.

It also included the painful budget-induced firing of Hood's number-two man, General Mike Rodgers, over a half year before.

Hood had done the best he could; he knew that. He had a shattered marriage to prove it. What he felt was that this place had somehow let him down. Like a child you love and raise and who falls short of what you expected or wanted or did not know you needed.

Hood had not seen the exhaustion coming. Rodgers had, though. Before he left, the general suggested Hood read about the British officers who had been hunting the German battleship *Bismarck* during the Second World War. Hood went on-line and found out why Rodgers had recommended it. In May 1941, when aerial reconnaissance informed the British commanders that the modern, fast, and very powerful vessel was in Grimstadfjord, Norway, they knew they could not afford to let it slip into the open sea. Despite the ultimate toll of hardware and manpower, the officers of the Royal Air Force Coastal Command and the Royal Navy threw every plane and ship they could muster at the *Bismarck*. They did not rest for the six days until it was sunk.

Those men knew the kinds of decisions, effort, loss, and attention that combined to flatten a man's spirit. Rodgers had seen it coming better than Hood had, the work it would take to resuscitate Op-Center. The effort required to inspire the people doing two or three jobs instead of one, learning new equipment, being unable to turn to associates who were no longer there. But then, Mike Rodgers had been in bloody battlefield combat. He understood sudden, often debilitating loss. Hood had only been in politics, the kind of combat where injuries could be repaired or ignored.

Scholarship had been Rodgers's way of putting the

world in perspective, and it was valuable to Hood during the years they had been together. Op-Center's intelligence chief Bob Herbert had a different way of seeing things. Herbert fired from the lip, which was hot-wired to the seat of his pants. Early in the rebuilding process, Herbert put Hood's life and labors in sharp perspective as only the candid, politically insensitive Mississippian could.

"You know what a bombshell can do," Herbert reminded him. "With just a look she can both fog your brain, clear your eyes, show you reality, and inspire a new one. But a bomb, Paul. That's pure destruction. It will break your spirit and body and will resonate through your soul. You'll hear the explosion and feel the shock wave every day for the rest of your life."

Like Rodgers, Herbert knew what an explosion could do. The former CIA field operative had lost his wife and the use of his legs in the Beirut embassy blast of 1983. But Herbert was right about the damage the bombshell could cause as well, and there was a reason he made the comparison. Several years before, Hood happened to meet his former fiancée, Nancy Jo Bosworth, in Germany. The great love of his life had turned Hood's head, literally, and when he looked back at his life, it was no longer the same, no longer comfortable or satisfying. It took a trauma—a United Nations hostage-taking involving his daughter Harleigh—and a few more years for his marriage to Sharon to end. Bitter though it was, at least there was time to adjust, to make the inevitable crash landing as gentle as possible.

The impact of the EMP was much different. It took everything from Op-Center in a flash. And the explosion didn't just necessitate the long and difficult rebuilding of Op-Center. The power of the electromagnetic disturbance showed Hood and his colleagues how vulnerable modern technology was to a lone gunman with the proper tools. They realized how important it was to get all of American security resources up to speed to protect the nation. That weakness made the rebuilding process seem even slower.

Now Op-Center's reconstruction was done, and however tired Hood felt, the real work was just beginning. Though he was eager to undertake it, he was also struggling to motivate himself for what was coming next, the Monday morning senior staff meeting. There was a curious and surprising conflict taking place in Hood's head. The NCMC had done some significant work over the years, but that was in reaction to events, not prevention. Running Op-Center was like bailing a rowboat. Success still left them deep in cold water with the sea pouring in.

Hood was unreasonably, inexplicably angry at Op-Center for that. Nothing like this had happened when he was mayor of Los Angeles. He got frustrated, yes, with the city bureaucracy but never enraged. But then, his staff in city hall were mostly career politicians more dedicated to themselves, to advancement and power, than to their responsibilities. The people of Op-Center were different. They had to be: they were ready to die for their work. It was as if their dedication, their sacrifice, had given this place sentience, a soul. A target for his frustration.

Op-Center was not supposed to get sick. The NCMC had been designed to be a constant in a world of changing dynamics and new challenges, with experts in every field and the technology to support their activities. Hood's people were devoted, and they were the best, but they required a support structure. They rallied after the explosion, but they were not able to do their jobs effectively for over half a year.

Not that Hood had discussed this with them. It was all rah-rah as technical genius Matt Stoll supervised the electronic recovery and upgrades. There were heavy doses of can do as they borrowed intel and data from other agencies so they could watch national and international hot spots. But through it all Hood was crying inside. Staff psychologist Liz Gordon probably would have told Hood that he was having a serious bout of transference, laying what he felt about his failed marriage onto Op-Center. Sharon Hood had let him down, too, in his mind. She had failed to support his dedication to his career, his responsibility to the staff and the nation.

Maybe it was true that Hood was shifting his feelings from one situation to the other. It did not change the fact that Op-Center had taken on water, and the man in charge was angry and disappointed.

To make matters worse, the bailing pail was smaller now. Fewer hands, less money. All Hood had wanted to do this morning was get the place on its feet and running. Instead, he finished his coffee, told his assistant Bugs Benet where he was going, and headed toward the elevator.

Benet rose inside his cubicle. "Do you know when you'll be returning?"

"I don't," Hood said. "Tell Ron to start the show without me."

"Yes, sir. Good luck."

"Thank you."

Op-Center was housed in a two-story building at Andrews Air Force Base. During the Cold War, this nondescript, ivory-colored structure was a staging area for flight crews known as NuRRDs—nuclear rapid-response divisions. In the event of a nuclear attack on the nation's capital, the job of the NuRRDs would have been to evacuate key officials to secret bunkers built deep in Maryland's Blue Ridge Mountains. With the fall of the Soviet Union and the downsizing of the Air Force's NuRRDs, evacuation operations were consolidated at Langley Air Force Base in Virginia. The building at Andrews was given over to the newly chartered National Crisis Management Center.

The two floors of upstairs offices were for nonclassified operations such as finance, human resources, and monitoring the mainstream news services for possible hot buttons, seemingly innocent events that might trigger crises. These included the failure of Third World governments to pay their troops, accidents such as a submarine ramming a foreign fishing vessel or yacht—which might not be just a fishing vessel or pleasure cruise, but a spy ship—the seizure of large caches of drugs that could harm the black economy of local provinces, and other potential domino-effect activities.

The basement of the former NuRRD building had been entirely refurbished. It no longer housed living quarters for flight crews. It was where the tactical decisions and intelligence crunching of Op-Center took place. This executive level was accessible by a single elevator that was guarded on top twenty-four/seven.

Hood acknowledged the guard with a nod. The red-cheeked kids were rotated every week to keep any of them from being tempted by foreign agents looking for access. Ironically, it was an individual with seemingly perfectly legitimate credentials who had been able to deliver the EMP bomb. In an era when a smart teen with a computer could shut down power grids, phone systems, banks, and military installations, passwords and swipe cards seemed quaint relics of a very distant time.

Hood stepped into the parking lot. The day was warming quickly. It helped to invigorate him. Hood knew it was partly a radiant effect of all the asphalt on the base, but he let himself think it was the sun. And it was a glorious spring morning, one in which the scent of the flowers that lined the security fence was actually stronger than the smell of the jet fuel coming from the airstrips.

Hood hoped the day stayed warm and welcoming.

In Washington, the weather had a way of changing unexpectedly.

FOUR

Alexandria, Virginia
Monday, 8:11 A.M.

Morgan Carrie always regarded her career as a classic good news–bad news situation.

One year before, at the age of fifty-three, Carrie was the first woman to earn the rank of three-star general in the United States military. It was a low-key promotion. The army wished to promote a woman without calling attention to it. As her husband, Georgetown University Hospital neurosurgeon Dr. T. H. Albert Carrie, put it, "They wanted to break the glass ceiling without the sound of shattering glass." That was all right with the woman. Since she was a kid playing war games with her four older brothers—she was usually the nurse, only occasionally the French Resistance fighter Mademoiselle Marie—she wanted to be the officer she had become. She outranked two of her brothers, both of whom were in the Navy.

At the same time, the career intelligence officer was passed over to head the National Security Agency in the new president's administration. Carrie had spent most of her career in Army General Staff, familiarly G2, the last five years as its head. Her office was concerned with all aspects of intelligence gathering, counterintelligence, and security operations. On paper she was more qualified than the man who got the job to oversee the organization that coordinates and executes the activities that protect American information systems and sources and generates foreign intel. But General Ted Dreiser was Air Force, and the new vice president, Bruce Perry, was former Air Force.

End of story.

Or so General Carrie had thought.

At eight P.M. the night before, the woman had received a call in her home in Alexandria, Virginia. She was being summoned to the White House for a short meeting with the president, the vice president, and Chairman of the Joint Chiefs Raleigh Carew. All she was told was that the president had a question for her.

A student of the history of American intelligence, Carrie knew that presidents rarely asked idle questions. At the very least, every query they made caused a snap-to ripple down the appropriate chain of command, just in case he decided to follow through. Sometimes, seemingly simple questions caused more dramatic responses. In 1885, President Grover Cleveland summoned Adjutant General R. C. Drum to the Executive Mansion to ask him a question about a foreign military installation. The officer was mortified to admit that he did not possess the information the president required, though he promised to get it. Drum did so and immediately organized the Military Information Division, which quickly grew from a single officer and four clerks to fifty-two officers, twelve clerks, and sixteen attachés. The MID collected data on geography and foreign armies and gave spying instructions to the attachés. The material the MID collected on military assets in Cuba, Mexico, and Samoa saved countless American lives during the Spanish-American War of 1898.

Carrie's driver took her to the West Wing, where she met with the three men for a total of ten minutes. There was, as promised, just one question. The president gave her until this morning to answer it. The question was a little larger than she had anticipated, but General Carrie took some comfort from the fact that she had five hours more to answer it than Adjutant General Drum had.

General Carrie was up before her husband, who was himself an early riser. That was when the doctor usually read his medical journals, from about five A.M. to six-thirty. The sixty-year-old Johns Hopkins graduate believed that a doctor was like a general: having a lot of degrees, like having a lot of soldiers, wasn't what made you effective. The trick was having the right ones, the best ones. Dr. Carrie was always on the lookout for those.

As requested, the general had responded to the president, in writing, by seven A.M. The letter was faxed to the White House and to the Pentagon. Original copies would be hand-delivered later in the day. For now, President Debenport had the answer he wanted. And General Carrie had a little more history in her dossier.

At seven-fifteen, Carrie received a call from the vice president's chief of staff. A new driver, a civilian driver, would be coming to get her at seven forty-five. He would be carrying instructions in a sealed envelope. She would have two days to get her footing before meeting again with the president.

It was all very quick and definitely very gratifying. And through it all, as ever, her husband of thirty-eight years held her sure and steady, as he held a scalpel.

A nondescript navy blue sedan pulled into the driveway at exactly seven forty-five. The tall, lean neurosurgeon had delayed going to the hospital to hug his wife before she left. The woman, five foot seven and jogging-slender, pressed her head to his chest. He put a big hand around her short-cropped white hair. Morgan Carrie had earned a bronze star for her work with the 312th Evac unit in Chu Lai, Vietnam—where she met her husband—and later ran special intelligence ops behind enemy lines in the Persian Gulf. Yet when her husband held Carrie like this, she felt like an alabaster doll, fragile and fair, and not a commander of fighting men and women. Which was fine. When her husband sat on the sofa with her and watched Italian operas on DVD, he was not a confident surgeon but a teary schoolboy with trembling hands. Forget sex: this comfort level was really what marital intimacy was about.

The doctor gave his general a parting kiss on the forehead and wished her well. She grabbed her leather briefcase from its spot beside the door. There was nothing in it but pens and a notepad and the originals of her letter. She knew it would not be so empty when she came home. The general stepped into the bright morning. The driver was standing beside the car and opened the door. He introduced himself as Angel Jimenez and told her there was an iced tea in the cup holder in the backseat.

"How did you know that is my drink, Angel?" the general asked.

"I sent the question up the ladder until someone knew the answer," the young man replied.

"And that person was?" she asked.

"Actually, General, no one knew. They called your military driver."

"I see." She smiled. "Well done."

"Thank you, General," Angel replied.

General Carrie slid into the unfamiliar car.

"There is a folder on the seat for you," the driver said.

"I see it. Thank you."

The general picked it up. She tore the red paper seal with an index finger. After years of riding in a Cutlass, the Saturn seemed small. Certainly the leather seat needed breaking in. But she did recognize the heavy-bottomed ride as the result of armor plating and the thick windows as bulletproof. She did not know if she were more or less a target than before, but she understood that the precaution was necessary.

General Carrie looked at the folder. The outside said Eyes Only. Inside were sealed manila envelopes. Each contained a concise dossier on the personnel of her new command. She flipped through them, looking for familiar names. As expected, there were only two: Bob Herbert and Stephen Viens. She knew Bob and his late wife Yvonne from the Middle East, and Viens from his years with the National Reconnaissance Office. Both were solid professionals, though she had heard that Herbert was more of a loose cannon than ever.

No matter. President Debenport wanted her to reconfigure Op-Center, to run a tighter command. Either Herbert would fall in, or he would be replaced.

Carrie started scanning the files to familiarize herself with the personnel she would be meeting today. Former political liaison, now deputy director Ron Plummer. FBI liaison Darrell McCaskey. Director of Tech Operations Matt Stoll. Psychologist Liz Gordon. The evaluations written by Paul Hood and his former number two Mike Rodgers suggested that they were all rather individualistic, what the army called rogues.

Hood seemed to like and encourage that. Rodgers did not. Carrie sided with Rodgers.

It would be a challenge to bring them around, but that was what Carrie had been waiting for her entire career. She did not intend to blow it. Besides, the general was representing more than just women in her new position. She was also a standard-bearer for the military. It was flattering, it was terrifying, and it was invigorating, all at once. And the only way she would get through this was to remember something her dad, a newspaper editor in Pittsburgh, had told her when she went off to enlist. He knew her better than anyone when he said, "The job is not about you or having something to prove, honeypot. It's about serving your nation."

She began reading the dossiers in greater detail as the car merged smoothly onto the Capital Beltway.

FIVE

Washington, D.C.
Monday, 8:29 A.M.

There was an unusual calm in the West Wing as Hood arrived.

The offices and corridors were never as busy as they were fictionalized on TV, people dashing here and there with purpose bordering on panic. But there seemed to be a bubble around Hood as he made his way through the security checkpoint and was greeted by the president's assistant executive secretary. Eyes would come near him and then slide away, like sand off a beach ball.

Maybe it was his imagination. Or paranoia. In D.C., those were not hindrances; they were tools.

Hood was taken directly to the Oval Office, where Chief of Staff Lorraine Sanders was leaning over the desk, talking with the president. Debenport waved Hood in, and Sanders disappeared into an adjoining office. When she returned, she was followed by a man in a white jacket. He was wheeling a two-tiered brass cart into the room. The wheels squeaked loudly.

The president rose and offered Hood his hand. Debenport was a slope-shouldered man of average build. He had thinning straw-colored hair and a quick smile. He looked like a country pastor. His centrist views and unflappable nature made him a dramatic contrast to his predecessor, who was tall and dynamic—and had come close to a psychological breakdown from which Op-Center had rescued him. Hood and the NCMC had also been instrumental in helping Debenport get elected, fighting off a threat from corrupt third-party candidate Donald Orr. That battle had earned Op-Center the deadly EMP attack.

"It belonged to FDR," the president said, nodding his chin at the cart. "I'm told the president wouldn't let his staff oil the wheels. They made his own wheelchair seem quieter, more presidential."

Hood believed it. On such details were image and power built.

"Sit," the president said, gesturing toward a red leather armchair.

Hood did so. The president waited until Sanders sat before he did. With any other president that would have been a power move. The equation was, "The taller the figure, the greater his authority." With the former South Carolina senator, it was simply good manners.

The president asked Hood about his children as coffee was poured and the tray of pastries was uncovered. More politeness, Hood suspected. Until the server was gone, they could not discuss national security matters. Hood told him that Harleigh and her younger brother Alexander were doing well.

"I can't believe it's been over two years since the United Nations siege," Sanders remarked. She was a lean five-footer with a frowning and intense look. "I was deputy director of the State Department's New York office at the time. We were working with the FBI to put a SWAT scuba team into the East River when you and General Rodgers ended the siege."

"Mike was really the one who ended it," Hood said. "I was just trying to get my daughter out."

Hood's voice choked as he spoke. He and Rodgers had been through a lot. He owed the general a lot. The men had not spoken for six months, ever since the general had become the head of the military-industrial firm Unexus, an international cooperative formed by Australian, British, Russian, and American interests.

The server left, and the door to the other room was shut. The president took a sip of tea and leaned forward.

"Paul, I asked you here because I need a favor," Debenport said. "I need you to take on a project for me."

The president had a talent for personalizing things. That made it difficult to refuse a task without insulting him.

"Mr. President, do you need Paul Hood or Op-Center?" Hood asked.

"I need you, Paul!" Debenport replied. His exuberant tone was the equivalent of a slap on the back. "I would like you to become special envoy to the president. The position entails international intelligence troubleshooting, unaffiliated with any group but with access to the resources of all of them. Your office would be down the hall from this one, and you would report directly to me through Ms. Sanders, not through the executive secretary."

Hood thought the last six months had been a lot to process. This was complete information overload. Hood found himself with a lemon pastry in his hand. He did not remember reaching for it.

"Mr. President, I'm flattered," was all Hood could think to say.

"Then you're on board?" the president pressed.

"I'd like to think a bit, sir. This would be a big change."

"I need someone *now*, Paul," the president told him. "Someone I can rely on. I want it to be you."

"What about Op-Center, sir?"

"No longer your concern," the president replied bluntly.

"Excuse me, sir?"

"I have given the post to General Morgan Carrie, formerly of G2," the president said, leaning forward. "Her commission is effective immediately." Debenport spoke now with some of the steel Hood remembered from his days as chairman of the CIOC. The pastor was gone, replaced by a higher authority.

"You're saying, Mr. President, that either I accept reassignment, or I'm fired," Hood said.

"Not at all, Paul," the president told him. "You can resign, effective as of eight-thirty A.M. this morning. You can say it was always part of your plan to get Op-Center on its feet and move on."

"At the risk of belaboring something you want to see over and done, sir, are you saying you need me here, or are you saying you need me *out* of Op-Center?" Hood asked.

"Both. Paul, the military is not happy with some of the budget initiatives this administration is taking. I have to equal the ledger."

"By giving them Op-Center?"

"In a word, yes." The president leaned back. "You're not a neophyte, Paul. You know that this is how things work. As for the new position, that's *my* way of maintaining balance. I need someone who will continue to interact with Op-Center on a personal level and who will form close relationships with personnel at other intelligence agencies here and abroad."

"You are saying, sir, that you want a personal intelligence officer."

"Cabinet level without the title," the president said. "And don't look so glum, Paul. That's a promotion."

"I understand, sir. Doesn't that interfere with the NSA and their mission?" Hood asked.

"You've met General Carew," the president said. He looked at Sanders. "How did the vice president describe him?"

"He said the general has brass ballistics," she replied.

"That's right," the president said. "And Vice President Perry ought to know. They served together in Vietnam. The point is, whatever Carew knows, the DoD will know."

"That doesn't answer my question, sir," Hood said. "How will General Carew take my being here?"

"He will like it about as much as General Rodgers liked serving under a civilian," the president replied. "But he will have to live with that. Your only contact with the general will be when you require information from the NSA. You will not be at their disposal."

"I see. What about staff, sir?"

"We have budgeted two assistants, both off premises," Lorraine Sanders replied. "We felt it best to have your telephones and computers located in a less trafficked area. We have assigned them space in the renovated basement of the Winder Building at 600 Seventeenth Street."

"The U.S. trade rep has offices there," Hood said.

"Correct."

"But the basement," Hood said. "Isn't that also where they held prisoners during the Civil War?"

"As I said, it's been renovated," Sanders replied.

"Right." Hood had gone from one basement to another. "Have you already hired the staff?"

"No," Sanders replied. She smiled. "We want you to be comfortable with your associates."

"This office will not be looking over your shoulder," President Debenport assured him. "What do you say? I need my own intelligence resource, my own confidant. I need Paul Hood."

Damn him, Hood thought. *Damn the president for making something expedient sound desirable.* And damn him for leaving Hood unemployed if he declined the offer. He had alimony and child support. Hood would not let indignation over the process affect his responsibilities.

"I accept the post," Hood told him.

"Thank you," the president replied, rising.

Debenport sounded sincere, which was something. It made Hood feel marginally better about having been shanghaied. Besides, the president was right. This was Washington, and Hood would have been lucky to make a lateral move, let alone enjoy an upkick in a new administration.

It still had not really hit him that he would not be returning to Op-Center, that the responsibility of running it—and the privilege—had been taken from his shoulders. Unlike the ending of his marriage, there was no sense of relief to counterbalance the sudden, encroaching emptiness.

Hood forced himself not to dwell on that. He had just accepted a new job. That was where his attention must go.

Hood and the chief of staff rose. Sanders told the new special envoy that she would show him to his office and come back around three, after she had arranged for help to organize and equip the Winder Building space. He thanked her while the president was still within earshot. Hood may have come from Los Angeles, but he had good manners as well.

As they walked down the corridor, the sense of avoidance Hood had felt earlier was gone. It had been replaced by a sense of courteous attention. Maybe it was all in his imagination, or maybe it was something palpable in his walk or his carriage, a stalwart if unconscious evidence of his new access to power.

Whatever it was, Hood resolved to ignore it. Yesterday he was the director of Op-Center. Today he was a special envoy to the president.

Tomorrow he could be indicted over a cheese Danish.

As they neared the area where the vice president had his small office, Hood felt one of his two cell phones vibrate. It was the one on his right hip, the secure STU-III unit he carried for Op-Center business. He slipped it from the loop on his belt and checked the number.

Hood replaced the phone without taking the call. He felt guilty about that, but it was the right thing to do.

Whatever Bob Herbert had to say would probably be better spoken—and heard—when it had cooled.

SIX

Durban, South Africa
Monday, 3:10 P.M.

The Gold Coast of Africa is no longer the gold coast of Africa.

The honor of being one of the richest, most profitable, and fastest-growing regions on the continent has passed from western Africa along the Gulf of Guinea to the eastern coast of South Africa, with the city of Durban as the anchor. Because of the subtropical climate, with high temperatures and significant amounts of rainfall, the area has always been a perfect environment for growing. Beginning in the middle 1850s, thirty years after the British first established a major port there, significant sections of arable land were earmarked for sugarcane. The crop was easy to cultivate and export, much in demand, and produced significant profits.

Over a century and a half later, sugar continues to play a prominent part in South Africa's agriculture, with Durban as the biggest sugar port in the world. Tourism has grown as well, with miles of beachfront having been developed into one of the most popular and celebrated vacation spots in the world. Along the Golden Mile, where summer lasts all year, the beautiful beaches are protected by shark nets, there are swimming pools with water slides, and there is an array of markets and merry-go-rounds, shopping centers, and world-class restaurants, nightclubs, and five-star hotels, all a few steps from the ocean.

Ever since the late nineteenth century, when a railroad was built to give inland regions access to the port, workers from the rest of the continent and from as far as India have come to work in the fields. Investors from other nations have come as well, creating an international mix unparalleled in most of Africa. Some of those individuals used the port and its resources to smuggle goods and receive cash. Men like the infamous drug lord Yakuba Balwon moved heroin through Durban, then laundered the money through the London-based Windsor Global Securities Bank. Others sold Rophy tablets, which was short for Rohypnol, an addictive relaxant that was most popularly used as a date rape drug.

Because of Durban's multinational nature, and because it has been an economic lifeline to blacks and whites alike, the city has been spared much of the violent racial tension that devastated other regions. None of the local workers, black or white, lived as comfortably as the plantation owners, investors, or tourists, but there is always money in everyone's pocket, and the end of apartheid, when it came, was peaceable. The only noticeable difference is the number of British and Afrikaner businessmen who are selling their interests in the port and portside concerns to financiers from India, Germany, France, and China.

Something that has not changed over the years are the sugar silos. Stuffed with raw brown sugar, they stand side by side in clusters across the landscape. Once made of brick and stone, the fifty-meter-tall towers are now constructed of aluminum and steel with a ceramic veneer to help control the temperature. They are connected at the top by enclosed bridges, which allow workers to move from one to the other with stampers, jackhammer-like devices with round bottoms that are used to compress the contents. The silos are rated by tonnage, not volume. Even if they are full, there is usually room for more sugar.

The air smells sweet around the structures, like cotton candy. Despite the presence of inner and outer doors, large, rough granules spill from hatches and cover the ground and the raised walkways. Like ants, the sugar is nothing by itself. En masse, however, the power of these twenty-five-ton mountains is immense. The silos are akin to the revered seven pillars of wisdom of many local faiths. South Africans regard the towers as the sentries of prosperity. They ensure economic security for this area, its investors, and its workers.

The largest of the sugarcane repositories are located along the Maydon Wharf. The workers here, mostly from Kenya and Nigeria, have unusually strong legs, the result of having to forcibly lift their feet hard when they move along the sticky walkways. They work in ten-hour shifts, with a half hour for a brown-bag lunch and two other fifteen-minute breaks. Their job is to see that the raw sugar stems move from truck or train to processing plant to silo to freighter in a timely and efficient manner with as little spillage as possible.

Twenty-two-year-old native of Durban Moshood Azwe was not concerned about losing a little "sweet gold" here and there. The silos attracted flies, and the loose grains kept the insects low to the ground, away from his face. That made him a more efficient worker as he directed trucks to the elevators that carried the sugar to the tops of the silos. These dump trucks backed up to funnels, which had filters to catch cane or other debris the processing plant had missed.

There were few deliveries at this hour. Most were made

in the morning, before the heat and dampness could affect the unsiloed sugar. Azwe was beginning to think about going to the João Tavern with his buddies when a dump truck arrived. It did not have a familiar logo from the de Gama Company or KwaZulu-Natal Shipping Associates, the firms that usually transported sugar to the silos. There was a loosely fitted tarpaulin stretched across the top of the truck to keep the sun off the cane. It would not be necessary to remove it. The flap in back would simply ride up on the sugar as it was dumped into the bin below.

Azwe was standing on the ramp that circled three-quarters of concrete bay three. It was located beside the centermost of the six silos in this section. As the truck backed in, Azwe held up his big hands so the driver could see. He was not supposed to allow anything to be off-loaded without first checking the bill of lading. The young man jogged over to the driver and jumped from the ramp to the driveway. He did not put his hand on the ramp lest the oil in his skin pick up sugar. The glaze was like glue, extremely difficult to wash away.

Azwe was a tall man. He put a hand on the side view mirror and dipped his head into the open window.

"May I see your documents?" he said. His voice had a clucking quality that was native to the region centuries before the arrival of the Europeans.

The driver, a young man who looked Madagascan, turned to another man who was sitting in the passenger's seat. The second man handed the driver a clipboard. He gave it to Azwe.

"Thank you," Azwe said as he looked at the document. He frowned deeply as he flipped through sheet after sheet. They were pages torn from the South African edition of *Time* magazine. "What is this?" Azwe demanded as he looked back into the cab of the truck.

The young Durban did not have time to react before a silenced Beretta that had been concealed beneath the clipboard put a raw, red hole in his forehead. He gasped softly as he dropped to the ground between the front wheel of the truck and the side of the bay. He was twitching at the wrists and hips as blood spat from the wound in the front of his skull. Azwe's eyes were open, blinking incongruously as red drops fell on them. After a few moments, they shut.

The man in the driver's seat jumped out. He stepped over the oddly angled body of the bay foreman and hurried to the back of the truck. The passenger also got out. He went to the elevator control box, which hung from a thick cable at the rear of the bay. As he pressed the blue button that opened the elevator door, the driver went to the back of the dump truck. He reached under the flap and removed a cooler. He popped the lid. The plastic container was packed with C-4. He pulled a detonator from his jacket pocket, set it for four minutes, and jabbed it into one of the explosive bricks. Then he took the open cooler and put it on the elevator as it rose from the floor.

He and the other man quickly removed four other coolers from the back and opened them. They contained a half-dozen bricks of C-4 each. He set the timers to blow five seconds after the initial blast.

When the explosives had been off-loaded, the elevator was sent back into the silo. It would travel under the ramp, then up an external chute before being dumped into the top of the silo.

The two men hurried back to the truck. They had watched the silos for several days from a motorboat and from the nearby Victoria Street Indian Market. The entire process would take three minutes. That would give them enough time to get away. When the blast occurred, it would not just impact the silos, it would destroy the security cameras and the shack where the videotapes were recorded. Nothing would be left to attach them to this action. All investigators would find was the abandoned truck, the

Beretta with its serial numbers filed off, and a torn copy of *Time* magazine.

One hundred seconds after the truck drove from the bay, the men were outside the chain-link fence that surrounded the silos. Moments after that, the C-4 exploded. The blast blew out the top of the silo as if it were a party favor. Steel and ceramic tile were flung outward, along with huge pieces of fused sugar. The jagged sheets caught the late afternoon sunlight and flung it in all directions—up, down, and around. The explosion sent the other coolers tumbling along the covered bridges on either side. They detonated as they reached the other silos, blasting out the sides and driving chunks of debris into the silos that were facing them along the northern side. Multiple booms echoed through the harbor. They were joined by sharp cracks as massive pieces of shrapnel ripped into the second row of towers, ripping off the tops and sending them into the water as powdery rain. Cracks appeared in the sides of all six silos, some hairline, some like vast geologic fissures. The three most heavily damaged silos on the south surrendered first, dumping sugar and pieces of themselves onto the ground and against the adjoining structures. The impact caused the smaller fractures in the northern towers to expand, bringing them down within seconds.

In less than a minute, the familiar Maydon Wharf landmarks were six distinct mounds of rubble beneath a cloud of smoke that smelled like roasting marshmallows. Though there were only a few small fires in the wreckage, firefighters rushed to the site to search for survivors. The KwaZulu-Natal Metro Police also arrived to search for clues. The silos were not heavily protected locations, because no one benefited from their destruction.

Until now.

SEVEN

Washington, D.C.
Monday, 9:11 A.M.

Nothing ticked off a career intelligence officer more than not having intelligence. And right now, Op-Center's intelligence director was extremely ticked off.

The people who glided past Bob Herbert's open office door would not have known anything was wrong with the forty-eight-year-old officer. Their quick, questioning glances and hushed conversation suggested they knew there was something amiss at Op-Center, though no one knew exactly what that was. They may have heard rumors from Bugs Benet or seen the new arrival when she strode through the hall. But no one knew what it meant.

Including Herbert.

The intelligence chief sat quietly behind his desk in his new, state-of-the-art wheelchair. His expression was neutral. He appeared to be a man very much in control. But physical peace was a hair-trigger condition that rested, like crustal plates, on a molten sea of emotion. And Herbert's emotions were bubbling.

Herbert had come to work a half hour before, after spending a long night overseeing the software setup of Op-Center's lean but crackerjack intelligence division. He had arrived expecting to experience an exciting start-up with his colleagues, the culmination of six months of team effort, *Sunrise at Campobello*. Instead, Herbert found something much different.

A few minutes after Herbert had passed the upstairs guard—who logged him as present, information that went to the computers of all the division directors—Bugs Benet called to inform him that there was someone in Paul Hood's office, a three-star general. A woman. She obviously had the creds to get downstairs, she had an ID card that gave her access to Hood's office when she swiped it through the lock, and she told Benet to call a meeting of the senior staff for ten A.M. in the Tank, the conference room at Op-Center. Then she shut the office door.

"That was the last I saw or heard of her," Benet told Herbert. "I'm calling you first."

"Where *is* Paul?" Herbert asked.

"At the White House," Benet said.

"Oh?" That did not sound good. Washington had a singular way of removing an individual from power and assuring a continuity of command. This was it. "Did you try calling him?"

"No. That will go on the phone log." Benet lowered his voice. "If Paul has been dismissed, his security status may have changed. I don't want to be accused of passing operational data to an outsider."

It was a valid point. Paranoid, but valid. Herbert asked to be put through to the general.

The woman took the call. She introduced herself as General Morgan Carrie, the new director of Op-Center, and said she would brief Herbert and his colleagues at the staff meeting. When Herbert asked what that meant for

Paul Hood, she told him she did not have that information and would see him in forty-five minutes.

And hung up.

Herbert tried to call Hood, but he did not answer his cell phone. Ticked off quickly became pissed off as frustration and consternation grew. Darrell McCaskey called, and Herbert told him what he knew. Liz Gordon suggested that they track him down using the GPS and intercept him somewhere.

"If he's been dismissed, we don't know what he might do," the staff psychologist said.

"I don't think Paul is the kind of guy who would off himself," Herbert said.

"Actually, those are exactly the people you have to worry about, the *über*-steady souls who guide you through a crisis, then don't have a place to put their key," Gordon countered. "Like soldiers who come back from war. The job is finished, the purpose is removed from life, it's time to check out. Though that's not what concerns me about Paul."

"What does?" Herbert asked. The intelligence chief was half-convinced that this was displacement, that Liz Gordon was upset and disoriented and looking for a place to put *her* key.

"He might turn his anger outward, at the thing he perceived has hurt him," Gordon said.

"The president?"

"Op-Center," she replied. "He could go to the press and complain, visit an old friend and divulge secrets without thinking, just get himself into a lot of trouble."

"I think Paul is a little steadier than that," Herbert replied.

"Do you." It was a statement, not a question. "Remember what a chance meeting with an old girlfriend did to him?"

"Liz, that was the love of his life."

"And what is Op-Center? This place *is* his life."

Liz had a point there. Herbert still thought the soul of her concern was psychobabble, and he was not ready to hunt Paul Hood down and put a tail on him. Still, Herbert agreed that they should revisit this question after the staff meeting. Hopefully, by that time, General Carrie would have more information about her predecessor or Hood himself would have gotten in touch by then.

Hood had to know they would be concerned.

The emotionally impervious Matt Stoll called to ask if the rumors of a new director were true and how Herbert thought this would impact his own staff and operations. Herbert said he did not know, but he was perversely relieved that someone, at least, was concerned about Op-Center and not about its people. It reminded him that, like it or not, they had a job to perform, a nation to serve.

And then it was two minutes to ten o'clock. Time to get intelligence.

Assuming, of course, that any of them still had jobs.

EIGHT

Washington, D.C.
Monday, 10:40 A.M.

At first blush the Tank struck General Carrie as a relatively spartan and unwelcoming chamber. The wood paneling was dark, the drop-down fluorescent lights were cold, and the rectangular table that dominated the room was heavy and plain.

The Tank got its name from the protection it afforded all electronic activity that was conducted within its walls. The room was completely surrounded by a barrier of electromagnetic waves that generated static to anyone trying to listen in with bugs or external dishes. The phone and computer lines were similarly protected. It was the only section of Op-Center that had survived the EMP blast, and it served as the field headquarters for its reconstruction.

General Carrie had selected this room for the meeting because it was impersonal. Though the director's office was large enough to accommodate everyone, there were photographs of Paul Hood's children on his desk and pictures of Hood and various individuals on the wall. That would have been a distraction. She was having Benet box those and messenger them to Hood.

Anyway, she told herself, *people make a room.* If these people were as sharp and stimulating as their dossiers suggested, the austerity of the place would not matter. She set her folder and notepad on the table. Although there were computers in the highly secure conference room, she would not be needing one.

The general had arrived precisely on time and nodded once at the guarded, unfamiliar faces. She had chaired hearings and run briefings countless times. Frequently, there was a percentage of officers or politicians in attendance who felt uneasy or amused to have a woman in charge, the sense that what she had to do or say was somehow less important than if she had been a man. And a white man at that. Carrie had no doubt that African-American and Latino officers experienced unspoken reserve similar to what she had always felt.

All General Carrie saw right now was concern in the faces of the five men and one other woman sitting around the oblong table. Some of that was probably about their own futures, and some of it was certainly worry about Paul Hood.

The general recognized the key tactical department heads from their photographs. Technical Director Matt Stoll was to her left, Op-Center attorney Lowell Coffey III was beside him, and Darrell McCaskey was next to him. Bob Herbert sat at the foot of the table with Deputy Director Ron Plummer to his left and Liz Gordon beside him.

There was a pitcher of water beside her computer. The general poured some into a glass. She asked anyone else if they wanted any. Only a few people answered to say no thank you. As usual, Carrie did not sit. She preferred to stand, not because it made her taller than everyone else but because it allowed her voice to carry. She did not have a classic baritone bark, as they called it at the Army General

Staff. She put her hands together in the small of her back and looked out at the room.

"I am General Morgan Carrie," she said to the group. "At the request of the president I assumed the directorship of Op-Center commencing at eight-thirty this morning. Unfortunately, I have no information regarding the disposition of former-director Hood. Perhaps one of you has spoken with him?"

Most eyes looked down. A few heads shook slowly.

"I will be pleased to share whatever information I am provided about Mr. Hood," Carrie said.

"We had our differences, General, but he is our friend," Bob Herbert said.

Carrie looked at him. "I am happy to hear that, Mr. Herbert. It gives me something to shoot for."

"That isn't why I mentioned it," Herbert replied. "When General Mike Rodgers was dismissed six months ago, Paul Hood was up front about it. He was unhappy. He was apologetic. And he was sensitive to the fact that none of us was going to like it. This team has never relied on information that was 'provided' to us. We dig it up. I want to make sure we know what happened to Paul, why, and how."

"Or else?" General Carrie asked. There seemed to be a threat in Herbert's tone. She did not like being challenged any more than she liked being patronized.

"Think of it as the intelligence equivalent of leaving one of your troops behind in battle," Herbert told her. "Leave unanswered questions lying around, and you will have a command, but you won't have trust or respect."

"That would be *my* problem," she replied sharply. "Your responsibility will be to do your job, not mine."

"My job description includes advising the director," Herbert said, unfazed. "I believe I have just done that, General Carrie."

Carrie unfolded her hands and leaned on the table. The annual evaluation Hood had written of Bob Herbert included a notation that the intelligence chief tended to challenge everyone. Hood saw it as an "often productive if frequently exasperating exercise." Hood had not understated the case.

"Do you have any other advice for me, Mr. Herbert?" she asked.

"None at present, General."

"Good. Then I have some for you. There is a line between advice and criticism, and you just crossed it. Sometimes it's a word or a phrase; sometimes it's a tone. But cross it again in my presence, Mr. Herbert, and I will be able to tell this team *exactly* what happened to the former intelligence director of Op-Center."

The general took a moment to study their reactions. She felt like the new Medusa: they were six faces cut in stone. Even Herbert. The irony was that she did not disagree with what Herbert had said. In the military, information was passed down through channels, not dug up. Op-Center was a civilian agency, more aggressive, more contraceptive than reactionary. She would have to get used to their way of doing things. But on her timetable, not his.

"I will be meeting with you all individually as time and responsibilities permit, starting with Bob." She looked at him. "Perhaps we can scroll things back and start fresh."

Herbert's cheek twitched, and he dipped his forehead quickly as though he were a base coach giving signals. She took that for a "Go." Lowell Coffey and Liz Gordon both smiled slightly. The general's attempt to reach out to Herbert apparently had scored points with them. Either that or they knew she was wasting her time.

She would find out soon enough.

"In the meantime, I need your help," General Carrie went on. She made that sound as conciliatory as possible without sounding weak. She opened her folder and looked at a printout. "There was an alert on my computer from Hot Button Operations upstairs. They looked into a pair of explosions that occurred this morning, one in Charleston, South Carolina, at five A.M. and the other in Durban, South Africa, at around five P.M. local time. The HoBOs suggest the attacks may have something in common. According to the Charleston Police Department, the ship that was blown up in their harbor was carrying illegal Chinese workers. The attack overseas three hours later destroyed sugarcane silos owned by a Chinese firm. The HoBOs suggest the second explosion was too swift to be retaliation, but both may be first shots in a broad war of some kind." She looked across the table. "Suggestions?"

"We had evidence that the Chinese were becoming increasingly involved in African affairs nearly a year ago," Ron Plummer said. "They were involved in diamond operations in Botswana."

"That was part of the attack on the Catholic church there?" Carrie asked.

"Yes. We believed at the time that some faction of the Chinese government would have benefited from destabilization in the region," Plummer said.

"We filed a formal white paper through our embassy in Beijing," Coffey told her. "Our ambassador received a response from the director of the International Security Committee of the National People's Congress. She strongly denied that Beijing was engaged in official activities on the African continent outside their embassies, and also disavowed any private misdeeds that might be going on."

"I should point out that the Chinese are usually pretty forthright about their involvements abroad," Plummer added. "When they feel possessive about something, such as the oil deposits in the Spratly Islands, they go after them openly."

"Which doesn't mean much in this case," Coffey said. "The letter from the DISC didn't preclude the involvement of private individuals inside and outside the government."

"You're talking about a black economy," the general said.

"Not just that," Plummer replied. "Many wealthy Chinese invest overseas because constraints on ownership of businesses and property are much less restrictive than in the PRC."

"But the illegal workers would have been what you suggest, General, a black market," Darrell McCaskey said. "They get smuggled in for an average price of two hundred grand each. They stay indentured, working as prostitutes or cheap labor, until that sum is repaid. Since half the money they earn is sent to relatives in China, they are effectively enslaved for life. The FBI has been playing catch-up with these undocumented Chinese workers for decades. The Bureau has actually been losing ground since resources have been shifted to Homeland Security and the tracking of illegals from Malaysia, the Philippines, and the Middle East."

"Maybe we need to change the way the search is carried out," the general said.

"What are your thoughts?" Herbert asked.

The intelligence chief sounded challenging rather than beaten. Carrie wondered if Bob Herbert knew the meaning of the word *defeat*. Or *humility*.

"HoBOs says that Chinese-Americans represent four percent of the national population," Carrie said. "Most of those people are concentrated in cities like New York, San Francisco, and Philadelphia. Those are not areas in which we want to see a potential conflict spread. I suggest we have a look to see if there's a war brewing. Who takes point on that?"

"That depends where we want to run the operations," Herbert said. "Two of our stringers, Dave Battat and Aideen Marley, are familiar with Africa. One of our local people can shoot down to Charleston."

"That's catch-up," she said. "I want to get ahead of this. What kind of resources do we have in Beijing?"

"A few stringers," Herbert told her. "Our contact with the Chinese has been in proxy settings."

"Korea and Vietnam redux," Plummer said.

"Well, we know how those turned out," Carrie said wistfully. "Maybe it's time to change the dynamics."

"Excuse me, General, but did you see action in Vietnam?" Liz inquired.

"Yes. Why do you ask?"

"It's the first time you looked away from the table," she said. "Like you were looking back."

Carrie felt exposed but decided that was not necessarily a bad thing. It told the group a little about her past, something that might start to earn her the respect Herbert had spoken about. Liz Gordon was wearing a slightly satisfied look, one that suggested it was exactly why the psychologist had asked the question.

The general leaned forward again. "Bob, maybe you can canvass the team and your resources, and we can have our sit-down over lunch in my office. We can go through whatever thoughts you have then and pin down a course of action."

Herbert nodded, this time more affirmatively.

The general closed the folder, then took a sip of water. "If there's nothing else, I want to thank you all for sharing your time and thoughts. I also want to assure you that we will never forget or slight the contributions of those who came before us—Paul Hood, Mike Rodgers, and especially the men and women who gave more than just their time and industry—Martha Mackall, Lieutenant Colonel Charlie Squires, and the heroes of Striker."

Darrell McCaskey pounded the table lightly with the side of his left fist, a gesture of tribute echoed by everyone else in the room.

Including Bob Herbert.

And for a moment, the Tank seemed almost like home to General Carrie.

NINE

Beijing, China
Monday, 10:46 P.M.

The twentieth-century Chinese Communist leader Liu Shao-ch'i once said that there could be no such thing as a perfect leader in China. The nation was too large, its population too diverse.

"If there is such a leader," the philosopher-politician posited in a collection of his writings, "he is only pretending, like a pig inserting scallions into its nose to look like an elephant."

Balding, stocky Prime Minister Le Kwan Po was not sure he agreed that China was ungovernable. But it was true that leading this nation of provinces with vastly different histories and needs required an individual of uncommon wisdom and resourcefulness. There is a tale told about the last dowager empress of China, Tz'u-hsi, whose reign was marked by the rise and fall of the turbulent Boxer Rebellion. The insurrection was named for the men at the center of the revolt, the secret society of the Righteous Harmonious Fists, which was founded in 1898 and fought to keep China from falling under the undue influence of foreigners. The empress approved of the modern conveniences brought by British, Russians, Japanese, and Americans, devices such as telegraphs and trains. But she disapproved of missionaries and foreign influence over Chinese affairs. It was a difficult balance to support them both.

One morning, a Boxer was captured after murdering a British businessman on his way to the embassy. The Boxer beat him to death in his carriage, the businessman's Chinese driver having run off at the sight of the attacker. One of Tz'u-hsi's advisers wanted the Boxer beheaded. Another counselor warned that to do so would only encourage the Boxers to hit harder. The empress allowed the execution to take place, though not for the attack on the foreigner. In her decree she stated that the man's actions had set one of her ministers against the other and disturbed the tranquillity of the morning. For that crime, and that only, he was to die.

Le Kwan Po contemplated the complexities of gestures and appearances as his state car pulled away from the government building at No. 2, Chaoyangmen Nandajie, Chaoyang District, in Beijing. His own life was full of such careful maneuvers. For example, the prime minister had two cars. One was a Chinese-made Lingyang, the Antelope, and the other a more comfortable Volkswagen Polo manufactured at the German-run plant in Shanghai. He rode the Antelope in Beijing, the Polo in the less populated countryside.

Always a balance for appearances, he thought. Please the nationalists while holding something out for potential foreign investors.

Except for the driver, the prime minister was the only passenger in the chauffer-driven car. Typically, an aide and a secretary rode home with the sixty-six-year-old native of the remote Xizang Zizhiqu province near Nepal. But the prime minister felt like being alone tonight. He wanted to reflect on the disturbing events of the day.

He looked out the window as the car drove past the lighted monuments and palaces surrounding Tian'anmen Square. It was a hot and rainy night. Large drops ran down the window. They smeared the lights of the city—fittingly, on a day when nothing was clear. The driver guided the small sedan through narrow side streets. At this hour, in this weather, the lanes were sparsely populated with the carts and bicycles that filled them during the day. The vehicle moved quickly toward Le Kwan Po's nearby Beijing residence on the top floor of the exclusive Cheng Yuan Towers apartment complex. The prime minister had another official home, a weekend retreat in the Beijing suburbs at the foot of Shou'an Mountain near Xiangshan Park. During the week the prime minister preferred to remain in the city. That allowed him to work as late as possible. It also permitted him to stay synchronized with the pulse of Beijing.

It enabled him to watch those who wanted his job or sought to remove him as a thoughtful, mediating influence.

The prime minister enjoyed the tranquillity of the countryside, yet that scenic, agrarian world was China's past. The future was in the increasingly cosmopolitan capital and cities like Shanghai, with their proliferation of students and businessmen—many of them from rich Taiwan, the supposed enemy. That was another act for an acrobat greater than any the Beijing Opera had yet produced: solving the Taiwan question. Chinese businesses were growing enormously due to investments coming across the strait. The Chinese military was being held to the budgetary levels of previous years as the threat from both Taipei and Russia was diminished. That did not make high-ranking career officers happy. Fewer commands meant fewer promotions. It caused grumbling up and down the ranks.

Though Le Kwan Po knew what the empress experienced a century ago, he did not have her wisdom. He had not fought wars and rivals, dealt with prejudice against his gender and heritage, nor had to guard against or formulate regicidal plots. He was simply a conservative career politician, the son of a schoolteacher mother. His father had been a village magistrate at twenty-one and had risen regularly to positions in town, county, municipality, province, and finally the central government. He was not the prime minister solely because of his experience in government. He was here because, unlike his colleagues, he had not made any serious missteps. His background was spotted and propped with careful alliances and cautious agendas.

Even more important than the ruthless will of the dowager empress, however, the prime minister did not have her unilateral authority to act. In addition to the president and vice president above him, there was a cabinet with very powerful and ambitious ministers and the National People's Congress with its proliferation of special interests, both local and personal.

The current struggle between Chou Shin, head of the secretive 8341 Unit of the Central Security Regiment, and People's Liberation Army hero General Tam Li was outside the prime minister's experience. According to reports Le Kwan Po had received from the Ministry of State Security—the Guojia Anquan Bu, or Guoanbu—the two rivals had begun a long-simmering face down today in two foreign ports. And that was just part of the problem. Tam Li was one of those officers who was unhappy with the lack of growth in the military. If his two displeasures converged, and he wished to express them at home, he could be a formidable threat to the stability of the nation.

It was just like it was in feudal times, when every man of importance had centuries of hate behind him. Then, even if a man was willing to look past personal differences with another, the shadow of their ancestors would not allow it.

It was quite a burden, the prime minister reflected.

It was also easier to defend clan honor centuries ago, when a man was surrounded by like-minded individuals, and vast distances made confrontation an occasional matter. Today, the few men who harbored different loyalties, who had different goals, were in very close proximity. For the most part they managed to work together in the name of nationalism.

But not always.

The rain tapped on the roof. The prime minister reached into the vest pocket of his white trench coat. He withdrew a case of cigarettes and lit one. He sat back. Whenever China finally managed to reverse the trend and spread its influence around the world, there were two things he hoped. First, that his people would learn to make a car as good as a BMW or a Mercedes. And second, that they could produce a cigarette as soul-satisfying as a Camel.

The prime minister did not know how he wanted to pursue this conflict between proud, stubborn, influential members of the government. It was not a matter he wished to present to the president or vice president. Disputes between officials, even those with international ramifications, were the responsibility of the prime minister. He was supposed to be able to settle them.

Le Kwan Po wished that securing peace was as easy as sacrificing a minor third party, the way the dowager empress did with the Boxers. Of course, that only delayed the inevitable, having to deal with the rebellion itself. The foreign powers sent their own armies to China to crush the nationalists. Not only did the empress decline to stop them, she embraced their Western ways.

China did not.

The dynasty fell shortly after Tz'u-hsi's death. Nationalist forces were so upset with her legacy that they blasted open the royal tomb, stole the riches, and mutilated her remains. The anti-imperial backlash allowed Dr. Sun Yat-sen and Chiang Kai-shek to come to power, each espousing a form of Western-style republic that opened wounds and created political and ideological chaos. It was not until Mao Tse-tung and the Communists came to power in 1949 that order was truly restored.

That had been a proud time, centuries in the making. Le Kwan Po remembered hearing his father read of the events from newspapers that were published in a tiny print shop in their small village of Gamba. The prime minister's uncle set type there in the evening. During the day, he worked in a quarry that was literally in the shadow of Mount Everest. The young Le could still vividly remember the joy in his father's voice as he read about the end to the civil war that had tortured a nation already bleeding from the long war with Japan. He was almost giddy about the victory of the Communists over the republicans—who had the temerity to call themselves nationalists—certain it would help those who had to work all day, every day, just to support a small family in an extremely modest lifestyle.

When the newspaper was closed by the new regime, Le Kwan Po's uncle was asked to stay on to typeset a new weekly publication, *Principles from the People's Administrative Council.* The young boy was as proud as he could be when he attended the new school that the Communists opened in Gamba, and he was selected to read the first issue to the class.

The senior members of the current government—this prime minister included—remembered the taste and feel of disorder. They did not want to see it return, not as a result of student demonstrations in Tian'anmen Square or from disagreements among powerful members of the government.

The prime minister exhaled smoke through his nose. He thought about the fake elephant of Liu Shao-ch'i. Somehow, he would have to convince the warring forces that he was a dragon. That the only way to defeat him was to put their differences aside and join forces.

Le Kwan Po did not know how he was going to do that. All he knew was one thing.

That it had to be done, and done quickly.

TEN

Beijing, China
Monday, 11:18 P.M.

Chou Shin, Director of the ultrasecret 8341 Unit of the Central Security Regiment, sat in his fifth-floor office of the old Communist Party Building. It was located in the shadow of the Forbidden City, site of the palaces of the deposed despots who had run China for centuries. The six-story-tall brick structure had been built in the 1930s on the site of the Yuan Chung Silver Shop, one of the oldest banks in the city. The Communists had torn down the pavilion-style institution to prove that the old ways were gone and a new era had begun. It was in Chou's very office that the war against Chiang Kai-shek was planned and executed.

The structure itself had brick walls, copper ceilings, and pipes that groaned with their inadequacy to cope with the demands placed on them. There were several small windows along one wall, but the shades were drawn, as always. The director had the heat turned on, not only to chase out the chill of the stormy night but to generate white noise. It helped to befuddle any listening devices that might be present.

The seventy-one-year-old Chou was waiting for an intelligence update from an operative in Taipei. What they were planning was dangerous. But as the day had proved, so was inactivity.

While he waited, Chou reviewed what he called his cobblestone data, intelligence that was pulled from the street. This collection was done by a combination of paid informants, operatives who habituated bars and restaurants, hotel lobbies, and train depots just watching and listening, and electronic eavesdropping. Vans from the CSR drove through the streets of Beijing listening to cell phone conversations and intercepting the increasing number of wireless computer communiqués. Although the CSR had sifters on the staff who went through the raw data, what ended up crossing his desk had still managed to double in the course of a year. He could not imagine what it would be like two or three years hence. Perhaps, like the American CIA, they would be forced to listen for just key phrases like *terror plot* or *bomb threat* and let the rest go by.

Years ago, the CSR list would have been a short one. During the late 1950s when Chou was recruited for the organization, the primary task of the 8341 Unit was to see to the personal security of Mao Tse-tung and other Communist party leaders. But the elite division of the People's Liberation Army was more than a bodyguard unit. It also ran a nationwide intelligence network to uncover plots against the chairman or senior leadership. Chou himself, a former telephone lineman in the PLA, was part of the team that had discovered electronic listening devices in Mao's office, hidden in the doorknob. The young man's first promotion was to the counterinsurgent unit, assigned with executing surveillance of Mao's rivals. The 8341 Unit was a key participant in the 1976 arrest of the Gang of Four, the group that attempted to seize power after the death of Mao. After that, the unit was officially disbanded. Mao's successor, Teng Hsiao-P'ing, wanted to make a point of "decommunizing" the nation and its institutions. However, hard-line Communists like Chou resisted the change. Unlike many leaders before him, Teng decided it was prudent to acknowledge the wishes of the Chinese people and not just the Chinese elite. The deputy premier quietly but quickly reinstated personnel and organizations he had removed. Most immediately, the one that was responsible for his personal protection.

Today, the 8341 Unit was responsible for uncovering plots against the regime. Their sphere of activity centered upon China and the breakaway republic. Since the Tian'anmen Square uprising in 1989, few dissidents had undertaken public displays against the government. Private activity was still relatively abundant but unthreatening, limited to pockets of philosophers, failed entrepreneurs, foreign-born firebrands, and disenfranchised youths who wanted fashionable Western clothes. At present, none of them represented a serious threat against the government. The only potential source of danger was the PLA, where one reckless, ambitious man might control the loyalty of tens of thousands of troops.

A man like General Tam.

Unlike the prime minister with whom he had just been meeting, Chou had no patience or sympathy for those who would betray the nation or the philosophies set out by Chairman Mao. Le Kwan Po was a mediator. He was a man committed to equilibrium, to compromise. Chou liked the prime minister and believed he was a patriot. But Le wanted to rule a China that was unified at any cost, even if it was a heterogeneous one and not a Communist one. Chou did not agree with him on this very significant point. The director still seethed when he thought of the beloved chairman's late wife, who was one of the treasonous Gang of Four. She and her three fellows had coerced members of the military to help cleanse the nation of ideologues. The Communist Revolution had been an uprising of ideas. They were good and necessary ideas. In the 1930s and 1940s, the military was called upon by Mao to defend the right of the people to hold those ideas. Jiang Qing corrupted that. She used the vicious Red Guard to enforce her ideas. Iron boot education never produces long-lasting results. It produces slaves, and eventually slaves turn on their masters.

That was something the Gang of Four learned during their long, televised trial in Beijing.

It was something General Tam Li would also learn.

The computer beeped. The short, bespectacled intelligence director closed the white folder and put it in a drawer. He looked at the monitor. The cursor prompted him to enter a password. He typed in the Chinese characters for *eagle* and *talon* and waited for the file to download. Chou had a collection of ivory dragons on a shelf in his office. He enjoyed them and had collected them since he was a boy. But they were also there to mislead his adversaries. Anyone who came into his office and tried to access his computer files would naturally search for dragon-related passwords. No one would ever think to look for another powerful predator.

It was a report from one of Chou's field agents in Taiwan. The CSR director had been expecting the information.

General Tam Li had gone into this day with a plan he had hoped would undermine the resolve of the man who was watching him closely. The general seemed to have thought that violence and the threat of personal exposure would turn the eyes of Chou Shin elsewhere.

Tam was not just wrong, he was decisively wrong.

As he would discover in less than an hour.

ELEVEN

Taipei, Taiwan
Monday, 11:49 P.M.

Lo Tek had a wonderful life. Part of that was due to the freedom he enjoyed, and part of it was the respect he had. Part of it was also due to the quaint simplicity of his world.

Born Hui-ling Wong, Lo Tek was a name given to him by his associates because he refused to use any sophisticated electronic communications devices. He believed in being surreptitious, and one could not work in the darkness with all the electronic lights of the modern age. Most days and nights the thirty-two-year-old spent on his ninety-four-foot ketch with its artful crew of three, sailing the waters of the Yellow Sea and the East China Sea. For the most part, his navigation was done the old-fashioned way, by wind and by starlight. His belief was that if it worked for his ancestors, it would work for him. Though he used a computer and DVD player for onboard entertainment, communication was conducted entirely with point-to-point radios.

Lo Tek rarely left the sea. That was where he found refugees—men, women, and youngsters attempting to go from wherever they were to anywhere else. Mostly they were trying to get out of Indonesia or the PRC and trying to get to Taiwan, Hong Kong, or Japan. More than half of the nearly fifteen thousand who set out each year perished on the water due to overloaded or inadequate boats, inclement weather, insufficient supplies, or pirates who robbed them of their few possessions, assaulted then killed the women, and sank the boats. Of the seven thousand or so souls who managed to survive on the seas, four thousand were turned away by coastal patrols, arrested, or sold by corrupt police to slavers who worked the docks. Typically, those were young women. Occasionally they were young boys. Invariably, they were never seen again.

Less than one thousand individuals managed to make it ashore. Of those, fewer than two hundred managed to find employment. The rest became thieves, prisoners, or corpses.

Lo Tek had a very special business. His agents ran shipping services that "helped" refugees achieve their goals. The boats brought the cargo to Lo Tek, who brought the finest of the women on board and sold them to high-priced brothels in Taiwan, Thailand, Japan, and Hong Kong. In exchange for their silence, Lo Tek made sure the rest of the passengers reached their destination.

In return for giving his boats safe passage from Chinese ports, Lo Tek made sure his contact in the PLA was well-paid. General Tam Li had been a valuable asset for many years and a frequent guest on his ketch.

The young man felt no guilt about what he did. As they had sailed the seas, the ancient Chinese also dealt in human cargo. It was an old and legitimate profession. Statistically, without him most of these girls would be dead within days or weeks. Lo Tek never abused them himself and left the training to the professionals ashore. He felt that he was doing the young ladies a favor, placing them in situations where they would be warm, fed, and given regular medical care. They would even earn money to send to their families, which was the reason most of them had left their homes.

When Lo Tek came ashore, he liked to visit the clubs with whom he did business. They always treated him like nobility. Excellent food and drink and a reunion with one or more of his women. For the orphaned son of peasants, who had sold his twin sister to soldiers and dockworkers in Shanghai for ten *fen* each, that was quite an accomplishment. He still sent her half the money he earned, which she used to run an orphanage back in Shanghai.

The Top of the World club at the new Barre Crowne Tower was actually a legitimate nightclub with dinner, entertainers, and dancing. Only select guests knew to ask for special treatment. There were elegantly appointed rooms on the floor below for men with the time and money for what the club called "exceptional treatment." These rooms could only be reached by a private elevator.

After two weeks at sea, Lo Tek was in the mood for *very* exceptional treatment. During that time the Chinese native had gathered a total of thirty women for clients along the Pacific Rim, including one private collector living in the Philippines who liked his companions tall and very young. Lo Tek arrived at the tower, was announced by the street-level doorman, and was greeted with an embrace from the manager when he reached the fortieth floor.

"You should have called ahead!" the manager said. "We would have had a lounge ready for you."

"You know how I work."

"Well just once, you know?" the manager said. "Give me a half hour, and I will have things arranged for you."

"Thank you," Lo Tek replied.

The men walked arm in arm as they went down a circular staircase into the main nightclub area. The manager, Chin Teng, was a thin man who wore heavy glasses and a film of perspiration across his forehead. Lo Tek imagined that he had the metabolism of a mouse, which would be fitting, given all the running around he did, attending to clients.

It was dark in the club, with a semicircular bar in the center and high tables scattered throughout. There was a raised dance floor behind the bar. The windows were floor-to-ceiling and covered 160 degrees of the circular room. They offered a commanding view of the city and the hazy lights of the harbor. Because it was still early, the club was relatively empty. Most of the customers arrived between midnight and one A.M. and stayed until dawn. A disc jockey was playing Asian pop standards from a booth overlooking the floor. Lo Tek knew that there were also security guards up there, watching through the smoked glass to make sure everyone behaved. There were two couples on the dance floor, three men and a woman in a group at the bar, and two young men bent over tall beers at one of the booths in the back of the room, away from the window. It looked like they had had a long day.

"What would you like to eat and drink?" the manager asked.

"I would like orange juice, freshly squeezed, no ice," Lo Tek replied.

"I'll get it at once," the manager said as he showed him to a booth in the corner, near the window.

Lo Tek slid into the deep leather cushion. The swaying of the sea had become natural to him. It felt odd being on solid ground.

A stunning young waitress in a short black skirt brought him water, macadamia nuts, and a brilliant smile. He smiled back. That was something else that happened on-shore: he did not look at a woman and wonder what kind of price she would bring. He saw her simply as a person.

The manager brought Lo Tek his drink, then left to check on "the rest of your order," as he put it with a wicked wink. Lo Tek took an appreciative sip of the juice. His mouth felt alive. He took another as he looked out at the club. He absently folded the cocktail napkin into a little sailboat. Origami was a hobby of his, something he had mastered to amuse and distract the younger girls who were briefly guests on his ketch.

He watched as the two men at the booth tossed several bills on the table and left. Neither of them carried a briefcase or backpack, which seemed unusual. He noticed, too, that both beer bottles had napkins around them. They were wrapped entirely around the glass, as though both men did not want to leave fingerprints.

Lo Tek wondered if that meant anything, or if his naturally suspicious nature were getting the best of him.

That was the last thought the slave trader had before his eardrums exploded, followed by the rest of the room.

A bomb had been left in a briefcase under the table and was triggered remotely. It consisted of six sticks of TNT bound with electrical tape and capped with a detonator. The sticks were packed in a bed of sugar.

From Durban.

The explosion fused the sugar into tiny shards, blowing them around the room like fireflies. The small table was shredded as the explosion slammed through the room. The force of the blast did not just pulverize objects and people, it knocked them about like a force five hurricane. Blood and alcohol were dashed against the walls, first by the TNT and moments after that by the exploding CO_2 canisters behind the bar. There were a few screams from below as the dance floor of the nightclub was shoved down into the exclusive rooms on the thirty-ninth floor. Moments later there were cries from the streets as the big picture windows flew outward. Particles of glass rained down thickly, like hail, clattering off rooftops, cars, and the street. Twisted barstools, along with broken bottles and glasses, were hurled toward the exterior wall. Most of the window frames were bent and dislocated, hanging at odd angles over the street. Some were still dropping larger pieces of glass to the pavement as dark gray smoke churned through them. The winds carried it over the harbor, an added pall on the already steamy night. People who were caught in the lethal rain were knocked to the pavement, some writhing with minor wounds and others utterly still, impaled by the larger pieces of debris.

The maelstrom lasted for less than five seconds. Sirens broke the muffled silence that followed, wailing nearer from all directions as scraps of paper and clouds of powdered pasteboard and brick continued to drift earthward. Some of the debris ended up in the harbor.

Including, fittingly, the paper boat Lo Tek had made.

It sank quickly.

TWELVE

Washington, D.C.
Monday, 1:01 P.M.

After Paul Hood was shown to his office, a young female intern who did not look much older than his daughter came in and cheerfully showed him how to work his computer. The lady—Mindy, from Texas money, he knew from her accent and her Armani suit—dutifully looked away after telling him how to program his personal password.

"A master program maintains a record of all your Web stops, Mr. Hood," the slender young woman informed him. "The president has asked us all to be circumspect about where we go."

Hood could actually hear the Southern-born president using a word like that, imbuing it with the proper balance of danger and piety. The young intern sounded very mature indeed, carrying forth that word from the commander in chief. At Op-Center, Hood used to tell people the same thing. It took him two words, though: "*No porn.*"

Mindy showed Hood how to work the telephone and

gave him a swipe card for the men's room. She was very professional about that, too. After the young woman left, Hood sat alone, with the door shut. Chief of Staff Sanders said she would come by at three. She wanted to review her thoughts with Hood on how the new office might work. She assured him, however, that the decision would be his, and he would have full autonomy on the final setup.

As long as you agree, Hood thought. Otherwise, the new special envoy would be removed, and someone else would get the job. That was how things worked in the nation's capital.

It was difficult to process everything that had just happened. Hood looked around and smiled mirthlessly. About the only thing today had in common with yesterday was that Hood still did not have a window.

Just an exit, if he needed it.

Hood felt alone, despite the people he knew were just a few feet away. He was at the seat of power, yet he felt strangely powerless. It would be odd not to receive hourly intelligence reports from the research rooms upstairs. It was frustrating not to have anyone of a Bob Herbert or Darrell McCaskey caliber to consult.

That is not entirely true, he reminded himself. Hood owed Bob Herbert a phone call.

It took a moment for Hood to remember how to work the telephone. He had to press nine, enter his department code, then punch in the number he wanted. At Op-Center it was the other way around.

"Paul, what the hell is going on?" Herbert asked after Hood had said hello.

"More changes," Hood replied.

"That's obvious. The phone ID says you're calling from the White House."

"I'm the new special envoy to the president," Hood replied.

"Special envoy to where?" Herbert asked.

"Everywhere. I am still an international crisis manager," Hood replied.

"Did you know that this was coming? Any of it, including the changing of the guard over here?"

"No," Hood said.

"Neither did I. And we're intelligence professionals."

"An attack always comes from somewhere you're not expecting it," Hood pointed out.

"Is that what this was?" Herbert asked.

"What do you mean?"

"An attack?" Herbert said. "Hell, I thought we were all on the same side."

The remark caught Hood like a palm-heel strike to the side of the head. Herbert had a point. Hood was obviously not pleased with how this had gone down, and he was not sure why. Not everyone got "fired" to the White House. He should be flattered, not angry. Maybe it was the idea that he was now working for someone. He had never done that in his career, not as the mayor of Los Angeles, as a financial adviser, or as the head of Op-Center. Though the Congressional Intelligence Oversight Committee watched what the NCMC was doing and how the money was spent, Hood *was* the superior officer. He did not report to one. The question he had to answer, truthfully, was whether he considered the president an enemy.

No. Lorraine Sanders, maybe, he decided. She struck him as being extremely territorial.

"How is everyone taking the change?" Hood asked.

"I don't know," Herbert admitted. "Numb, I guess. We had a staff meeting this morning, and everyone was pretty quiet. But I haven't really talked to anyone. I've been looking into this situation we have."

"Can you talk about it?" Hood asked. He wanted to put on his professional hat as soon as possible. Dwelling on personal issues was not going to get him anything but deeper into them.

"Sure," Herbert replied. "You've still got your security clearance, right?"

"Yeah," Hood said. Herbert was not joking. That bothered Hood, but like everything else, he was not sure why. Herbert was just doing his job, following a protocol that Hood had helped to establish.

"Someone out there is capping Chinese interests abroad," Herbert told him. "There have been three incidents in one day. General Carrie wanted to know if they are connected or if we need to be concerned about that."

"Do you?" Hood asked.

"It's too early to say," Herbert replied. "Charleston police report finding the remains of Chinese stowaways in the harbor. An hour ago there was an explosion at a nightclub in Taipei. Special guests received special treatment there—"

"From mainland Chinese girls," Hood said.

"You see where this is going," Herbert replied. "We do not believe that someone is attacking men and women who leave China. We suspect the target is the enabler, whoever is helping them to get out and making money from their sale in Taipei or the United States. Darrell just got off the horn with a friend in the Taipei Municipal Police Department. The Section Four Bomb Squad, attached to the Xihu Police Substation, was at the site within minutes. They found a badly wounded fellow who has since been identified as Hui-ling Wong, a suspected slaver. He died on the way to the hospital, but they found his boat in the harbor."

"Did they get any phone records, computers?"

"Nada," Herbert said. "The guy never used any of those. He had a nickname, Lo Tek. All his deals were conducted in person or arranged via ship-to-ship or ship-to-shore communications."

"Sensible."

"The harbor police did get his radio operator, though. They're hoping he'll be able to tell them something."

"Do you think Hui-ling was the target?" Hood asked.

"No," Herbert said. "It would have been just as easy to take out his ketch. He was probably just a bystander who happened to deserve what he got."

"So the business was the target," Hood said.

"Yes, but Ron and General Carrie both think there might be a proxy war being fought here. I'm inclined to agree."

Those words were not a slap. They were worse. Hearing Herbert mention Ron Plummer and General Carrie in the same sentence was like hearing his former wife talk about her new boyfriend. It reminded Hood, painfully, that forces beyond his control had wrested him from people and events that had defined his life. It was an effort to speak, let alone to speak unemotionally.

"Why do you think that?" Hood asked flatly.

"The PRC has an enormously high rate of illegal emigration," Herbert said. "In terms of sheer numbers, it's higher than that of any other nation. Those refugees were the people Wong reportedly hunted. He would not have been able to pluck people from offshore vessels without the tacit approval of the People's Liberation Navy. Not in a ketch that size, in those waters, in a perpetual state of silent running. That alone would have caught the attention of every radar station along the coast. Wong had to be paying people off."

"Do you have any idea who?"

"Not yet," Herbert said. "But we may have a back door to that information. The attacks in Charleston and Taipei bookended the bombing of sugar silos in South Africa. According to public records in Durban, one of the investors in that refinery is the Tonkin Investment Corporation, a group of Vietnamese shipping entrepreneurs who have close ties with members of the Chinese government. Specifically, they handle official government investments managed by Chou Shin, who is the vice chairman of the Chinese Communist Party's United Front Relief Fund. The Chicom UFRF manages funds for the survivors of soldiers who died in the struggle to put the Communists into power and keep them there. Chou is a hard-liner, an acolyte of Mao who also happens to be the director of the 8341 Unit of the Central Security Regiment."

"I've heard of them," Hood said. "They're extremely low profile."

"Very. Their job is to spy on political and philosophical enemies of Chicom at home and abroad. Chou has deep files on students, radicals, black marketeers, and plutocrats."

"A kind of anti–J. Edgar Hoover," Hood suggested.

"Exactly," Herbert said. "Chou also has the resources to attack the trade in illegal émigrés."

"For what reason?" Hood asked.

"Defense. Spite. The profits could be used to finance rival factions in Beijing, or maybe he has a grudge against some minister or general. What's interesting is the timing of the events. The first two, the blasts in Charleston and Durban, happened relatively close together."

"You mean someone might have had the silo scenario primed in the event of an attack on the émigrés."

"Right. But the blast in Taipei came significantly later—possibly a response to the bombing in Durban."

"That isn't a proxy war," Hood said. "It's gods hurling thunderbolts at one another."

"Not giving a damn about collateral damage, I know," Herbert said. "In any case, Maria has Interpol connections who deal regularly with the National Security Bureau in Taipei. They've got people inside Beijing. We're trying to find out who is on the top of Chou's hit list, someone who might have the resources to have the counterstrike in Durban ready and waiting."

Maria Corneja McCaskey was the Spanish-born wife of Op-Center's FBI liaison Darrell McCaskey. She had retired from Interpol to come to the United States with her new husband. She had not settled comfortably into domesticity and was retained by Op-Center to interface with the global police agency and its affiliates.

"So who are we rooting for?" Hood asked. "The slaver-capitalist or the repressive spy who's watching out for war widows?"

It was a rhetorical question, and Herbert took it as such. "The sad thing is, people end up suffering either way," the intelligence chief remarked.

"I hope there's something you can do to minimize that," Hood said.

There was a short silence as Hood worked through another painful moment. In the past that would be the start of a discussion between Hood and one of his senior staff, not the end.

"Are there any resources you can bring to bear?" Herbert asked.

"I'll find out," Hood said. "Hell, Bob, I'm still learning how to work the telephones."

"Didn't they give you an assistant?"

"I get to hire two," Hood said.

"Hey. That's a step up from Op-Center."

"Not really," Hood said. "I have no idea where to find them."

There was another short silence. It grew into a long one. Herbert was not one for small talk, and Hood felt as if the intelligence chief had been extending the conversation unnaturally.

"I guess I'd better let you go," Hood said.

"Sorry," Herbert said. "I was just checking my caller ID. There's an incoming call I'd better take."

"Sure," Hood told him. "I'll have a look into this Chinese situation and get back to you."

"Thanks," Herbert said. "Hey, Paul, have you heard from Mike lately?"

"I haven't spoken to him since he left Op-Center," Hood told him. "Why?"

"Because that's who is calling me," Herbert replied.

THIRTEEN

Washington, D.C.
Monday, 1:13 P.M.

"Hello, Mike Rodgers," Herbert declared as he took the call. "How are things deep in the heart of Unexus?"

"The company is doing well, and so am I," Rodgers replied.

The firm for which Rodgers worked was located in Arlington, Virginia, not far from the Pentagon. The two men had last spoken a month before, when they met for dinner at the Watergate. The 600 Restaurant was one of Herbert's favorites, as much for where it was located as for what they served. The hotel was a monument to presidential arrogance, to the notion that the nation was still a democracy. That thought gave Herbert a warm feeling. It reminded him of the values he himself had paid such a high price to uphold.

"Is there something quick and dirty I can help you with, or can I give you a shout in about an hour?"

"Both," Rodgers said. "What are you hearing about China?"

Herbert had been playing with a loose thread on his cuff. He stopped. "Why do you ask?"

"We've got a very important project about to launch with Beijing," Rodgers told him. "I was wondering if the explosion in Taipei is an isolated event."

"Do you have any reason to think it wasn't?" Herbert asked.

There was a brief silence.

Herbert smiled. Rodgers knew the drill. Herbert's first obligation was to Op-Center. Their job was to put puzzles together, not provide the pieces for others. Not even for an old friend, a *trusted* friend. With Herbert that was not a territorial imperative. It was his definition of professionalism.

"All right. I'll go first," Rodgers said. "Unexus has designed a Chinese telecommunications satellite that is going to be launched on Thursday. The prime minister has asked the head of the Xichang space center to provide him with an overview of security operations. Director Lung says that has never happened before."

"Is this the first job you've done with them?"

"Yes, but that does not seem to be what is driving the prime minister's caution," Rodgers told him.

"Will the telecommunications satellite be used for civilian purposes only?" Herbert asked.

"We don't know," Rodgers said.

"Plausible deniability," Herbert replied.

Rodgers ignored the remark. "The prime minister has asked that the security information be sent by courier, directly to him. Ordinarily these matters are reviewed by the Guoanbu."

"The Ministry of State Security," Herbert said.

"Bypassing them in a review of this nature is very unusual," Rodgers said. "Director Lung was also instructed to make sure that one of the guests be accompanied by a Xichang official at all times."

"What guest?" Herbert asked.

"General Tam Li of the PLA," Rodgers told him.

"Is the army involved with the launch?"

"Only as observers," Rodgers said. "We hope to be doing more business with them in the future, though I'm not at liberty to say more than that."

"Is there any reason at all to think that this General Tam Li is a threat?" Herbert asked.

"That's why I'm calling," Rodgers said. "The prime minister must think so."

"When did the prime minister request the security plans?" Herbert asked.

"Saturday morning, Beijing time," Rodgers said. "Now tell me. Is there anything you can add?"

"Is this for your ears only, or will it get back to the prime minister of the People's Republic of China?" The question tasted like ash. But Mike Rodgers had new employers now, and he had always been a good and loyal officer.

"Do you even have to ask, Bob?"

"Unfortunately I do, Mike. You're a good friend. You're also a private citizen working with the government of a foreign power, possibly with the *military* of a foreign power. My boss would scowl at swapping spit with the enemy."

"Tell Paul I am the same man I was—"

"Paul Hood is not my boss," Herbert said. "Not anymore."

It took Rodgers a moment to process the information. "What are you talking about?" he asked.

"I wish I knew," Herbert admitted. "I came to work this morning and found out that Op-Center had a new director, effective immediately. General Morgan Carrie. Do you know her?"

"I know of her," Rodgers said. "First woman to earn three stars."

"That's the one," Herbert said. "From what I gathered, Paul was 'invited' to work for the president in some new capacity."

"Classic occupation ploy," Rodgers said.

"Excuse me?"

"The German army used to roll into a village and appoint a puppet government from among the population," Rodgers said. "The new leaders and their families would get preferential treatment as long as they did Nazi dirty work, like ordering searches and ratting out resistance fighters. When that leadership had been squeezed dry, they would be executed."

"I'm not sure I see the parallel, Mike."

"The CIOC had Paul cut Op-Center back, then turned the knife on him," Rodgers said.

"True, though I wouldn't equate a West Wing job to being terminated," Herbert said.

"Did Paul sound happy?"

"He sounded uncertain, dislocated—" Herbert said.

"That's as good as it's going to get for him," Rodgers said. "If you're not part of the inner circle to start, you aren't likely to get in. That's the same as a political execution."

"I don't know if I agree, and I don't think Paul is concerned about that," Herbert said. "He cares about the work."

"Bob, that's how the work gets done there," Rodgers said. "Whether it's at 10 Downing Street, in the Kremlin, in Beijing, or in Havana, it's all about having the sympathetic ear of the core group. If I were to cold-call the CIA, do you think I'd get someone at your level willing to talk to me?"

"I hope not," Herbert said. "You're a patriot, but you're still a civilian."

"Exactly. It's about access, Bob."

"And trust," Herbert reminded him. "Access gets a Bob Herbert on the telephone. Trust is what gets you information. And whatever I—we—think about Paul Hood personally, he has never been dishonest or unreliable."

"No," Rodgers agreed. "And Robert E. Lee disliked war. That didn't prevent four years of ferocious bloodshed."

This conversation was taking them down a rutted path Herbert did not want to travel. The men had never really discussed it because they did not want to let loose the resentment they both felt. But here it was, sneaking out the back door. Herbert had not approved of the cutbacks Hood had made or the effective dismissal of Mike Rodgers as deputy director. But those issues, those emotions, did not need to be on the menu right now.

"We can talk about precedent over a cup of joe," Herbert told Rodgers. "Meanwhile, here is what I can tell you about the Chinese. It isn't much, but I'm working on it. General Carrie called a meeting first thing this morning. She introduced herself and asked us to look into two, now three, incidents involving targets with a Chinese connection. The freighter that blew up in Charleston harbor, a sugar silo that was attacked in Durban, South Africa, and an explosion at an upscale brothel in Taipei that sent body parts sailing into the harbor."

"Do you think those are all related?"

"Slave labor was involved in the harbor and brothel attacks," Herbert said. "A spymaster, Chou Shin, apparently ran holdings in the sugar processing facility that was destroyed."

"I've heard of Chou," Rodgers said. "He's a real hard-liner."

"That he is. Have you heard anything else about him?"

"Not really. His name showed up a lot in a white paper on the Tian'anmen Square uprising."

"You remembered it just from that?"

"Oh yeah," Rodgers replied.

"Why?"

"He was out there running plays for the police, pointing out individuals he wanted for interrogation," Rodgers said. "They call him the 'eagle' because of the way he just looked down from a balcony and plucked people from the square."

"I don't understand," Herbert said. "Why would a die-hard Red invest in capitalist enterprises?"

"The Unexus think tank was all over that question when we got involved with the Chinese," Rodgers told him. "There are parallels regarding Middle Eastern, Colombian, and Japanese investments. What we view as naked capitalism Beijing regards as a means of control. Think about it. How does a foreign country gain influence in the United States? Through real estate holdings, owning businesses, even laundering money through banks. They help to drive our economy. That helps elected officials stay elected. It gives you their very attentive ear. How does a foreign government make money for those often extravagant enterprises? They invest in something people will always need, like sugar or tobacco, diamonds or gold."

"I guess that makes a kind of lopsided sense," Herbert admitted. "As long as you don't become what you seek to destroy."

"You know as well as I do that a lot of sleeper agents and fifth columnists are seduced by a better life and a big bankroll," Rodgers said. "That's always been a problem when foreigners infiltrate the United States. They try to recruit sociopaths and ideologues, but those kinds of people tend to stand out."

"Okay. I understand why Chou might have invested in a sugar refinery," Herbert said. "What I don't understand was whether this attack was against the silos, the investment, or Chou himself."

"I have no idea," Rodgers said. "I just don't want to worry that our satellite is in jeopardy."

"Do you expect China to be a big part of your business in the future?" -

"We hope so," Rodgers said. "But that's not my biggest concern."

"What is?"

"The satellite has an RTG," Rodgers told him.

Herbert grunted. An RTG is a radioisotope thermoelectric generator, a lightweight, very compact system that provides energy through the natural radioactive decay of Pu-238. Though the plutonium is encased in a lead-ceramic alloy that would survive a crash or explosion, there was always the chance of an accident. One that could spread lethal radioactivity across a wide swath of the countryside.

"Is it a DoE component?" Herbert asked. Before plutonium-powered spacecraft were banned, the Department of Energy had built all of the RTGs used on American missions.

"No," Rodgers said. "We built it."

"So nuclear power is going to be a part of what Unexus offers in the future."

"I can't really talk about that, Bob."

"I understand. It's too bad you're not tighter with the prime minister," Herbert said. "You could put the question to him."

"Do you think Paul might want to take a swing at that?" Rodgers asked. "You said he's looking for something to do, and the White House has ways of communicating with the prime minister that we don't."

"Good point. Call him," Herbert suggested.

"I will," Rodgers said.

The intelligence chief did not want to phone Hood and say, "I was talking to Mike, and we were wondering . . ." That would seem like charity. It would carry more weight if Rodgers broke six months of silence with the request.

"Meanwhile, I'll see what else Darrell and our overseas allies have come up with," Herbert said. "Hopefully, the prime minister is just being cautious."

Rodgers thanked him, and they made a dinner appointment for the following week. Herbert hung up feeling very strange. Here he was, doing his duty at Op-Center, while the guys who left were in a much better position to set the world on fire—one of them literally.

Obviously, doing the right thing is not the way to get ahead in the world, he thought. You had to leave government service and shit-can your friends to do that. *But then you abandon the principles for which your wife died and you gave up your legs.*

To hell with that. Bob Herbert picked up the phone and called Darrell McCaskey.

He had a job to do.

FOURTEEN

Beijing, China
Monday, 2:27 A.M.

Prime Minister Le Kwan Po went home to his wife and a late snack of tea and apricots. Ever since he was a child he had liked dipping fruit in tea. The apartment in Beijing was a privilege of office. The very tart Mongolian apricots were his one indulgence.

They had also been an education.

The delicacy had taught him the joy of mixing elements to produce something new. It had showed him that different blends produced different results. It had proven to him that two of anything is superior to one. What he had still been puzzling over was how to convince Chou and Tam Li of that fact.

The prime minister sat across the table from his wife Li-Li. They were in a small dining alcove off the kitchen, Beijing spread below them. The rain had stopped and the streetlights shone like candles in the misty night.

Li-Li was a handsome woman with a round face framed by long, gray hair worn in a bun. She was dressed in a red silk robe and matching scarf. She was smoking a cigarette. When Le Kwan Po finished his apricots, he would join her in another smoke. Throughout Le Kwan Po's adult life, Li-Li had been his most valuable and trusted friend and adviser. She possessed a calm wisdom that was characteristic of those who had been raised in a temple. In the case of Li-Li, it was the seventeenth-century Qingshui Yan Temple in the state of Fujian. Her widowed mother cooked meals for the priests, the acolytes, and the pilgrims. The women lived in a very small room behind the mountainside structure. Some might have described it as a boring life. To Li-Li it was a reflective life. She met her future husband when he came through the region with fellow soldiers. The mountain unit stayed at the temple for nearly three weeks while they pursued remnants of the *Guomindang,* the nationalists who were hiding in these remote regions. "The soldier and the lady," as her mother called them, quickly discovered they shared a love of two things. One was the mountains. They enjoyed being where they could look up at the sun yet down upon the clouds. They enjoyed the grandeur of the sharp-edged peaks and the flora that dug its roots into the rock to thrive there. Li-Li marveled that such a small, delicate tendril could split stone.

Just as the revolutionary ideology of Mao did in 1919. He did not work and study in Europe as all the other Communist leaders did. He moved among the peasants to invent his own form of government. He put small roots in the rich soil of the Chinese working class where they grew into a powerful nation.

A hybrid, like apricots and tea.

The other thing Li-Li and Le Kwan Po enjoyed was a lively discussion. She was always confident, soft-spoken, but very, very sure of her point of view. Some would say smug. Perhaps that was because Li-Li was raised in an environment where rules were incontrovertible. Le Kwan Po was more balanced in his thinking, more willing to listen to all sides.

The prime minister and his wife had been discussing the radical differences between the two men. She believed her husband should work behind the scenes to undermine the men.

"Remove their support structure, and they will fall," she counseled. "What you must do is relocate their aides, their allies, their confidants."

"This does not need to be so complicated," he replied dismissively.

"Not this," she agreed. "But you are not doing it just to stop these men. This situation is about the future. By undermining their network of conspirators, you will discourage others."

"Fear is not a deterrent," Le replied. "Even overwhelming force can be resisted, if not at the moment, then over time. The only thing that causes a permanent change is reason."

"We have had this discussion before," the woman reminded him. "The stakes are higher now. Do you believe you can convince these men that compromise is better than whatever they are after?"

Le nodded once. "They want power. But apart from that, men want to survive."

"You just said fear does not work."

"Not the act," Le replied. "But the threat. That is different."

Li-Li took a long puff on her cigarette. "What can you do to threaten their security? You cannot dismiss them. You cannot demote them."

That was when De Ming Wang, the minister of foreign affairs, called on the prime minister's cell phone. De Ming informed him about the explosion in Taipei. Le was not happy to learn of the disaster nor to hear of it from De Ming. The foreign minister wanted very much to become prime minister. Typically, De Ming withheld information to make rivals look ineffective. If the foreign minister were providing information, it was to maneuver someone into a situation that could prove difficult or embarrassing.

"Three incidents in one day," De Ming said in conclusion. "We need to contain this situation immediately."

His motives did not change the fact that the foreign minister was right. Which is what made him a danger.

"Was this Chou's doing?" Le asked. "Those clubs in Taiwan host disreputable sorts—"

"This was very elite, and it employed girls from Guangdong province. The freighter this morning carried workers from Guangdong."

That was not proof. But it was not a good sign.

"I will handle this," the prime minister said.

"What can I do to assist?" De Ming asked solicitously.

Le lit a cigarette, blew smoke, and thought for a moment. This was a delicate situation. If De Ming were directly involved in any talks, he could sabotage the prime minister's efforts at peacemaking. If De Ming were not involved, and those efforts failed, the foreign minister could go to the National People's Congress and ask for a no-confidence vote on the prime minister. In a situation like this, Le felt it might be best to keep his enemy close.

"I will call Chou and Tam Li and arrange a meeting," the prime minister replied. "I would like you to attend."

"Certainly. When would you like to meet?"

"I will let you know," Le replied cautiously. He folded away the phone and tapped it as he looked across the table at his wife. He told her what had happened. "War between these two men will force others to take sides," he concluded. "I need to do something about it."

"You are anxious. You should wait until morning before contacting them," Li-Li suggested softly.

"I cannot afford to let the situation escalate."

"You are also tired," his wife insisted. "Mao said that a dull-witted army cannot defeat the enemy."

"They are tired as well."

"Not so tired that they won't perceive this as what it is," Li-Li said.

"Oh? And what is that?"

"Desperation, not strength. Wait. And let the foreign minister wait."

Le Kwan Po shook his head. "There is a difference between someone who is desperate and someone who is decisive. I have to find out if either of these men were involved in the attack."

"Why would they tell you?" Li-Li asked. "You were reluctant to pressure them earlier."

"I have no choice now," the prime minister said. "The foreign minister will use this against me."

"Then you *are* desperate."

Le took two quick puffs, then reached for his phone. "I am motivated," he replied.

"What will you say to them when you meet?"

"I will reason with them," he replied. "That is what I do."

"Please. If you must, call them now but see them tomorrow," Li-Li urged. "If you sit together tonight, they will say nothing or throw charges at one another. You will simply be a mediator."

"What will I be tomorrow?"

"More in control of the situation," she replied. "They will wonder why you waited to see them."

"They will wonder with good reason. I myself don't see the sense of it," Le protested.

The prime minister was not comfortable playing these psychological games. His success in politics was due to evenhandedness. He possessed a tireless devotion to the party but a willingness to allow that what worked in the twentieth century could not be cleanly adapted to the twenty-first.

Still, Li-Li was correct. These were very different circumstances. Chou and Tam Li had always fought for position and influence, but they had never resorted to murder or attacks on one another's holdings.

But silence? he thought. The prime minister regarded his wife. *How does one turn silence into a perfect weapon?* he asked himself. Silence is like clay. Others can read into it what they wish. The question Le had to ask himself was whether his wife was correct, and the men would perceive it as strength. Or whether he was right, and they would regard it as weakness. He continued to look across the table. Li-Li looked back. Her sweet face was visible through the snaking smoke of their cigarettes, through the fainter mist of their tea. Her eyes were impassive, the thin lips of her mouth pulled in a firm yet delicate line. Le did not know for certain what she was thinking. He assumed it was critical of haste.

You assume the worst based on her silence. That supported what his wife had been saying about the value of silence. *But you know her,* he reminded himself. *You already know how she feels.*

Unfortunately, the men he was dealing with would regard his silence as indecision. He had to confront them.

Le crushed his cigarette in the ashtray and picked up his telephone. He scrolled through the stored listing of cell phone numbers.

"You are calling them," his wife said.

"Yes."

"To meet when?"

"Now," he replied.

"To reason with them?"

"At first."

Li-Li stubbed out her own cigarette. "They will not listen. And what will you do if it fails?"

Le Kwan Po regarded her before accessing the first number. "Three nations suffered covert attacks today. As the prime minister of China, I have ways of passing information to those nations. Information such as the names of the people who organized the bombings. I need never soil my hands."

Li-Li smiled as she rose. "I like that reasoning," she said as she left the small kitchen area to give her husband privacy.

FIFTEEN

Arlington, Virginia
Monday, 2:44 P.M.

Since his days as a military commander in Vietnam, Mike Rodgers maintained that there were two phases to any operation. This belief was borne out during his tour of duty at Op-Center, where the general was both deputy director under Paul Hood and commander of the elite rapid deployment military unit Striker. It was also proving to be true at Unexus.

The first stage of a project was the booster phase. Whether it was a military incursion, a research program, or even a business deal, it always started with heavy lifting. Someone had to have and then sell an idea. Once it was successfully off the ground, it entered the pitch-and-yaw phase. That was a time of fine-tuning. The project had a life of its own. All the creator could do at that point was make sure it did not crash or self-destruct.

In science, the pitch-and-yaw rockets were on different sides. That was how the projectile kept its balance. In every other venture, opposing forces were not always beneficial.

The Chinese operation, as Rodgers called it, was in the pitch-and-yaw stage. The scientists had specific requirements, the investors in Europe and the United States had needs, and now the Chinese had concerns. Some of them conflicted, such as the propulsion engineers needing access to the booster and the Chinese not wanting them entering the gantry area without Chinese scientists, who had their own ideas about how things should be done.

Rodgers was kept from addressing the launch security matter as he worked to settle these problems. He was aided by fifty-one-year-old Yoo-Jin Yun, his translator, who had the most singular background of anyone he had ever met. She was the daughter of a suspected North Korean spy who was repeatedly raped by her South Korean interrogators. Her mother was fifteen years old at the time. Yoo-Jin was born nine months later. She was raised to believe that communication was the key to world peace—and to survival. Mandarin and Cantonese were two of the twenty-seven Pacific languages and dialects she spoke. The short, trim woman sat in the office next to Rodgers's on the top floor of the six-story Unexus tower. Just being around her gave Rodgers a sense of world access he had never before experienced. And meeting her mother, Ji-Woo, had also enriched him. The older woman lived with her daughter and often drove her to work. She had relocated to Seoul in 1955 and raised her daughter on her own, cleaning office buildings at night and the Sangbong bus terminal by day to put her through school. Ji-Woo had nursed the beauty that had come of tragedy. Bob Herbert could take lessons from her about living with adversity.

So could I, Rodgers had to admit. Testosterone had a way of overpowering intellectual equanimity and good intentions.

Rodgers rose from behind his opaque glass-topped desk. He went to a small stainless steel refrigerator hidden in a dark corner of the office and got himself a ginger ale.

He was dressed in shirtsleeves, a tightly knotted black silk tie, and Bill Blass slacks. His sharply pressed suit jacket hung on a wooden hanger behind the door. Rodgers always wore it when the door was open or whenever he was video-conferencing. He felt strangely powerless without a uniform of some kind. The retired general had come to this job after serving on the abortive presidential campaign of Senator Donald Orr of Texas. It was the murder of a British computer magnate, William Wilson, that precipitated the senator's downfall. The founder of Unexus, industrialist Brent Appleby, knew Wilson well. Appleby attended the trial and was impressed with Rodgers's frankness and composure. He asked the retiring general to become president of the new operation. Rodgers accepted with a handshake on the steps of the District of Columbia Federal Circuit Courthouse on Madison Place NW.

Rodgers returned to his desk with the can of soda and a cork coaster. In addition to the usual distractions, Mike Rodgers was not sure how he felt about calling Paul Hood. Rodgers had been allowed to resign from Op-Center after it was downsized. Though the cutbacks were not Hood's fault, Rodgers felt the director had not fought hard to keep him. He understood why. Paul Hood had the larger picture in mind, the continuation of Op-Center in the wake of severe budget cuts. Striker had been decommissioned after a successful but costly intervention in Kashmir. At that time there was not a great deal for an army general to do.

But understanding and forgiving were not the same.

Now Paul Hood had been replaced. Maybe the White House position was better for Hood in some ways. But it was still a very sudden take-it-or-leave-it offer, not the kind of move that fattened a man's ego. Rodgers did not need to gloat. That was in Bob Herbert's nature, not his own. However, he also did not want to be a friend to Hood. That was a status Hood had never earned.

As soon as there were no other emergencies to handle,

Rodgers was finally able to call the White House switchboard. They put him right through. That was how Rodgers knew that Hood was reporting to the Oval Office. He had been given cabinet-level treatment. Someone had literally walked his extension information to the switchboard rather than E-mailed it, where it might go unattended for hours. The name Paul Hood had been placed before the bank of operators so they knew who he was, where he was, and what his title was.

It also puts the president's fingerprints all over Hood, Rodgers reflected. Unlike Op-Center, where a man was measured by his abilities, Hood's fate was tied to that of the new chief executive. Whatever Hood himself did, he could be elevated or scapegoated at the whim of Dan Debenport.

"This is Paul Hood."

"Christ, Paul. Didn't they even give you an assistant?"

It took a moment for Hood to place the voice. "Mike?"

"It is," Rodgers replied. "Bob told me where to find you."

"Jeez, I'm glad he did! How the hell *are* you?"

"I'm doing terrific," Rodgers assured him. "The change has been good for me."

"I can imagine," Hood said. "Unexus ain't small potatoes."

"No. Lots of starch here," Rodgers joked, glancing at his jacket.

"How does it feel being in the private sector for the first time?"

"I'm happy, and my bank account is happy," Rodgers admitted. "Speaking of changes—"

"Yeah. This is a big one. A *sudden* one," Hood said.

"Are you okay?"

"I'm tucked in the corridors of power without an assistant," Hood said. "I'm told there will be a couple of them waiting in my other office down the road. An office that has a window, I hope."

"That would be nice," Rodgers said. He had a fleeting *screw you* moment as he looked out his own large floor-to-ceiling window. The Washington Monument rose in the distance, stone white against a cloudless blue sky.

"Bob tells me you're enjoying what you're doing," Hood went on.

"I'm still fighting with powers from across the sea but usually with less bloodshed," Rodgers said. The banality of this conversation was painful. Still, after six months of silence the quasi-hail-fellow-well-met dialogue was necessary. "So what can you tell me about this new position of yours?"

"Not a hell of a lot, yet," Hood said. "*New* is the operative word. The job is just some five or six hours old."

"Has it got a title?"

"A lofty-sounding one. I'm special envoy to the president."

"Which is what, exactly?" Rodgers asked.

"Well, I'm still a bit unclear about that," Hood admitted. "The position was described as 'an international intelligence troubleshooter, unaffiliated with any group but with access to the resources of all of them.'"

"What about political access through the president?"

"You mean working heads of state?" Hood asked.

"Exactly. In particular, I wonder if that includes getting the ear of the Chinese prime minister?"

"I don't know. Does it pertain to intelligence troubleshooting?"

"It does," Rodgers said.

"Impacting the private or public sector?"

"Public there, private here."

"'Here' meaning Unexus."

"Right," Rodgers said.

"Maybe you had better give this to me from the top," Hood suggested.

Paul Hood had never been an evasive, cover-your-ass bureaucrat, and that was not what was happening here. He sounded like a man who really did not know the mechanics, let alone the parameters of his job. Since it had only been in existence for one morning, that was understandable.

Rodgers told him what had happened with Le Kwan Po and the Xichang space center and the exclusion of the Guoanbu from the equation. Hood seemed surprised to hear that. Unlike Washington, Chinese intelligence agencies shared information with each other and with the impacted ministries.

"What you really need to know is whether the prime minister has specific information or concerns that your satellite may be a target," Hood said.

"Their satellite, our subcontract," Rodgers said.

"Right. Sorry. I thought we could shorthand it."

"I'm a little sensitive about that," Rodgers said. "When I was a general, they were the enemy."

"Aren't they still?" Hood asked. "Or is North Korea funding its own nuclear program?"

"I've got a new office, Paul, one with a window," Rodgers replied. "Things look different. They have to."

The comment came out more explosive than illuminating. Rodgers might still be looking at things from a general's perspective if Hood had not forced him to change offices. He decided to ignore his own minioutburst.

"It's three days until launch," Rodgers continued. "I'm hoping the prime minister is just being cautious. But I would like to know."

"What does Bob say about all this?" Hood asked.

"He's going to sniff around from downwind," Rodgers said. "But you know what our HUMINT resources are like."

Like most intelligence agencies, Op-Center had cut

back on expensive human intelligence and relied primarily on ELINT, electronic intelligence. That was fine, as long as adversaries used cell phones and E-mails, or spoke in public places where the agencies had VARDs—videographic or acoustic reconnaissance devices. If not, the analog fish slipped through the digital net.

"Lorraine Sanders will be here in a few minutes," Hood said. "Let me talk to her about this, see what she thinks."

"She's a smart lady," Rodgers said. "I assume she's helping you to integrate into the system."

"That, plus I'll be reporting to the president through her," Hood said.

Rodgers was surprised. "Does she have veto power over your operations?"

"No. Only the president, to whom I report."

"But if the chief of staff controls the flow of information—"

"Conveying information in a timely fashion is part of *her* job description," Hood replied sharply. "Mike, is there something we need to talk about? Apart from this, I mean?"

"No," Rodgers said. "Why?"

"Because that's the second kick in the ass you've given me in as many minutes," Hood replied.

"That was not my intention," Rodgers assured him. "I'm sorry if it came out that way."

"This isn't easy, Mike. Being here, talking to you, none of it. The six months of silence—that wasn't something I wanted."

"Okay," Rodgers said. "But out of curiosity, Paul, if you didn't want the silence, why the hell didn't you pick up the phone?"

"Embarrassment? Discomfort? Maybe a little envy because I left the high road and you still had it?"

"You could have talked to me about that," Rodgers said.

"We talked when you left. It didn't change anything,"

Hood said. "I wasn't happy about the way things went down. Who could be? Then it became awkward because so much time *did* pass."

"And now?" Rodgers asked.

"Has this been easy for you?"

"No," Rodgers admitted.

"There's your answer," Hood said. "Look, I've got Sanders coming, and I want to get into this situation of yours. I'll be in touch after the meeting."

Rodgers thanked him and hung up.

Conflicted did not begin to describe how Rodgers felt at the moment. It began to look as if Hood had been demoted upward. Part of Rodgers felt bad for him. A smaller, more insistent part of him did not. Yet what had been the oddest part of the conversation had nothing to do with that. It happened when they were talking about Herbert and his limited HUMINT capabilities.

Rodgers had called them "our" resources.

Even six months later, it was difficult not to think of them all as a team. Hood, Herbert, and Rodgers had gone through a lot together, more than most men got to experience in a lifetime. The deaths of coworkers, family crises, fighting the clock to prevent civil wars and nuclear attacks. Maybe Op-Center was an idea as well as a place. Maybe it was hardwired, like Rodgers's need to wear a uniform of some kind even if it was a suit. Perhaps they always would be a team, despite working from different places toward different ends.

And perhaps what the sage once said of divorce was also true of Mike Rodgers and Paul Hood. That going separate ways wasn't a sign two people didn't understand one another but just the opposite.

An indication that they had begun to.

SIXTEEN

Washington, D.C.
Monday, 3:18 P.M.

Of all the people General Carrie had met at Op-Center, the one she had enjoyed the most was Liz Gordon. The two women sat in facing armchairs in front of the desk. Carrie felt it might make these talks less intimidating than if she were behind the desk. Liz was the only one who moved her chair, turning it so that she was facing the new director rather than sitting at an angle. The staff psychologist also offered her viewpoints without having to be asked. She was the only one who did not say exactly what she thought the new director wanted to hear. They talked about Paul Hood and his impact on the organization before moving on to the existing personnel.

"The senior staff is going to want to please you," Gordon told Carrie a few minutes into their informal chat. "But they will also resent you."

"Because I replaced Paul Hood or because I replaced a man?" Carrie asked.

"Both," Liz said. "And also because you were given the job most of them would have wanted."

"I earned this position," Carrie replied. She jabbed the desk with an index finger. "I also earned the three stars I'm wearing, something no other woman ever accomplished."

"You see, General, that is part of the problem," Liz replied. "You are a woman with three stars. I know Bob, Darrell, Lowell, Ron, and Matt. I know them very well. To the first two, at least, your promotion represents a bone to our gender and not a real accomplishment."

"That would be their problem, not mine," Carrie said. "Do you think they will work less for me than they did for Hood?"

"As I said, they still need the director's approval if they want to keep their jobs. I'm sure they feel as if they are all on probation."

"They are," Carrie replied.

They were interrupted by a call from Bob Herbert. He brought Carrie up to date on the conversation with Mike Rodgers. Rodgers had also spoken with Paul Hood and had phoned to tell Herbert about that. Hood was going to see what he could do about getting intel from the Chinese prime minister.

Carrie thanked Herbert and hung up. There was a very strange mix of resentment and suck-up in Herbert's brusque but meticulously complete briefing.

"None of them is in danger of being dismissed, and I don't care whether they like me or not," the general went on. "But I want to be sure I can count on them to give the job everything they've got."

"You can," Liz said confidently. "Bob and Darrell are competitive with each other and themselves, so they will always overreach—"

The conversation was interrupted by a beep on the intercom.

"Yes?" Carrie said.

"General, Darrell McCaskey and Matt Stoll are here to see you," Bugs Benet informed her.

"Thank you. Send them in," Carrie said.

"I'll leave," Liz said, rising.

"I appreciate your input, Liz. We'll finish this later."

"I look forward to it," the psychologist replied.

Liz stepped out as McCaskey walked in. Carrie noticed McCaskey fire the psychologist a short, narrow look. It was the kind of look soldiers going into interrogation gave to soldiers leaving interrogation: *Did you crack? Did you tell them something I should know about?*

The moment passed quickly. As McCaskey entered, he was back on the job. Matt Stoll came in behind him. Carrie had not yet met the scientist alone. The MIT graduate was a lumpy man with eyes that saw elsewhere. Stoll struck her as a man who used his senses to guide him through this world while his mind lived in another, far more interesting place. He was carrying a compact disk on his index finger.

Carrie stood and went behind her desk. She did not want to be an armchair general when she received an official update.

"We may have caught a break," McCaskey said. He stopped in front of the desk and remained standing. "There was a man at the club who Interpol and the Taipei police were watching. He was a reputed slave trader by the name of Hui-ling Wong, aka Lo Tek. He died in the blast. The coastal patrol had seen his boat arrive, and officers were dispatched to all the clubs he usually frequents."

"Why didn't they arrest him en route?" Carrie asked.

"Because they have no evidence," McCaskey said. "The agents were at the nightclub with acoustic devices, hoping he would say something that would give them a reason to arrest him."

"Did he?" Carrie asked, looking at the CD.

"No," McCaskey replied. "But the agents were wearing wide wires, digital, wide-frequency recorders that collect every sound in a room and send it to a central location where the extraneous noises are removed."

"That's the only way to collect specific conversations without using a parabolic dish," Stoll said.

"The agents were killed in the blast, but everything they recorded was sent to a mobile unit not far from the club," McCaskey said. "Through my Interpol connections we got a copy."

Stoll held up the CD on his finger.

"The explosion destroyed everything within one hundred yards of the epicenter," McCaskey went on. "The bombers would have known the blast radius and made sure they were beyond that. But they would have had to be within three hundred fifty yards to detonate a radio-controlled device. Matt executed a thorough acoustic search in that window and managed to pick up the very faint trigger ping, the signal sent to activate the bomb."

"We got the guys talking on the stairwell, Madam General," Stoll said, "They were breathing hard, moving real fast, and speaking Cantonese."

"So they were probably from the mainland," the general remarked. "What did you get?"

"Until the blast killed the wide wires, we managed to pick up their names," Stoll told the general. He smiled a little for the first time. "More important, we got remarkably clear voiceprints."

"There was no one else in the stairwell at that point," McCaskey noted.

Like fingerprints, voiceprints were unique to every individual. Stoll placed the CD on the general's desk.

"We passed those charts back to Interpol and the Taipei police," McCaskey said. "They've mobilized all of their ELINT units, including those of the military. They've sectored the city and are scanning every cell phone call being made. Which, at this hour, is not a lot."

"They don't actually have to listen to the calls," Stoll

explained. "All they need is to find a frequency that matches either voice."

"Yes. I've worked with voiceprinting before," the general said.

"Sorry," Stoll said.

"So we have PRC bombers working in Taiwan," Carrie said. "Hired hands?"

"We believe so. The working theory is that it's the Tong Wars redux, right down to fighting of brothels and the trafficking of slave girls," McCaskey said. "Foot soldiers working for gang leaders. In this case, though—and it's the worst-case scenario—the leaders could be Beijing heavyweights. It will be tough to get to them."

"Maybe," General Carrie said. "Do you remember how Jack Manion dealt with the tongs?"

"Not actually, General."

"His background was required reading when I went over to G2," the general said. "In 1920, a gentleman named Dan O'Brien took over as San Francisco's chief of police. He put his childhood friend Manion in charge of the Chinatown Squad. Inspector Manion recruited Chinese to infiltrate and inform on the warring factions, on shipments of heroin, on contracted hits. He made sure his men were there to intercept and interdict. He even came up with early electronic surveillance devices, such as electrified doormats to let him know how many people were inside a room. Manion also made protecting his sources a high priority. He always had his own men on the street where spies could go with information or for protection. Not only did Manion end the violence, but after ten years in the precinct, the grateful Chinese refused to let him leave. He stayed there until his retirement in 1946." She leaned forward. "We need that here."

"In China or in general?" McCaskey asked.

"Both. Our immediate concern will be making sure that we've got a blast shield for whatever is blowing up in

China," Carrie said. "I don't care if they kill each other. But like Manion, I don't want that spilling into the streets. Not the streets of Charleston or the streets of Taipei."

"I still don't see how we're going to get close to the Chinese leaders," McCaskey said. "We don't have a deep well of HUMINT personnel and none over there. Are there resources you can call on?"

"There may be," she said. "Let's wait and see what the CA patrol turns up over there."

CA was a chase and apprehend mission. In Carrie's experience it was more often than not a full-fledged CAT operation: chase, apprehend, and terminate. Most spies and enemy infiltrators did not like to be apprehended.

McCaskey and Stoll left. Carrie slipped the CD into the computer and listened to the exchange between the bombers. The back-of-the-throat sound of the Chinese language was strikingly unfamiliar, but it was clear that both men were talking. They were definitely equals. They had been hired by someone else.

The prospect of facing a crisis this big on her first day in the director's seat both scared and invigorated the general. She could not help but wonder if someone at the Pentagon or the White House had anticipated this.

"Toss it to the chick with three stars. See how she handles the long ball. . . ."

She would handle it just fine. Not only because her career depended upon it but because of something more important.

Lives did.

SEVENTEEN

Taipei, Taiwan
Tuesday, 4:22 A.M.

Senior Inspector Loke Chichang and Lieutenant Hanyu Yilan were partners at the Taipei Municipal Police Force CID—Criminal Investigation Division. Chichang was a twelve-year veteran, Yilan a five-year man. Chichang came from a family of soldiers and had extensive training in judo and marksmanship. Yilan was a graduate of the Central Police University with a doctorate in criminology. Chichang was a wide, burly man with muscle stacked on muscle. Yilan was barely 115 pounds of bone. Chichang had a wife and three children. Yilan did not.

But both men had at least one thing in common. A passion to protect their homeland.

They had been at home when they heard the explosion in the harbor. They immediately went to the stationhouse, fearing that Taiwan might be under attack. That had been ruled out by the time they arrived—not through detective work but because nothing else blew up. A report from Interpol provided additional information: the bombing was the work of two men. Listening squads in vans were being positioned about the city, scanning cell phone conversations to find a match for their voice patterns. Chichang and Yilan joined one of the units, sitting in patrol car seventeen behind a van. The precinct commander wanted a police presence around the city. That was not just to reassure the population but to force the perpetrators to hide.

To compel them to use a wireless phone.

Voiceprints, radio triangulation, and similar technologies both impressed and frightened Chichang. The forty-year-old reasoned that if the police could watch lawbreakers, criminals could also watch police. That was one reason he did not use a cell phone. When he needed to call home, he pulled over to one of the increasingly rare pay phones and put his coins in the slot. The other reason was that he already had enough gear hanging from his belt, from his gun to his radio to pepper spray and a baton. Moreover, he did not want to carry something that might beep or vibrate as he moved into a hazardous situation. His point-to-point radio was easy to turn off with just the press of a button. After that, it stayed silent and still.

"We've had a hit in the Daan District," the CID dispatcher said over the phone. "One hundred percent match over a cell phone."

Yilan was at the wheel. He pulled the patrol car from the curb and quickly headed west.

"The target is in the Cho-Chiun Hotel," the dispatcher went on. "Cars three, seventeen, twenty, and twenty-one are closest. There is an underground parking structure. That is the rendezvous location. A bomb squad and backup are on the way, coming in silent, headlights only. Everyone else is to be turned away."

That was not just for safety, of course. One of the incoming cars could be the bombers' ride.

Chichang removed his snub-nosed .38 from its shoulder holster. He checked his weapon. Taiwan was not a society accustomed to guns and shoot-outs. Even among the police, pistol craft was a low priority and infrequently needed. Most crime was committed by thugs with clubs or knives. Homicide was relatively rare because it was difficult to get away from the crime scene and from the island nation. Chichang was a rarity, a true marksman. He had recently scored a 98 percent, the department's highest ever, in the yearly handgun test. The examination involved eight points of ability: decision shooting against pop-up targets, reduced-light shooting, hitting moving targets, the use of cover when under fire, shooting to disable, alternate position shooting, reloading drills, and malfunction drills. The inspector would have earned a perfect score if a pigeon had not flown onto the range. Chichang did not think the bird was part of the test, but he could not be sure. He chose to shoot it. It was the wrong choice.

The gun was loaded, the safety was off, and the hammer mechanism was functioning free and clear, as his father used to describe it. The former army officer was the one who first taught his son how to shoot. Chichang slipped the weapon back into the holster as his heart began to speed up. The inspector had discharged his gun only once in all his years on the police force. That was during a raid on a drug factory in a harbor warehouse. He had wounded a pusher in the shin when the individual swung an AK-47 toward him. The victim was fifteen. He was sentenced to the same number of years in prison. Chichang was commended for his restraint.

The patrol car tore through the misty morning. They reached the hotel in under five minutes. Two of the other cars had already arrived. They parked in the small underground garage. As the ranking officer, Chichang was in charge of the operation. He told the two hotel security men to make sure all the exits were locked, including roof and cellar doors. Then he went to the front desk. According to the concierge, 418 was the only room in which two men were registered. Chichang asked the bellman to describe the layout of the floor. The room was relatively near the elevators. The two men might hear the bell if he went up that way.

The hotel was one of the older structures in the district, and there was only one stairwell. There were two windows, which overlooked the rooftop of a small grocery store. It was a two-story drop. Chichang instructed one of the police officers to go to that roof. He had one of the housekeepers go with him to point out the window of 418. If either of the men tried to escape, the officer was to open fire. His goal was to keep them inside, not to kill them.

The inspector took a master key from the desk and ordered Yilan and two other men to come with him. He sent one of the men to the fifth floor so the bombers could not go up. He left the other man on the third floor to block their descent. He and Yilan exited on the fourth floor. Yilan's job was to make sure that if the two men got past him, they did not try to get into another room and take hostages. The bombers had taken a corner room beside a linen closet. The room on the other side was occupied by a couple from England.

"I'm wondering if we should wait for the bomb squad and body armor," Yilan said. "They may have more explosives."

"If we're quick, they won't have time to prime them."

"They may already have done so," Yilan observed.

"If we wait too long, they may hear the quiet, start to wonder if something is wrong. We need to move quickly if we want to surprise them."

"What about a chain on the door? Surely they would have used one."

"That's why I need you here," the inspector said. They reached the door, and Chichang removed his handgun. He handed the brass key to Yilan. "You open it," he whispered, pointing toward the room. Then he hunkered his right shoulder toward the door and put his weight on his right leg.

Yilan nodded in understanding.

He put the key in the lock as carefully as he could to make as little noise as possible. He turned to the right. The deadbolt slid back, and the door popped open. The chain was not on. But there was a very thin wire between the door and the jamb. It moved when the door swung inward. It pulled a plug from a detonator cap. The cap was stuck in a wad of plastique. It blew the top half of the door and the frame outward, slashing the two police officers with pieces of wood ranging from splinters to large fragments. They screamed and were tossed backward by the blast. Yilan took the brunt of the explosion, which tore a large, lethal hole through his rib cage. Chichang lost most of his face in the initial explosion. He also lost his right hand when the gunpowder in the shells detonated. He lay on the floor, his legs stretched across the carpet as his own blood mingled with that of Yilan.

The two bombers tossed aside the bedspread they had been holding over their heads. They pushed open the shattered door, stepped over the two bodies, and ran down the hall. They had been alerted by a call from the front desk. The Guoanbu maintained a covert sleeper presence in several Taiwanese businesses. This hotel was one of them. The concierge had no idea how the bombers were pinpointed. The only thing they could think of was that the cell phone had been compromised in some way. They had placed a short call to a relay boat in the East China Sea, letting their employer know that they had escaped the site. If they had been injured or captured, it could have led investigators to Director Chou.

The linen closet was unlocked, and the two men ducked inside. The officers who had been stationed on the staircase came running when they heard the blast. The bombers waited until they heard the men talking beside the blown-out door. Then they pushed open the closet door and ran to the stairwell. The door afforded them the moment of cover they needed to get away.

The two men hurried down the concrete steps. They got off on the second floor, which had a ballroom and a small kitchen. The doors were unlocked. They went inside, swung around a butcher-block island, and went to an emergency exit. It was there in case of fire in the kitchen. The steps were inside and led to a nondescript door near the Dumpster in an alley. Unless someone knew it was there, they would not think to look for it. The men listened, heard nothing, then opened the door a crack. There was no one in the alley. The CID had done a classic off-premises entry. The patrol cars were probably parked in a place where they would not have been heard or seen.

The two men walked into the damp, chill, early morning mist. They had arrived that same day and had no luggage. The explosives had been provided by a mainland loyalist in the Taiwanese military. They had planned to leave Taiwan the same way they came in, by a China Airlines flight through Tokyo. They would still do so, only now they would spend the next few hours at the White Wind all-night bar on Kunming Street instead of in their hotel room.

They had no way of notifying Director Chou that they had escaped. The cell phone had been attached to the plastique they applied to the door. The concierge had said he would call the boat with news of the getaway.

The men walked to the bar and went directly to the lavatory to wash the distinctive tart smell of the plastique from their hands. The bedspread, at least, had prevented their clothes from being covered with dust. They had walked off any traces that might have stuck to their soles.

Dawn came quickly, burning off the mist and allowing the two bombers to slip away, like human vapor.

EIGHTEEN

Washington, D.C.
Monday, 5:00 P.M.

Paul Hood felt mortified after talking with Mike Rodgers, though he was not sure why.

Horseshit, he scolded himself in a flash of candor. *You know damn well what the reason is.* He was humiliated because Mike Rodgers had come out on top. The guy who had been dismissed had not only landed upright but next to a ladder that let him scurry right back to the top. And beyond. Hood had landed on his ass and had to be picked up by the president and dusted off by the chief of staff. As Hood discovered, and as Rodgers had intimated, that was not a pleasant experience.

Lorraine Sanders came to Hood's office as scheduled. She entered after knocking but before he told her to come in. He did not have time to put on his blazer, which was hanging from the back of his chair. Sanders's mind was obviously somewhere else as she informed Hood that two temporary assistants were getting an on-site briefing at the new office. They would be prepared to take Hood around in the morning. She said that he was free to spend as much time in either office as he wished. A car would be at his disposal, though Hood told Sanders he preferred to drive himself.

"Are you trying to make the rest of us look bad?" the woman asked with a critical grin.

"Just a preference," he replied.

"You'd be the only senior staff member without a driver," she pointed out. "There are also security issues. We'd feel better if you used him."

" 'We' as in the president? Are you speaking for him?"

"I know that is what he would want," she replied.

"I'll think about it," Hood replied with a smile only slightly less insincere than her own.

What she had said to him was close to the truth. If he did not use a driver, someone in the press or the General Accounting Office might notice. They might wonder why anyone but the president and vice president needed a chauffeur. Perks might have to be sacrificed to keep the peace. Hood had always used that drive time to think. When he was mayor of L.A., he took public transportation to encourage its use. And Hood did not like the fact that Sanders was speaking for the president without even having discussed this with him.

Sanders's smile evaporated as she gave Hood a CD containing intelligence matters that concerned the president. Hood promised to review them.

"I would also like to talk to him about a matter involving the PRC," Hood told Sanders.

"Talk to me," she said.

"Prime Minister Le Kwan Po has requested information about an upcoming satellite launch at the Xichang space center. The satellite was built by Unexus, the firm run by my former deputy Mike Rodgers. He's concerned that there may be an attempt to sabotage the booster."

"Unexus is a firm with a minor American component, isn't it?"

"I don't know the exact proportion—"

"Why should this administration be concerned about what is basically foreign-built hardware for a potentially hostile government?"

"The trajectory will carry the rocket over the Pacific," Hood said. "If it blows up after launch, radiation from the plutonium power source is going to hit the atmosphere like Mardi Gras confetti. Some of that could come down in Hawaii or along the West Coast."

"I see," Sanders said. "And do you really think the prime minister will tell us what he knows?"

"The Chinese obviously have some kind of spitting contest going on," Hood said. "He may be ready for a hand."

Sanders nodded and looked at her watch. "The president will be finishing his meeting with the Joint Chiefs in about five minutes. I'll pass this along."

"Fine. But before you go, tell me why I had to stand here and justify my request," Hood said. "It was my understanding that 'I'd like a minute with the president' was all I needed to tell you."

She smiled more sincerely now. "You think too much," she said. "I'll let you know what the president says."

The phone beeped as Sanders was leaving the office. The room was small enough so that Hood could grab the call and tap the door shut with his foot at the same time. He was aware of a sharpness in the little kick, a little *Stuff it* gesture to the retreating chief of staff.

"Paul Hood," he said. He began rolling up his shirtsleeves like he used to do when he got to work at Op-Center or on a construction site in Los Angeles. Only now there was nothing to do.

"Paul, it's Bob. The Taiwanese screwed up."

"How?"

"The bombers got away," Herbert said. "They killed two cops and blew up the cell phone when they did. We aren't going to be hearing from them again."

"Aren't the police still looking?"

"No one saw them," Herbert said. "No one who survived. And the descriptions from the hotel workers are not giving them enough to go on."

"What are the implications?" Hood asked, adding, "I don't just mean for Mike's launch."

"That's tough to say, Chief," Herbert said. Was the use of the title a lapse or a sign of respect? Hood did not know, but it was nice to hear. "It's not likely that these were the same people working in Charleston or Durban. They'd be two very tired men, and you don't want tired men handling explosives. If there's a network of bombers, and they were already positioned only in soft targets—for whatever reason—I would say the rocket launch is safe. But these three blasts could be the warm-ups for one or more big attacks. Perhaps the prime minister has insight we lack. We need to find out."

"I agree," Hood said.

"Did you make progress on your end?"

"I'm about to," Hood replied. He was still standing beside his desk. He glanced at the closed door as if it were an enemy.

"I don't follow."

"I'll call you when I get back from Olympus," Hood promised.

The new special envoy to the president hung up the phone and left his office. He did not bother rolling his shirtsleeves back down. He had something to do, and it was in the Oval Office.

The Joint Chiefs were making their way down the corridor like a green glacier. They were talking quietly among themselves, ignoring the nonmilitary staff that moved past them. If the president were Zeus, then these were the Titans, anchored by Army General Raleigh Carew. The Minnesotan stood six foot five and carried himself even taller. Hood sidled by. At the end of the hallway he entered the office of the president's executive secretary, Julie Kubert. They had not been introduced earlier, but she knew who he was and greeted him by name. The door to the Oval Office was open to her left. Debenport was on the phone.

"I'd like to see the president," Hood said.

The white-haired woman looked at her computer. "How is tomorrow morning at ten fifteen—"

"Today," Hood said. "Now would be good."

The former executive secretary to the publisher of the *Chicago Tribune*—which supported Debenport—looked over. "The president of Laos is waiting in the Red Room, Mr. Hood."

"Appropriate," Hood remarked. He cocked his head toward the Oval Office. "Is he speaking with Ms. Sanders?"

"Mr. Hood—"

"Has she been to see him?"

"Mr. Hood, they are scheduled to review the day at six-fifteen, as always. Now, do you want an appointment for tomorrow or not?"

"Ms. Kubert, there's something going on that I must discuss with the president, and soon."

"If it will shut you up, Paul, come in," Debenport said.

"Thank you," Hood said to Kubert. Then he turned and entered the Oval Office. "I'm sorry, Mr. President, but I need to speak with Prime Minister Le Kwan Po."

"The Chinese fence-sitter," the president said. "Why?"

"He may be sitting on intel we need," Hood replied.

Lorraine Sanders rushed in. She obviously had been alerted by Ms. Kubert. The chief of staff said nothing as she took up a position beside the president's desk. Arms folded, she glared at Hood.

Hood ignored her. When the president was still Senator Debenport, and head of the Congressional Intelligence

Oversight Committee, he would often pit factions one against the other, then step aside as they slugged it out. The survivor was someone he wanted on his side. Hood did not know if that was the case here. It would not be a bad tactic to put sinew into a new administration. If this were a gladiatorial showdown, Hood did not intend for it to end with Sanders's foot on his neck. Either he would win or leave the arena.

Hood told the president what he had already explained to Sanders, adding the new information from Bob Herbert. He made the presentation as concise as possible. The president listened, then rose and walked from behind the desk. He came around the side opposite from where Sanders was standing.

"Ms. Sanders, have Ambassador Hasen look into a meeting," the president said. "Paul, get yourself over to our embassy in Beijing."

"Sir?"

The president stopped beside Hood. "If there's infighting in Beijing, we need to know. It might help to have General Rodgers with you. He can go to observe the launch, I presume."

"I don't see why not."

"As for Op-Center, I want you to talk to General Carrie before you leave. The Joint Chiefs were just in here. They mentioned something in passing that obviously dovetails with this."

"What's that, sir?" Sanders asked. It was an obvious effort to become part of a project she had not felt was terribly important. Until right now.

"General Carrie has requested that a small group of marines be seconded to Op-Center for a possible security mission in Beijing," the president told Hood. "One that will be defined as information becomes available."

"Did she say what kind of security mission it would be?" Hood asked.

"The president said it would be defined later," Sanders said.

"What I mean, sir, would it be at the launch site, at the embassy, or a black ops action somewhere else?" Hood asked the president, ignoring Sanders.

"The Joint Chiefs did not tell me, and I did not ask. There was no point. As I told you before, Paul, General Carrie was pushed on me as the head of Op-Center. If the military is planning some kind of new and covert direction for Op-Center, I want to know what it is—not what they *tell* me it is."

"Understood," Hood said.

"It's good you have someone you trust on the inside," the president told him. "Tell Herbert to keep one eye on the NCMC . . . and one on his ass." He winked, then did not look back as he headed toward the door.

Hood looked over at Lorraine Sanders. Her arms were still crossed, and her expression was still sour. Debenport's inner circle had a reputation for resenting outsiders. If Hood let that bother him, he would never be able to do his job.

"I'll have the travel office arrange for a ticket to Beijing," she said to him.

"Thanks."

She walked toward the door, stopping beside Hood. "If you do that again, I'll feed you to General Carew. I swear it."

"Are you working for him? Should the president be concerned?"

"No," she replied thickly. "I just happen to know the general likes chewing up starchy little bureaucrats."

She crossed the blue carpet with its gold symbol of the presidency, leaving Hood alone for a moment in the Oval Office. He had always understood why presidents became paranoid, why they installed recording devices in the West Wing. He just hated being a part of that intrigue. The people at Op-Center had always pulled together toward a single goal: protecting the United States and its interests from chaos. Here, they helped to create it.

As he left the Oval Office and the pointedly averted eyes of Ms. Kubert, Hood was suddenly more afraid of his own team than he was of the Chinese.

NINETEEN

Beijing, China
Tuesday, 4:40 A.M.

Li-Li would be proud. The prime minister arrived at his office shortly after three A.M. His visitors were already there. Le Kwan Po had made them wait.

Blinking hard to chase away the fog of exhaustion, he looked over data that had been sent from the Xichang space center, hand-carried by his aide and placed in a safe. Against opposition, Le Kwan Po had supported international involvement with the project. It was not just a matter of having a sophisticated communications satellite at their disposal. It was a question of being able to deconstruct the technology, study it, and build the next generation of homegrown Chinese satellites.

A number of old-school members of the government did not like the idea of commissioning work from other nations. Stealing blueprints and technology was acceptable, a legitimate function of the state. Paying for it was to admit a need, to show weakness. A technologically advanced satellite could not compensate for a bowed head. Men like

Chou Shin were unyielding in matters like that. What Le did not know was whether they were willing to promote internecine warfare.

The security arrangements were no different than they were for other launches. Unless he could forge some kind of peace very soon, that would have to change. Chou and Tam Li both had access to the old codes. They knew the standard distribution of manpower throughout the site and what areas engineers would be watching as the countdown progressed.

They knew that this was the centerpiece of the National Day celebration honoring the founding of the People's Republic of China.

Something would have to be done about this. Le would try reasoning with the men, though that had never worked in the past. Perhaps now, with their feud becoming public, their attitude would be different. A news report from Taiwan had just arrived. It underscored the need for someone to take control of this situation. Bulletins from the breakaway republic were automatically sent to all Chinese government officials. Le read about the attempted arrest at the Taipei hotel. The Cho-Chiun was a safe house for Chinese spies. There was no doubt in his mind who the police had been pursuing. He would be interested to find out how they tracked the men there. He called the vice chairman of the Standing Committee on Regional Security to see if he knew anything more. The vice chairman had been up since hearing of the nightclub bombing. He had confirmed through intercepted radio transmissions what Le had suspected, that the Taipei Municipal Police had been given assistance by Interpol. The SCRS did not know who had provided the international police with their information.

To clear his mind, the prime minister also reviewed an updated guest list for the reception he would be hosting the following evening. A few ambassadors had been added, and several journalists had been removed. Leading academics in the sciences and arts would also be attending. Le's daughter Anita was among them. The forty-year-old woman was a professor of literature and head of the doctoral arts program at Beijing University. Poised, articulate, and lovely, she was a favorite of the premier. Le often said, only partly in jest, that it was her status that had given him job security rather than vice versa. The cocktail party was in honor of the fifty-eighth National Day. The reception was an opportunity for people to mingle and exchange ideas.

At least, on the surface.

When he was ready, Le Kwan Po lit a cigarette and went to the sitting room adjoining his office. The foreign minister was pacing, Chou Shin was sitting in a red leather armchair with his chin on his chest and his eyes shut, and General Tam Li was tucked against one side of a white sofa, his right arm poised on the armrest as he stared straight ahead. He was smoking a hand-rolled cigarette stuffed with strong Hongtashen tobacco. He was catching the ashes on a copy of the newspaper resting under his elbow. Only the foreign minister reacted to the prime minister's arrival.

"Is everything all right?" De Ming asked solicitously.

"We would not be here if it were," Le said as he shut the office door. He walked toward the men. The prime minister did not apologize for making them wait. General Tam Li continued to stare ahead. Chou woke and sat up straight. "Did any of you see the latest report from Taipei?" Le knew they had not, since the time stamp was 4:29 A.M. They all looked over.

"What has happened now?" De Ming asked. The man's hovering attentiveness was replaced by real concern. Not just about the event but for knowledge the prime minister possessed that he did not.

Le sat in a rocking chair. He leaned forward and took an ashtray from the coffee table by the sofa. He told the three men about the explosion at the Taipei hotel and the subsequent escape of the bombers.

The men seemed surprised by the news—for different reasons, the prime minister suspected.

"Do the Taiwanese police know who the hotel guests were?" Chou asked.

"Which information is the director of the Guoanbu concerned about?" General Tam Li asked as he blew smoke from the side of his mouth. "The names of the men or the fact that Taipei might have identified them?"

Chou did not reply.

The prime minister regarded the spy chief. "I would like to know the answer to that, Director Chou."

The seventy-one-year-old hard-liner snickered. "Is that why we were called from our beds? To be interrogated by an amateur?"

"The technique is not important. The information is," the prime minister replied. "It is no secret that the distinguished director of the Guoanbu and one of our most honored soldiers are not getting along. The foreign minister has kept me informed about attacks against Chinese interests abroad. These incidents do not seem to have been random. I hope both of you can tell me more about them."

The foreign minister did not look happy. The prime minister did not care. Le wanted these men to know that De Ming Wang was a self-serving opportunist and not a potential ally.

"My interest in Taipei is professional," Chou replied. He regarded Tam Li for the first time. "As for this honored soldier, the general and I have a very different vision of China and its place in the world. My views are in accord with the values and policies of the *Zhōngúo Gòngchandang*. His are not."

Chou was near reverent when he mentioned the Communist Party of China. The spy master obviously did so to suggest that an attack on him was an attack against the nation itself.

"General?" Le asked.

"I do not intend to sit here as my devotion to our nation and its party are questioned," Tam Li replied. His mild surprise at the news from Taipei had diminished. He continued to look ahead and not at anyone in the room. "Director Chou has failed to answer the prime minister's question. I would like to know the answer as well. I would also like to know whether the resources of the Guoanbu are being used in ways other than their regulations permit."

"Is there evidence of this?" the prime minister asked. He looked from the general to the spy chief. Until Le had more information—*any* information—he did not wish to take sides. Ultimately, there might not be a need to. Not if he could get the men to do that work for him.

Neither man spoke. Le did not bother asking the foreign minister. De Ming would not say anything, even if he knew.

The prime minister drew on his cigarette. He exhaled slowly. He had the authority to empanel a Special Bureau of Investigation to examine these matters. The ten-member group would be hand-picked by the minister of justice from among the representatives of twenty-three administrative divisions of China. Because the members came from outside the executive branch, the legislative branch, and the military, an SBI was generally unbiased and untouchable. The representatives were prohibited, by law, from seeking higher office. They had nothing to gain by coloring their findings.

But an SBI would not act quickly. And the prime minister needed immediate results, especially if the launch might be at risk. He also needed to keep the foreign minister from moving against him.

"Does the foreign minister have any comments?" Le asked.

"Chinese citizens were killed in the United States and Taipei," De Ming said. "I would suggest at the very least an oversight committee be formed to collect information from foreign sources."

"To place blame or redirect it?" General Tam Li asked.

Le regarded the officer. "I ask again, General. Do you have information you wish to share?"

"None," Tam Li told him. "Only an observation. Absent détente, this situation will escalate."

The prime minister did not bother to ask him how or when. No one seemed to want to say anything incriminating, something that might help an opponent. "What would it take to establish peace?" Le asked.

"There can be no peace without a singular vision," Chou said. "We have a system of beliefs in China, one established by great men. One put in place through the sacrifice of millions of lives. There can be no deviation from that."

Tam Li rolled what was left of his cigarette between his fingers. His pale eyes were fixed on the glowing tip. "The number of smokers in China surpasses the population of the United States. Should all of us smoke the same brand? Should those who do not smoke be forced to do so? I am told by my physician that millions of souls have died for that right as well."

"Your comments are sickening," Chou snapped. "They diminish the sacrifice others have made."

"I had hoped to provide perspective," Tam Li replied quietly.

"You failed," Chou said. "Mr. Prime Minister, this meeting is pointless, and I am tired."

"You should consider retiring," the general said and then looked at the spy chief. "To bed, I mean."

Chou Shin regarded the prime minister. "Is there anything else we need to discuss?"

"Not at the moment, thank you," Le replied. The spy chief had just given him what he needed.

The head of the Guoanbu bowed slightly toward the foreign minister, then to the prime minister, then left.

"Ideologues are easy to bait," the general said.

"Why did you want to?" Le asked. "You do not advocate our political philosophy?"

"I support the land," Tam Li replied. "I support China, whatever form that takes. One day it is a dynasty, an empress, one day it is a party called Communism. The next day we are all looking the other way as Hong Kong and Taiwan force us to tolerate new ideas."

"Not everyone tolerates them," the foreign minister pointed out.

"No. Director Chou does not. Others do not. As a general, I have been trained to watch and evaluate the currents of battle. This one, the one Director Chou is fighting, is a losing one."

"Do you think the director loves China any less than you, less than any of us?" Le asked.

"No. But he is a jealous lover."

"A violent one?"

General Tam Li smiled self-consciously. He put the stub of the cigarette between his lips, then carefully folded the paper full of ashes. He stood and dropped the paper in a wastebasket. Then he walked over to the prime minister and put his cigarette in the ashtray.

"No, Mr. Prime Minister," the general said.

"He is not a violent man?" Le asked.

"No—I will say nothing more," Tam Li continued. "Director Chou and I share this much: the belief that a man fights his own battles."

"Such battles could hurt China," the prime minister pointed out.

"Internal struggle, however painful at the time, invariably strengthens the host. It builds new defenses, discards aspects of a system that do not work. If the system fails, it was not healthy to begin with."

"We are talking about escalating attacks on Chinese holdings, not debates in the People's Congress," the prime minister complained.

"You are just giving us idealistic words and sweeping ideas," the foreign minister added impatiently.

"What is Communism if not that?" Tam Li asked.

The foreign minister threw up his hand in disgust. Then he excused himself and left the room. The prime minister set the ashtray aside and rose. "General, I don't care whether you and Director Chou claw each other to pieces," he said. "I am not worried about the survival of China. I am, however, very concerned about the launch of the *Red Eagle* on Thursday. Your command will use it to link communications that are currently using landlines."

"That is a piggyback function," Tam Li replied.

"One of many, yes," Le said. "That is why the Ministry of Science turned to a foreign firm to build the mainframe. Their design allowed us to plug in multiple utilities, to consolidate what would have been several launches into one. I am concerned that your conflict with Director Chou may affect that launch."

"I don't see how I can help you," Tam Li said. "We have a strong philosophical difference."

"Yes, and it has taken physical form, like the spirit in the old story of *Zong Dingbo and the Ghost*," the prime minister said. "In that form the ghost was able to destroy and to *be* destroyed."

"As I recall from my childhood, it was a careless ghost," the general said. "But a ghost must be a ghost, whatever the consequences."

"The satellite is bigger than your dispute," Le said angrily. The prime minister was too practical for this. Like

Director Chou, Tam Li was a man who would follow principle through the gateway to hell.

"Do you know what our argument is about?"

"You sell people," Le said. "At least, that is what I am told."

"It is not true, Mr. Prime Minister. I collect an honorarium for advice, for helping other men conduct trade."

"Slave trade—"

"Not to me and not to them," Tam Li said. "These are people who want to leave China, people who do not want to be a part of Director Chou's world. Like me, they want to make more money. Unlike me, they leave. I collect my legal fee for the same reason that my soldiers gamble or occasionally traffic black market goods. Because we do not make enough money to raise and educate our families. In Russia, men in my position are selling outdated weapons. In the United States, some men sell military secrets. China benefits from both because our government is willing to pay them. We, who offer our lives in the defense of our nation, must make do with what the government has left. Which is not very much."

"Soldiers are always underpaid," Le said. "But they do not have to depend on crops or tourists or the whims of commerce to earn a living. Their salary may not be substantial, but it is regular. They are never hungry, and they always receive medical attention."

"Until new technologies reduce our numbers," the general said. "You know as well as I that even exotic hardware like the *Red Eagle* is going to reduce the need for communications units. The new Song-class submarines require half the crew of the older models. In my lifetime I may become redundant. I do not farm. I do not weave. I will not beg to give Japanese and American visitors a tour of the Great Wall. You may not like it, and Director Chou absolutely does not like it, but I stand for many, and I will not back down. Tell me, Mr. Prime Minister. Are you asking me to do so because I happen to be the last one here, or do you agree with Director Chou?"

"I cannot sanction what you do, but I do not support Chou's actions."

"You won't tell him that, though, because he represents the party, and the party is the embodiment of Mao," the general said. "To challenge him is to challenge the great revolutionary."

Le said nothing.

"Then I suppose I stand for you as well," Tam Li said. "I will resist the assault of Director Chou Shin because his China belongs to another century. We evolve, Mr. Prime Minister. We always have. With our diversity of people and cultures and even climates, we have no choice. If we don't, we will fracture." He smiled. "What kind of love can exist without a big and enlightened embrace?"

Tam Li left, his shoes squeaking as he crossed the blue carpet. New shoes. The prime minister looked down. His own shoes were not new.

And his ideas? the prime minister wondered.

Le went back to his office. He looked out the window at the soft arrival of dawn. He did not know what he had accomplished by bringing everyone together, other than to confirm what the two men were thinking, feeling, and in some cases doing. His desire to separate them and then reason with the one he hoped was the more tractable had not worked. He had not even neutralized a potential threat from the foreign minister. De Ming had been driven, slightly, toward the side of Director Chou. The general was a closet capitalist, someone who still performed his job and was a danger to no one who did not get in his way. Chou was an idealist, someone with the means and allies to attack anyone who did not share his vision.

That could include the prime minister. It could include a scientific project that enriched foreign corporations.

But the night was not a complete loss. Le had realized something. His problem might be bigger than he imagined. General Tam Li stood to lose something, too, with the successful launch of the *Red Eagle*. What the PLA gained in efficiency it surrendered in manpower. And as Tam Li had suggested, a general without troops is not a general. He is a retiree.

Tam Li and Chou Shin both had something to gain by the destruction of the satellite. Unfortunately, this was also true:

If either of them won, Le Kwan Po lost.

TWENTY

Washington, D.C.
Monday, 7:00 P.M.

Paul Hood was baffled by the president's comments about marines being seconded to Op-Center. For one thing, the ambassador would have told the president if he had requested additional security for the embassy. For another, that was an expansion of the NCMC, not a scaling down. Perhaps it represented a honeymoon period for General Carrie, a chance to let her reorganize according to her own vision. But Maryland Senator Luke Murray, the new head of the Congressional Intelligence Oversight Committee, was even more frugal than his predecessor Debenport. Hood did not see anyone convincing the senator to spend money, let alone to revive a military contingent that had recently been abandoned.

Unless there was something going on that Hood knew nothing about. That was certainly a possibility. It was also possible that the president had not been informed. Not every intelligence operation was written up and placed on his desk. Hood hoped to find out more by seeing General

Carrie. He called before leaving the White House. Bugs Benet had been happy to schedule the appointment, but there was a new formality in his voice. That was understandable. Bugs had a different boss now. Each man asked how the other was doing. There was something guarded and unnatural about their responses. Perhaps Carrie discouraged familiarity in her team.

The drive to Op-Center was also both familiar and strange. Hood knew the roads, the nuances of the traffic, the colors of the trees under the streetlamps, and the moods of the early evening sky. He recognized the homeless man who stood by the highway and peddled coffee-cup sculptures from a makeshift stand. Hood had once stopped and bought one because he felt bad for the guy. The man, Joe, had used three cups to make a replica of the Capitol. It was not bad. The problems Hood pondered while driving were the same he always contemplated: what to do about an evolving situation overseas that impacted the homeland.

But the drive was not the same. Going to Op-Center was like visiting Harleigh and Alexander. He was going to a house that used to be home. Rules were not made, they were followed.

Upon reaching Andrews AFB, Hood had to stop at the gate. He knew the sergeant who talked to him from the bulletproof guard booth. They had just seen each other that morning. Hood still had to wait while a digital picture was taken by a driver's-side camera. He had to wait for the guard to check his name on the computer list. He had to wait while the security gate was rolled open. The identity card that was still in his wallet would not have worked in the slot.

Hood parked and entered the upper lobby. The guard knew him, too, but still had to call ahead to let Bugs know that Hood was there. Hood was handed a pass that would work the elevator for just one day. Bugs met him downstairs. The men shook hands. It was no longer just formal. It was damned awkward.

"It's good to see you," Hood said.

"Same. The general is waiting."

Bugs was wearing a smile, but there was no joy in it. There was something else. He looked different. Hood noticed then that his long sleeves were rolled down, and his tie was tightly knotted. Hood had always allowed him to wear it loose with the top button opened. Perhaps Bugs was waiting to be told that was okay. Perhaps he had already been told it was not. It was not a big thing, but a mosaic like Op-Center was built on details like that. One tessera did not change without affecting all the others. A knotted tie might induce formality in Bugs that was passed to others, from their appearance to their work. It had always been Hood's contention that someone who was bundled too tight would be less inclined to look for—and deliver— fresh insights.

Employees were surprised to see their former boss. There were Bugs-like smiles and a few big hellos, but no one stopped to talk. No one had information for him or a question. Some people might find that liberating. Hood found it disturbing. More and more he felt as he did when he left Sharon and the kids. As though he had not just relocated, he had been dislocated. He needed someone to pop him back in his socket, and it was not happening.

Hood was shown to his office. Or rather, what used to be his office. It looked different. It *smelled* different. Carrie was a tea drinker. It sounded different. Carrie kept the door closed. Hood did not even have time to thank Bugs before he was shut inside with the general. She stood and shook his hand across the desk. General Carrie did not look like Hood had imagined. She had sharply defined features and a disarming smile that pulled up slightly to the right. Her eyes were soft. So was her voice, though it was not weak.

Nor was her handshake.

The general gestured to one of the armchairs that Hood himself had picked out. She offered him a beverage, which he declined. He sat after she did. That might be politically incorrect, but Hood did not care. Morgan Carrie was still a woman, and women sat first. That was how it went.

"I imagine this is a little strange for you," the general said.

"Somewhat."

"Is there anything I can do to help?" she asked.

"Just treat my people well," Hood replied earnestly.

"I meant, for you," she said.

"That would help me," Hood assured her. "Since we never got to do a proper transition, my people—*these* people—work best in a relaxed atmosphere. When the world is falling down, the NCMC can be a haven. For example, Bugs is a great aide. He doesn't miss a thing."

"Mr. Benet seems to be a very effective and knowledgeable man," the general concurred. "He has helped a great deal today. Of course, there is going to be an evaluation process. I may bring in some people from G2. But I would like to keep as many of the current staff as possible. In any case, Paul, I won't be making any immediate changes."

"I understand that," Hood told her. He felt uncomfortable. He had not intended to get into any of this, but here he was. "It's more a matter of day-to-day efficiency. Take Bugs again. It's a small thing, but he works best with his sleeves rolled up and his tie open."

"He's free to do so," Carrie replied. "This is not the army. I stand by the civilian dress code."

Hood looked at her. "Oh. Okay," he said. He felt stupid. Obviously, Bugs had tied his tie and buttoned his cuffs to try to please her.

The general leaned forward and folded her hands. "Believe me, Paul. I'm aware of my situation here. I'm in a trial period as well. The man who sat in this chair before me did the brutally difficult job of pleasing a president *and* his own staff for years. That's a hell of an accomplishment. My team at G2 was assigned to me. Like it or not, that was their command. Your people were mostly civilians. They stayed because they wanted to. Op-Center did not always run smoothly, I know. Nothing does. But it ran well and effectively. I would be happy to have that on my résumé."

Now Hood really felt stupid. And also flattered and proud. He had been expecting Mike Rodgers, someone for whom every meeting, every conversation was a form of combat. That was not General Carrie.

The officer sat back again. "Bugs said that the president asked you to come in and talk with me," she said with her little half smile. "I do not imagine the subject was shirtsleeves."

"No," Hood told her. "I am here because I am about to leave for Beijing. Both Bob Herbert and Mike Rodgers are concerned about the launch of the Unexus satellite. The president is more concerned about the stability of the government. He wants me to assess the situation."

"It is a dangerous one," Carrie said.

"Was G2 watching any of the players?" Already, Hood felt himself acting like an outside intelligence operative. He did not say, *"Were you watching General Tam Li?"* He was guarding his information.

"We collected whatever we could on all the major military and intelligence figures," she replied, equally vague.

"Does anyone stand out?" Hood asked.

"Several," she replied.

Except for Hood asking, *"Who?"* they had reached the irreducible and in some ways the most absurd level of intelligence conversation. The you-show-me-yours point. It seemed to be a silly game for adults to be playing. Unfortunately, silly as it might be, it was not a game. In a world where knowledge was power, everyone did it. Even when they were supposed to be on the same team.

Carrie picked up the phone. She tapped the intercom button. Hood had always put it on speaker.

"Send them in," the general said.

The door opened behind Hood, and Bob Herbert wheeled in. He was followed by Darrell McCaskey. Herbert stopped to the right of Hood's armchair. The men shook hands. Herbert's smile was tight, his eyes blood-shot. The man was totally shot. McCaskey also looked a little drawn as he shook Hood's hand and dropped into the other armchair. Herbert's tie was open at the top. Darrell's was not.

"I asked Bob and Darrell to join us," Carrie said. "I thought it might be useful if we were all on the same page."

The general looked at the men. *At her men,* Hood thought. At the men she had made a point of calling at her discretion. Either General Carrie had wanted to show Hood that he could be isolated or made part of a team. In any case, her point was clear: the call was hers to make.

"Paul is going to Beijing at the request of the president," Carrie told Herbert and McCaskey. "President Debenport asked him to stop here first. Paul was about to tell me what information he needed."

That, too, was very smooth. She was a natural at the wielding of authority. McCaskey and Herbert looked at Hood. Now he had to tell them something.

"Actually, I'm here to find out why a contingent of marines is being dispatched to the embassy under the aus-pices of Op-Center," Hood said.

Carrie seemed surprised by the question. "They are go-ing to gather intel," she replied.

"In Beijing?" Hood asked.

"In Beijing and elsewhere," the general told him. "They're all of Chinese-American heritage. G2 has been training them for years to infiltrate Chinese society, get jobs in and around the seats of government."

"That's a good idea," Herbert said. "We need HUMINT resources who can blend in."

"Individuals who are not local with variable allegiance that could compromise missions, the integrity of intelligence, and the safety of other operatives," Carrie replied. "We have been training groups like that for service in dozens of ethnic regions." She regarded Hood suspiciously. "The Joint Chiefs were aware of that. The president could have asked them."

"I suppose he could have, but he asked me," Hood replied innocently.

"It would be unfortunate if the president did not trust his own advisers," she said incredulously.

"I've been a White House crisis manager for less than twelve hours. I cannot say who President Debenport does or does not trust." Hood replied. He tried to lighten the mood, which had suddenly turned heavy and suspicious. "Maybe my visit here is the equivalent of a West Wing hazing. Toss the new guy into a maelstrom and see what he can do."

"That's possible," Carrie agreed. "Though to me it's more of a street gang mentality, where you have to pull off a crime before they accept you. Usually it's against a friend or high-visibility target to prove your loyalty."

"Did I just miss something?" McCaskey asked uncomfortably. "Are we no longer playing nice?"

"We're not playing anything, Darrell," Herbert replied. "I think a second front just got opened."

Herbert may be tired, but he was not oblivious. Nor anyone's fool. It was an unsettling thought but, like China, these men were in fact a battleground. Hood had assumed he had been sent here to get inside information about the marines and also to show G2 that there were outside eyes on Op-Center. But what if he was sent not to anchor the White House in the marine operation but to provide a wedge? Perhaps Debenport saw Hood as someone who could divide the loyalties of those who worked at Op-Center, forcing Carrie to keep a balance between the White House and the military—or risk alienating Hood and his people, and having to replace the rest of the battle-seasoned team that was loyal to them. It was a new level of intrigue, one that gave a fresh definition to domestic intelligence.

He was spying on the home team.

"Surely we have larger issues to deal with," McCaskey said.

The FBI liaison was correct. Unfortunately, the situations were not mutually exclusive. Hood and Carrie locked eyes. He was not sure how he got into yet another conflict with a woman he did not know, but here he was. And here she was. Now they had to see it through.

"Getting back on topic so I don't miss my flight, will the marines be reporting to G2 or to Op-Center?" Hood asked. That was something the Joint Chiefs would not necessarily have shared with the president.

"Op-Center is chartered to run military and paramilitary operations," Carrie replied carefully. "G2 is not. As you know, the funding for Striker was rolled back but not the commission itself."

"They'll have to report directly to you," Hood said.

"Of course," she replied. "I'm the only military officer on staff."

What the president obviously feared became clearer: that G2 would strip-mine Op-Center for use in its own operations. That would shift the control of intelligence from the federal sector to the military.

Unfortunately, Hood was forced to put all of that aside for the moment. There was still a crisis bubbling abroad. And whether it served the needs of G2 or not, Hood had to admit that the infiltration was a good idea and, just as important, a timely one. Everyone on the inside would be on guard, and people on the outside—from news vendors to bicycle salesmen—would be more inclined to comment on that unrest. In such an environment, the alternately inquisitive or inherently tentative actions of spies would not stand out.

"Will I have access to your team when I'm in Beijing?" Hood asked.

"They have several targets," Carrie said. "What are yours?"

"I won't know until I get there," Hood said.

"That would be the time to discuss it, then," General Carrie said. "You will, of course, have whatever support and cooperation I can provide, as I'm sure our team can count on yours."

"Naturally."

"Bob tells me that General Rodgers hoped you could tap into resources the prime minister may have," Carrie said. "He assumed, correctly, the president would have better access."

"That is true," Hood replied. This had to be awful for Herbert. The intelligence chief was looking down. He was playing with a loose thread on the armrest of his wheelchair.

"You'll make a connection through our ambassador?" Carrie asked.

"That's the plan," Hood said. "I won't know for certain until I get there."

"We still don't know why the prime minister is suddenly worried about the launch," McCaskey said.

"Or even *if* he is," Herbert added. "In a politically tense situation, keeping the Guoanbu out of the loop on a major project may be the prime minister's way of putting them in their place."

Like the Joint Chiefs or G2 not giving the president the full story about a marine group seconded to Op-Center, Hood thought. He knew Bob Herbert well enough to detect a subtext in anything the intelligence chief said. From her expression, Carrie did as well. It struck Hood—after just half a day—that this was no different than being a wife or adviser to Henry VIII. Inevitably, your head was vulnerable to wide swings of the ax, whatever you did. The positions to which men and women naturally aspired required an exhausting combination of brawn and diplomacy. If American children knew the truth about being president or anything close to the Oval Office, they would cling to their sane, youthful dreams of being a firefighter or an astronaut.

"Well, I suggest we talk again when you get to Beijing," Carrie said. "We'll have a better idea then about how the various scenarios might play out. Bob, do you want to be point man on that?"

"Sure," he said.

"Very good." Carrie looked at Hood. "Was there anything else?"

"At some point I'd like to get my photographs and mementos back," he replied, gesturing toward the desk and wall.

"I've asked Bugs to see to that," she said. "Would you like the items sent to your apartment or office?"

"Office, please," Hood replied. It was another small thing, but he wanted her to know he intended to be there for a while.

Carrie rose. McCaskey did as well. The general shook Hood's hand across the desk. "Have a safe and productive trip," she said.

"Thank you."

"Ditto," McCaskey said, offering his hand.

"Yeah, good luck," Herbert added. "I'll see you out."

The men left together, followed by McCaskey, who shut the door behind him. The three moved along the narrow corridor toward the elevator.

"What the hell was all that about?" Herbert asked.

"Which part?" Hood replied.

"For starters, the stuff about the Joint Chiefs. Are we worried about a military coup?"

"Not per se," Hood replied.

"What does that mean?" Herbert asked.

"I'm not sure."

"For 'not sure' there was a lot of thrust and parry going on back there," Herbert said, cocking his head toward Carrie's office.

"I think the general is more 'sure' than I am," Hood said.

"Paul, she was appointed by the president," McCaskey noted.

"Who was yielding to pressure from the Joint Chiefs," Hood said, his voice low. "I get the sense there is a realignment taking place," Hood went on. "Administration changes affect the top levels of the executive branch, but the military is unchanged."

"Except for the figurehead positions like the secretaries of the different forces," Herbert said.

"Right. This is a realignment that may have been going on for a while. Debenport probably saw it coming as senator. Now he's making his own moves to ensure the White House isn't entirely dependent on the military for intelligence."

"Which could be self-serving," Herbert said. "Report instability somewhere, predict a war, get a budget increase."

"Right again."

"But the president still has the CIA, the FBI, and the NSA," Herbert said.

"For now," McCaskey said. "I didn't think anything of it before, but over the past two or three years, the Bureau has been recruiting heavily from the ranks of the mustered-out. The HR people say they value the fitness and discipline of the modern American soldier."

"Why wouldn't they?" Herbert asked. "I think you're both being a little paranoid. When I was in Beirut for the Company, I had military advisers and contacts."

"You were reporting to a civilian then," Hood said. "You're reporting to a three-star general now."

"Mike was a general."

"And President Lawrence made a point of not putting him in charge," Hood said. "The president kept the Op-Center command with a civilian."

"Well, maybe the balance was off in favor of civilians," Herbert said. "Maybe this is a necessary correction."

"If this is as far as it goes, I might agree with you," Hood said. "Obviously, the president has concerns."

"Well, I think we all need to take a few steps back," McCaskey said.

"My grandad used to say if you step away from the bear, you may step in the bear trap," Herbert said.

"We haven't defined anyone as a bear yet," McCaskey pointed out. "All I'm saying is, let's see how it plays out over the next few days."

"I agree," Hood said. The men had reached the elevator. Hood swiped his temporary card to open the doors. He entered.

"Paul? You know I'll do what I can to get those marines if you need them," Herbert said.

"I know you will," Hood replied. "That's why I want you to watch your ass."

"What do you mean?"

"I think the general knows it, too," Hood said as the doors slid shut.

TWENTY-ONE

Beijing, China
Tuesday, 8:11 A.M.

When he was a boy, Tam Li was self-conscious about the ruddy mole on his left temple. His mother told him it meant he was special, that he had been kissed by the sun. She said this little gift from the sky would watch over him, help him to find his way. She added that she was counting on her "little flame" to lead the way for all of them. His mother meant the family, of course. Tam Li took it to mean something bigger than that. After all, where the sun moved the earth followed.

General Tam Li was gratified when he left the prime minister's office. Le Kwan Po was not a hard-liner. He was a pragmatist. He was effective at keeping a balance between the old guard and the new without disturbing or affecting either.

That was why the struggle between himself and Chou would continue a little longer. Just long enough to give the general what he really wanted. It had nothing to do with the small profit he made from the slave trade. That was a laboratory. That was how he learned who he could trust and who he could not. The real profit was in doing what men like Tam Li did best: fighting.

The general went from the prime minister's office to his car, which was parked in the underground garage. He was on the topmost of three levels. During the day, Tam Li had an aide drive him to meetings or airfields. There had not been time to arrange for that now.

The garage was empty at this hour, and the general could see out into the street and watched as a farmer stopped his truck on a street corner and delivered produce to restaurants. His son, who could not have been more than seven or eight, was there to help him. When they were done, they would drive home, and the boy would go to school while the father went into the fields.

Tam Li came from a world like that. His family grew corn on a small farm thirty-five miles from Beijing. They made long drives every day during the seven-month growing season. Their clients were military installations, which was where the young Tam Li became fascinated by the crisp uniforms, the smart salutes, and the imposing weapons. He also learned how officers demanded kickback for allowing vendors onto government property. It was an accepted way of doing business.

Tam Li drove to the small apartment he kept in the city. The apartment was at the top of a four-story structure built in the early 1960s, part of the vast modernization program instituted by Mao. Former military personnel got first pick of the new apartments, an incentive for young men to join. It was a comfortable and spacious residence that he shared with his elderly mother. She had sold the farm three years ago when his father died, and she spent most of her day chatting with women in the courtyard or sitting on the rooftop embroidering. She was a very heavy sleeper, which made it easy for Tam Li to return at any hour.

Attached to the Beijing Military Base Joint Command,

and serving a second four-year term as a vice chairman of the powerful Central Military Committee, the general spent half his time in the city and half his time in the field. He got back as the sun was coming up. Tam Li was more alert now than when he had been awakened by the prime minister's call. He did not want to go back to sleep, even though he had to be well rested for what was to come.

He went into his small office and turned on the radio. He removed his army jacket and hung it carefully in a small freestanding bureau. The office was a windowless alcove off his bedroom. The walls were painted white, and there were no pictures. The desk was bare save for the radio, telephone, and the computer. Tam Li was not a hoarder. He was not sentimental. His vision was external, about the future. He lit a cigarette, sat back in the desk chair, and contemplated the future as he listened to Beijing People's News, a round-the-clock station of international events. They were still talking about the attack on the police in Taiwan.

Tam Li could not prove that Chou Shin was behind the assaults. Not that proof was required. The men had been adversaries for over twenty years, ever since they met at the Tianjin military base. Over two hundred cadets had come down with a severe case of food poisoning. Tam Li was the officer in charge of the mess, and Chou Shin was an investigator with the PLA internal police detachment. Chou discovered that Tam Li had bought tainted pork in exchange for a sizable payoff from the farmer who had produced it. The inspector was never able to prove that Tam Li knew the meat was bad. In fact, he did not. But another kind of poison had been generated between the two men, a toxic suspicion that was fueled by their very different political beliefs. As the men rose through their respective services, their mistrust and finally hatred also grew. Chou watched Tam Li, and Tam Li did everything he could to put false leads under the intelligence officer's nose.

This time, however, Chou Shin had tried a different approach. Instead of trying to attach evidence of wrongdoing on Tam Li, he destroyed the offending target altogether. He had struck back with his own reserve plan, the blast in Durban. Chou Shin had retaliated in Taipei. He was trying to show the general that he would not only match his actions but surpass them. Unfortunately, while the Guoanbu director had demonstrated determination, he had not shown sufficient insight.

What Tam Li had told the prime minister was true. Soldiers were not paid enough for the work they did. But for Tam Li, the transportation of indentured women was only a profitable hobby. The real work was being done in a way that Chou and the prime minister would not see.

Until it was too late. While Chou Shin chased prostitutes, slave traders, the general had the real prize tucked somewhere else. Somewhere Chou Shin and Le Kwan Po would never think to look.

The general listened to the weather. It was not true that he only looked ahead. Sometimes he experienced flashes from the past, like now. His father used to stop by the house of old Chan Juan on their way back to the farm. She had a tube filled with mercury, which told them whether the next day would be cloudy or clear. They paid her an ear of corn for her report. It was not just the primitive barometer she used to make her predictions. She also observed the birds and insects and kept careful records from year to year. She was rarely wrong.

Today meteorologists used computers and satellites to generate forecasts. Their predictions were no better than those of Chan Juan. New ways were not always superior; they were simply more complex. In the old days, the general would have challenged a rival like Chou Shin to combat with sword, spear, or staff. Their conflict would be resolved in just a few minutes.

He shook his head as he lit a new cigarette with the old.

Such a tiny red ember, the general thought as he passed the fire from one tip to the other. Yet unchecked, this spark had the power to level a city and, in so doing, bring down a nation. In effect, the only difference between a little flame and a big flame was the amount of time it had to do its work unchecked.

Finishing the cigarette, Tam Li shut the radio off, and then he shut his eyes. A drowsy sense of contentment had come over him, and sleep followed quickly. When he woke, he could hear his mother moving about in the kitchen. He looked at his watch. Two hours had passed.

His legs complained a little when he stood. He ignored them the way his father had ignored his daily aches and stiffness. The general put on his jacket and went to greet his mother. It was late, but not too late to have breakfast with her. After that, he would shower and drive to his office. He had work to do before he had his weekly meeting with the other members of the Central Military Committee.

So they could finalize their plans to do what had to be done while Chou and his old-school dinosaurs prepared to become extinct.

TWENTY-TWO

Arlington, Virginia
Tuesday, 8:12 A.M.

It was the first time in a long time that Bob Herbert had not felt like getting out of bed. That was odd, considering that he was going to see his longtime friend and coworker Mike Rodgers.

Herbert had always enjoyed the general's company, whether it was at work or over a butcher-block tray covered in sushi. He had enjoyed it more than he enjoyed being with Hood or McCaskey or any of his other colleagues. The general was openly bitter about aspects of his life, and Herbert related to that.

Now, though, it was Herbert who felt unhappy and abused by life. That was why he had called Rodgers at home the night before and asked to meet. To talk, to see if Paul Hood was seriously off target about the military or if Herbert was being uncharacteristically naive.

The men were meeting for breakfast at a diner that used to be a Hot Shoppe forty-plus years ago. They had fresh-squeezed grapefruit juice and ample handicapped parking for Herbert's large, custom-built van. The intelligence chief required two spaces for the "pig," as he called it. The vehicle was also large enough to let him pull off the road and take a nap. He often did that when he felt like scooting home to Mississippi and did not want to be bothered looking for a wheelchair-accessible motel on the way. The van also accommodated the computers and secure uplink equipment he required when he was out of the office.

Rodgers was already there, sitting in a corner booth and reading the newspaper. The former general was one of the few people he knew who not only read several dailies but read the print versions. A pot of coffee sat beside him. If Rodgers had been there more than five minutes, it was already empty.

Herbert wheeled himself along the sun-bleached linoleum toward the booth. It was odd seeing waitresses and truckers, interns and realtors going about their business. He himself felt as though he were in a science fiction movie, one of those films from the 1950s where just one man suspected that aliens might be plotting a takeover. Back then, the science fiction aliens were a metaphor for Communists. Now, the imaginary aliens were a metaphor for the U.S. military.

Rodgers folded away his *Washington Post* when Herbert arrived. The intelligence chief sat at the end of the table in the aisle. They had taken the back table so he would not be in anyone's way.

"I appreciate this, Mike," Herbert said.

"Sure."

"Do I look as crappy as I feel?"

"Pretty much," Rodgers replied. "What's wrong? The new boss or the old one?"

"Both." Herbert laughed.

"Crunched in the middle of a sudden transition?"

"That's not it," Herbert said. "The work is the work. I'm more concerned about what's behind the transition."

The waitress came, and the men ordered. Rodgers got a fruit plate and whole wheat toast, no butter. Herbert went for the pancakes deluxe with sausage and grapefruit juice. When the waitress left, the intelligence chief hunched forward. Even though the adjoining table was empty, secrecy was a habit many people formed in and around D.C. Everyone, even Herbert, had an ear out for what other people were saying. Not just spies and reporters but everyday people. There was always someone who knew someone who would want to know such-and-such.

"Paul thinks there may be a power shift taking place," Herbert said. "He's concerned that the sudden appointment of General Carrie to Op-Center may be a harbinger of a military takeover of national intelligence."

"That's a pretty big leap."

"That's what I thought," Herbert said.

"Anyway, he's the guy close to the president, and the president is the one who made the appointment."

"Under pressure from the Joint Chiefs, apparently," Herbert said.

Rodgers shrugged. "Compromises happen. That doesn't necessarily mean a seismic shift."

"No, but as I was thinking about it last night, there was one thing that bothered me." Herbert leaned even closer. "Debenport was the head of the CIOC. He was getting ready to run for president at the time. If he thought this was something he wanted to do, why did he put your name on top of the downsize list?"

Rodgers frowned. It was obviously still a painful memory.

"Sorry," Herbert said. "If you don't want to talk about this—"

"I don't, Bob. But let's follow it through," Rodgers said. "Maybe Senator Debenport wanted to clear the path for a woman. General Carrie may have been on his radar as the most qualified individual. If he had just kicked me out and put her in, that might have been perceived as reverse discrimination. A lot of members of Congress and the military would not have approved, and Carrie would not have enjoyed the legitimacy that position demands."

"Possible, although you credit Debenport with more forethought than I do," Herbert said. He glanced around casually, then spoke in a voice barely more than a whisper. "She's also got Striker back."

"What?" That surprised him.

"She's sending four Asian-American marines to Beijing, undercover, through the embassy."

"For covert or intel activity?" Rodgers asked, also whispering.

"The latter," Herbert said.

"We had people who could have done that," Rodgers said.

"Exactly. Two well-trained Asian-Americans from your field staff," Herbert said. "They weren't even contacted."

"You offered their names?"

"As part of my initial sit-down with Carrie," Herbert said. "It was a short meeting because we had the Chinese situation to check on. But I gave her all the names, from David Battat to Falah Shibli. Our South Korean and Taiwanese associates were in there as well."

"Has Carrie worked with these marines before?"

"Until yesterday morning she was crunching data at G2," Herbert said.

"I see."

Their food arrived. Herbert was silent until the waitress was through. When she left, the intelligence chief took a swallow of juice. The wonderful tartness made him wince. He took a second slug. It was odd that he craved in food what he had no patience for in people.

"Maybe this *is* just a realignment," Herbert went on. "Maybe there are too many civilians in the intel business. The Joint Chiefs complain, the president capitulates. But if it was just about equilibrium, why would he create a new post for Paul, one that keeps him very close, unless it was to keep an eye on the brass intel expansion?"

"You mean the president would have just put him out to graze, as he did with me," Rodgers said.

"Or to stud, depending on how you want to use your time," Herbert said.

Rodgers held up his wheat toast in answer. "At my age, the penne is mightier than the sword."

"That's all in your head." Herbert grinned. The smile faded quickly. "What about *this* stuff? Is it all in *my* head?"

"I don't know," Rodgers said as he chewed his dry toast.

"What does your gut tell you?" Herbert pressed. He could tell Rodgers was thinking about it. Thinking hard. He recognized that familiar, unfocused look in the man's steel gray eyes. It was as though Rodgers were gazing through you, past you, at a hill his unit had to take or a town they had to infiltrate.

"My instincts say there's something to Paul's concerns," Rodgers said. "It's like Patton after the war in Europe was over. He wanted to start a new conflict with the Soviet Union because the troops were already there, and he reasoned we would be facing them eventually. Most of all, though, he wanted the war because conquering territory is what generals do."

"So what do we do?" Herbert asked. "Paul and me," he added. This was not Mike Rodgers's problem, and he recognized that.

"There is one way we might find out more," Rodgers said.

"What's that?"

"It's been suggested that I go over for the launch," Rodgers said. "I think I will."

"Why were you undecided?" Herbert asked. "It's your satellite."

"That's why," Rodgers said. "As you know, there are elements of the Chinese government who do not want to be reminded of that."

"Paul's going over. He's probably already en route."

"Right. If I go, I might be able to help keep an eye on the marines. Especially if they go to the Xichang space center."

"Apart from ticking off some of the Chinese, is there a downside for you?" Herbert asked.

"Only if the rocket blows up," he said as he took a bite of melon.

Rodgers called his office and asked his secretary to get him on any flight bound for Beijing that afternoon. Then the men sat and talked about Unexus and its plans for the future, which included a satellite that would image the earth in three-dimensional pictures, allowing for unprecedented recon. Herbert promised to keep that one a secret.

What was no secret was how much happier Rodgers was now than even a month ago. Joy would never be a chronic condition for either man, but Rodgers seemed more alive and content than ever. Perhaps he had been steeped too long in the underground world of Op-Center, both physically and emotionally.

As they finished and the men headed back to their cars, Herbert knew one thing for certain. Despite his own great loss a quarter century before, his own journey into that heart of darkness was not nearly as close to a resolution.

If anything, it was just getting under way.

TWENTY-THREE

Washington, D.C.
Tuesday, 8:48 A.M.

Before today, Morgan Carrie had only been to Andrews
Air Force Base once. That was two years ago, when she
was part of a receiving line for a foreign ruler who was
making her first trip to the White House. Carrie had been
the token two-star at the time. It was not the kind of invitation an officer turned down; it was an order. But it felt dirty
to be on display.

Things had changed since then. Carrie was in charge,
and others were coming to see her.

The marines, for example.

Carrie did not meet them in the NCMC headquarters
but in a ready room beside Hangar 5. It was not a short
walk from Op-Center, so she took the golf cart. She would
have preferred to walk, but the marines were on a schedule.

The idea of bringing marines into play was hers. It was
enthusiastically endorsed by Joint Chiefs Chairman General Raleigh Carew. He said that one of the failures of Op-Center had been the difficulty Hood, Rodgers, and Herbert

had in attracting human intelligence operatives in foreign lands. There were the historic problems: fear of repercussions among potential spies and difficulty trusting even those who agreed to help. The answer, Carew believed, was sending what the intelligence community called "passables," outsiders who could blend in with the local population and were quick studies on customs, fads, and colloquialisms not covered in their training. They were designed to serve as both "spec-tar" units, staying long enough to hit specific targets and then leaving, or as sleeper cells. The military had been working on PITs— Passables Infiltration Teams—for several years. To date, small PITs had been fielded in Iraq and the Philippines under the auspices of G2. They were necessary because local recruits were too easily counterrecruited to spy on Americans. The idea for the PITs was inspired by the German action against Allied forces during the decisive Battle of the Bulge in World War II. Paratroopers dressed, equipped, and trained to speak like Americans were dropped behind Allied lines. Their mission was to destroy gas stores, slash truck tires, disable tanks, and send troops into ambushes; anything to slow the enemy advance while German forces attempted to retake the key port of Antwerp. Hitler also gambled that a long and bloody fight in the winter months would cause the weak alliance between American, British, and Russian soldiers to fray. That would give his newly supplied troops a chance to pick at one side while his diplomats stalled the other with insincere overtures of peace.

When Allied commanders became suspicious of the deception, sentries not only demanded passwords from soldiers but asked questions about baseball teams back home. Men who could not answer were arrested. Sufficient numbers of infiltrators were apprehended, and the push to crush Hitler was successful.

The general arrived at the hangar. The mission coordinator, Captain Tony Tallarico, saluted and showed her into the ready room. The four marines were dressed in civvies and sitting on folding chairs in the center of the small room. Beside them were nondescript backpacks. The three men and one woman had been driven over from Quantico, where they had trained. After Carrie had spoken with them, they would be taken to Dulles for an All Nippon Airways flight to Tokyo. There they would transfer to Air China for the trip to Beijing.

The marines got to their feet and saluted when the general entered. Carrie returned the salute and told them to sit back down. They were all in their early twenties but had eyes that were much, much older.

The general dismissed Tallarico. Soldiers had a formal, somewhat rote way of addressing familiar officers. She wanted to see them fresh, the way the Chinese would see them. Before coming over, she had only had a few minutes to glance at their records, both their real dossiers and the identities G2 had given them. In everyday Chinese life the marines would be posing as two history students, a bicycle repairman, and an electronics technician. She wanted to make sure she could picture them that way before sending them undercover.

"As of this morning you have all been seconded to the National Crisis Management Center," the general said as she looked from one eager face to the other. "We are the people who stop wars so that people like us don't get killed. The two of you posing as students—you understand what that job may entail?"

"Yes, sir," the two replied as one.

She looked at one of them, the woman. "Second Lieutenant Yam," she said to the woman. "A student confides that he or she is publishing an anti-Communist newspaper. What do you do?"

"I collect as many names as possible, sir, and file them with the NCMC."

"What if we decide you need to ingratiate yourself with local party functionaries?" the general asked.

"I will provide those names to said functionaries, sir."

"Even if it means a lengthy period of jail time for people whose politics you support?"

"Regrettably yes, sir."

General Carrie nodded. "This is not always pleasant work, and it is rarely fair. It is a battle in which innocent lives are regularly lost. The rewards are often very difficult to see. They cannot be measured in terrain won or in an enemy's quick surrender. This war requires ruthless patience. If you don't have that, if the life of someone's son or daughter will cause you to hesitate, I want you to speak now. I will replace you without prejudice. I would rather have to change a tire than drive on three."

No one spoke.

"Very well then," she said. "Does anyone have any questions, any last-minute requests or ideas?"

"No, sir," they all replied.

Their voices were loud and proud, as she expected. These four had been very carefully selected and trained for the maximum-one-year mission. She was lucky to get them. Four others were being trained to back them up. If they were compromised and had to leave China suddenly, the others would be ready to go immediately.

"Just a few spot checks for my own peace of mind," the general said. "You've all got your cover stories as well as the scientific credentials lined up to get into the launch site if that should be necessary?"

"The papers and passes have already been delivered to the embassy," said one of the men. "One of the female diplomats will make the delivery tomorrow at noon at a popular dumpling stall. She will make a pass at me, and we'll do the switch."

"Tough job," the general said.

"Well, sir, she is *considerably* older—"

General Carrie's expression registered quick displeasure. Only then did the marine realize what he had done.

"Sir, I mean—"

"Exactly what you said," the general replied. "Some older women could teach you a great deal, Lieutenant Lee."

"Yes, sir, General, sir."

"You *are* my contact, Lieutenant Kent Lee?" Carrie went on.

"Yes, sir." Lee had recovered his go-get-'em demeanor immediately.

"The electrician."

"Correct, General," Lee replied. "I hope to get a position fixing cell phones and computers."

"To facilitate recon," the general said.

"That is the plan, sir. And also repairs to our gear, if necessary."

The team would be communicating by text-messaging. Lee would collect and summarize reports in regular E-mails to the general. The messages would be routed through the computer at the home of Lee's "sister" in a New York apartment. The space was actually a CIA surveillance site near the United Nations. If Lee's computer were ever stolen or the account hacked, a pogo-mail address for one Andrea Lee is all the thief would find. Nor would there be anything suspicious about the contents of the E-mails to or from Ms. Lee. The computer would be employing a HIPS program to encode the messages. The hide-in-plain-sight encryptions took all the words of the message and earmarked them, then dropped them into longer messages. The longer message was deleted at the other end. Anyone reading them would see nothing unusual, nor were there any patterns to look for.

"You have all got your exit strategies if that becomes necessary?" the general asked. She knew the details from her years at G2 when the routes and plans were established.

"We fall back to the embassy or to the safe house behind the North Train Station near the Beijing zoo," said Lee.

"Apartment?" she asked the woman.

"Basement, sir," the marine replied. "Seven steps down, door to the right, three knocks, then two knocks."

"And you've all studied the space center if you're asked to go there?" the general asked. Carrie had looked at the map before leaving the office. A key to maintaining morale among subordinates was for a superior to know as much as possible about a mission. It made operatives feel as though there was a vetting process, a careful and knowledgeable eye watching over them.

"We've gone through it in virtual sims, General," Lee said. "We know that place better than we know our own barracks."

"Where is the launch center relative to the technical center?" the general asked, pointing to the shortest man in the group.

"North, sir. Three point four kilometers," he added.

"And the tracking station relative to the tech center?" she asked the only marine who had not spoken.

"Four kilometers to the southeast, sir," he told her.

She looked at Second Lieutenant Yam. It was odd. The general did not see herself as a new recruit. This woman projected a fearlessness that Carrie had not possessed. Maybe the new generation of women was openly competing with men, not bracing themselves for impact with the glass ceiling.

"Latitude of the launch tower?" she asked Yam. She had saved the toughest question for the young woman. Despite what Yam might think, the playing field was not a level one.

"It is twenty-eight degrees fifteen minutes north, sir," the second lieutenant replied.

"Elevation?"

"Eighteen hundred feet, sir," Yam replied.

General Carrie smiled and nodded. That felt good.

There was no time to chat further, nor any need. Carrie had seen all she needed to see. They were four sharp, enthusiastic marines. A little young, but that was all right. Youth had energy and clarity uncorrupted by cynicism. They would need that as reality started peeling away the layers of idealism.

Wishing them well and saluting them proudly, the general brought Captain Tallarico back into the room. She congratulated him for his work, then returned to her golf cart.

As she headed back to the NCMC, General Carrie was confident in the group but a little uneasy about their inexperience. There was no way to get it, other than by being in the field. But she was suddenly much more aware of the fragility of the four tires than she had been driving over.

TWENTY-FOUR

Beijing, China
Wednesday, 5:22 A.M.

Hood reached Beijing surprisingly refreshed and exhilarated. He had slept for most of the flight, and he had left having done something that made him feel good. Something that had nothing to do with work. Not directly, anyway.

Whether he was the mayor of Los Angeles or the director of Op-Center, Hood had always tried to spend time with his kids before traveling anywhere. This was especially true on Op-Center business, when he usually went away for more than just an overnight visit. Hood used that time to plug tightly into his family. He craved it, and the kids seemed to enjoy it. Sharon Hood had never really been a part of that. She allowed her husband to give his attention to the kids.

As he thought back on it, that was how they did everything after Harleigh was born. Their love was funneled to their daughter and then their son. They never gave any to each other. Maybe Sharon was doing what she thought the kids needed. Hood's time at home was limited, and she wanted the kids to have full access to their father. Whatever the cause, over time their life became all about kids and career, with Sharon spending her free time working on her cable TV cooking show. The events that subsequently rocked their personal lives simply accelerated the sad, lonely drift.

The state to which they had deteriorated was evident whenever Hood went to see the kids. It was not just how snippy Sharon was with him. It was how openly affectionate she and her new lover were. He did not think their hand-in-hand walks around the yard or hugs in the window were an act for his benefit. But he did see that Sharon was capable of more than she gave him.

Then again, the new man was around a lot more. Jim Hunt was a caterer Sharon had met on her show. The former Mrs. Hunt was an electrician Jim had met, the kids told him, when she was repairing an oven in a restaurant. Hunt had been the one who divorced her. He had come to the relationship with Sharon bearing full closure with his past and a white tablecloth ready to spread on their happy relationship banquet. An emotionally free and available caterer who made his own hours. It was a recipe that had to make Sharon Hood weak with need.

Hood had pondered all of that, again, as he drove to the house from Op-Center. He had called to make sure the kids would be there before heading out. Then he also did something impulsive that only made sense because he was angry at just about every woman he knew, from Lorraine Sanders to Julie Kubert to General Carrie Morgan and Sharon Hood.

He turned, irrationally, to one for support. One he believed might actually want to hear what he had to say.

He guessed that the number of the former Mrs. Jim Hunt was the same as her son's, for whom he had gotten an internship at Op-Center six months before. He called. A woman answered. Hood asked if this was the former wife of Jim Hunt. She asked who wanted to know.

"Paul Hood, the former husband of Sharon Hood," he replied.

There was a silence so long he thought his phone had died.

"Hello?" he said.

"Hello," she replied. "This is Gloria Lynch-Hunt. Is everything all right with Frankie?"

Frankie was her son, her only child. Of course she would assume that was why he was calling.

"Actually, as of yesterday morning things were very well with Frankie," he said. "The truth is I'm not at Op-Center anymore. I'm working on special projects for the president."

"Oh," the woman said. "Does he need a recording system installed in the Oval Office?"

"Excuse me?" It took a moment for Hood to understand what she had said. Gloria was an electrician. She was making a joke. Hood was caught off guard. He was also surprised by her voice, which was very soft and very high. It was not what he imagined a female electrician would sound like. Not that a female electrician should sound like anything, he knew. But he could not help having imagined her as smoky-voiced and a little hulking, albeit slimmed down because she would be dating again after years of complacency in marriage and eating her husband's rich foods. "No," Hood went on. "I'm not calling about the president, Mrs. Hunt. Gloria. I'm calling to see if you want to have lunch or coffee."

There was another long, long silence. This time Hood *had* lost her. He pressed Redial. He wondered if she would still be laughing or if she would not bother to pick up at all.

"Hello?" she said.

"Hi. Sorry. Lost the signal there."

"That's okay. I was thinking this might have been a joke," she said. "Maybe it is, I don't know."

"Why?"

"Because you come up as Unknown Caller on the phone ID, and my former husband is a dick. This is the kind of stunt he would have one of his restaurant or chef buddies pull."

"To what end?" Hood asked. He understood the idea of postdivorce payback, but that seemed excessive.

"Mr. Hood, you're a stranger. Maybe you won't be, after the dinner you're going to buy me—at a restaurant of my choosing, where I know my ex holds no sway. Until then, 'my former husband is a dick' will have to suffice. The details are bloody—and personal."

"Understood," he said. It was odd. He felt no need to warn Sharon that her beau might be "a dick."

"I have to say, this still seems kind of strange," she said.

"It is completely strange," he admitted.

"Do you even know what I look like?"

"No," he admitted as a jolt of concern flashed through him. "And this isn't an us-against-them alliance," he added. "You know what I think I was subconsciously thinking?"

"No. I'm not even sure I understood what you just said."

He smiled. "I think, Gloria, that I reasoned: Sharon and I did not get along. Sharon and Jim *do* get along. Therefore, you and I may get along."

The third silence was the shortest. "I'll buy that," she said. "Sort of a nearsighted date. When do we find out?"

Hood thought he detected a hint of excitement in her voice. It took him a moment to get this joke, too. They were not quite blind dating.

"I'm actually headed overseas now for a couple of days," Hood told her.

"Any place exciting?" she asked.

"Yes."

"But you can't tell me."

"Right."

"Sexy," she said.

That made Hood feel both good and uncomfortable at the same time. He actually choked on saliva as he said, "Can we chalk it in for Saturday?"

"Consider it chalked. That'll save me a DVD rental," she said.

"It's been that way for me, too," Hood said.

He hung up feeling pleased with himself. Not because he had made the call but because he had actually had a constructive conversation with a woman. He was upbeat as he reached the house, stayed upbeat as he talked to the kids on the back patio, and even smiled as he waved good-bye to Sharon and Jim as they did the dishes together, laughing as they scrubbed some kind of sauce from cooking implements he did not recognize. It was the first time in a year that Hood did not feel like sticking a steak knife in Hunt's raw heart.

Maybe that was because he had, though the "dick" did not yet know it. He loved having a secret that would cause Jim a little confusion and discomfort and probably some jealousy, even though he would never admit it.

Screw him.

And now, invigorated, Paul Hood was ready to tackle a world crisis. He did not know whether it was sad or remarkable that such a small thing as a date with this one particular woman could have such a large impact on his outlook. And he realized as he moved through a short diplomatic line that it had nothing to do with Gloria Hunt per se. It had to do with Paul Hood taking control of his life.

As revelations go, that was something an international crisis manager should have realized long before this.

TWENTY-FIVE

Beijing, China
Wednesday, 5:23 A.M.

Hood was met at the Beijing Capital International Airport by a car from the embassy. The driver introduced himself as Tim Bullock. The young man looked to be about twenty-four or twenty-five.

"How long have you been in Beijing?" Hood asked as they waited for the two pieces of luggage he had brought.

"Four months, sir. I have a poli-sci degree from Temple University."

"You're from Philadelphia?"

"Yes, sir. Birthplace of the nation. That's what got me into political science. When I understood what those men did—Mr. Franklin, Mr. Adams, Mr. Jefferson, and the others—the risks they took so their countrymen could live free, I knew I wanted to have a positive impact on people's lives."

"Is it difficult for you to watch Communism at work in China?"

"No, sir. It is another form of the kind of duress these individuals have always lived under," Bullock said in exquisite diplomatic-speak. "But they will overcome that, I believe. It is a strong and fascinating country."

"So you like this assignment?" Hood asked.

"Very much, sir," Bullock replied. "Dating is problematic, but the day trips are not like going to the Jersey shore. And this is a choice position for someone who wants a career in the dipco."

Dipco was the diplomatic corps. Or as Op-Center's late political liaison Martha Mackall used to call it, the "fifty-fifty" corps. You spent half the time trying to do your job and half the time trying to stay alive. In her case, her frank misanthropic view of the profession had proved sadly accurate. Bob Herbert had another name for it: the "diplomatic corpse." Happily, there were still men like Bullock who had stars—and stripes—in their eyes. At least, for now.

Bullock carried Hood's bags, told him there were beverages and snacks in the car, and said the eighteen-mile drive to the American compound at Xiu Shui Bei Jie 3, 100600 would take under a half hour. He asked Hood if he needed to use the rest room before they departed.

"Thanks," Hood told him. "I went before I left."

Bullock did not acknowledge the joke. He was in a mode Hood recognized: the focused, efficient "dipco-proby" mode. A career in the diplomatic corps meant doing everything right during his six-month probationary period, especially when it came to collecting and delivering VIPs in a timely and efficient manner. Hood had never possessed that kind of polish. Then again, he never had the kind of career vision Bullock seemed to have. Hood had planned on a career in finance. He fell into politics and felt his way from post to post as he moved between the two fields. He always tried to do what was right, not what was expected.

Until six months ago, he reflected. That was when he

fired Mike and made a deal with Senator Debenport to work more closely with the White House. At the time, he had no idea how closely that meant. It was strange. Here he was feeling used and compromised, yet the kid in the front seat would probably sign away his soul to be doing what Hood was doing. The president's special intelligence envoy did not have the heart to tell Bullock that would probably *be* the price.

Hood sat back in the deep leather seat of the bulletproof sedan and looked out the window. The driver pointed out a few landmarks but was respectfully silent the rest of the time. Beijing was not what Paul Hood had expected. Even through the pollution, the pale yellow disc of the rising sun brought out the rich, earthy reds and browns of the stones and tiles that comprised the ancient structures. Except for these old walls and pagoda-style rooftops, and the billboards of Mao that were still surprisingly plentiful, the capital of the People's Republic of China looked like a modest-sized American city. There were a few newer highrises, some well-preserved turn-of-the-century buildings, and a great many trees and plazas. There were paved roads and cobbled roads, all of them still relatively uncrowded this early in the morning.

The sedan pulled up to the high iron gates. There was a marine sentry in a guard booth inside. He pressed a button, and a small oblong panel slid down in one of the columns of the gate. There was a dark glass inside. Bullock rolled down the window and pressed his palm on the clear vertical screen. A narrow green line scanned his palm from the top to bottom, then from the left to the right. A moment later, the gate popped open. The box closed, and Bullock drove through. The marine had never left the safety of the booth.

"They had a retinal scan installed for a few days," Bullock told Hood. "But it was very difficult to lean that far from the car."

Good old government planning, Hood thought as they

drove along the curving drive. Hood was quite aware of a four-story bunker-style building to the right of the compound, just outside the gate. He had no idea what the Chinese characters said, but it did not matter. Whether the building was supposed to be the Institute for Cultural Exchange or the Department of Petroleum Research, it was in fact a listening post. The eastern side, which overlooked the embassy, had eight windows. They would all take direct sunlight until about one or two P.M. The shades were drawn in all but one, which had the widest view of the grounds. There were probably a number of still and video cameras concealed within the room. Everyone who came or went at the United States embassy was photographed, their conversations recorded. A number of satellite dishes and antennae were crowded on the roof, more than an ordinary office building would require. All of that raw data was stored and analyzed.

The Chinese did not make a secret of the building's true purpose, nor did the Americans erect a wall to block the view. It was all part of the polite game of overt surveillance that nations played, like parole officers checking on ex-cons. The real spy work against the embassy came from the police officers who patrolled the streets or the delivery men who bicycled past or even the traffic helicopters that flew overhead. These people were no different from the "nannies" in D.C.—the CIA operatives who dressed as ordinary citizens going about their work sweeping streets or vending postcards and hot dogs or pushing babies in carriages. In reality, they were watching the embassies and their ambassadors, creating charts of their movements throughout the district. Profilers could often extrapolate more from this data than they could from cryptic conversations between emissary workers. The Chinese in the building next door would spend hours going over anything Hood might have said to the driver while they waited at the gate. The Chinese analysts would come up with nothing or with a misguided interpretation of an innocent conversation.

It seemed, suddenly, a very silly business for grown men and women to be conducting. In that moment Hood understood the squirmy frustration Mike Rodgers used to feel at meetings in the Tank or in diplomatic offices. There was nothing vague about combat. One side lost, one side triumphed. Soldiers lived or they did not. It was not a back-and-forth patty-cake; it was decisive. Hood also got a sense of the direction Op-Center would be taking with a general in command and marines on the payroll. There would be fewer second opinions and more surgery.

The car continued to the front door of the main building, a Victorian-style mansion. Hood was met by a man who seemed to be about Hood's age. He was short, thin, with a closely cropped mat of salt-and-pepper hair and a smartly tailored suit. His eyes were narrow and his forehead creased. He seemed too tense to be a diplomat.

"Mr. Hood, I'm Wesley Chase, the ambassador's executive secretary," the man informed him.

That explained it. This was the man who did all the work. Hood shook his hand and entered the embassy ahead of him. A marine guard sat at a desk in a large, open foyer. There was a six-foot-high omniglass wall in front of him—thick and explosion-proof. A blast in front of it would be directed back outside. The wall ran the length of the big receiving area. The only way in or out was a revolving door to the right of the desk. Mr. Chase told Hood to stand in the doorway. He placed a card on the scanner to the left. The door turned once, sweeping Hood with it. Chase stepped into the next slot, placed the card on the scanner, and the door moved again.

"You have to be quick or you lose your arm," Chase said with a laugh when he reached the other side.

Hood knew that all this security was not just to protect

the embassy from bombers and assassins. It was also to keep defectors safe. Several times each week, Chinese nationals came here seeking asylum. Some were dissidents, some simply wanted to be reunited with family in Taiwan, others wanted a better life in the United States. Rarely was political haven granted. Refusal was not simply a matter of accommodating the host government but of thwarting them. It was difficult to know which refugee was sincere and which was a potential spy. That was why so many Chinese ended up on the boats of people like Lo Tek.

The two men passed a large antechamber that was already beginning to fill with both American and Chinese citizens looking for help. The application fee for a visa cost one hundred dollars, whether the request was honored or not. Still they came, the Chinese who earned twice that a month—if they were lucky.

Hood was shown to one of the guest quarters. Chase told him the ambassador would be down to breakfast with him in about an hour. Hood's luggage arrived as Chase was leaving. Tim Bullock set up a stand and hoisted the large bag on top. He asked if Hood wanted anything hung up or set out.

"No thanks," Hood replied, and Bullock turned to go. Hood called out to him. "Hold on. Your tip."

"Sir, we don't—"

"Not that kind," Hood said. He approached the young man.

"I know you said it's 'problematic,' but don't neglect the dating. It's not enough to have professional acquaintances, even close ones. To make it through this business you need a home and a partner. The *right* partner."

Bullock smiled. Maybe he was pleased with the sentiment or just with the fact that someone had actually paid attention to him. Drivers tended to be the most invisible people in the dipco.

"Thank you for the tip, sir," Bullock said. "I'll get to work on that. Are you sure I can't help with your baggage?"

Hood grinned and shook his head. Bullock left, leaving Hood with his suitcase—and his baggage. Hood hoped the kid would take his advice. Nancy Jo had once inspired him to overachievement, and a chat with Gloria Lynch-Hunt had helped get him through a miserable day. The attentions of former Op-Center press secretary Ann Farris had forced him to take a closer look at the health of his marriage.

Not that a relationship is the solution to everything, Hood thought as he unpacked. The kid's single-mindedness underscored the strength but also the weakness of individuals who entered politics. It was like a Chinese ceremony he had witnessed when he was mayor of Los Angeles. A fifty-foot-high tower had been erected off Alpine Street. A young lady sat on top in a gold and white gown. She was the morning princess. A dozen warriors dressed in black and red robes fought to reach her. The man who made it to the top took the princess as his bride. The ceremony in Chinatown was choreographed; in ancient days, the battle was to the death.

Politics was a lot like that. The prize was at the top, and the participants became seduced by the heights and the worldview. Some of their senses were numbed by the rarified air. As they became more and more cloistered in the high tower, they also became protected by layers of security until the scrutiny of a Watergate or Irangate punched through and took lives. The intelligence community managed to avoid that problem because their coin was not personal access but information.

But perspective was a lesson Bullock would have to learn himself, if he learned it at all. He had ideals from Philadelphia, but he was already in the system and speaking the lingo. Faced with opportunity, ideals could be postponed or forgotten. Most career politicians Hood had known went a lifetime without ever looking back on the good reasons that may have brought them to public office.

Hood finished unpacking, then stretched out on the twin bed. It had been a very long time since he had traveled. It felt strange to put his head on a pillow that was not his own.

Perspective.

Getting out of Washington gave Hood a chance to look back on the events of the last few days. As much as he did not like the way things had played out, he could hardly consider himself abused. He was abroad in the service of the president, of the nation, of the world.

Again.

Intelligence personnel had to catch the balls that slipped through the gloves of the diplomats. Men like Hood and Bob Herbert and General Carrie went to work so that other Americans could pursue their lives without fear or compromise. It was difficult work. It was also dangerous and exhausting. And there was no one to grab the balls they missed. But there was one thing of which Hood never lost sight. The work was stressful and damned difficult, but it was not a burden.

It was the playing field of Franklin, Adams, and Jefferson. It was a privilege.

TWENTY-SIX

Zhuhai, China
Wednesday, 11:00 A.M.

Though General Tam Li held all his bases in high regard, he preferred the facility to which he was headed now. The Zhuhai base was the home of the PLA's Macao forces, key players in his master plan. Macao was only six square miles, a narrow peninsula connected to the mainland by an even narrower isthmus. It was the oldest European settlement in China and had been administered by Portugal since 1557. Yet most of the inhabitants were Chinese, and the hilly, rocky peninsula adjoined the Guangdong province in southeastern China.

Tam Li wanted it for China. And one day he would have it. But first, his larger objective must be realized.

The general traveled to Zhuhai on board a Gazelle helicopter gunship. He did not do so for his personal security. He did it because ordinary citizens enjoyed seeing military aircraft. They always stopped what they were doing to look up. It inspired them, and it made them feel safe, more productive.

Soon it would give them much more.

The trip from the isolated military sector of the Beijing Capital Airport took a little over three hours, with a quick refueling stop in Wuhan. The general was at his desk by nine-thirty for the eleven o'clock meeting.

The other seven members of the Central Military Committee arrived at different hours throughout the morning. The generals and admirals had come from Beijing, Shanghai, Hong Kong, and other cities across the nation. They came separately and discreetly, by air. This was not one of the committee's regular monthly meetings, and the men did not want to attract attention by gathering in Beijing or traveling together. Besides, the way Chou Shin was attacking Tam Li's interests, the officers did not want to be out and about with him. None of them put it past the Guoanbu to assassinate the general. Especially if Chou found out what Tam Li was planning.

The irony, Tam Li knew, was that Chou would probably approve of the plan but for one thing. It would shift the balance of influence in Beijing from the old-line Communists to the more capitalistic-minded military. That was something Chou Shin would never permit.

The officers had all assembled by eleven. They gathered in the small tactics room down the hall from Tam Li's office. The pale green walls were covered with maps printed on plastic sheets. Military planners could write on them with grease crayons, which could then be erased. The budget of the People's Liberation Army did not include wall-size monitors linked to computers.

Nor should it, Tam Li thought as he sat at the large, round table in the center of the windowless chamber. He had heard that an electromagnetic pulse bomb effectively shut down the American National Crisis Management Center. The same thing could happen to the Pentagon or any facility that was absolutely reliant on electronics. What any organization needed was balance through diversity.

Each of the men had brought folders containing different aspects of the plan. If any one of these files had been lost or confiscated, it would make no sense. All of them were required for the plan to be clear.

"Has there been any change in the Guoanbu plan for the launch?" Tam Li asked as he sat down.

The general's question had been addressed to Rear Admiral Lung Ti. The fifty-three-year-old officer ran the Third Department of the People's Liberation Navy, which was in charge of naval intelligence. The division was linked closely to activities in the other intelligence agencies. It was an alert from the rear admiral that had triggered this plan three months before.

"There is no change," Lung Ti replied. He paused to light his pipe. "Even if we did not have whispers from inside the Guoanbu, a man like Director Chou does not undertake a project unless he is sure of his mission."

"He is very sure," Tam Li agreed.

"How do you know?" Lung Ti asked.

"I was just with him," the general replied. "When the prime minister learned of the explosion, he called us to his office."

"So soon after the event?" laughed a youthful-looking general of the People's Liberation Army Air Force. "I did not realize that Le Kwan Po could make a decision in less than a day or two."

"He summoned us well after midnight, along with the sycophantic foreign minister," Tam Li said. "Le Kwan Po showed uncharacteristic displeasure as he pressed us both for an explanation. Chou gave none and left the meeting before it was ended."

"Did Chou mention the satellite launch?" Lung Ti asked.

Tam Li shook his head once. "He spoke about a 'singular vision' for China and refused to condemn the attacks on my private-market economy. That was the extent of his contribution."

"Was Chou feeling any pressure at all?" asked the rear admiral.

"No. He was angry to be there, to have his motives questioned," Tam Li replied.

"The old bastard is still upset by the end of *hukou*," said Lung Ti. He snarled, showing a gold tooth. "He does not let anything go."

Hukou was a form of census-taking and infrastructure maintenance. Each household was registered, and identification was issued to every individual. He or she could only get employment in the issuing district. That kept the main roads relatively free of traffic, allowed local planners to know exactly what kind of medical or police services they would need, and—perhaps most important—kept radical ideas from spreading. Radio and television broadcasts could be monitored. Conversations in the square or in a marketplace could not.

"That would suggest a crisis point is very near," said the rear admiral.

"What a waste of effort," another man said.

"It is a counterproductive effort," Tam Li said sadly. "Do you remember Chou's last contribution to our economy? He made the deal to sell tens of thousands of machetes to Hutu killers in Rwanda during the Hundred Days of Slaughter."

"Now he's killing again," one of the generals remarked. "That is how Communists move the economy."

The general's comment was a simplification, but it was true. Chou refused to fully embrace capitalistic solutions. He saw increasing numbers of beggars in the streets and opposed allowing more foreign corporations in to hire them. He watched the way minor international powers faced China down on peninsulas and islands in the region. He knew that foreign banks and corporations were assuming Chinese debt in exchange for more and more collateral properties. Yet his wish was to maintain the system that allowed these things to flourish.

"I say once again that we should put a bullet in the back of his neck and move on," Lung Ti said.

"A bullet won't get us everything we want," Tam Li reminded him.

"It will get me what I want," the officer grumped.

"What is Le Kwan Po going to do about Chou's actions?" another man asked.

"What does Le Kwan Po ever do?" Tam Li replied. "He functions as a buffer between the ministers and military on one side, and the president and vice president on the other. He does not solve problems. He merely prevents them from colliding."

"Then you do not believe he will try to stop Chou?" Lung Ti asked.

"I do not believe he will," Tam Li said. "We proceed with our own plans but I will have my own security people on alert in case Chou gets in our way. We will follow his staff and learn who his contacts and workers are. We will use them ourselves."

Tam Li looked at the rear admiral as he spoke. It was Lung Ti's intelligence that had suggested there would be assaults in Charleston and in Taipei as a prelude to an attack on the rocket. His people had become aware of the comings and goings of explosives experts from safe houses in the United States and Taiwan. That had been the first indication of fresh initiatives, as aggressive new intelligence actions were called. Once the individuals were flagged, the PLN3 watched them. There were requests for detailed maps, which went through a central logistics center. And travel documents. There was one other site on that list: the Xichang space center.

"We do not have a lot of time before the launch," Tam Li went on. "I want to make certain that our operations are coordinated."

He proceeded to review the PLA response, code named Sovereign Dragon. Twenty-four hours before the launch,

Taiwan would put its military on alert. Any Chinese rocket launch was an excuse to scramble Taiwanese air and sea forces. Taipei would say the launch could be an act of aggression, a potential intercontinental missile strike. Typically, launches like these were a chance for the nationalists to strut their muscle without fear of reprisal.

Typically, but not this time.

Throughout their career, these seven veterans had watched the Chinese military become *shangsheh*—more and more of less and less. Though the PLA received budget increases, that money went to updating hardware in an attempt to gain parity with foreign forces. By that time, the enemy had advanced even further. China would always be behind in everything except manpower. That would be used for the backbone of Sovereign Dragon. Unfortunately, there were very few barriers to which that manpower could be effectively supplied. Over the past twenty years, China had become increasingly isolated and marginalized, militarily. To the north they were bordered by slumbering but still dangerous Russia. To the east was Japan, which was on the verge of deploying a ten-billion-dollar missile shield in conjunction with the United States; nearer to home were an increasingly Western-leaning Vietnam and the smouldering Koreas. To the south and west were India and Pakistan, whose Hindu and Islamic rivalry could become a nuclear showdown at any time. If China did not make a move soon, there would be no moves to make. The job of the PLA would become purely defensive, to keep other wars and nations out, not to enhance China's international standing or power base. Without those, China would become what it was during the Boxer Rebellion: a carcass to be picked at by foreign powers. To Chou and his people, that was acceptable. Closing the doors and keeping the Communist vision pure was a victory. To Tam Li and his allies, that was an unacceptable loss of face as well as a slow death.

So they went over their plans and timetables, fine-tuned the specifics. They would begin with a response to the Taiwanese action. The PLN deployment would be modest and not unprecedented. But this time things would be different. Taiwan would be accused of capitalizing on a tragedy that was about to befall the PRC. As a result, the deployment of PLAN ships would be followed by the launching of PLAAF squadrons over the Taiwan Strait. While the world watched the buildup there, the PLA would seek—and obtain—the authority to establish buffer zones inside the current borders of Laos, Vietnam, and Burma to prevent opportunistic actions by those governments against coveted Chinese lands. The Central Military Committee would be granted those powers because they feared other terrorist actions like the one that was about to take down the Xichang rocket.

While all of this was happening, Taiwan would be blockaded. The United States would be told that an attack on the PLA would be met with devastating force. If they chose to move against China, China would invade the bordering states. Not even India could withstand an invasion of that magnitude. Either the United States had to accept a reintegrated Taiwan or face a massive war on many fronts.

They would press for, then accept, a negotiated settlement that joined a healthy capitalistic society with a dormant giant. The symbiosis would allow both to grow exponentially. And in a very few years, China would be the greatest power the world had ever known.

General Tam Li wondered how Chou Shin would react to the sudden, wrenching change in Chinese society. How could anyone react negatively to their nation going from a Third World economy to one of the most viable on earth?

The PLA and the rest of China were about to find out. And then Tam Li would make certain of something else: that Chou Shin was arrested and executed for treason.

TWENTY-SEVEN

Washington, D.C.
Wednesday, 2:00 A.M.

Morgan Carrie did not go home when Op-Center's night crew came in. She waited until she had received messages from each of her marines that they had arrived. As she was leaving, the general learned that she was not the only one who was working late. Bob Herbert was still in his office, which was next to hers. The intelligence chief was looking at a series of figures on his computer on his desk to the left. It presented his profile to the general.

"Staying the night?" she asked, leaning in.

"There's a crisis, I'm a crisis manager," he replied without looking over.

"Do you have something new?"

"If you consider confusion as something new, I have it," the intelligence chief replied.

Carrie was feeling more than a little hostility from Herbert. She did not know him well enough to determine whether it was her, the pressure, or overwork that was bringing it out.

"What's the problem?" she pressed.

"I know what we're looking at," Herbert told her. "I don't know what we're looking *for.*"

"Pertaining to what? The bombings?"

"The trail from Charleston to Xichang," Herbert said.

"You assume there is one."

"No, that's just something I have to consider," he told her. "Putting aside the satellite launch for a moment, we seem to have this tit-for-tat struggle taking place between two men, a general, Tam Li, and an intelligence officer, Chou Shin. What we do not know is why. It could be nothing more than personal animus, manifested as attacks on their reputation, sovereignty, or economy. But there is also the possibility that it's a proxy war between those two groups."

"That's unlikely," Carrie said. "A struggle between the military and intelligence communities would be counter-productive. It's also rare. Intramural wars are usually fought between rival intelligence units or military divisions."

"A fight for funding or the ear of the leaders," Herbert said.

"That's a simplified view, but yes."

"I agree," Herbert said. "It does not appear as though the general wants to take over Chou's position, or vice versa. There is nothing in their backgrounds to suggest that kind of personal ambition or professional interest."

"So where does that leave us?" Carrie asked.

"With a prize that we have not yet identified," Herbert replied. "To try to find that, we have to take a large step back and look at the picture of China overall. Before they went home, Ron Plummer and his hardworking assistant Robert Caulfield shot me a State Department bullet-point overview on China. What they are about, where they are going. One thing stands out, what State calls the Hong Kong Factor."

"Which is?"

"The success of democracy as an economic spur," Herbert said. "Since the Chinese takeover in 1997, Hong Kong has underscored the lie that Beijing has been promulgating for over sixty years, that Communism works." Herbert scrolled to some figures. "Hong Kong has six million extensively educated citizens. The society is multilingual and highly Westernized, with a low crime rate. Here's the fascinating part, though. At $24,750 in per capita annual income, the citizens of Hong Kong are twenty-five times wealthier than mainland Chinese."

"Has Beijing tried to explain the discrepancy?" Carrie asked.

"They say that Hong Kong is not a fair laboratory for China," Herbert said. "It is small and relatively homogeneous. China is too vast, too uneducated, and too culturally diverse to embrace the kind of democracy that has worked in Hong Kong and, of course, in Taiwan."

"All true."

"As far as it goes," Herbert said. "It's also true that if people got to vote, most of them would probably toss the Communist leaders."

"Which would result in a fracturing of China in much the same way that the Soviet Union came apart," Carrie said. "Every province would vote for policies that brought industry or agriculture to it."

"Or new military bases," Herbert said. He looked at Carrie for the first time. "That would give young people jobs, and older folks would run the support services that feed and equip it."

"Perhaps," Carrie said. "For China to build and modernize its military would require the kind of economy it simply does not have. We studied this at G2, extensively. It's one of the great problems of our age. If the different regions are not held together by force, or do not get an across-the-board influx of prosperity, we will have another Africa or Middle East or Pakistan with warlords and tribal leaders coming to power and fighting one another. No one wants to see one-fifth of the earth's population pitched into that kind of chaos."

"Which is what puzzles me," Herbert said. "Apparently, someone in China has figured out another way."

"The Mob," someone said from the hall.

Carrie turned. Darrell McCaskey was behind her. His eyes were half-shut and his five o'clock shadow had become a thicker-looking five A.M. shadow.

"You're cracking your head on this, too," Carrie said.

"It's what we do, Bob and me," McCaskey said. "Ron sent me the same data. We review it separately. If we come up with a lead or idea that matches, chances are it's worth following."

"So which mob are you referring to?" Carrie asked.

"The one with a capital *M*," McCaskey replied, moving into the doorway. "The Cosa Nostra, 'Our Concern.' The one that runs its organization, its empire, just like China."

"I didn't think of that one," Herbert said.

"You weren't a G-man," McCaskey said. "That's why I was coming over to talk about it. The Mob has a bloated hierarchy, just like China. And how do they support it? By constantly moving into new businesses. They leave it pretty much alone and shave cash from the top. Then they plug that cash into diverse new businesses, some of them legitimate, so they can stay afloat in any economy."

"I'm not getting your point," Carrie said.

"It's the other Hong Kong Factor," McCaskey said. "China took the colony over, learned some new tricks about running a capitalistic society, and put some of the profits into the Bank of Beijing. What's the next logical step?"

"Expand that into China, except—" Herbert said.

"That would not work," McCaskey said. "The process would be too slow and too jarring to the current system, as you've said."

"So you need more of the same," Carrie offered.

"If you're going to grow, yes," McCaskey said. "But if you're an old-school Red like Mr. Chou, you are going to resist that."

"I wonder how he stood on the Hong Kong takeover," Carrie said.

"He was for it, but with deep, deep reservations," Mc-Caskey said. "He sent a very detailed white paper to the National People's Congress and to the leadership of the Chinese Communist Party warning against allowing more 'water under the foundation,' as he put it."

"Do we have a copy of that paper?" Carrie asked.

"A summary," McCaskey said. "The FBI has a listening device at the NPC. Chou read excerpts pertaining to intelligence issues pertinent to folding a British colony into China."

"The success of that merging, which relies on a hands-off policy, would obviously not sit well with him," Carrie said.

"To say the least," McCaskey agreed. "He would watch it closely, and he would also watch for other signs of erosion. He would use the system to provide funds for his own purposes, as in South Africa, but he would not want to see that free enterprise concept expand."

"Especially among the people who are sworn to uphold the old ways," Carrie added.

"We can be pretty sure his concerns about the slave trade have nothing to do with humanity," Herbert observed. "Not with the way he has been blowing people up."

"Which leaves us, still, with no idea what the endgame is," Carrie said.

"I wouldn't say 'no idea,'" McCaskey said. "Getting back to the Mob analogy, if skimming off one society works, what is the next step?"

"Take another, as long as you think no one can or will stop you," Carrie said. It was not so much an answer as the general thinking aloud. "Take another" was not just the approach of Mafiosi but of greedy heads of state. It was the way Saddam Hussein had taken when invading Kuwait. All the research G2 had conducted suggested that if it came to building or saving face—either because they were challenged or because they wanted something—China would not hesitate to stand up to the United States. The U.S. military could blockade the Chinese coast and enforce no-fly zones for a time, but what would we do if two or three million men suddenly moved into Burma or Laos? Fight another Vietnam War?

"The region is full of tempting targets," McCaskey went on. "South Korea, Taiwan, Japan. Even Vietnam is coming back, thanks to us."

"But taking them over would further pollute the system, at least in Chou's eyes," Herbert said. "He would never stand for it. Presumably, he has allies in the Communist Party."

"There might even be enough support that he might attack the interests of someone who was promoting the idea of territorial expansion," McCaskey said.

"Support or arrogance," Herbert said. "The Chinese Reds don't lack for that."

"Darrell, I assume you're referring to the interests of Tam Li," Carrie said.

McCaskey nodded.

"What I don't get is, where does the rocket tie in to all this?" Herbert asked. "Assuming it does."

"I don't know," McCaskey said. "That's got me puzzled."

"The satellite will serve a military function," Carrie said. "It also represents a foreign foothold in China. Chou would want to undermine both of those."

"Do you really think he would compromise Chinese security to make a point?" McCaskey asked.

"Not security. Prestige," Carrie said. "And socialists don't really care about that. Look, Chou has the same intel we do. He knows that China will not be attacked militarily.

What he fears is the end of China as a philosophy. He would risk a great deal to preserve that."

"But Chou has to see that Communism is a losing battle," McCaskey said. "If he keeps a market economy from the mainstream, it will flourish underground."

"Maybe not, if Tam Li loses," Herbert said. "It will be nickel-and-dime trading at most. People will go back to selling cigarettes and DVDs from trucks instead of slaves from boats."

"Besides, no extremist ever sees a battle as lost," Carrie said. "And this struggle is far from over. The Chinese Communist Party still controls the apparatus of government and, as far as we know, most of the military. A decisive defeat of Tam Li would enhance Chou's standing."

"I still say there's a lot of guessing going on," McCaskey said.

"Hopefully, Paul can find out more," Herbert said. The intelligence chief regarded Carrie again. "Of course, all of this would go counter to what we were saying about a struggle between the intelligence and military factions."

"It would," Carrie replied.

"Maybe there's a new world coming, one with new alliances, new rivalries, and new rules."

"It's possible," the general agreed. "Is this going anywhere?"

"Just thinking out loud," Herbert replied.

"The military frowns on too much thinking," she said. "I guess that's something I'll have to get used to."

"Unless the rules change," Herbert said.

Carrie was not entirely sure what he was getting at, and she was too tired to deal with it in any case. "I'm going home," she said. "Call if you have anything solid before the morning."

Both men said they would.

Carrie left, wondering if she had just gotten a taste of her own little Chou-like rebellion.

Maybe it's just the man's exhaustion and the regime change talking, she thought.

General Carrie hoped that was the case.

Bob Herbert would be a difficult man to replace.

TWENTY-EIGHT

Washington, D.C.
Wednesday, 2:16 A.M.

"What the hell was that all about?" McCaskey asked when General Carrie had left the floor.

"What do you mean?"

"Please, Bob. This is me you're talking to—"

"We were just having a discussion," Herbert insisted.

"You were baiting her."

Herbert said nothing for a long moment. Why bother? Herbert did not see challenging the general as a bad thing. This was *not* the military. He had a right to question his superior. But he did not want to debate that with McCaskey. Not at this hour with all they had to do.

"Shouldn't we be more concerned about the other general?" Herbert asked.

"Yeah. We should."

"If Tam Li has got some kind of expansionistic ideas in his head, we need to gather intel on him. We should also figure out who to support in this showdown." Herbert snickered. "Some choice. An aggressive general or a backward-looking Commie."

"You know, we could *use* a little military-style discipline here," McCaskey went on.

The former G-man was obviously not ready to talk about Tam Li.

"What makes you say that?" Herbert asked. "Not just *my* big mouth—"

"Someone slipped us an e-bomb a couple of months back," McCaskey said. "Maybe that would not have happened if we had been sharper."

"That was done by a CIA-connected son of a bitch," Herbert said. "He had the resources and credentials to put that baby wherever he wanted."

"He put it *here*."

"Do you think General Carrie or anyone could have prevented that?" Herbert asked.

"I don't know," McCaskey said. "Since yesterday I've been thinking about what Op-Center would be like under the military."

"Blindly aggressive," Herbert said.

"Bullshit," McCaskey said.

"You think so? I'm not a big Paul Hood fan right now. I don't like what he did to Mike, and I did not appreciate a lot of the crap he brought to his relationships with Liz, Martha, and Ann. Hell, he didn't get along with women in general. But apart from the e-bomb, the roughest times we've ever had involved operations that were under the command of Mike Rodgers, Charlie Squires, and Brett August. All military personnel."

"That's what happens when you get things done," McCaskey said. "There's a price."

"A higher price when you rush in without sufficient intel," Herbert said. "You know me, Darrell. I'm not against kicking ass. What I don't like is doing it without forethought. I think a lot of what Mike did was knee-jerk. It was his way of carving a corner of Op-Center independent of Paul. One of his earliest missions, to North Korea, was undertaken without an okay from Paul."

"They both had issues," McCaskey agreed. "And they're both gone. We're starting fresh. And the question is, what's the best way to deal with crises today? Not five or ten years ago, but *now?*"

"And your solution is what? Shoot first?"

"More like fire first," McCaskey said.

"You lost me."

"When we sense a crisis coming, we should ignite it in such a way that we're able to direct the flow," McCaskey said. "It's like smoke eaters who set backfires to control bigger ones."

"Which they do in conjunction with using water and flame retardant," Herbert pointed out. "Sometimes those backfires get out of hand."

"That's where intel comes in," McCaskey replied. "We look at a situation and determine which tactic will work best. Sometimes, the fire-first method is the best. To date, Op-Center has been like the forest ranger in a tower who sees the smoke, watches the wind, observes the flames, sends out warnings, and finally acts. By that time you can lose half the forest. You know what all this keeps slugging me back to, Bob? When we were kids and there was all of the information about how life would be under Communism."

"That was propaganda," Herbert said. "It was in the comic books I read, it was even in the goddam *World Book Encyclopedia*, little cartoons of Stalin controlling people like puppets." He moved his fingers as if he were playing with marionettes. "It was shameless overkill, Darrell."

"No. It was education. A crash education in a real danger."

Herbert shook his head. "That's like calling segregation a means of classification. Yes, the Reds were a danger. But so were the witch hunts, and they were happening right here! The cure was worse than the disease. We were being frightened, Darrell. On purpose, by those in power so they could remain in power."

"We have a major disagreement there, friend. There were opportunists and tyrants, but most of the people I knew were patriots. Veterans of World War II and Korea who knew firsthand that Communism was a threat. They were the reason I became an FBI agent. I was scared by the thought of being manipulated and cornered, and I wanted to fight it. The operative word is *fight,* Bob. We went against the Chinese and their agents in Korea, in Vietnam, and we scraped to a standstill. We outspent the Soviet Union on an arms race until they imploded. But never once have we taken the war to them. We parry. We react. We don't put anyone on the defensive. I get the sense General Carrie will do that. She was here less than a day, and she fielded a Special Ops team."

"Great. So we become 'Ops-Center,' with a little Stalin controlling the strings of her agents and sleeper cells."

"I don't quite see General Carrie as Joseph Stalin."

"Yet. Or maybe Stalin is waiting in the Joint Chiefs."

"Bob, you are way overreacting," McCaskey said.

"I'm way tired," Herbert said. "Maybe that has something to do with it."

"I hope so, because we are only doing what our enemies are doing," McCaskey said.

"That's a moral strike against it."

"It's an amoral world!" McCaskey replied. "Either we become part of it or we take more and more hits. Bob, these marines are no different than the regional Op-Center we tried to get going a couple of years ago, except that the troops are mobile and stealthy. Their job is to gather information and act if they have to. Set backfires. You'll see, Bob. This is going to work."

"You're aware that *backfire* has another meaning," Herbert pointed out.

McCaskey frowned. "Now you're just being ornery."

"I prefer *realistic*."

"You can prefer what you want. You're cynical and pessimistic. I have more faith in our system than that."

"Oh, I have faith in the system," Herbert replied. "It's some of the people who scare me. You know what's the weirdest thing of all?"

"I'm afraid to guess."

"I'm relieved that Paul Hood is in the field, too," Herbert said. "We've got some maturity and restraint out there."

McCaskey grinned. "There was a time when Bob Herbert would have described that as being a pussy."

"It is," he replied. "Maybe that's what you need when there are soldiers running around half-cocked."

There was an awkward silence, not because the men disagreed. They had disagreed many times in the past. The silence was because of the bad pun.

"I think I'm going to pull a Carrie and head home," McCaskey said. "If I'm lucky, Maria won't wake up and want me to brief her on what's been going on here."

"I'll be interested to know what she says about all of this," Herbert said.

"I can answer that," McCaskey said as he headed for the door. "She's going to want to know why she wasn't on the field team."

"Tell her they were all of Asian descent."

"She'll just want to organize a team of Spanish descent," McCaskey said as he headed out the door. "Good night."

"Night."

Herbert sat there. He was not looking at the monitor. He was reflecting on the last comment McCaskey had made about him, that the old Bob Herbert would have signed up for militancy. That was true. He still favored offense, only the venue had changed. It was no longer about a force of arms but a force of ideas. That was the war brewing in China, a conflict of the old way versus a new way.

Meanwhile, there is still some old-way crap going on, Herbert reflected. Explosions around the world and a possible attempt to blow up a rocket carrying a nuclear-powered satellite. They were all being distracted by the larger picture, which was being dictated and defined by the apparent militarization of Op-Center. The immediate question was how to put out this fire, which was itself apparently a backfire against some internal problem they did not yet understand.

Herbert turned his tired eyes back to the monitor. As he looked back over the data, his mind kept switching to Striker and the actions they took. Preventing a war between the Koreas. Stopping a coup in Russia and averting civil war in Spain. Sacrificing their lives to prevent India and Pakistan from going to nuclear war. All successes, as far as the bottom line goes.

Quick, expensive, decisive victories, he thought. *Who could argue with that, other than the widow Melissa Squires and the families of the dead?*

Herbert was confused. But there was one thing he held to, and that was the value of intelligence in making decisions and planning actions. There was no arguing the wisdom of that as a course of action.

It was, after all, called *intelligence.*

TWENTY-NINE

Beijing, China
Wednesday, 2:00 P.M.

The ambassador never showed up.

Paul Hood waited in the room for two hours, then finally went for a walk to find out what was going on. He bumped into Wesley Chase, who, as it happened, was on his way to see him.

"I'm so very sorry, Mr. Hood. The ambassador was on the telephone for quite some time and then left the embassy," Chase told him.

"Is something wrong?"

"This is an embassy, sir," Chase smiled. "Something is always wrong. But Mr. Hasen said that if he does not see you before then, he will see you tonight at the reception."

"For—?"

"The start of the celebration of the fifty-eighth Chinese National Day," Chase informed him. "He will be there, along with the prime minister and other dignitaries. He said this will give you a chance to talk to Mr. Le Kwan Po."

"Does he speak English?"

"No. But there will be translators, including his daughter Anita. I will give you a full briefing on the personnel before you go. In the meantime, he asked that an office be placed at your disposal. The driver who met you at the airport will also be free to take you anywhere you may want to go."

"I may take you up on the sightseeing later," Hood said. "In the meantime, I'd like to go to the office."

Chase extended an arm down the hallway. Hood went back to his room to get his briefcase. Then he let the ambassador's executive assistant show him to the guest office.

"Is the ambassador available by phone?" Hood asked.

"The ambassador went to see the prime minister with his translator, no one else," Chase told him. "The president and I have a cell phone number in the event of a crisis. Short of war or a death, neither of us would interrupt the ambassador during a mission of state."

"Don't you usually go with him to these meetings, just in case someone has an emergency that does not quite qualify as a crisis?" Hood was not being facetious. It was unusual for an aide not to be present to tug on an ambassador's sleeve in case information or an opinion were needed.

"I usually go with him but not this time," Chase admitted.

"May I ask why?"

"You may, but I don't have an answer," Chase said. "The ambassador did not ask me to go."

"Is there anything you *can* tell me about the ambassador's morning?" Hood pressed.

"To tell the truth, Mr. Hood, I do not know very much, and what I do know I am not at liberty to discuss. I am sure you understand."

"Actually, I don't. I am here at the request of the president—" Hood went silent. Suddenly, he understood. He was here to talk to the prime minister, which was typically the ambassador's job. Joseph Hasen had gone to see the prime minister first. He was probably being territorial if not downright preemptive. "You know what? It isn't important why he went," Hood said.

Chase gave him a puzzled look as they walked. Hood ignored him. The former head of the underground NCMC was going to have to get better at being an aboveground diplomat.

The office was located just around the corner, past the oil portraits of former ambassadors. The large canvases were hung on ivory white walls. The walls were plain, save for the ornate crown molding along the top. The door to the office had marble pilasters topped by a frieze of junks sailing from east to west. Hood tried not to read any warnings of conquest into that.

"My intercom number is four twelve," Chase said as he left. "Is there a message in case the ambassador calls?"

"Only that I'd like to talk to him as soon as possible," Hood replied.

"I'll tell him," Chase promised.

The aide left the door open behind him. Hood closed it. The office was actually a desk stuck in a small library. There was no computer, just a phone on the desk. Visitors probably brought their own laptops. Hood felt a chill of disorientation. The office underscored how different his life was now from only two days ago. He walked slowly across the Persian rug. It was a silk tribal rug from K'om, patterns of dark earth colors surrounding the portrait of a woman. There were burn marks along the edges and bloodstains on the woman's cheek. Hood had read about the rug in the briefing folder. It had once been in the ambassador's office in Teheran. Hasen's brother-in-law had been an attaché there when the Iranians took over the embassy. He managed to escape by pretending to be Iranian. He had wrapped the body of a dead "freedom fighter" in the rug and dragged it out to make his story more convincing.

There wasn't an office like this at Op-Center, one with

history on the floor and volumes stacked on seven tiers of built-in bookcases. Even the records room was mostly digital. It was erased during the e-bomb attack, then replaced with copies from other agencies. Looking around, Hood got a sense of the magnitude of loss the Egyptians experienced when the library at Alexandria burned.

When was that? Hood wondered.

That information was somewhere in here, in one of the encyclopedias or dictionaries. He would have to go and find it if he wanted to know, not plug keywords into a search engine.

Like this mission, he thought. He had to go somewhere, and now he had to search for information. That was his new life. He would no longer be struggling against the chairman of the Congressional Intelligence Oversight Committee for funding, he would be trying to run the ball around ambassadors and their staff, heads of state and their staff, and every organization in Washington that had information he might need. The size of the task suddenly became very apparent.

And daunting, bordering on frightening. It was astonishing that anything got done. He looked down at the rug. He did not approve or sympathize, but he understood the frustration that pushed radicals to do what they did.

"Which means you've got to push back," he murmured.

As he thought that, his brain shifted to a default setting: Sharon. He did not like the fact that his subconscious apparently regarded her as an anarchist. He felt ashamed. He went to the desk and sat in the leather seat and decided to push back. At the real enemy, not the one in his head.

It was very early in the morning in Washington. Hood called Bob Herbert at Op-Center. If he did not find the intelligence chief at the office, he would not bother him at home.

Herbert was there.

"This is why bureaucracy sucks," the intelligence chief said.

Declarative statements like that passed for "Hello" from Bob Herbert, especially when he was working on a project. Caller ID had liberated him even further. It allowed him to vault right into a complaint without the inconvenience of having to wait for an answer to "Who's this?"

"What's wrong?" Hood asked.

"The retooling of Op-Center, which was done to streamline our operation, has left me with all my old associates plus a new one," he said. "It's a good thing I'm in my chair, because this Mississippi boy ain't finding his footing."

"You want to talk about it?" Hood asked.

"No. I'm done."

Herbert was always blunt and aggressive, but he never whined. And he did not displace his anger the way Hood did. He smacked the source, hard.

"Are we getting anywhere?" Hood asked.

"No, as I just told *Frau Feldherr*," Herbert replied.

Well, at least Hood knew who had triggered this outburst. General Carrie had been at Op-Center two days, and Herbert already saw her—or the people she represented—as the gestapo.

"I heard from Mike a few minutes ago," Herbert went on. "He's in Beijing at the Grand National Hotel. He was going to catch some winks, then meet up with his Xichang people. What about you?"

"Apparently, I won't know anything new until I go to the National Day reception tonight," Hood told him.

"I wonder when we're going to know anything, and if we're going to like what we find out," Herbert said.

"You lost me."

"About Op-Center," he said. "Maybe you and Mike are lucky to be out there, doing something else."

"Did something happen?" Hood asked.

"Not really. Some words with Carrie, then with Darrell."

"That's nothing new for you, Bob," Hood said.

"I know. I just get this sense that something is ramping up," Herbert told him. "Something not good. The DoD effectively takes over Op-Center, and the president pulls its top guy out to keep him close. That doesn't sound like rewarding Paul Hood for services rendered. Plus, we've got marines at our disposal. I was talking to Mike about that before. Striker redux. It sounds like a strategic realignment."

"That could be," Hood agreed. "Why do you assume that's a bad thing?"

"When I was a kid back in Neshoba County, we had a problem with the deer population after a dry spring. They were moving in on the resorts, the golf clubs, eating everything they could. The mayor and the board of aldermen of Philadelphia recommended that we send a team of environmentalists into these areas to do a complete study of the problem. Most of those guys were hunters. By the end of the summer the deer population was no longer a problem. In fact, it was damn near invisible. Except in the venison counters at the meat markets. You can solve problems or you can pick off the parts of them that are unlucky enough to show their heads. I'm afraid that we're starting to look for quick fixes instead of permanent ones."

"Whacking the weeds instead of uprooting them," Hood said.

"Yeah. Same thing, if you like aphorisms instead of folksy narratives," Herbert joked.

"That's my years as a homeowner talking," Hood replied. And as soon as he said it he felt that pinch of anger at Sharon again. He always liked doing the lawn, especially when the kids were younger and went out to "help" by pulling up dandelions or raking leaves to jump in. Hood got himself out of that place quickly. "Look, Bob. The future of American intelligence is not our concern at the moment."

"True, true," Herbert said. "I'm letting it go. But the operative phrase is 'at the moment.' I don't want to be caught

with my drawers down when it does become our concern.
It's the Big RB. It's Liz Gordon's white paper."

"I know," Hood said.

"There are moral issues at stake, but more importantly,
there are tactical ones," Herbert said. "I'm not a patriot for
a paycheck, Paul. If I think something is wrong, I'm going
to fight it."

The words "And I'll be fighting at your side" snagged in
the back of Hood's throat. He was not afraid to take on the
DoD. What scared him was civil war between American
government factions at a time when the nation needed to be
united. Even if the weeds were not eradicated, containing
them was better than ignoring them while the intelligence
departments fought.

"I hope it won't come to that," Hood said.

"Spoken like a newly minted diplomat," Herbert
replied.

Hood could hear the disappointment in Herbert's voice,
but he refused to let it bother him. This was not about Bob
Herbert's approval. It was about preventing the nation
from being drawn into Chinese politics.

If that's even possible, Hood thought as he said good-
bye and hung up. Herbert himself had taken to calling the
world the Big RB—the big rubber band ball. That was his
view of globalization, a tight intertwining of finance and
culture and religion. It was an apt description. All of the
strands were still distinct. United, they were a potentially
powerful force. But remove one of them, and the neighboring strands would start to slip. If they did, then the entire
structure would pop. Psychologist Liz Gordon had done a
profile of the planet called—rather more academically—
The Forced Unity of Disharmony. She declared that slip-
page was inevitable. One passage in the book-length study
asked the reader to imagine what would have happened if
the Sioux and Cheyenne who battled Custer had, instead,
been dropped into New York City. Would the so-called

"hostiles" have fought to keep from being captured, or would they have surrendered to superior numbers? Would they have taken hostages? Would they simply have scattered, gone underground to reconnoiter and then strike at night, at will? Would the police have tried to contain them—or kill them outright, the way the Seventh Cavalry did? How would ordinary citizens have reacted to a much different culture? With fear, curiosity, or a confusing mixture of both?

"The problem with globalization," Liz wrote in a cautionary summation, "is that all of those worlds do intersect now, and in more layers than anyone can successfully isolate, study, and chart."

In other words, like Bob Herbert said, it was a Big RB ready to pop. And maybe, Hood thought, the DoD was preparing to deal with it in a way that did not isolate, study, or chart.

Hood took his laptop from his briefcase and booted it. He wanted to have a close look at the party list, make sure he knew the players. He also had a walk around the library. He pulled out a current encyclopedia yearbook so he could read up on National Day. He was a guest in a strange land and wanted to know something of their history and customs.

As Hood did his research, he could not help feeling that his efforts were sluggish and obsolete. He did not feel like a hunter. Perhaps he was experiencing some of what Herbert felt.

If you're not a hunter, you're venison.

THIRTY

Yu Xian, China
Wednesday, 2:11 P.M.

After ten years in the business, Shek had talked his way out of a job. He was happy it turned out that way.

When he was a boy, Yuan "the Emperor" Shek used to look forward to his mother coming to his room and singing him a good night song. His favorite was "The World Beneath the Stone of Farmer Woo." It seems the farmer had to move a large stone in his field in order to plant corn. But when he did so, he found all manner of insects and tunnels, nests and roots, and even a family of field mice. Food came and went in organized supply lines, "Many ants with many legs in service of the empress." At the end of the song the farmer replaced the rock and grew his crops around it.

Young Shek lived in the back of the schoolhouse where his mother was the only teacher. His father was a soldier who was rarely home. There were plenty of rocks in a field behind the school. Most of them were too small to conceal more than a few bugs or small snakes. Shek was not strong enough to move the larger rocks, where he imagined the riches to be much greater.

One day, when his father was home, the older man showed his son how to get the rock to move. Not with a lever but with gunpowder. Carefully placed in cracks or under the edges, the tiny charges made Shek the master of the field. He even wrote a little song about himself, "The Emperor of the Empress Ant."

Explosives became a very big—and profitable—part of Shek's life. From a soldier friend who sometimes visited with his father, the boy learned how to manufacture explosives using fertilizer and other ingredients. Shek put them to work moving rocks for fun, creating popping toys to celebrate birthdays or holidays, and even for pest control. He taught himself how to set off charges using a slight amount of pressure applied to a trigger plate—in this case, pieces of bark peeled from trees. His small Emperor Mousetraps were a big seller in the village. He pedaled them from a small, flat rock along the main road until his mother found out what he was doing. She lent him a card table from the school.

She believed in doing things right.

Shek's father died in a truck accident when the boy was twelve. Teaching had never been very profitable for his mother, and the widow's pension from the military was extremely meager. Shek's sideline became an important part of their income. He made increasingly sophisticated fireworks, flares, and even custom demolitions for local builders. Without the benefit of an education, Emperor Shek became a master of his craft. Best of all, there was no record of his skill in military or scholastic records. He was what the intelligence trade called an invisible.

When Chou Shin learned of this talented young man, he hired him for the 8341 Unit. Chou immediately set Shek and his mother up in a small but comfortable cottage in Yu Xian, a Beijing suburb. The structure was isolated and had a shed out back for Shek's work, which was building bombs for the Central Security Regiment. The explosives were not simply for use by the CSR. Many of them were employed by the military for covert land and sea mines, illegal armaments that would not be traced to Beijing. Even more were given over for off-the-books ballistics. These were passed to rebels fighting in foreign lands, where destabilization benefited Beijing by involving enemy forces in distracting struggles at home.

Shek was always busy, though he was never rushed. His employer recognized that he was an artist who could hide explosives inside donuts for transport or bake them into ceramic goods that would explode spectacularly in a microwave oven or conventional oven. Those were good for assassinations.

Director Chou—who never made his requests by phone or computer but always visited the laboratory personally—had commissioned Shek to make very specific bombs over the last week. He wanted something small and powerful that could blow out the hull of a thirty-thousand-ton freighter. He wanted something else that would detonate cold: destroy a room on top of a high-rise structure without setting a fire or causing collateral devastation below. That required a briefcase-sized device with interior deflectors, steel ribs, and titanium mesh that would release the explosion without scattering superheated debris. Shek never knew where these devices were headed, nor did he care. Chou took care of him and his aging mother. Like his father, Chou was a military man and a loyal Communist. That was all Shek had to know.

A few days ago, however, Shek received a visit from someone else. Another military man who had learned of his work for Chou and needed a secret device of his own. He asked if an explosive could be prepared that would endure heat reaching 2,500 degrees Fahrenheit without detonating. Shek told him the real problem was not detonation but evaporation. At that temperature the medium carrying the chemicals would vaporize, causing the explosive to malfunction. Shek said it would be possible if the package were encased in a low-density, high-purity silica 99.8-percent amorphous fiber similar to the material used in the thermal tiles of the American space shuttle. Shek said he had something similar to that in his equipment closet. By that time Shek had guessed that the explosive would be used on a rocket, probably a ballistic missile, and foresaw a more difficult problem.

"The charge itself can be small, but the added weight of thermal shielding will immediately cause a missile or rocket to shift course," Shek told him. "Even some of the larger fireworks I built had no tolerance for imbalance."

"Added weight will not matter," the individual said, smiling broadly and showing a gold tooth.

"But sir, it will cause the rocket to veer."

"Mr. Shek, I want you to create the device. How long will it take?"

"Ten hours, maybe a little longer."

"Good. I will return then. You will be generously rewarded."

Shek did not care abut that. He did not mind killing people here and there, anonymously. They were enemies of the state or they would not be targets. But ever since he began making fireworks, Shek had been a student and devotee of space flight. He did not know what kind of rocket the man wanted to destroy, or why. But he did not want to be a part of it, whatever nations were involved.

"You will do it," the visitor replied coldly. "If you refuse, your mother will be brought here and shot in front of you. In the legs first. Then the arms."

Shek began assembling the man's bomb. He finished it on time. He did not ask what it was for. He did not want to know.

Now, however, he was watching television while he worked on a design to inject fuel into a lightbulb so it would explode when it was turned on. He saw a television newscast about the next launch from Xichang. It would take place the following afternoon, on National Day. A Long March 4 rocket would be used to carry a communications satellite aloft. Shek used his low-level security password to look up the project on-line. He read that the manufacturer was the Unexus Corporation and that the power source was plutonium.

Shek felt sudden nausea unrelated to the gas fumes. At a height of seven miles, as originally proposed, the destruction of the satellite would have caused the resultant radiation to remain primarily in the upper atmosphere. There, air currents would have diluted the effect and disbursed it over a wide area. An explosion under three miles would cause extensive fallout, much of that directed downward by the blast.

What this man planned was worse.

Far, far worse.

THIRTY-ONE

Taipei, Taiwan
Wednesday, 7:32 P.M.

The commander in chief of the Taiwan Armed Forces, based at General Staff Headquarters, Ministry of Defense, in Taipei, sat in a conference room. With him were the commanders of each of the services. Except for short rest periods, the six men would be in this room for at least the next twenty-four hours.

Exactly one day before any rocket launch on mainland China, the 427th Taiwan Flight Wing, based at Ching Chuan Kang Air Base, went on alert. The nationalist Chinese did not expect an attack, and the planes did not leave the field. But the pilots all went to the ready room, and the radar was put on double data status. This meant that the sophisticated new American-built strong-net radar systems at Ching Chuan Kang were interlocked with the systems at Pingtung Air Base North, home of the 439th TFW. That gave the military overlapping pictures of the mainland coast. Instead of receiving a blip with each sweep of one system, incoming images were constant. The double data system left holes in Taiwan's northern coast, but high command was not overly concerned. If an attack came from North Korea, Seoul would let them know.

Not that the Taiwanese high command expected an attack. Rocket and missile tests by the People's Republic of China were more an opportunity for a drill than an anticipation of hostilities. It was a chance for the Taiwanese Armed Forces to show their across-the-strait military adversaries that they were watching.

And ready. Twelve hours after the radar scan had begun, Taiwanese Fleet Command would dispatch one cruiser each from the four major naval facilities at Kenting, Suao, Makung, and Keelung. Two recently commissioned diesel-powered submarines would be launched from the new mountain stronghold in Hengchung on the southern coast. Six hours after that, in Tsoying, the Taiwanese Marine Corps would prepare for deployment by sea and air. On the books, their mission would be to recover anything that might land in Taiwan's territorial waters. But each man knew that in the event of a real crisis, their target could be anything from the vanguard of the PRC fleet to a coastal base or industrial complex.

In all, just six vessels and under three thousand men would be activated in this initial phase of national defense. If the TAF subsequently identified an actual threat from the PRC, the military would move from EWI—the early warning and information phase—to an aggressive electronic warfare phase. This would constitute a massive blocking of mainland communications and reconnaissance systems. Concurrently, Taiwan would launch its forces in a strategic counterblockade capacity to ensure that the waterways and air lanes would be kept free for the TAF and its allies. Anti-ballistic armament would be launched to intercept any missiles fired from the mainland coast. One hundred fifty F-16 fighters were the cornerstone to this capability. The

American-made jets were faster and more powerful than the sixty French Mirage 2000-5 jets that formed the backbone of the PLAAF.

This information and counterattack superiority would form the basis of the initial Taiwanese thrust. It would be followed by a fully synchronized, multiservice and extremely quick response to any sea or land assault, or even the hint of one. There was no doubt in Taiwan that an initial thrust from the PRC could be met and stopped. Their entire strategy depended upon decisively repelling a first strike and holding a second wave. If a struggle went beyond that, and the United States did not intervene, the PRC would simply overwhelm them.

No one expected it to come to that. War benefited neither nation. Taiwan and the PRC did a great deal of business with one another. Not just black market activities but legitimate investments and industrial development. And those numbers were increasing exponentially. The only ones who objected to that were the vintage Communists and the military hard-liners. Both groups were losing ground to the young entrepreneurs. Ironically, these young men and women were a product of a successful Communist policy: the decades-old one-child-per-family rule. Family planning prevented an estimated three hundred million births, which would have taxed the infrastructure and kept Chinese mothers out of the workforce. But it also created a generation of pampered, entitled Chinese. These young adults wanted what their Taiwanese counterparts had: brand-name clothes, electronic toys, and high-end automobiles. Neither Communism nor militarism was going to give them that.

Nonetheless, the commander in chief and his staff still put the Taiwanese military through its carefully planned defensive motions. There was always the chance that someone in Beijing would think the future looked better draped in red instead of silver and gold. Reason and greed were powerful motivators. Unfortunately, so were habit and vanity. That combination could be catastrophic, especially if a political or martial cause to which someone had dedicated their life was in danger of being extinguished.

THIRTY-TWO

Beijing, China
Wednesday, 8:00 P.M.

Being a guest in China was a little like making a soufflé. If you opened the door at the wrong time, the result wouldn't be a happy one.

Unlike their counterparts in Washington, dignitaries in China did not arrive fashionably late for a party. Not only was it considered extremely bad manners, it assured the latecomer that he or she would be ignored. The Chinese were very good at turning away from or looking through someone who was ungracious.

Arriving early was also considered discourteous, an imposition on the host's charity. The result, of course, was an inevitable bottleneck at the door. But there was a benefit to that as well. People were obliged to meet and chat with whomever was standing around them under the long, long canopy that led to the street. The canopy was only erected for receptions. It was a gesture so guests would not feel as though they were waiting outside, exposed to elements and passersby. That would have been considered bad manners.

In Hood's case, he ended up chatting with two people he did not know. A third individual was one he did recognize, a Chinese national who worked for the Beijing bureau of the *Washington Post*. Hood did not want to talk to him. The man did not recognize Hood, and he wanted to keep it that way. A good reporter would not simply accept, "I happened to be in Beijing, and the ambassador invited me," as a reason for being here.

Presenting his back to the reporter left Hood facing the Brazilian ambassador and his wife. They looked to be in their sixties. The woman was wearing a small diamond engagement ring, which suggested that she was the original Mrs. Ambassador. The man was a former architect who was admiring the Huabiao, an ornamental marble pillar engraved with twining dragons and ominous clouds. He said that the origin of the Huabiao dated to the legendary kings Yao and Shun, who ruled some 4,000 years ago. He said that they were originally wooden columns used as landmarks for travelers.

His wife smiled benignly. She was a historian, a professor at Pontifícia Universidade Católica do Rio de Janeiro. The handsome, gray-haired woman was on sabbatical to be with her husband during his tenure.

"The Biaos were not that," she said, addressing Hood. "They evolved from a pole called a *Biao*, which was used in building much more recently, around 700 B.C. The Biao was placed in the ground to determine plumb and to mark the boundaries of construction. As larger structures came to be built, stone Biaos were used. By 400 B.C., they had become part of the structure."

"While we are here, we are collecting data to ascertain which of us is right," the ambassador said with a smile for his wife. He added pragmatically, "Whichever of us wins or loses, scholarship benefits."

Hood smiled. There was something sweet about their rivalry. The couple had found an activity that allowed them to be together yet still individual. He envied them that.

They made it through the door and into the ballroom after nearly ten minutes. Their names were checked against a master list by men wearing formal black Chinese military uniforms. Though Hood and most of the guests were dressed formally, the Chinese made no attempt to evoke the dynasties or Western styles. This was a show of traditional Red Chinese influence and authority. Inside, the Chinese leaders were dressed in tuxedos with necks reminiscent of the high-collared Mao jacket.

The American ambassador was already working on a martini as he chatted with the prime minister through a young female interpreter. Hood felt a flash of anger, not because the man had Le Kwan Po's ear but because Hasen did not have to wait in line. The feeling passed when the ambassador saw Hood and waved him over. Simultaneously, Hasen excused himself and walked toward Hood. He was glad to see that. Hood did not know who he was supposed to be or why he was here. That was something he was to have discussed with the ambassador before coming. He knew only that he was posing as an observer attached to the embassy.

The room was already loud with chatter, the voices a combination of English and everything else, most notably the clucking sounds of the Chinese tongue. The ambassador put a hand on Hood's shoulder as he brought him forward.

"Sorry I couldn't meet you earlier," Hasen said. The very tall, round ambassador spoke softly, his voice nearly swallowed by the din. "The prime minister wanted to meet with someone, and I had to arrange it quickly."

"Someone obviously more important than a special envoy to the president," Hood said with a trace of sarcasm.

"In this instance, yes," Hasen said. "It was a friend of yours, actually. General Mike Rodgers."

Hood frowned. He had not yet conferred with Rodgers about coordinating their work here, because he was not yet sure what needed to be done. Obviously, that had not stopped Mike.

Hood did not get to follow up because they reached the prime minister's side. Le Kwan Po had been distracted by someone who was speaking through his own translator. The Russian ambassador, from the sound of it. The man looked vaguely familiar, and Hood wondered if they had met before. It was possible. He had been to Russia and had worked closely with Sergei Orlov, his counterpart at the Russian Op-Center in Saint Petersburg.

My former counterpart, Hood reminded himself. Orlov was still running that facility.

Hasen took that moment to present Hood to the young woman who had been translating for them.

"Paul, allow me to introduce Ms. Anita Le, daughter of the prime minister," Hasen said. "Ms. Le, this is Mr. Hood. Paul Hood. He is a presidential aide sent here and there to make sure administration policy is being upheld."

"The president should have more faith in his ambassadors," Anita said to both men.

"Some of us fall victim to a variation of the Stockholm syndrome," the ambassador remarked.

"You start to empathize with your hosts," Anita said.

"Speaking of hosts, I'm going to see if I can recapture the prime minister," Hasen said. "Will you excuse me?"

"Of course," Anita said.

Hasen left, and Hood asked Anita if she would like a drink. She said yes and motioned to a waiter. The white-jacketed young Chinese hurried over. She asked for champagne. Hood ordered a Coke.

"Do you not drink?" the woman asked.

"Rarely," Hood replied. "I like to remember what I hear. More important, I like to remember what I said."

"Moderation, Mr. Hood."

"Not something Americans are very good at," he replied.

"I understand. When I was in school I read novels by Mr. Hemingway and Mr. Fitzgerald. The men were always drinking too much."

"The authors, too, I fear."

The woman smiled. Anita Le was a striking woman. She was dressed in a sequined white gown that did justice to her slender, athletic figure. She had straight black hair with hints of red and a round, open face with large eyes. She looked to be in her late thirties or early forties. She had poise that came from years of negotiating the sharp edges of life.

Hood glanced over at Hasen. He was still trying to insert himself into a conversation with the prime minister. The crowd around him had grown considerably.

"Is this your first visit to Beijing?"

"It is," Hood replied. "Do you work full-time as a translator?"

"No. I teach literature at Beijing University. You can tell a lot about the ethos of a culture from its fiction."

"Do you follow contemporary literature or just the classics?"

"I stay as current as time allows," she said. "Though I must confess I have no particular interest in most of the work being produced by your country right now. Most of it is wish fulfillment for women and men, with very little to offer both. That divides rather than unites a culture."

"You mean romances for the women and spy stories for the men."

"Yes."

"I look at that stuff as aspirational," Hood said. "It creates idealized heroes and heroines that make us want to be better."

"They are comic books for adults," Anita replied dismissively.

"What's wrong with that?" Hood asked.

"Popular literature is more about superficial external desires, to be strong or beautiful, than about internal growth,"
she replied. "There was a time in the nineteenth and early
twentieth century when American authors like Herman
Melville and John Steinbeck and Upton Sinclair addressed
social and psychological issues instead of fantasies."

"Fantasies have truth in them," Hood said. "*Moby-Dick*
is a fantasy."

"Only as far as the whale is concerned," the woman
replied, "and it is not to be taken literally. The white whale
is a personification of Captain Ahab's destructive desires."

"I'm sure many of the enemies in contemporary American literature can be seen that way."

"No," the woman replied with a firm shake of her head.
"The Chinese are inevitably portrayed as enemies, as are
the Russians. These are very specific references in all your
spy novels, your James Bond adventures, and they distort
reality in a quest for propaganda."

"James Bond is British," Hood pointed out.

"An irrelevant detail. The mentality is still Western."

"To some degree," Hood admitted the truth of that.
"You have read James Bond novels?"

"Only *Dr. No*," she said. "I saw several of the films.
Comedies, really. *Dr. No* was a villain born in Beijing, a
member of several tong gangs, a man with a translucent
yellow skin with a Chinese Negro bodyguard. Destroying
American missiles with a laser beam while posing as an
exporter of guano. Mr. Hood, have you ever met a Chinese
like that?"

"No," he had to admit.

"Or a dazzlingly brilliant spy like Mr. Bond, who an-
nounces his identity to everyone he meets while moving
through the world in a tailored tuxedo?" Anita said. She gestured vaguely at Hood's attire. "A spy would be discreet."

"One would think," Hood said uncomfortably. He saw

Hasen returning with the prime minister. Hood's own powers of subtle intelligence gathering were about to be tested.

Hood did not know if they would ever find common ground where literature or literary protagonists was concerned. But the woman spoke English magnificently, and while she had the aggressive confidence of an academic, she listened when he was speaking. There was curiosity at work.

Anita's manner changed instantly when the men returned. She moved between but slightly behind her father and Hood. Her chin was no longer high and proud but lowered, like her eyes. It was not subservience but respect. Hood wondered if the writers Anita disliked so much would have bothered to note the dynamics between a father and daughter, a prime minister and translator.

Not the ones who had made Le Kwan Po a Fu Manchu-style tyrant, he reflected.

Hood and the prime minister shook hands.

"Mr. Hood. Mr. Hasen says you wished to meet me," the prime minister said through Anita.

"Yes, sir," Hood replied. "Is there someplace we can talk for a moment, privately?"

"Right here," the prime minister said. "No one can hear us, and most do not understand English. If you speak and I listen, we will be secure."

"All right," Hood said.

"But, Mr. Hood—I know your name. Why is that?" the prime minister asked.

"I've been in government for quite some time," Hood replied.

"In what capacity?"

"Most recently as the director of the National Crisis Management Center," Hood replied.

"Yes, of course. The renowned Op-Center. Your spies uncovered plots around the world, prevented wars."

Anita looked at Hood as she finished translating. Her expression darkened, and Hood felt a flush.

"Then you know, of course, General Michael Rodgers," Le Kwan Po said.

There was an edge to Anita's voice that had not been there before. Anita had to feel as though Hood had been leading her, patronizing her.

"Yes, sir. I worked very closely with General Rodgers for years."

"Are you here at his request?"

"Only partly, sir," Hood admitted. "The president also had reasons for sending me."

"I would like to hear those reasons," Le Kwan Po said. "President Debenport seems to take a harder view of our government than his predecessor."

"Harder in what sense, Mr. Prime Minister?"

"Black and white," Le Kwan Po replied.

"I cannot answer for the president, sir," Hood said. "I can tell you that his regard for you personally is very high. As is mine."

"Thank you," the prime minister replied. He looked at his watch. "The toasts do not begin for another forty minutes. Perhaps we had better go elsewhere."

"All right."

Le Kwan Po led the way through the crowd toward the back of the ballroom. Well-wishers bowed or clasped his hand. Le smiled politely and patiently as he continued moving forward. It was a tremendous political asset, being attentive without stopping, giving a moment of your time without breaking stride. Le did that and one thing more: he did not show any favoritism. Everyone got the same smile, the same moment of contact. Debenport—and James Bond—might see the Chinese as black, but Le Kwan Po was definitely gray.

And his daughter was definitely annoyed. She was still walking behind her father, which meant she was walking behind Hood. He caught her sharp stare whenever he maneuvered around someone in the packed hall.

The group reached the back of the hall. A soldier wearing a formal black uniform opened a door for the prime minister. Le extended an arm, urging the ambassador and Hood to enter. They did, followed by the prime minister and his daughter.

Hood would talk to Anita later. He would try to explain that she was not wrong about so much spy fiction—though what is often distilled for narrative convenience is not necessarily false.

Maybe you can invite her to go whale-watching, Hood thought. That would keep his record of wrongheaded approaches to women intact.

For now, though, Hood had more important matters to deal with. Which was one way life and fiction differed very dramatically. Despite the tuxedo and impressive résumé, he doubted that any spy could attend to a crisis and a woman at the same time.

THIRTY-THREE

Beijing, China
Wednesday, 8:22 P.M.

Le Kwan Po found it strange that so many Americans knew about his investigation. There was a cultural difference between the nations, one encapsulated in the saying, "Tell one American and you have told them all." Chinese were not talkers. To the contrary, they were hoarders. They kept information as though it were fresh water on the high seas. They would share it only if it would bring an exponentially high return or was necessary to save face.

But Americans talked to a stranger as if he were their best friend. Diplomats were a little better, depending upon their experience. Most of the men sent to China, including Mr. Hasen, had a good deal of experience in government. But Le had met ambassadors who had been newspaper publishers, actors, and even a professional bullfighter before being sent to represent their nations. These men loved to talk. Only occasionally did they listen.

Paul Hood seemed different. The three men settled into

the century-old easy chairs in the antechamber. Anita sat between her father and Hood. The American's beverage arrived, and he accepted it graciously. By his expression, his easy carriage, the few words he had spoken, even the way he paid attention to Anita, Le could see that Hood was neither obsequious nor pretentious.

If there were such a thing as the typical movie-hero American, General Rodgers embodied those aggressive, masculine characteristics. If there were such a thing as an average American, Paul Hood seemed to possess those more modest traits. There was something fair but resolute in his eyes. Hood certainly seemed far more open and approachable than General Rodgers had been.

"Paul, why don't you tell the prime minister why you're here?" Ambassador Hasen urged.

Anita translated for her father. Hood leaned forward in his chair, his hands folded in front of his chin. It looked as though he were praying.

"Mr. Prime Minister, I am here at the request of the president," Hood said. "He has asked me to offer whatever help we can to assure a successful launch of your new communications satellite."

"Does he have reason to believe the launch is in jeopardy?" Le asked.

"There is intelligence to suggest you think there is a danger, Mr. Prime Minister."

"General Rodgers expressed that concern, but he had no information," Le said. "What can you tell me?"

"We believe the explosions in the United States, South Africa, and Taiwan may be related," Hood said. "With respect, sir, we believe that the perpetrators may be elements within China."

"Is your information vague, or are you simply being reticent?" the prime minister asked.

"I am a guest in your country, sir. I did not come to make charges against individuals, merely to offer help."

"What form would that help take?" the prime minister asked.

"I would like to come to the launch," Hood said. "Represent the president at a historic moment for China."

Le laughed. "We have launched many communications satellites before this."

"Not one built with the help of American industry," Hood said.

The American ambassador leaned forward. He looked very sincere. "As I have said before, Mr. Prime Minister, President Debenport wishes for a closer détente with Beijing."

"You *have* said that before, Mr. Ambassador. Yet only recently your government has made arms sales to the rebels across the strait."

"The Taiwan Relations Act is for purely defensive use—" Hasen said.

"Gentlemen, I doubt we will solve the issues of this region right now," Hood interrupted. "But I hope we can establish some degree of trust regarding this launch. Mr. Prime Minister, you know my background. I would like the honor of standing at your side."

The prime minister sat silently while he considered Hood's offer. He was studying the American.

"General Rodgers made the same offer," Le said after a moment. "He said he wanted to 'watch my back.' "

"It's a popular expression."

"I understand," Le assured him. "It would also suggest personal weakness and mistrust of our own security forces if I had a small force of Americans looking out for me and for the launch. I told General Rodgers I would consider his offer. In the name of this new détente, I will allow one of you to attend. You understand the situation. Please work it out between you who that will be."

"Mr. Prime Minister, it would not be unprecedented to have a representative of the manufacturer and a foreign government present for a launch," the ambassador pointed out. "And it would show the world that we are approaching a new age in the Sino-American relationship."

"Many members of my government would find that an unacceptably generous leap," Le said, "especially when both representatives spent years working together at an American intelligence agency." The prime minister rose and regarded Hood. "I must return to my guests. I will expect your answer in the morning."

Hood stood. "You will have it. Thank you, sir."

Le left the antechamber, followed by his daughter and the two Americans. They walked slowly toward the ballroom. "What is your impression of this man?" he asked Anita.

"Unexceptional," she replied.

"Yes. The best spies are, you know," Le told her. "They should never stand out."

"Do you think he is spying on us?"

"Almost certainly," the prime minister answered. "The American president already has an ambassador. Why send another? Besides, a man with his credentials is always watching for new faces, new dynamics, new technology. Yet he may be sincere in his desire to want to help protect the launch."

"Why?"

"If something happens, it may have repercussions throughout the region," the prime minister said. "His government might not wish to be forced to participate. Hopefully, we will know more in a minute."

"How?"

"You will ask him a question." Le smiled.

"*I* will?" she said.

The prime minister nodded once. "Mr. Hood virtually ignored his own ambassador during our chat," Le told her. "Yet Mr. Hood was watching your reaction very closely."

"I was translating—"

"Interpreters are usually invisible, you know that," Le said.

"He was simply being polite."

"The ambassador was watching me, and he was watching Mr. Hood," Le told her. "You must have impressed him. I would like you to find out why this launch is so important to him. He may confide in you."

"Father, I am not a diplomat," she protested.

"Neither is your mother. But I trust you both, and you are intuitive in ways that I am not."

The prime minister squeezed his daughter's hand to signify that the conversation had ended. They had entered the ballroom. A number of people were now within earshot, and they spoke Mandarin. He did not want his thoughts or concerns to become part of a public debate.

Anita seemed a little confused by his observation. That was all right. It was good for her to step from the armor of academic absolutes now and again. He was not sure whether he trusted Paul Hood entirely. He seemed likable and sincere, but the interests of the United States in this matter were curious. Le had listened, but he had not learned much. The White House should not be so concerned about a multinational corporation like Unexus. Not to the extent that they would send a high-level troubleshooter to check on its interests. And this was not a diplomatic issue. Otherwise, the ambassador could have handled it.

Unless it is not the satellite that really concerns them, Le reflected. Paul Hood had come directly to see him. Le wondered what they might know or suspect beyond what he already feared. At the moment, the only casualty on Chinese soil had been his own credibility. If he could not make peace between Director Chou and General Tam Li, the president and influential members of the National People's Congress would lose faith in him. That was not something that would matter to the United States. And the destruction of the rocket would not impact them directly unless it affected one of their allies in the region.

Hopefully, there would be a way to find out.

Le was approached by Australian ambassador Catherine Barnes and her husband. At the same time, from the corner of his eye, the prime minister saw Hood making his way toward the door. Excusing himself from Ms. Barnes, the prime minister turned to his daughter.

"Anita, go to Mr. Hood before he leaves," the prime minister whispered.

"Will you be all right on your own?"

"Ambassador Barnes speaks passable Mandarin, and it is almost time for the toasts. Go."

Le released Anita's hand, and she made her way through the crowd. She followed Hood as he left the ballroom. Hood had his cell phone in his hand, possibly preparing to call General Rodgers.

There was something a little dirty about it, Le realized. Part of what may have appealed to Paul Hood was the fact that his daughter was an attractive woman. If so, he was using her in an unseemly manner. But while that could be part of it, that was not all of it. Le's sense of the brief meeting was that Paul Hood might be a new kind of spy. He was somewhere between General Rodgers and Ambassador Hasen: a covert bureaucrat, an ambassador without borders.

Testing a new kind of spy required a new kind of counterspy. Anita, an educator-interrogator. In a world where there were rumors of an American physician-assassin, the rules were definitely changing. Perhaps for the best. Le believed that Hood may have come for the reasons stated: to collect intelligence without prejudice and to begin forming a strategic international alliance. Whether that union lasted for as long as it took to protect the launch, or whether it was the start of a new détente remained to be seen. Even if that was not why Hood was here, the prime minister might be able to use him in that way. That would make this like any relationship in politics or in life. If it was successful, it did not matter who had contributed what and why.

It would be ironic, though, Le thought as he chatted superficially with Ambassador Barnes. A fight between two Chinese officials spills into the global arena. The one who stops it is a member of the audience. What was it Li-Li had said just two days ago?

"This situation is about the future."

His wife may have been wiser and more prophetic than she knew.

THIRTY-FOUR

Alexandria, Virginia
Wednesday, 8:41 A.M.

General Carrie did not get very much sleep.

She came home, sat on the sofa to go through the mail, and the next thing she knew, her husband was very gently nudging her awake.

"You must have been tired," Dr. Carrie said.

The woman opened her eyes. The general was lying against the armrest, her feet on the floor. Her husband's brown eyes were staring down at her.

"What?" she asked, still groggy.

"I said you must have been tired," he repeated. He held up an envelope. "You actually opened a 'You Won a Millions Bucks!' come-on."

General Carrie's eyes shifted from her husband to the envelope. She did not remember opening it. She did not even remember sitting here. She looked at the clock on the digital video recorder. It was coming up on nine A.M. It was late.

"The housekeeper will be here in twenty minutes," Dr. Carrie said.

"Yeah. Thanks," his wife replied. She moved stubborn limbs in an attempt to get up. Her husband helped her. He was already dressed, which meant he had showered, and she did not hear him. She smelled coffee. General Carrie did not hear him make that, either.

"Can I get you anything before I leave?" he asked.

"Tea, thanks," she said. "Also, a kiss."

He bent over and planted one on her lips. It did not work as well as caffeine, but it was a start.

The neurosurgeon brought his wife her tea, then left. Carrie rose and took a long slug of the strong Earl Grey. She felt as tired as she did when she had come home. She heard the car pull from the driveway and savored her daily moment of solitude. She checked her cell phone. There was just one message. It was from the Andrews dispatch sergeant, probably wanting to know when he should come and get her. She was glad someone had been there for her the night before. That was the great thing about working on an air force base. There was always a driver in the staff pool. She called him and told him she'd be ready to leave at 9:30.

The general took off her uniform, showered quickly, and felt better when that was done. The housekeeper had arrived and let herself in. Patricia Salazar was a young single mother of two who went about her work with easy efficiency. It had occurred to Carrie years before that Patricia would be a perfect spy. She had the run of the house, and who would ever suspect a Portuguese-speaking housekeeper of being an agent for a third party?

Which was exactly the point. Carrie had her G2 staff run a background check. Although Patricia had been married to an NCO in an army signals regiment seven years before, he had left her—and the children—for another woman. Phone logs were checked, as were travel records.

Patricia was watched for several weekends. The Salazars apparently had no contact after Patricia came to Maryland to live with her sister and brother-in-law.

Carrie had not felt bad about doing that. A clean house—and a happy housecleaner—were not more important than national security. But caution was a part of her profession. The general did not usually discuss work at home and never took sensitive documents to the house. But she did not want to go to work with a bug concealed in the heel of her shoe.

Carrie poured another cup of tea into a thermos, then glanced at the news on-line before the car arrived. There had been no explosions during the night. That was both good and bad. Good because no one had been hurt. Bad because each new event would give them more information to work with.

The driver arrived, and Carrie left with two things that were at her side constantly: her laptop and her secure phone. As soon as the general was comfortably settled in the car, she raised the glass partition between the seats and switched on the telephone. She entered the password neurodoc, then punched in 1*. That speed-dialed the cell phone of someone she spoke with almost every day, the man who had helped her rise through the military. The man who had ensured her promotion and made the transfer to Op-Center possible. General Raleigh Carew, Chairman of the Joint Chiefs of Staff.

"You did not call since you started," Carew said.

"I was settling in, getting the overview."

"And what's your impression of Op-Center?"

"Most of the people are dedicated, hardworking, and extremely burned out," the general informed him.

"Burned out in what way?"

"They work long hours, they take their cases home with them, and when they are not involved in a crisis, I'm told they are busy looking for the next one."

"Told by whom?"

"Liz Gordon, the staff psychologist," Carrie said. "That last factor is the one that's killing them. There is no downtime."

"What's going on there? The Napoleon syndrome?" Carew asked.

"I do not get the sense they are trying to compete with the big boys of intelligence," Carrie told him. "At least, that's not their primary motivation. It is more like a bunker mentality. They see themselves as a key line of defense— which they are. But according to Liz, Paul Hood made them feel as if they are the only line of defense. His personal line of defense."

"Against what?"

"Mediocrity," she replied. "Liz thinks that Paul Hood used the NCMC to fix the world in ways that he couldn't fix his life."

"General Carrie." Carew sighed. "Are you going to sit there and give me a lot of psychobullshit?"

"Mr. Chairman, I was not the one who brought up the Napoleon syndrome," Carrie remarked.

Carew was silent for a moment. "Touché," he replied. "Go on."

"Liz says that the big problem is the way Hood integrated everyone into the crisis management process on every level. Military planning was plugged into tech, intelligence gathering was hot-wired into the political liaison office, legal worked with psychological, everyone hands-on everywhere. I saw that happening myself around two this morning. I was talking to Herbert and McCaskey, and they were overanalyzing everything they had picked up that day instead of acting on it. The guiding principle is that the team takes risks but not chances."

"Everything comes from the brain, not the gut," Carew said.

"Exactly," Carrie said. "Whereas we encourage our intel people to explore from within, these people investigate from without. They started a unit of field agents under Mike Rodgers, but it never worked out. Liz says that Hood couldn't let go. I discovered that Hood is also one reason that Liz back-doored a recommendation to then-Senator Debenport that Mike Rodgers be the first one downsized. Hood's number two was burning out big time."

"That's because he's a soldier, not a bureaucrat. He took the full frontal hits for Op-Center, all of them in the field."

"Liz doesn't think Hood realized the damage he was doing to General Rodgers or to the rest of the staff," Carrie continued. "If he thought about it at all, he would blame it on being understaffed."

"Where was the CIOC in all this?"

"The Congressional Intelligence Oversight Committee didn't seem to care how Hood ran the organization as long as he got results," Carrie said. "And he did. Hood was one reason the CIOC felt they could cut his budget. Debenport knew that Hood would make it work. What I don't understand, though, is if he was so important to the mix, why did President Debenport pull him away?"

"So Hood could do the same thing for the West Wing that he was doing at the NCMC, pulling together an intelligence community under the direct control of the president," Carew said. "Debenport knows we want to create a greater structure allied with G2. Hood is his countermove."

"And his spy."

"What do you mean?" Carew asked.

"Hood is using personnel from Op-Center on the situation in China."

"Of course. The president had to realize Hood would do that," Carew said. "He would use long-standing relationships to tap Op-Center's resources and confuse their loyalty."

"Liz feels the danger to Op-Center goes deeper than that," Carrie said. "She says that Hood's command style not only connected people professionally but emotionally—in a common, often open dislike of Hood. Rodgers, Bob Herbert, attorney Lowell Coffey, and FBI liaison Darrell McCaskey all manifested extreme resentment from time to time. But she thinks that instead of being relieved by his absence they're feeling lost. These people don't have a familiar commander—or a place to put their frustration. In the absence of that, Hood can cherry-pick the personnel he needs in his new position. Whether intentionally or not, that will divide their loyalty."

"Keep us from solidifying the unit."

"Right."

"Whether or not that's true, and whether or not this was all Hood's fault, how long will it take to fix?" Carew asked.

"I'm going to work on that with Liz today," Carrie said. "We're going to see who we can retain and retrain."

"Are you sure Liz Gordon was not affected by all this?" Carew asked.

"Very sure," Carrie replied. "Hood did not trust profiling or psychology very much. He says as much in his own reports. Liz stayed aloof and apart from much of what went on at Op-Center."

"Sounds promising," Carew said. "Don't hesitate too long to do whatever is necessary to get the NCMC healthy."

"Of course not. China should be a good shakedown cruise for us."

"Speaking of which, what's the latest? G2 has nothing new on the Taiwan front."

"I'll be following up on that when I get to the office," Carrie said. "If something had happened, the night staff would have let me know."

General Carew said he would speak with her later. Carrie hung up and looked out the tinted window. She believed what she was doing was right for Op-Center, for the intelligence community, and for the nation. When Carrie first took over G2, it was an efficient collection of groups that tended to act unilaterally. The overall mission was to collect and disseminate military intelligence and counterintelligence, and to oversee military security and military intelligence training. After the Iraq War, Carrie had been charged with improving the organization on the tactical level. She planned and supervised a restructuring from battalion through division to allow G2 to effectively execute its mission in war and peace. During peacetime, she arranged it so that operations were centrally consolidated with outflow controlled by her office under the daily control of her number two, Lieutenant Colonel Scott Denny, the assistant chief of staff. In support of war, the intelligence assets were jumped directly to the tactical command post, the main command post, and the rear command post. This dissemination was executed by units Carrie had handpicked: the 640th Military Intelligence Battalion, the 210th Weather Flight, Air National Guard, the 1004th/1302nd Engineer Detachment, which specialized in terrain analysis, and the Quickfix Platoon C/1-140AV.

Of course, at G2 Carrie had the entire United States military at her disposal to accomplish that goal. The challenge of Op-Center was to do the same thing with a mostly civilian group and a relatively small budget.

It was a challenge she was looking forward to. There would probably be some casualties, though she hoped to minimize those with Liz's help. Burned out was not the same as passed away. This team had done some remarkable work, and she wanted to try to keep them intact.

The big challenge was not Bob Herbert or Darrell McCaskey or any of their teammates. The big challenge was the goal.

General Patton had once decried the short-sighted decisions of those "temporary residents of the White House." International policy and national security were too important to be left to upgraded senators and former governors.

The objective of General Carrie was to help strengthen the United States by making military intelligence a bigger and more integral part of America's defense structure.

On the way to that goal, however, another challenge suddenly presented itself. One that was smaller but tactically and morally important. According to Liz Gordon, Paul Hood was not burned out. Why would he be? Whatever his flaws, Hood had built and used a strong, hardworking support structure.

It would be quite an asset, Carrie thought, to have the president's personal intelligence officer work with the military to achieve their goal. Fortunately, by relying on his old Op-Center personnel, Hood had given her a head start in that direction.

THIRTY-FIVE

Beijing, China
Wednesday, 8:44 P.M.

Paul Hood stepped into the warm, damp night. There was a clinging mist in the air, and it caused his cell phone to crackle. He could only imagine what kind of pollutants were in the air.

He stepped away from the canopy to call Rodgers. Hood stood with his back to the reception hall, a finger in his ear to block out the sounds of traffic. The general was in his hotel room having dinner.

"Chinese food isn't Chinese food," Rodgers said. "I'm sitting here eating chicken kidneys and shark fins. What are you doing?"

"I'm standing outside a reception where I've already missed the hors d'oeuvres," Hood said.

"That's probably a good thing," Rodgers said.

The repartee was strained. Neither man was very good at this with one another. Hood got to the point. "I spoke with the prime minister. He said that one of us could attend the launch."

"You should be the one to go," Rodgers said.

"Why?" He had not expected Rodgers to come all this way and surrender that privilege.

"I'm looking into other aspects of the situation," Rodgers told him.

"Is it anything you can talk about?" Hood asked. "Not over this line, I realize, but maybe later—"

"Maybe later," Rodgers said with finality.

That was also unexpected. Rodgers had delivered a clean, unapologetic kick in the teeth.

"All right then," Hood said. "I'll make the arrangements for my visit. I'll let you know how things progress."

"Thanks."

"Will you give me a call when you can talk?"

"Sure," Rodgers promised.

Hood flipped the cell phone shut. He stood looking ahead at the oncoming traffic. He could not see the faces of the drivers, but he felt as though every eye was looking at him, laughing at him. He knew they were not, yet he had never felt as exposed and vulnerable as he did at that moment. He had never felt so adrift.

Since the night that his fiancée Nancy Jo Bosworth had left him standing alone on a street corner, waiting for a movie date that never materialized, he had never felt so alone.

"The man without a country," he muttered.

"Edward Everett Hale," came a soft voice from behind him.

Hood snapped around. Anita was standing there. She was holding a Coke and smiling. At least one of them was for him.

"Thank you," Hood said as he took the glass.

"Philip Nolan, an American exiled for treason," the woman went on. "Is that why you are here? Are you in exile?"

"Are you referring to here being outside or here being

Beijing?" Hood asked. He took a sip of cola. There was no ice.

"Let's take outside first." She smiled.

There was no ice in Anita now, either. Hood was suspicious, though he liked it better on her than he did in the warm beverage.

"I came out to make a call," he said, holding up the phone.

"Professional?"

He nodded.

"So you feel exiled in Beijing, then," Anita said.

"Not really," Hood told her.

Anita's big, open forehead crinkled. "I'm confused."

Hood smiled. "Me, too."

"But you said—"

"It was just a reverie," Hood said.

"Not a lament?"

Hood smiled. She was perceptive. But then, an interpreter would have to be. Many translations depended upon nuance, not just the literal words.

"Whatever it was, it's passed," Hood lied. "Is there something I can do for you?"

"Accept my apology," she said.

"For what?"

"For coming on a little strong earlier," Anita said. "I am sure you are under a great deal of pressure here. I should not have added to it."

"You did not upset me," Hood assured her. "To the contrary. I was sorry the Asian stereotypes upset *you*. There is no defending them."

"Time and perception change, and culture changes with them," she said. "It is both fortunate and unfortunate that the works themselves survive. Unfortunate in that the stereotypes survive. Fortunate in that we can measure how much more enlightened we have become."

"That is true," Hood said. He glanced back at the

canopy. "We should go back. We are probably missing your father's toast."

"Do you really want to hear it?"

"That's a loaded question," Hood said.

"Answer it truthfully." She smiled.

"I want to show respect for the man and his position."

"A perfect diplomatic response." She laughed. "You do your president honor."

"Thank you," Hood said. "But before we go back, I would like to ask you something."

"Certainly."

"You don't have to answer, if you think the question is out of line."

"Lao-tzu once said, 'There is no such thing as a stupid question. Only stupid answers.'"

"True enough." Hood smiled. "I'm wondering what caused your attitude toward me to change."

"May I answer freely?"

"Of course," Hood said.

"You spoke to my father with great deference," she replied. "You did not fawn or bluster the way other ambassadors do. In fact, you did not even act like someone from an embassy."

"Diplomats have a job to do."

"As I said, you do it differently."

"Thanks," he said.

Hood's radar had picked up the blip. He had only sensed it a moment before, when she first complimented his manner, but now it was big and green and closing in. Anita had come out here to find out what exactly he was doing in China.

He offered her his arm. "Shall we go back inside?"

"I was thinking a walk might be nice."

"All right," Hood agreed. He continued to offer his arm. She took it with a smile. Now he knew Anita was playing him.

The woman was obviously inexperienced at this. But Hood would play along. He was certain that her father had sent her to talk with him. The prime minister might be angry or insulted if Hood brought her back too quickly. Even though it could hurt the launch, he might withdraw permission for someone to attend. However, if Hood and Anita stayed out for a short while, the prime minister might shift the failure of this maneuver from Hood to his daughter's inexperience.

"I wonder. Did you ever think of writing a novel?" Anita asked.

"No." Hood laughed. "I would be too self-conscious."

"Why?"

"When I was a kid, I read *Tom Sawyer* and *Treasure Island*," Hood told her. "When my parents weren't looking, I read the James Bond stories. I loved them. Then I found out that Mark Twain and Robert Louis Stevenson and Ian Fleming made them up. They didn't happen. There was no Huck Finn or Long John Silver. That really upset me. Not because they weren't real, but because someone sat down and spent all that time to lie to me."

"You felt betrayed?" Anita asked.

"Betrayed, cheated, and stupid," Hood said. "Assuming I had the time and patience to write a novel, I think I would be distracted by the fact that I was lying to thousands and thousands of people."

Anita laughed. "You are aligned with Confucius."

"How so?"

"He did not like novels or novelists," Anita replied. "He felt they were on the low end of society, the opposite of truth and honor. Fiction writers started with a lie and went from there. I maintain that fiction is an internal search for truth that the artist shares."

"Well, that process doesn't interest me as a purveyor or observer," Hood said. "I prefer to read a newspaper and draw my own conclusions."

"Then how do you relax?"

"I listen to music or go to a museum," Hood said. "Until fairly recently I used to hang with my kids."

"They are grown now?"

"I'm divorced," Hood said. "I don't get to see them very much."

"Oh. I'm sorry. I did not mean to intrude."

"You didn't. I offered," Hood said, smiling at her as they continued to walk down the wide street. He was uneasy but willing to spend personal information to keep this conversation going. Besides, Hood knew what her eventual follow-up question would be. That part of the talk would be brief.

"What about nonfiction? A professional memoir?" she asked. "That would not be a lie, and I am certain it would be fascinating."

"Why are you so sure?" Hood asked.

"A man does not reach your position without a certain level of accomplishment," she said.

Hood chuckled. "Mr. Hasen's brother-in-law was a stockbroker and a tennis buddy of the vice president. That was how he got into the diplomatic corps. He lasted about two years. Unlike your father, many Americans in government service are not professional leaders or emissaries."

"Were you someone's tennis buddy?"

"No," Hood said. "I was dumb. I worked my way up the ladder."

"That is admirable, not foolish. You must have things to write about, stories to tell."

"I don't know. Even if there are, I don't have the narcissism to talk about whatever white whales I've hunted."

"But there must be experiences that deserve to be recorded, passed on to people who have not lived your life, enjoyed your career, who have not even been to Beijing," Anita said. "There is a long tradition of political memoirs that has nothing to do with vanity. Mao's thoughts were the foundation for a nation."

"He was a leader," Hood replied. "It's a tradition I will leave for presidents and prime ministers."

"Not ambassadors or revolutionaries or even men of intrigue?" she pressed. Anita spoke the last words leaning toward Hood, as though they were sharing a secret.

Hood grinned. "There would be no intrigue, would there, if a man walked into a room and said, 'My name is Bond. James Bond.' Some things are best kept private." He thought for a moment. "Though maybe there is one story I would consider telling."

Anita brightened. "May I ask what that is?" She obviously felt that she had her in.

They had reached the corner. Hood stopped and faced the woman. Her face stood out sharply, remarkably against the misty glow of the streetlamps.

"It's the story of my own daughter," he said. "She was taken hostage a few years ago at the United Nations by rogue peacekeepers."

"I remember that siege," Anita said. "Your daughter was there?"

"Harleigh was performing music with a youth group," Hood said. "She came out of it with severe post-traumatic stress and has worked very hard to regain her footing. A son's accomplishments are invariably measured against those of the father, but a daughter's courage and devotion stand alone."

Anita smirked. "That may be a first, Mr. Hood."

"What is?"

"It's the first compliment I have heard about a woman's character that I would consider sexist," she said.

"It is not meant to be," Hood said.

"You would have to convince me of that," she said. The challenging tone from the reception was returning.

"Are you familiar with the American dancer Fred Astaire?" Hood asked.

"From films?"

Hood nodded.

"Yes," Anita said. "That is an odd question."

"Not at all. He is considered the finest ballroom dancer of his generation," Hood told her. "He had a partner, Ginger Rogers. She did everything he did but in high heels and backward. It is not sexist to say that women have to work harder than men, and that they possess—or have developed—a different set of physical, emotional, and psychological skills in order to do that."

"You make us sound freakish."

"I'm saying that you are special," Hood said.

"In context, there is no distinction," she charged.

"I believe there is," Hood said. "Most women are a little scary to men. I think your father would agree."

"You think I *frighten* him?" she asked with a trace of annoyance.

"Not you, Anita. I meant in general. Your father obviously loves and trusts you a great deal."

Anita was frowning and silent. Hood could see her trying to determine whether his observation was calculated or innocent. He had meant it as a bit of a dig—perhaps carelessly, in retrospect—and he did not want her going back angry. Her father would not be happy about that.

Hood nodded toward the canopy. "We should go back. Your father is a fascinating man, and I want to hear what he has to say."

That was not an invitation Anita could resist. The couple turned and walked back in silence. Hood was relatively certain that he had achieved his goal. He had stymied Anita's mission, and he did not think she would go into detail with the prime minister. Le probably would not approve of his daughter having been distracted by a feminist debate. He might not be surprised, Hood suspected, but the prime minister would not be pleased.

Now that he had a chance to think about it, Hood was not too happy with all of that either. Until he had said it, Hood had never articulated the idea that he found women to be scary. From confronting Nancy Jo way back when to dealing with the romantic workplace tensions with Ann Farris to his talk with General Carrie, he had not been as comfortable as he was saving the world alongside Mike Rodgers and Bob Herbert. But that was something he would have to consider another time.

Unlike Anita, Hood did not want to be distracted from his mission. The idea that a nuclear-powered satellite could be blown up was pretty scary, too.

THIRTY-SIX

Washington, D.C.
Wednesday, 9:38 A.M.

Loyalty. In the end, that was the one irreducible value of life. It defined one's sense of honor and priority, of sacrifice and industry. The only question the individual had to decide was to whom—or what—loyalty should be given.

General Carrie spoke with Bob Herbert as she scrolled through her E-mail. The intelligence chief had no new information from China. He was frustrated by that fact and complained that Op-Center had no senior-level executive over there representing their interests.

"Just two former bosses, both of whom have their own agendas," he said.

"I am working on the problem," she assured him.

"How?" Herbert said. "We don't have the money." He sounded irritable and distracted.

"Let me worry about that," she replied.

There was nothing in her mailbox that needed immediate attention.

Not yet. Op-Center needed a makeover of personnel *and* procedures, both of which she would begin today. Since she had the time, Carrie asked Liz to come and see her. Profiling the entire team before contemplating cuts and reassignments was her priority.

The psychologist had just walked in when the phone beeped. The general motioned for her to shut the door behind her, then gestured to an armchair. The call was a surprise. It was from Mike Rodgers. The phone ID said that the general was calling from China.

"It's a pleasure to speak with you, General Rodgers," Carrie said.

"Likewise, General Carrie. Congratulations on your promotion and the move to Op-Center."

"Thank you," she said. "Are you in Beijing for the launch?"

"Yes, though I won't be going to the Xichang space center. I just spoke with Paul. He's going to be Washington's unofficial representative."

"What will he be doing?" Carrie asked.

"I am not sure," Rodgers admitted. "The game plan seems to be to stay close to Prime Minister Le, to watch and see what those around him are doing and who is not present."

"The von Stauffenburg scenario," she said.

Rodgers agreed. That was a name given to any plan to cause a catastrophic event to one's own team. Colonel Claus von Stauffenburg was the German officer who placed a briefcase with a bomb under a conference table at Hitler's command post in Rastenburg, East Prussia. After triggering the timed explosive, Stauffenburg left. The heavy table saved Hitler's life when the explosive detonated. Stauffenburg was arrested and executed. Obviously, if an officer or government minister were planning to cause the Unexus rocket to explode, he would not be anywhere in the neighborhood of the blast.

"What will you be doing, then?" Carrie asked.

"That's the reason I'm calling," Rodgers said. "Bob Herbert told me there is a field team. I would like to borrow it."

Carrie was not pleased that Rodgers knew, but she was not surprised, either. It underscored one of the strengths and drawbacks of Paul Hood's tenure here. His people were more devoted to one another than they were to the organization. That would have to stop.

"For what purpose?" Carrie asked.

"Paul Hood is going there to watch people," he said. "I want someone watching the rocket and the payload."

"What makes you think the Chinese would agree to let outsiders near the hardware?" Carrie said. "Isn't that what Le is worried about?"

"My Unexus tech people can talk to the Chinese tech people," Rodgers said. "We can try to get private security in openly or off the books. I'd prefer the latter, just to maintain surprise, and I think I can sell that to some of the chief scientists."

"If Le found out, they could lose their jobs."

"The only way Le will find out about a covert ops team is if something goes wrong and your guys save his butt," Rodgers said. "Even if the science team leaders are dismissed as a result, it is better than the alternative."

Rodgers had a point, and it spoke to a different kind of loyalty: that of the Chinese scientists to their mission. Their allegiance was not to individuals or to a nation but to the hardware, to the science. Carrie could not decide whether that was enlightened or provincial.

She took a moment to consider the ramifications for the United States. Her marines had gone to China to be ready for this kind of mission. But the prep time for the Xichang operation would be distressingly brief. If they undertook what Rodgers proposed and were discovered—especially if their operation failed—her career would be over. Carrie quickly put that thought aside.

Loyalty, she reminded herself.

The general was not serving in this office to practice loyalty to Morgan Carrie. She was here to do what was best for America and Op-Center. In that order. A failed mission could hurt the NCMC and result in her dismissal. It would cause the Congressional Intelligence Oversight Committee to impose stricter controls on Op-Center, at least cosmetically. But most important, what was the downside for the nation? Risking American lives to help protect a Chinese launch was a no-lose situation. They would not be accused of spying. Not with Hood there as an invited guest. Not with technology that was provided by the West. The upside was a historic first, a demonstration that American intelligence could be used to help other nations.

Perhaps it was also kismet. Hood had made his reputation at Op-Center by boldly preventing an attack against an American space mission. General Carrie could do the same.

"Here's the deal," Carrie said. "If you demonstrate that my team can get in and out of the facility, I will give you a go. But I want the names of the sympathetic scientists in time to run a background check. I want to know how you intend to get them to the facility. I want to know how you're going to get them in and then out of the facility. If there are security cameras, their faces will be on file. We will have to pull them, whether they act or not."

"I plan to move them in by truck, with other scientists," Rodgers said. "No security cameras."

"Most important is the exit strategy," Carrie said. "If they are forced to act, you will need to get them to safety until everything is sorted out. We cannot have them arrested, held, and interrogated."

"Paul Hood can help with that, if you have no objections."

"I do not," she replied. "But if the numbers fall too far short of one hundred percent, I will not authorize this."

Rodgers told her he understood. Carrie hung up and regarded Liz. There was something different about her. Carrie saw at once what it was. The psychologist had not been wearing lipstick the day before. She was now.

"Did you know that our late political liaison had a nickname for this place?" Liz asked.

"That would be Martha Mackall?"

"Correct."

"No," Carrie said. "What did Martha call it?"

"OTS-Center," Liz told her. "It stood for zero to sixty. Nothing in crisis management ever accelerates slowly."

"It's just a different avatar of national defense," Carrie said.

"How so?"

"Intelligence work is action of the mind, crisis management is action of the hands," Carrie told her. "One of the reasons I am here is to make sure said defense is an action of one well-trained and fully integrated body."

Liz considered that in silence. Something in her eyes said she approved.

"You heard what transpired," Carrie went on. "We have talked about other former employees. What is your impression of General Rodgers?"

"Mike Rodgers is a bulldog with a high percentage of bottom-line success in the field," Liz told her.

"Is that a spin doctor way of saying, 'Pyrrhic victory?'" Carrie asked.

Liz laughed. "Maybe."

"From everything I've read, Mike Rodgers is like Ulysses S. Grant," Carrie said. "The Union won battles because he kept throwing men and ordnance at the enemy until they caved. Compared to Robert E. Lee, Grant's losses were always improportionately high."

"Mike's units do take casualties," Liz admitted. "In his

defense, he rarely had more than the duration of a plane flight to prepare and often with limited intelligence. Yet he always found a way to get to the end zone."

"This time will be different," Carrie said. "Op-Center needs human intelligence operatives on the ground in potentially hostile nations. If Rodgers is going to borrow my team, I want to see a game plan that is more Lee than Grant." Carrie ended the conversation by opening the staff dossier on her computer. "There is just one person we have not yet talked about," the general said. "My psych officer. Are you ready and able to take on increased responsibilities in profiling and forensic projections about the mental health of my team?"

Liz started slightly. The psychologist obviously did not expect the attention or the question.

"General, I have been waiting years for a director of Op-Center to ask for my input and mean it," Liz said. "I would be happy to be more fully integrated with NCMC command and its missions."

"NCMC command meaning this office?"

"If you are asking the extent to which analyst-patient privilege applies—"

"I am asking whether you will implement without question any and all projects not expressly forbidden by the chartered mandate of the NCMC."

" 'Not expressly forbidden,' " Liz said. "Interesting choice of words."

"These are interesting times," Carrie replied.

"I never do anything without question," Liz said. She smiled. "But my questions are only meant to stimulate discussion. You're the boss."

"Very good," Carrie said. She closed Liz Gordon's file and opened two others side by side. "Then let's talk about Bob Herbert and Darrell McCaskey. I will want you to watch them closely over the next few hours. I want to know how they are handling the demands of this Chinese project.

Whatever Rodgers comes back with in terms of a plan, this is a good way for me to see how the team functions under pressure."

"They will be watching their front *and* their rear," Liz said.

"Because of me, you mean?"

"Yes."

"I am counting on it," Carrie said. "I do not want personnel who will crack under the strain, but I do not want a team that is complacent, either. Hood ran this place as if it were a town meeting. I will not."

"Order is the basis of creation," Liz said. "I'm all for it."

They began by going over Herbert's file in detail. The impact of the Beirut explosion on his work, how the loss of his wife might affect the way he related to women, and more. But Liz's remark stayed in her mind. Carrie had always believed in one of the Nietzschean cornerstones: "Out of chaos comes order." But the follow-up was equally true: from order comes progress. For Carrie, the order was simple. We were one nation under God.

And below Him, organizing creation, would be the watchful eyes and sure, powerful hands of the DoD.

THIRTY-SEVEN

Washington, D.C.
Wednesday, 9:51 A.M.

Bob Herbert was stumped. Worse than that, he was idle.

Op-Center did not have resources with an extensive background in China. Before speaking with General Carrie, Herbert was on the phone with Kim Hwan, Director of the Korean Central Intelligence Agency. As deputy director, Hwan had been an important part of Op-Center's successful Korean action several years before. Hwan's sources had confirmed what Herbert suspected, that General Tam Li and Director Chou Shin were engaged in what he described as "acts of purpose."

Herbert took that to mean a pissing contest.

But Hwan had no new information. Herbert had also contacted Sergei Orlov, director of the Russian Op-Center. Orlov's agents in China also anticipated the power struggle but had no idea about where it might erupt next. Herbert believed Orlov. The two countries shared 4,200 kilometers of border. If the situation in Beijing or Xichang worsened, or if the nuclear-powered satellite did in fact explode, violence or refugees could turn the region into a no-man's-land.

After talking to the men, Herbert wondered how and why this had become strictly an American situation. There was the involvement of Unexus, but that was an international concern.

Once again, a global crisis has become Op-Center's problem, he thought. By extension, the intelligence gathering became his problem. Ordinarily that would be a challenge. At the moment, it was also distracting. Herbert had a sense that he was being graded on his performance. General Carrie's questions and the fact that new officers tended to make changes had him feeling defensive, insulted, and definitely off his game. He had not even been that paranoid in Beirut, where there was every good reason to be. And apparently, this was Op-Center's problem alone. Herbert received on-line intelligence summaries twice daily from Homeland Security, part of their IDEA program: intelligence data, external access. The mailings offered headlines from every major division of the CIA and FBI as well as the National Security Agency and the National Reconnaissance Office. No one had the Chinese satellite on their agenda. Even the FBI, which had the Charleston explosion on their active-investigations list, had logged the attack as "having the earmarks of an intranational conflict that happened to fall on American soil." That was probably true. The FBI had obviously read the report Herbert and his small staff had filed on the IDEA Web site the day before.

A call from Mike Rodgers lifted Herbert's mood considerably. The sound of Rodgers's voice from Beijing held the promise of information. More, it momentarily returned him to a time when the mission itself was more important to him than how it—or he—were perceived.

Herbert's soul deflated when he heard that Rodgers was phoning to follow up on a conversation he had just had with General Carrie.

"She's giving you command of our field team," Herbert repeated when Rodgers had briefed him. The intelligence chief could not help but wonder if this was general to general or if Carrie would have given Paul Hood the same access. His instincts told him Hood would not have gotten the team.

"This is a loan, in case it's necessary," Rodgers said.

"How will they get in?"

"I have notified my associates to provide entry codes and passes for your people," Rodgers said. "I have also asked them to identify all access areas to the rocket and the satellite. The NRO will be sending me up-to-date images of the facilities and will also be watching for unusual activity. What I need from you are photographs for the IDs and a patrol pattern our unit can pursue."

"You want photographs of our undercover HUMINT personnel," Herbert said.

"The Chinese will see their faces anyway—" Rodgers said.

"But Chinese functionaries will be uploading them into a computer to print badges. They will remain in Chinese computers."

"The work roster will list them as on loan from various universities to help with different facets of the countdown," Rodgers said. "Their real local covers will not be blown."

"Mike, you don't think the Xichang director will check that?"

"He's the guy who's helping me organize this," Rodgers said. "He will sign off on their credentials. When this is done, the photographs will be deleted."

"So he says," Herbert said. "Your boy may end up looking for a budget increase by turning in spies."

"Spies that he allowed in," Rodgers said. "There is no gain for him. Look, Bob, there are risks in any operation. These are worth it."

Mostly to Unexus, Herbert thought. Rodgers may have

turned in his uniform, but he was still a gung ho general. He had substituted one team for another and was ready to make any sacrifice for them. Arguing against that was pointless. What Herbert had to do was find a way to minimize the damage.

"We disagree about that, but if Carrie has given you the okay—"

"She has."

"Then it's my job to help make it work. I will ask her to let me send you the photographs. You've got a secure Ethernet link?"

"Unexus equipment is more secure than what they've got at the DoD," Rodgers said.

"I will send you the photographs with no information, not even the names," Herbert said. "Then I will sit down with Darrell and go over the layout of the facility. We will send a patrol plan ASAP." McCaskey used to organize and run stakeouts for the FBI. He had a good eye for creating effective zone management.

"Thanks," Rodgers said. "I will meet them somewhere outside the facility. I will let you know where. I'm having our HQ send over radios so I can communicate with the team."

"And those won't trigger alarms?" Herbert asked.

"The Xichang radios all operate between 121.5 and 243, AM frequencies," Rodgers told him. "We will be running our communications at 336.6, piggybacking on a NORAD signal. Unexus has an arrangement with Cheyenne Mountain to use one of their carrier waves for sensitive operations."

"Really? The DoD is okay with that?"

"We designed the system components that allow NORAD to interface with NATO for quick response in matters pertaining to Homeland Security," Rodgers said proudly. "The Pentagon actually appreciates having us test that international system from time to time."

"I see," Herbert replied. "Mike, are you sure that's a good idea?"

"What?"

"Having this kind of symbiotic relationship with the military?" the intelligence chief asked.

"What's wrong with it?" Rodgers asked. "It benefits everyone. The more Unexus knows about field operations, the better we can protect our personnel. That's one reason Unexus hired me. No one but me is going to know the specifics of the Op-Center field action. You don't have to worry about the mission being poisoned by other civilian eyes and ears."

"I'm not," Herbert said.

That was true. Mike Rodgers knew how to quarantine information. But Rodgers was very wrong about one thing. The plan did indeed trigger a signal, this one in the head of Bob Herbert. The intelligence chief knew that NORAD had changed its mission over the last few years, from watching the skies outside American borders to watching the skies for terrorist threats. To this end, they received a steady flow of data from every airport in the nation. Any significant deviation from a flight path would result in fighters being scrambled and the aircraft destroyed. But Herbert did not know that NORAD had become tight with civilian agencies. He was willing to bet that the firewalls protecting the military from private industry were formidable. But in their desire to land lucrative government contracts, how defensive were companies like Unexus? How tapped in were places like Cheyenne Mountain and other facilities into the nonmilitary world? What kind of access did the DoD have to civilian records, surveillance, other capabilities? Herbert was willing to bet these tendrils were extensive.

"Bob, do you know what I think?" Rodgers asked.

"Usually."

"In this case, you're overthinking things as usual,"

Rodgers said. "Trust me. This is a controlled, highly focused operation. It's not like the old days when field ops were jury-rigged. And Bob? I'm glad you're working on this."

"Me, too," Herbert said. His statement was unenthusiastic, but it was not a lie. With the military presence at Op-Center and what he had just learned about NORAD, a picture was starting to form. An unsettling one.

Herbert called McCaskey when Rodgers hung up. The FBI liaison had just arrived and said he would be there in a few minutes. While Herbert waited, he went to the files of the field officers to send their pictures. He felt as though he were betraying each one of them. Yes, risk was part of the job. Herbert and his wife had known that when they went to Beirut. But this was different. He was helping to put these people in the line of fire, not for the stated mission but for what he sensed was a larger scenario. A scenario he did not yet understand. Herbert needed to find out what it was. Then he had to decide what the hell to do about it.

Herbert then phoned General Carrie to get permission for Mike's request. She granted it, with the implicit warning that Herbert's credibility was on the line. The intelligence chief was no longer in a slump. Unfortunately, a potential fight with his own people was not the boost he had been hoping for.

THIRTY-EIGHT

Zhuhai, China
Wednesday, 10:00 P.M.

General Tam Li sat looking out the open window of the large office. The windows were clean, despite the dust from the constant winds that blew from the strait. He allocated manpower to clean them and to keep the grounds spotless. When American spy satellites looked down on them, he wanted them to know that he ran a very smart, proud installation. That was also the reason every man wore firearms, and they never lounged in public. The Americans had to see that the PLA was constantly alert and ready, as well as strictly disciplined. They were not like the Third World forces Americans had been sparring with since the surrender of Japan.

The night was clear except for some low, sporadic clouds. They were lit from above by a full moon. The treetops moved gently below the fourth-floor window. Their motion and sound were relaxing. The lights of the office were off. There were no distractions but the view, the trees, and the general's own thoughts and ambitions. The sky and sea could not compete with those, he thought proudly. He had always had a rule about that. If a man could not dream greater than the things he could see, he was not much of a dreamer. And a man who did not dream was closer to the apes than to the stars.

The leaders of Taipei, for example. They were short-sighted, narrow-minded, and infallibly predictable.

The Taiwanese military reacted the way Tam Li knew they would. The commander in chief of the Taiwan Armed Forces put his Air Force and Navy on alert right on schedule, with all the same maneuvers. That was a Taiwanese show of strength as well as their exit strategy. As long as the Navy and Air Force did nothing different, Taipei assumed the Chinese would not perceive it as a threat. Beijing had never responded in kind, so the situation would not escalate.

Tam Li did not see it as a threat. But what if something happened that made it a threat? What if someone like Chou Shin were seen as wanting to seize this moment to weaken the military by blinding its new eye in the sky? What if Chou shifted the open war between himself and the general from an international staging area to a national one? Beijing would be distracted. Might not Taipei use the disaster as well to make a move against the legitimate Chinese government?

Of course they might, Tam Li thought. In fact, he was counting on it.

The sea spread darkly outside the open window. A sea wide and deep with promise, the stage for his dreams to be realized. There would be a temporary setback and a loss of face while the government dealt with Chou Shin's treason. But Tam Li would seize the moment as well as the spotlight.

There was a respectful rap at the door.

"Enter," the general said without turning from the window.

There was a click. The door opened. His security direc-tor entered.

"Sir, the enemy has begun moving out," he said.

"Is there any change from the normal pattern?" Tam Li asked.

"None, sir. It is as you said."

"What of the yachts?" Tam Li asked.

"Your associates from Japan have radioed that they are in position," the security director informed him. "The third target, from Australia, will be at his coordinates in an hour."

"You confirmed the escape plans?"

"The owners will all depart the yachts by helicopter, fearing for their safety, at precisely the time the enemy fleet appears on their radar," the security officer told him. "The vessels themselves will turn and follow when it be-comes clear to them that they are the targets."

Tam Li smiled. "The yachts will broadcast one another to that effect?"

"Immediately, sir."

"And we will record and intercept the transmission?"

"We will."

"Thank you," the general replied. "I will come down to the command center in a few minutes."

"I will let them know, General."

Tam Li heard the door click. A moment later the moon came out clearly and splashed light on the sea. It was a beautiful sight, but not as arresting as it would be in just a few hours.

He and his generals were quietly organizing the largest military counterstrike in modern Chinese history. It had been planned in phases so that absolute secrecy could be maintained, even from his own government. Over one hun-dred PLAAF and PLAN fighter jets were on regular and continuous patrol of the Chinese coast. Shoreline security was the primary function of Chinese military pilots. Long before the Taiwanese aircraft reached their fail-safe lines, before they could double back, eighty Chinese planes would be diverted in a targeted attack on the rearmost Taiwanese aircraft. That would cut the forward squadrons from retreat and allow them to be picked off by a second wave of Chinese aircraft, consisting of the remaining twenty airborne jets as well as another fifty that would immediately be scrambled from bases along the eastern seaboard. At the same time, three of the modern Song-class submarines, already at sea, would maneuver behind the Taiwanese Navy. The escort ships in the battle groups would be sunk and the destroyers surrounded.

By then, of course, Beijing would have learned what was going on. But it would be too late to recall the attack without losing face. Taipei would protest, saying that the patrol was routine. But the protest would be too little and much too late. Based on information provided by Tam Li, Beijing would argue that the Taiwanese expeditionary force was far from a standard patrol. The enemy intended to launch a surprise attack after the accident they would be suspected of having caused. The general's suspicions would be sent out at once. The panicked audio recordings from the yachts would also be released. They would make the first impression. It would put Taiwan on the offensive.

That, too, was a showdown they could not hope to win.

The Taiwanese sailors would be brought to China and held until the grand gesture of their release could be used for political gain. Chou Shin would be tried, convicted, and executed for masterminding that explosion as well as the blast in the United States. That would rid the general of one nemesis. At the same time, the Taiwanese would suffer a swift and decisive defeat in the strait. Because of their defense pact, the United States would be forced into a confrontation they, too, could not hope to win. The best the

Americans could hope for was a standoff. One that would diminish their status and elevate Beijing.

Tam Li thought very little about the price of the "trigger," as he called it: the destruction of the satellite. The rocket would blow up on the launch pad, where the blast and the radiation would kill or poison all of the Chinese leaders in attendance. It would distract the government while the military moved against the Taiwanese expeditionary force. In the days to come, Tam Li and his allies would be very visible defenders of the realm. They would be populist heroes.

They would become the leaders of a new, militarized, and expansive China.

THIRTY-NINE

Beijing, China
Wednesday, 11:08 P.M.

Mike Rodgers had the plans for the Xichang space center spread on his bed. The detailed map was nearly the size of the blanket. Satellite photographs of the facility were arrayed on his laptop. Rodgers had printed out blueprints of the rocket and payload. Those were on the floor with a map of the region beside them. The map was marked with public transportation that came virtually to the southeastern gate of the facility. Most of the scientists lived on site for convenience and security.

The former general stood in the middle of the papers. He was looking down at all of them, his eyes moving from one to the other. Rodgers had always solved problems best by "grazing the options," as he called it. He would get a first impression from one and move to the next. Those initial ideas were usually the best ones.

Assuming there was to be an attack on the rocket, he felt comfortable with one of three scenarios. First, that the rocket would be destroyed over a specific target. That would contaminate the region below with radiation and cause a long-term setback to the use of plutonium-powered satellites. That would be a loss to General Tam Li and would boost his rival Chou Shin in the long term. Second, that the rocket would be destroyed upon takeoff. That would take out a chunk of the Chinese command as well as their capability to launch any kind of rockets, military or domestic. Both men had their eye on power. Both men would gain from a temporary power vacuum. The third possibility was that the satellite itself would be targeted once it was in orbit. That would be a setback for Unexus but not the Chinese military. That, too, would help Chou Shin, who was an advocate of isolationism.

Any of these were plausible. The question was how to pull it off. Rodgers's eyes drifted toward the blueprints of the rocket. His technical staff had marked off places where a bomb could do the most damage. Rodgers would have the Chinese science crew inspect them all.

Paul Hood would have to let him know who showed up and who left early. That would give the team some indication whether an attack would take place at launch. With an explosion of this magnitude, a potential mastermind would want to be a considerable distance away. Even so, Rodgers was planning to be close by to prevent the individual from leaving and supervise the counterattack.

There was a call from Op-Center. It was Bugs Benet. He gave Rodgers contact information for the leader of the field team.

"He will come to your hotel in about an hour as a messenger," Benet said.

Rodgers thanked him. "How are things going for you?" he asked.

"Tentative," Benet answered. "General Carrie will be wanting a military aide. We are pretty lean right now. I'm not sure there is any place she can shift me."

"Can you go to work for Paul?"

"He has not asked," Benet said.

"Maybe he will," Rodgers said. "If not, I will talk with the people in my organization."

"I appreciate that, sir," Benet said.

Rodgers put away his cell phone and went back to studying the documents. He bent low over them in case the room had video surveillance. Whenever he walked away, he folded them over. Rodgers used a grease pencil to mark spots on the rocket that his scientists had told him were not just vulnerable but relatively invisible. Bombs in these locations would weigh the rocket down without necessarily destabilizing it. Even five pounds of explosives, positioned off-center—on a stabilizing fin, for example—would pull the rocket quickly off course. That would only help an attacker if the goal were a near-site explosion. Then he folded the blueprints and turned to studying the plans of the launch complex. He had four marines to cover 1,200 square kilometers of terrain. If they ruled out a possible attack from a rocket-propelled grenade, they could limit the patrol area to just the launch pad. Could they afford to make that assumption?

We might have to, he thought.

Besides, a rocket-propelled grenade was not the modus operandi of either man. There was also a chance that a one- or two-man team would be spotted by Chinese security forces. They had to assume that any attack would be executed as close to the rocket as possible.

Working on these scenarios, Rodgers felt less like an officer of Unexus and more like an officer of Op-Center. Despite the risks to his employer, he liked the excitement. He also liked the fact that he was in this with a military professional and not Paul Hood. General Carrie may not have liked what he requested, but she asked the right questions and reached the right decision.

Now he had to do the same thing.

Rodgers ordered room service as he worked on the map.

He circled several points around the pad and gantry where virtually all the personnel would be visible going about their activities. An explosive device might be placed late in the countdown to avoid detection. If so, they might be able to spot it from these positions.

Exactly an hour after Benet's call, the front desk called. There was a visitor to see Mr. Rodgers. The former general asked who it was.

"A messenger with a package from a man named Herbert," the caller informed him.

Rodgers asked to have the messenger sent up. He took a bite of seared tuna from his neglected dinner tray, then walked over to the TV and turned it on. He did not know whether the rooms of foreigners were still bugged in Beijing. He did not intend to take the risk.

The young man who appeared at his door was exactly what Rodgers had expected. Dressed in an olive green jacket with a reflective orange stripe down the back, he was a somber young man with hard eyes, full shoulders, and a ramrod-straight posture. He looked like someone who rode a motor scooter around town and then bench-pressed it. He handed the general a package and a clipboard.

"I require a signature, sir," the messenger said.

Rodgers invited him in. The young man entered, and Rodgers looked down the hall.

The messenger pointed to his own eyes then made a zero with his fingers. That meant he had checked, and no one was there. He also understood that the room might be bugged.

Rodgers nodded and shut the door. He went to the television.

The messenger followed. He looked down at the papers as they walked past the bed. They were unfolded now, but shielded by Rodgers and the new arrival. His eyes were like little machines, stopping on each for a moment before moving on. It was a standard reconnoitering process: floating data. If the marine saw anything important, he would keep it in his head until he could mention it or write it in a secure place.

The former general did not ask the marine his name or any other personal information about himself or the team.

"What do you know of this situation?" Rodgers asked.

"We were told you would brief us," the young marine said.

"The plan is still evolving," Rodgers said quietly. He threw a glance at the papers. "I will be working on it for at least another few hours. There's a map. I want to pick a spot to meet you before we go in—"

"Sir, General Carrie has ordered that there be no civilian component to our mission," the marine told him.

Rodgers did not know quite what to say. He said nothing.

"I am sorry, sir. I assumed you understood," the marine added.

"No," Rodgers said.

The marine had spoken without emotion or apology. Rodgers expected no less. Marines regarded themselves as representatives of their commanders. As such, they were unfailingly proud and loyal. For his part, though, Rodgers was anything but unemotional. He did not like being left out or outsmarted. He had already agreed that Hood could represent them in the viewing area. If Rodgers did not go to Xichang with the marines as one of the new "technical advisers," he had no way of getting in. And if he tried that, Carrie might pull her team.

"Wait here," Rodgers said and went to get his cell phone. "And help yourself to some dinner. I don't feel like eating at the moment."

Rodgers grabbed the phone from the bed and went into the bathroom. He shut the door and turned on the shower so he would not be heard. Then he called General Carrie's office. Benet put her on the line.

"I understand my messenger is there. Have you got all the answers I asked for?" Carrie asked.

"Nearly," Rodgers informed her. "First I have one more question. Why was I excluded?"

"You were not *ex*cluded. You were never *in*cluded. This has always been members only," she said. She was still being vague, thus reminding Rodgers that they could still be overhead.

"I would like to change that."

"No," Carrie replied.

"Ten eyes are better than eight. They are better for the work and for security," Rodgers insisted.

"My view is that two or more eyes will be on you, making sure you are all right. That is a net loss, not a gain."

"You act like I've never gone into business with new partners," Rodgers said through his teeth.

"I am not in a position to rate your performance, which is why I am denying your request."

"Talk to August," Rodgers said.

Colonel Brett August was the head of Striker, the former military detachment at the NCMC. When Striker was disbanded, he went to work at the Pentagon.

"I have my plate full reviewing current personnel," she said. "Talking to a former employee about another former employee is not at the top of my to-do list. Do we have an understanding or not? I have a lot to do."

"Of course we do," Rodgers said. The security of the rocket had to come first. "But I can help them."

"I believe that is why the messenger is there—"

"Would you leave this up to him?" Rodgers asked suddenly.

"No," she answered.

General Carrie hung up. Rodgers closed the phone and slowly tucked it in his pocket. He had a hand on the white porcelain sink. His fingertips were white. He had not realized how tightly he was squeezing the rim. He released it and flexed his fingers. He glanced at the door. He thought he saw a shadow move on the highly polished parquet floor. Rodgers did not know if the marine had been listening. Nor did it matter. There was nothing to hear. Rodgers considered calling Hood to try to rescind their agreement. But he had probably already told the prime minister. In any case, Rodgers was unsure of his own motives. At this moment he did not know whether he wanted to protect the rocket or whether he wanted to go just to shout a big "screw you" at General Carrie. He turned off the shower and went back into the room. Rodgers stood beside the TV, facing the marine. The former-general's eyes were on the floor.

"Is everything all right, sir?" the marine asked.

Not entirely, Rodgers decided. He wanted to be there to look after the Unexus payload, and he wanted to teach Carrie manners. He understood her protectiveness but not her intransigence. Military protocol gave leeway for civilian involvement. At Op-Center he had often worked with outsiders on missions. In Vietnam, he had helped to recruit them as guides. Even though Rodgers no longer wore the uniform of his country, he had served it with his life and his blood, his mind and his soul, for decades. He deserved better than Carrie's cool dismissal.

What was worse, he needed a place to put the increasing anger he felt about it. But that was not this marine's problem.

"Let me go over the data with you," Rodgers said.

"Yes, sir."

"And let me ask you something," Rodgers said. "How old are you?"

"Twenty-six, sir."

"I was a soldier for more years than that."

"I know, sir."

"They gave you a file on me?"

"Yes, sir," the marine said.

"What was your impression?"

"Sir, it's not my place—"

"I asked," Rodgers said.

"Sir, I'm humbled by your question," the young marine replied. "If I serve half as well as you did, I will consider my life very well spent."

That was a surprise. "You're not just blowing sunshine?"

"I took your request as if it were an order, General. May I add, sir, that for someone who wasn't a marine, you surely kicked some tail."

Rodgers could not help but smile at that. He felt the sword leave his hand. It was not yet sheathed, but he did not feel the need to lop heads.

"Are you sure you wouldn't like some food, a beverage?" Rodgers asked.

"Thank you, no."

"Then let's go to my command center," Rodgers said, patting him on the shoulder as they walked to the papers that lay on the bed and floor.

FORTY

Washington, D.C.
Wednesday, 12:00 P.M.

Liz Gordon left General Carrie's office to check her E-mail and her voice mail. She had her PowerBook under one arm and her coffee mug in the other hand. Between them was a heart that was drumming just a little more than she would have liked, and a shortness of breath that alarmed her.

Liz did not know whether the cause of her anxiety was the topic of her own employment or something else. Liz knew that she would have to undergo the same kind of scrutiny the others were getting. What the psychologist did not know was whether she would be part of that self-evaluation process or not. It would be interesting to see how the general handled that.

Interesting and possibly humiliating, she thought.

Liz had never seen her own dossier. The file was only available to the director of the NCMC and to the head of Human Resources. But Liz knew one thing that had to be there. Because of the potential one-strike nature of the offense, Paul Hood would have been obligated to record it.

Liz swung into her sparse office. The safe, familiar surroundings allowed her to relax a little. Liz did not have, nor require, nor want a human assistant. The Chips Family did everything for her. That was how she anthropomorphized her computers. Her former roommate, an artist, drew little Post-it faces for her to affix to her office equipment. The blue pen drawings were the various foodlike avatars of the microprocessor. Potato Chip stored her audio messages, Corn Chip stored her E-mails, Paint Chip managed her calendar, and the infamous Buffalo Chip held sway over her personnel files. Blue Chip kept track of her budget here, which was easy. Except for occasional outside consultants, there was no budget beyond her salary. Black ops files, including profiles of foreign and domestic leaders, were the province of Chocolate Chip. Those files were comaintained by her and Bob Herbert.

The Chip Family did their work without prompting and without taking time off. They even replied with a variety of messages, spoken and typed, when Liz was away from her desk.

For a psychologist it was a mixed blessing. There were never any disputes, just an occasional ailment that Matt Stoll and his team could easily repair. But there was also no human interaction, no laboratory experiment she could follow day after day. When she was a student coming to terms with her own nontraditional life, Liz would turn outward and watch others as if they were a living soap opera. The drama was satisfying, and her prediction rate for how people would react and how situations would evolve was exceptionally high.

Liz would be returning to General Carrie's office for a working lunch. She was happy for this respite, not because she needed a break from the profiling and reviews, but because she needed more coffee and her nicotine gum.

She also needed a short break from Morgan Carrie.

Thinking about the general caused her breath to shorten again. And this time it had nothing to do with whatever was in Liz's dossier.

Damn that, she thought.

The thirty-five-year-old woman put the PowerBook and mug on the desk and plopped into her swivel chair. She landed harder than she expected and nearly fell backwards. Her arms shot out in front of her.

Balance, the woman thought as she sat up. She pulled a square of gum from its wrapper and pushed it into her mouth. She did not have equilibrium at the moment. She took a breath, brushed curly brown hair from her forehead, and tried to distract herself by scanning her E-mail. The words flashed by without registering. Her heart began to speed again.

The general was an impressive woman. After Paul Hood and his dull consensus management style, Carrie's ability to make a strong decision, whether informed or intuitive, was refreshing.

Is that all it is? Liz asked. *Refreshing?*

Liz stopped going through the E-mail. She would only have to do it again later. She poured black coffee from the pot behind her. The morning brew was bitter. She did not care. She winced as she took a sip, then resumed chewing her nicotine gum. Feeding one habit while crushing another.

Shit, Liz thought angrily. Her life made no sense. She had ended one relationship because it was too much to handle. Now her imagination was flashdancing into another that would never be. And even if it could, it would be a professional disaster. As a psychologist, she knew she was being reckless. Unfortunately, she was also a human being. Understanding the problem and being able to do something about it were very different things.

Liz grabbed her mug and went back to the general's office. The only way through this was straight ahead. She once had a fast crush on a teacher at college. She would deal with this as she dealt with that: as long as she did not think about anything but her job, she should be all right.

Bugs had sent out for sandwiches. Liz sat back down and opened her egg salad. Carrie had selected roast beef. Liz's heart had slowed, but not much. The general was looking at the computer monitor when Liz arrived. Liz poked her gum on the edge of the wrapper before she ate.

"There is only one person we have not talked about," Carrie said.

"I know," Liz said. Her heart was at maximum. She felt exposed, not just because of whatever Hood had written but where the questions might lead. She had to trust that Carrie would recognize and respect the boundary between the professional and the personal.

"Paul Hood had very little to say about you," Carrie pointed out.

"As I said, Paul did not think much about what I had to contribute," Liz replied. But "very little" was not "nothing." The psychologist was anxious as she waited for what had to be coming.

"He does mention a conflict between you and the late Martha Mackall," Carrie said.

There it is, she thought with an anxiety that settled in the small of her back. "What did Paul say?"

"That Ms. Mackall formally requested you and she attend separate briefings," Carrie said. "She rescinded the request the same day."

"There was a little accidental tension between us."

"Paul wrote that Ms. Mackall initially found your presence a 'complete and irreconcilable distraction,'" the general replied. "Those are strong words for a little accident."

"Martha was a strong woman."

"Paul writes that he denied her request, which resulted in her withdrawing it," Carrie said. She looked at Liz. "Do you want to tell me what that was about? It's your call."

"I believe in full disclosure," Liz said. She set her sandwich down and hunched forward. "Martha was convinced that I had made an amorous advance toward her." The word *amorous* snagged in her throat, a lump of truth she could not easily get around.

"Did you?"

"No. But there was a moment, General—it was stupid, I admit," Liz said, "and it was completely inadvertent. We were all about to go upstairs to Andrews to greet Striker's plane from North Korea. Martha and I had been working very closely for—Christ, it was about thirty-six hours straight. What happened was that I forgot myself. I blanked, literally. There was a woman standing next to me, I was tired, and I thought she was my roommate. I put my arm around her waist and pulled her toward me the way I do—*did*—with Monica. Martha freaked."

"Did you explain?"

"Of course, and I apologized. But we were with Bob and Darrell and others, and Martha was very image conscious."

"Was Paul there?"

"No. She went to him when we got back. Paul smoothed it over, but Martha still wanted it recorded as a one-strike situation. Paul refused."

"Kind of him. He could have used it to close down your position."

"I know. I always appreciated that," Liz said.

"But I understand Martha's point of view, too," Carrie acknowledged. "Her complaint was her form of cover your ass. The glass ceiling for women is tough enough. For gay women, it's worse."

"Yes," Liz said. She wanted desperately to ask how Carrie knew that. Maybe another time.

Carrie closed the file and took a bite of sandwich. "Okay. HR says there has been no change in your personnel file for seven months."

"Correct."

"That was when you changed your insurance form from a domestic partnership to a single."

"Right," Liz replied quietly. The alarm in her back was now a small tickle.

"In other dossiers you remark on the impact of marriages and divorces—extensively in the case of Paul Hood. But there is nothing about yourself."

"There was nothing to say."

"Nothing that would affect your work, the way you wrote about Paul's divorce or Darrell's marriage?"

"No."

Carrie regarded her. She chewed slowly, her mouth closed, her jaw making strong, purposeful motions. It seemed connected to the general's thought process, as if she were mulling something over.

"All right," Carrie said. She clicked the file shut.

That's it? Compared to the scrutiny the others had received, Liz felt she was getting off easy.

"Are you sure you're all right with this?" Liz asked as her heart slowed.

"I wouldn't have said so if I weren't," Carrie assured her. "Are you?"

"Sure," Liz said.

"If you're concerned, I do not think there was anything wrong with what you did. In fact, I am a bit resentful that it is in your file at all. If you had put your arm around Lowell or Matt, no one would have mentioned it."

Liz appreciated the support, though it missed the point. She would not have put her arm around any man by accident.

It also did not change the fact that there was something about General Carrie that Liz found very appealing. The confidence was a large part of that. Monica Sheard had been an extremely insecure, anxious woman. Liz had been drawn to her talent and her sensitivity, but the artist's low self-esteem and jealousy drove them apart. Since the breakup, Liz had not dated and, like Hood and Herbert, had spent most of her time at Op-Center. She had once remarked, not in jest, that the intelligence community would benefit if it were comprised entirely of people who had lost their significant others.

Carrie shifted the subject to the second tier of workers, men like Bugs Benet and Kevin Custer in Elec-Comm. Part of Carrie's goal was to find individuals who could multitask in a crisis, such as the EMP bomb attack on Op-Center. Liz's profiles of the team during that crisis were a valuable guide for Carrie. Former serviceman and MIT graduate Custer—a distant relative of General George Armstrong Custer, through the general's brother Nevin—seemed in particular to catch and hold Carrie's eye.

The palpitations and self-imposed pressure waned as the day grew older. Carrie and Liz hit a comfortable groove that gave her a good feeling about her future here, and also the future of the NCMC.

It also allowed Liz to focus on professional matters instead of personal issues.

For now, anyway.

FORTY-ONE

Beijing, China
Wednesday, 12:33 A.M.

In Chou Shin's business, two days was a long time.

The head of the Guoanbu lay on the thin cot in the situation room. He was dressed in a silk robe, a fan blowing on his desk. For the second night in a row he did not go home to his wife, their daughter and son-in-law, and their grandchild. Chou Shin missed the little one. He missed the boy's innocent eyes and gracious smile. He even missed the sincerity of his tears.

His world had been flat and silent since the explosion at the Taipei nightclub. There had been no response to the blast from General Tam Li. The absolute silence alarmed Chou Shin even more than the odd intelligence reports he was receiving about unusual troop allocations along the eastern coast. Surely Tam Li had more than the Durban counterattack prepared. The general had allies in the military, men who would do anything for a price and do it quickly. And he was not the sort of man to back down or allow an insult to go unanswered.

Perhaps Tam Li was waiting for a shot at the enemy himself. That was why Chou Shin did not want to go home. If he were to be the next target, Chou Shin did not want his family to be hurt. He did not think Tam Li would attack his family directly. That would be dishonorable.

The intelligence officer looked at his watch. In less than twelve hours he would be in Xichang alongside General Tam Li and the prime minister. Maybe the general was waiting until after the launch. A successful mission would elevate Tam Li in the eyes of the military. Perhaps he was holding out for retaliation that was less dramatic but far more effective: a high political post.

No doubt it would be the position Chou Shin wanted for himself, the prime ministership. An effective prime minister ran the country. While the president and vice president were concerned with foreign affairs, the prime minister could make deals with ministers and representatives. He could control banking, communications, utilities, even the military. With his access to information, Chou Shin could woo or blackmail anyone he wanted—provided he had a clear path to a new job. Otherwise, he was just a wooing, blackmailing intelligence chief. That was something that would appeal to Tam Li but not to Chou Shin. The director of the Guoanbu wanted power for Communist China, not for himself.

Chou Shin was outraged that he should have to fight for that. The battle was fought decades before, and won. Tam Li was a traitor.

There were two things Chou Shin did not do well. One of them was to operate in an intelligence vacuum. Information about everyone and everything was out there. If the data were not in his possession, there was something he or his people were doing wrong. The other thing Chou Shin did not do well was wait. The two attacks he had organized were designed to spur an instant overreaction from Tam Li. He did not understand why that had not happened. For

Chou Shin that was a double failure: an intelligence vacuum and having to wait.

The intelligence officer rose from the cot. He lit a cigarette and paced the bare tile floor of the basement office. An aide had once warned Chou Shin that this was a dangerous place, a room with just one way out. That was all right with the director. It also had just one way in. He had several handguns and automatic weapons in a locker at the head of the bed, along with a gas mask and rations for five days. It would be difficult for anyone to get to him through the iron door.

It was a spartan room, with bare walls painted green and just a few hanging lightbulbs. There were no electronics down here, and the furniture was sparse. It was a place where strategy and intelligence could be discussed in absolute secrecy. Hiding a bug or Web camera in here would be virtually impossible. Only Chou Shin and two trusted aides had access to the room. During the heyday of Mao Tse-tung, the basement was an interrogation room used to "reorient" dissidents. Their broken spirits gave the place a spiritual character the director could feel. Now and then Chou Shin would take a sketch pad and charcoal from the desk and draw. He sketched images in his mind, odd shapes or scratched shadows that were the outlines of shapes. Sometimes he would look at them and try to figure out what they were, as though they were windows to his subconscious. They were like inkblots to him. And it was only fitting. Others had been interrogated here. Why not himself?

Mao himself had come down here often in the early days of the regime. He did not question prisoners himself. Most of his enemies wanted to stand proud in his eyes, to show him that the opposition had heroes as well. Mao would come down, speak to one of the interrogators without looking at the prisoner, then leave. His disinterest suggested to the captive that he was not important, that his information was unnecessary. Few men were willing to die for a trivial contribution to a cause.

Chou Shin did not know if the spirit of Mao were here, but that thought always energized him. It gave him direction and purpose. And as Chou Shin paced the room he wondered if it might have given him something else.

An idea.

Chou Shin had walked out on Tam Li the last time they were together. That had not produced information or further communication. How would the general react if Chou Shin reversed himself now? Would he welcome a chance to talk, or would he be guarded? There was one way to find out.

The intelligence director went to the telephone on the desk. There was just one line. The only other items on the desk were a notepad and several pencils, a pitcher of water, and a glass.

Chou Shin called his nighttime assistant and asked him to locate Tam Li. Since the general was going to the launch, he was probably in Beijing or already at the site. The director was surprised to find that he was at neither place.

"According to the command roster he is in Zhuhai," his aide reported.

"What is the explanation?"

"The log line says that he is monitoring the current movement of Taiwanese forces, sir."

"Why? Taipei always fields assets prior to our launches," Chou Shin said. "He never watches those."

"The roster entry does not say, sir."

"Call over. Find out his schedule for the rest of the week."

"Yes, sir," the aide replied.

Chou Shin placed the phone in its cradle. Over the past year there had been eleven Chinese missile launches. Each of them had triggered a response from Taiwan. The intelligence community had individuals inside the Taiwanese military who monitored these movements. They were officers whom Mao had sent to the island as young men, soldiers who masqueraded as firebrand separatists. Now they, or their sons, were deeply entrenched in key areas of the enemy military. If Taiwan were going to move against China, Chou Shin would know about it.

These troop movements were deemed presentational, designed to show the world that Taiwan knew what was happening across the strait. Chou Shin had seen nothing unusual in the daily intelligence briefings.

The aide rang back.

"Sir, the general's office says he will be flying directly to the launch from the base," the aide reported.

"Why is he there *now*?" Chou Shin asked.

"They do not say, sir."

"Put me through to his office," the intelligence director demanded.

"At once, sir."

Chou Shin stood beside the desk. He tapped his right foot impatiently. Ordinarily, Tam Li's whereabouts would not be on anyone's radar. Even if they were, most members of the government would accept the explanation that the general was visiting the base to check on possible outside military action against the rocket carrying his payload. But Tam Li did not need to be present to do that. And there were the reports of scattered troop and asset relocations to China's eastern coast. Perhaps the rotation was routine. But what if it was not?

"General's office, Captain Feng Lin—"

"This is Director Chou Shin of the Ministry of State Security. Please put the general on the line."

"I will let him know you are calling," the captain said.

There was a considerable loss of face for Chou Shin to

go to the general, and also to be kept waiting. But all information cost something. Especially if that intelligence was worth having.

The captain got back on the phone. "Sir, the general would like to return your call at a more convenient time."

"When would that be?" Chou Shin asked.

"The general did not share that information with me, sir."

"Do you know if Tam Li is still going to the launch tomorrow?"

"It is still on his calendar, sir," the captain replied.

"What arrangements have been made for his transportation?"

"I do not have that information, sir," the captain said. "Shall I connect you with the transportation office?"

"No, thank you, Captain," Chou Shin said. "And it will not be necessary for the general to phone."

"I will tell him, sir."

Chou Shin pressed a finger on the bar to disconnect the call. Sometimes the absence of information was enlightening, like the negative space that defined one of his silhouettes.

Tam Li had to be curious why his rival was calling. Yet the general did not want to speak with him. That suggested he was more afraid of answering questions than of learning the reason for the call. The only question he would be afraid to answer would be why he was at the base.

Chou Shin raised his finger. He called his aide.

"I want immediate air transportation to Zhuhai," the intelligence director said.

"I will arrange it, sir."

"This is a Code Six internal investigation," Chou Shin added. "I want two armed officers to accompany me. Have the aircraft wait for a return trip to Xichang. Also, call the transportation office at the base. I want to know what arrangements have been made for General Tam Li's trip to Xichang."

"At once."

"I want hourly updates on the status of that aircraft, even if it is just sitting on the field."

"Yes, sir."

Chou Shin hung up. He had a feeling that something was happening at the base, something more than just watching the Taiwanese go through the motions of self-defense. He wanted to know what Tam Li was doing.

If the general were overseeing standard operations, they would both go to the launch, and nothing would be said. But if the general were planning something—perhaps a retaliation for the Taipei attack—Chou Shin intended to stop him.

The Guoanbu had the power and authority to investigate the use of military resources for any and all actions. That fell under the jurisdiction of what the intelligence community called "exposure": whenever troops or hardware were moved, the enemy was presumed to be watching. It was the job of the Guoanbu to minimize their acquisition of useful information. Chou Shin would not hesitate to invoke those powers.

Indeed, it would be his pleasure.

FORTY-TWO

Washington, D.C.
Wednesday, 2:55 P.M.

Stephen Viens, Op-Center's liaison with the National
Reconnaissance Office, knocked on Bob Herbert's door.
Viens had been an NRO director until he took the fall for a
black ops budget of which he had been unaware. Hood immediately hired the surveillance expert. Hood took heat for
the appointment, but he did not care. Viens had been a
good and loyal friend to the NCMC. He continued to be
one of Op-Center's most valuable assets.

"We've got some very strange blips on the Pacific Rim,"
Viens said as Herbert ushered him in.

Herbert had been checking the database of everyone
who had access to the Chinese rocket during its construction. He was comparing those names to individuals with a
history of dissidence or contacts with foreigners. Even scientists with a foreign education were suspect. It was
strange to be looking for someone who might actually be
an American ally working against Beijing's interests.

"What kind of activity are you seeing?" Herbert asked.

"It's too early to say, but it looks a little more aggressive than the mainland military usually gets in situations like this," Viens said.

He handed Herbert a small stack of satellite photographs. The black-and-white images were labeled and covered the coasts of both Chinas as well as the Strait of Taiwan.

"Routine chin-first strut from Taipei," Herbert said.

"Right."

Herbert continued to go through the pictures. He came to a group that had been marked with orange grease pencil. Objects had been circled in all of them.

"PLA assets," he said. Fighter jets were being moved into launch formation at both the Shanghai Dachang Airbase and Jiangwan Airfield. They were the backbone of the eastern air defense. Jiangwan was home of the most advanced fighters in China. A third air base, Weifang, was also represented. That was the home of the powerful short-range 5th Attack Division. Photographs also showed PLAN activity. Men were loading additional ordnance onto destroyers and frigates that were part of the East Sea Fleet based in Ningbo. Ships were also being readied in Wusong and Daishan. "It looks like the Chinese are getting ready for a fight," Herbert said. "These sites are early response positions for an attack on Taiwan."

"An attack on Taiwan, yes," Viens agreed. "But they are also ERPs for an attack from Taiwan."

"The PLA can't believe that Taipei's maneuvers are the beginning of an offensive," Herbert remarked. "Beijing may just be getting ready to drill in response, or immediately after."

"They rarely do that," Viens pointed out. "The chance for a mishap with two opposing forces in the field is too great. All you need is someone on either side looking to provoke a fight."

"Maybe it's rare, but that is obviously what is happening," Herbert said. He looked at a few of the Taiwan images. "Taipei has nothing unusual in the pipeline. No extra planes or ships being readied. Obviously they do not expect a Chinese attack."

"You're right. So why would Beijing move forces into position?" Viens asked. "Why now?"

"Maybe they assume the nightclub explosion may have made everyone in Taipei a little edgy," Herbert suggested.

"Edgy as in looking to retaliate?"

"It is possible," Herbert said. "Maybe they think the Taiwanese could 'accidentally' fire a shell toward Shanghai during a drill or lose a mine in Chinese shipping lanes or fishing waters."

"Something that is not aggressive enough to start a war but would allow Taipei to win face."

"Exactly," Herbert said. "Or the PLA preparations could have nothing at all to do with the Taiwanese deployment. Beijing may be looking to scramble assets in case the rocket goes haywire. They may need to recover the payload and seal off a section of the sea."

"Because the satellite has a plutonium power source," Viens said.

"Yeah."

"The Taiwanese always go through maneuvers when there's a Chinese rocket launch or missile test," Viens said. "The Chinese military action could have nothing to do with the rocket per se."

"That's possible," Herbert agreed.

Both men were silent as Herbert looked through the pictures a second time. He did not see a national effort throughout the mainland. At other naval bases and airstrips visible along the fringes of the photographs it was business as usual. Of course, that could change quickly if hostilities erupted.

"What would happen if the rocket blew up on the launch pad?" Viens asked.

"There would be a bunch of job openings in Beijing," Herbert replied dryly.

"With the military, I mean," Viens asked. "Would they be needed to keep order in a power vacuum?"

"The loss of the prime minister and a few ministers and generals would not have that serious an impact," Herbert said.

"What if Taiwan were responsible for that kind of an explosion?"

"Then the PLA might very well strike back," Herbert said. He shook his head. "You know, Stephen, the more I look at these, the more I wonder if we are being sucker punched."

"How do you mean?"

"There's no activity at the Dinghai or Nantong naval bases. None at all. It's the opposite of business as usual. It's the same at the air bases in Shanghai Longhua and Wuhu."

"Suggesting what?"

"You ever watch police put down a riot?"

"No," Viens admitted.

"The frontline guys come in to try to control the perimeter. They use hoses, maybe some gas, nightsticks. That takes some of the steam from the rioters. Then the heavy-duty troopers arrive from vans with shields, body armor, rubber bullets. They don't slip that stuff on in public. They do it in private, then they really tear into the main body of the assault."

"You're saying these other bases are arming in hangars and dry dock?" Viens asked.

"I am saying they could be," Herbert suggested. "Considering how I've been mucking about the last two days, getting nowhere, I would not put a whole lot of faith in that."

"What kind of action would primary and secondary military strikes be considering?" Viens asked. "Who would be the rioter?"

"I don't know. But now you've got me thinking the rocket could be a precipitating event somehow."

"Or at least a participating event," Viens suggested. "If it isn't the trigger, it could be a distraction. Like a magician getting you to look the wrong way when he does a trick."

"Possibly."

"Well, it seems worth presenting to the new chief," Viens said. He leaned closer. "How is she?"

"You haven't had your audience yet?"

"Tomorrow," he said. "Is that what it is? An audience?"

"When a grunt meets with a general, you don't call that a meeting," Herbert said. "We shook hands, but it might as well have been a salute."

"Formal?"

"Rigid and commanding," Herbert said. "I get the impression that until proven otherwise, we're all grunts."

"Without the job security," Viens said.

"I think Madam Director wants to test our mettle under fire before she makes any decisions," Herbert said.

"Madam Director," Viens repeated. He chuckled anxiously. "You remind me of my grandfather Jacques."

"How?"

"He used to tell me stories about the Reign of Terror and how the instrument of justice was called 'Madame la Guillotine.' It was a title of respectful fear, not genuine regard."

"Let's just hope your analogy is a bad one," Herbert said. He was still looking at the photographs. "This is good, Stephen. I'm going to bounce these scenarios off Paul and Mike and see what they say."

Viens lingered. "It sucks," he said.

"What does?"

"We've got surveillance in space, we've finally got HUMINT resources in the target area, Op-Center is lean and focused and fully functional—and we're worried about our future."

"No. We're *anticipating* being worried about our future," Herbert said. "We have to screw this operation up first."

"Good point," Viens said. "Well, I'm all thought out. I'll keep an eye on the satellites and see what else they can tell us."

The NRO liaison left, and Herbert tossed the pictures aside. He was frustrated, not just by the Chinese game plan but his own distraction with office politics. There was conflict and occasional drama under Hood, but that was easier to manage than not knowing where you—or the boss—stood.

It was the difference between democracy and tyranny.

It was the primary reason people rioted.

And it occurred to Herbert then, with a realization that chilled his neck, that General Carrie might only be the first wave of whatever was coming here.

FORTY-THREE

Shanghai, China
Thursday, 4:42 A.M.

The People's Liberation Army Naval Flight Unit was based at the Shanghai Dachang Airbase. Thirty-one-year-old Lieutenant Commander Fa Khan was proud to be here, though he knew that assignment to Dachang was considered less prestigious than deployment at the Shanghai Jiangwan facility.

The two airfields were neighbors. Their importance had nothing to do with proximity to the coastline or to the heart of Shanghai. Jiangwan received more funding and the newest aircraft and radar because of ancient family ties between key military officers and members of the government.

Prestige was much less important to the pilots of each base. They saluted one another whenever they flew close enough to have cockpit visual contact. To them, the pride was the shared honor of being the homeland's first line of defense.

Dachang was a staging area for the PLANFU while

Jiangwan was primarily used by the People's Liberation Army Air Force. Fa Khan was an eleven-year veteran of the PLANFU and knew this as well: the sharpest fliers were stationed with him at Dachang, where the technical and logistical facilities were the weakest. Though that kept him from piloting the newest fighters like the J-13, with its stealth capabilities, Fa Khan and his squadron could nurse miraculous maneuvers from the aging MiG-21s at Dachang. As he once explained it to his father, who repaired automobiles in the city, pilots recognized every groan and hesitation, every burp in the engines or response time variance from the stick. The Dachang pilots knew just how to compensate and how to get the most from their machines. The MiG was flown by a man, not by a computer. It had been designed for quick and cheap construction, like the earliest biplanes. It was the ideal craft for an air force that wanted to throw overwhelming numbers at an enemy. That concept of war had been the Russian and Chinese mind-set for centuries. The MiG-21 was simply a mechanical expression of that tactic.

Besides, he had joined the PLANFU to fly, and he had achieved that goal. He experienced renewed joy each time he pushed himself into the sky. The takeoff and flights were never the same. Indeed, change was something very keenly felt by Fa Khan and his fellow fliers. The clouds changed from second to second, the colors changed from minute to minute, the air currents changed from hour to hour. The landscape below changed from day to day, and the political situation shifted from week to week. The preflight briefing indicated that there was tension with Taiwan now. In a few days it could be South Korea or Vietnam, Japan, or even the United States. These struggles always played out in the air or upon the sea to the east.

He was a part of all that, and he was also apart from it, like one of the gods of old China. He had insight into what was coming and the tools to affect it. He was also vulnerable to these events. The thrill was constant.

As long as all the gear worked, Fa Khan was happy. Not many men got to sit where he was. As he prepared to take off into a sun-drenched morning, he did what he did every day: he cherished his life and work.

Fa Khan's patrol sector was Sector Seventeen. That took him northwest for 200 kilometers and then east 150 kilometers over the Yellow Sea. He returned via a southward course over the East China Sea, then east again in a long loop that brought him west to return to base. It was a 1,400-kilometer round trip, 200 kilometers within the MiG's maximum range. If Fa Khan spotted uncharted sea traffic—smugglers were a primary target—or if he faced an engagement with the enemy, he would be able to meet them, hold them until reinforcements could arrive, and still return to base.

These patrols were vital to national security. China did not yet have the satellite capabilities of the United States, Russia, and their allies. That would begin to change later this morning with the launch from Xichang. If he was lucky, he might be in a position to spot the flames of the launch and the mighty contrail as the rocket sped into the heavens.

Lieutenant Commander Fa Khan had only been aloft for a few minutes, his heart still racing from the G forces he took during his sharp climb, when he received a coded communiqué from the tower. It was a series of five double-digit numbers, followed by a time code in letters, followed by another number. He put the MiG on autopilot as he wrote the figures on a pad that hung from a chain below the altimeter. Since he was still in his ascent to 22,000 feet, the pad was hanging slightly toward him, the always-reliable low-tech plumb in his cockpit. The tower asked Fa Khan to repeat the numbers, which he did. When the radio officer confirmed that the read-back was accurate, the lieutenant commander signed off. He referred to a thick but compact map book in a lockbox beneath the seat.

There were four maps on each page of the volume. The numbers referred to a section number, a page number, a map number, and then two coordinates. The last two numbers pinpointed a patrol zone.

Fa Khan raised the visor of his helmet as he looked at the map. He checked it against the numbers. Twice. Then again.

There was no mistake.

He went back to the pad and worked out the letters. The corresponding numbers were six, zero, zero. Six o'clock in the morning. That was a little less than two hours from now.

The lieutenant commander had no idea what was up, but he knew how much time and fuel it would take him to reach the target zone. He calculated backward so he would arrive exactly at six A.M. He would also keep an eye open for other aircraft that would be converging on the target, a point just outside the territorial waters of the breakaway republic of Taiwan. The last number of the series indicated that Fa Khan would be joined by seventeen other fighter jets from Dachang. That was the remainder of his squadron as well as two other squadrons.

Apparently, this was a day when change was coming a little faster than normal.

And yet, one thing did not change: the determination in his eyes and spirit as he altered his flight path slightly in preparation for the rendezvous.

FORTY-FOUR

Beijing, China
Thursday, 5:11 A.M.

Paul Hood woke early.

The car to take him to the airport was arriving at six. From there, he would fly to Xichang. He lay in bed for a while, hoping to get back to sleep. But his mind was instantly on patrol, marching toward problems on the near and far horizon.

He did not want to think right now. There was no new information and no way to get it. He grabbed a book he had packed, a biography of the explorer Richard Francis Burton. It had arrived at his apartment shortly before he left. It was in a box of books his former wife had sent him. Sharon was still packing up his things and shipping them out when she had the time. Presumably, to make room for the stuff her boyfriend was leaving at the house, like his videotape collection of the Washington Redskins' greatest games.

He stopped reading when Burton took an African spear through both cheeks. The graphic attack by tribesmen did not induce sleep. Hood set the book aside and just sat there. He was jet-lagged but overstimulated by his frustrating lack of information. He was used to having people to turn to, a team, specialists. None of that had been set up before his departure. Hood was in the midst of the evolving situation, yet he knew very little about the scenario or the dynamics between the different players.

He thought about Anita instead. She was completely devoted to her work and to her father. There did not appear to be room or need for anything else. Men at the party did not seem to notice her. Most probably knew who she was. Perhaps they had tried talking to her before and were put off.

Not everyone is a professional small-talker, Hood reminded himself.

Anita apparently stayed in the two worlds where she felt comfortable: ivory-tower politics and academia. If anyone wanted to be with her, it had to be within those two disciplines. There was something to be said for that. Although it made her a poor spy, as she had demonstrated, it would be very difficult for anyone to take her by surprise, intellectually or emotionally.

The secure cell phone was set on Silent, so the light flashed without ringing. Hood reached over and picked it up. It was Bob Herbert.

"Hope I didn't wake you," Herbert said.

"No. What's up?"

"An unusual Chinese military buildup in response to a traditional Taiwanese military exercise," Herbert said. "Have you heard anything about that?"

"No."

"Is there anyone you have met who might know about it?" Herbert asked.

"I can ask the prime minister later, with the caveat that it probably won't do any good," Hood said. "If he does know anything, he might not be inclined to share the information with me. Have you talked to Mike?"

"Not yet," Herbert said. "I'm frankly at a loss here."

"You sound like it."

"Is it that bad?"

"You sound winded."

"Maybe. I feel like I'm sitting on the sidelines, though I don't know if I'm catching my breath or scratching my butt," Herbert admitted.

"It's that dry out there?"

"Arid," Herbert said. "You know how Chinese politics are. No one says anything to anybody."

"Yes. I experienced that firsthand," Hood admitted.

"All we see are the shadow results of conflicts, the explosions in Charleston and South Africa. Our associates in D.C. and Interpol have no more information than we do about what is behind this or what might be next. Sergei Orlov had some background on the key players. Chou Shin was considered a moderate because he was trying to reconcile the 'brother' Communists of China and the Soviet Union. When the S.U. fell, he turned on Moscow with a series of pretty riled-up speeches."

"The spurned lover," Hood said.

"Yeah. Communism is a religion to him, and he will die for it," Herbert said. "According to Orlov, the other nutcase—General Tam Li—is not a martyr. But he is an aggressive bastard who will risk his life or the lives of others to increase his power base. All of which tells us what we already know: these guys are dangerous. We need to try to find out if the Chinese action is related to the Taiwanese drill, the rocket launch, or something else."

Herbert's frustration came through the phone. It sucked hope from the room, from Hood.

"There is not much we can do about the armies," Hood said. "We should concentrate on the rocket."

"I figured Mike would be all over that with his marines," Herbert said. "I got General Carrie to lend them to him."

"I'm not surprised."

"He's not in command, but they'll listen to him."

"Of course." Hood felt marginalized. But the general-to-general sympatics was inevitable.

"What about you?" Herbert asked.

"I did not get anywhere with the prime minister or his daughter, and I'm frankly at a loss what to do next."

"Hence being awake at a few minutes after five in the morning."

"Exactly," Hood replied.

"What was the daughter like?" Herbert asked. "Businesslike and severe?"

"Businesslike yes, but very feminine."

"Is there something there you can work?"

"I don't think so," Hood said. "Her father comes first. Everyone else comes a very distant second. I'm stumped, Bob."

"Didn't this sort of thing play out differently once upon a time?" Herbert asked plaintively.

"You mean, 'Remember when we used to win these things?'" Hood asked.

"Well, I'm not willing to write this one off—"

"Nor am I," Hood assured him. "But we did seem to have more control hunkered in the Tank with Striker in the field."

"That was the hub. Now we're in the fringes."

"Not by choice," Hood pointed out. "We've been pushed out by younger or more aggressive individuals with stronger beliefs. Or if not stronger, they put more muscle behind what they *do* believe."

"Christ, Paul. You sound like an old soldier."

"Bob, I am—*we* are," Hood insisted. "We have been marginalized by people of passion, by people who want to build a career or an army or an ideology, or else destroy one."

"I never thought I would hear you call me a moderate," Herbert joked.

"You are devoted to your people," Hood said. "Loudly, fiercely, but completely. That keeps you from watching your own ass, from elbowing your way to the front of the line."

"I like where I am. And I do not see anything wrong with being one of the guys who holds it all together from the middle."

"Which is exactly what I'm talking about," Hood replied. "No one is a centrist anymore." Hood was starting to get annoyed. Not with the vague, imagined usurpers but with himself. There was resignation in his voice, and he did not like that. "Look, I've got to get ready to go. The government car will be here soon."

"And I have to take another walk around the intel we have collected," Herbert said. "Have you thought about your own safety at the launch?"

"Not really. We'll be in a bunker—"

"The concrete will protect you from an explosion, not from radiation," Herbert cautioned.

"I guess we will just have to make sure that nothing happens," Hood said.

"That's a goal, not a plan," Herbert said.

"I know."

Hood's conversation with Bob Herbert was different, too. There was a time when the men would have been discussing very specific options about evolving situations. Ideas would be on the table, intelligence would be in the data stream, and answers would emerge. Instead, they sat here complaining, like old men on a park bench reminiscing about the good old days.

Hood did not like that, either. He had always prided himself on being a professional. And for him, by definition, that was someone who did his best, even when he did not feel like it. Maybe it was post-traumatic shock about being plucked from Op-Center, but he was not doing his best. He and Herbert were like mice in a maze, moving along a route they did not know to a goal they could not see.

That had to change.

Now.

"Bob, we need to take another walk around this situation. There has to be something we've missed."

"Such as? We've gone over the launch site, the schedule—"

"There must be something in the individuals, their personalities, their past actions that we can use."

"Sure," Herbert said. "Say, are you okay?"

"Why?"

"A minute ago you sounded down," Herbert said. "Now you sound like you're speeding."

"It's a new day and an important one," Hood explained, rising. He had not intended that to be metaphorical, but it was both literally and figuratively true. "You're right. We don't have a plan, and we need one, something better than planting my ass in a concrete bunker and waiting for something to happen."

Herbert was silent for a moment. "How about this," he said. "Don't go to the bunker. Ask to go somewhere else."

"Where? A representative of the president of the United States will not be given an all-access pass."

"Will Le's daughter be there?" Herbert asked.

"Yes."

"What if you could convince her that the prime minister is in danger?" Herbert asked.

"And use that how?"

"I am isolating potential targets at the launch site for Mike's team," Herbert said. "Maybe you can have a look at them as well. Between you and the marines, we can cover more territory."

"I think Le and his daughter might go for that," Hood said. "I'll talk to them when I get there."

"I like it," Herbert said. "I'll send the likeliest sites to your laptop. If you check it en route to the facility, I can talk to Mike about dividing the duties."

"Absolutely," Hood told him. "If I have any questions, I'll give you a shout."

"I'll be here," Herbert assured him. Now the intelligence chief sounded energized as well.

Hood hung up and took a quick shower. The water invigorated his body the way the ideas had invigorated his mind. Both contributed to the much-needed renewal of Hood's spirit.

At least one thing had not changed over the years: Hood's capacity to bootstrap himself and those around him. What the old Op-Center team may have lacked in zealousness they made up for in endurance and dedication.

That was not nothing.

At the moment, it could be everything.

FORTY-FIVE

Zhuhai, China
Thursday, 7:18 A.M.

Tam Li was dozing at his desk when the intercom came on. He did not start at the sound, because he never slept very deeply. It was a habit soldiers acquired if they wanted to survive. He picked up the phone.

"Go ahead."

"General, an aircraft is approaching from Beijing," the orderly reported. "It is carrying Chou Shin of the Guoanbu."

"How do you know?"

"We advised the pilot that the base is in a lockdown situation because of the maneuvers off Taipei," the orderly replied. "The pilot insisted that command did not apply to his passenger."

That was not good. Not at all. "Are they landing?" the general asked.

"They said they will, with or without assistance from the tower," the orderly informed him.

"Bring them down," the general said. "Send two security units to meet the aircraft and take them all into custody."

"Arrest the Guoanbu director?" the orderly asked.

"And everyone with him."

"Yes, sir," the orderly said. "The security detachment leader will need to know the charge."

"Murder," Tam Li said without hesitation.

"Sir?"

"Chou Shin has committed homicidal acts of terrorism abroad."

"Yes, sir," the orderly said. "If there is resistance?"

"Tell the detachment leader to resist back!" the general shouted. He slammed the receiver into the cradle and looked at his watch. He did not need to prove the charges or even make them survive the morning. All he needed was for Chou Shin and the leadership at the launch site to be out of the way for the next few hours. After that, there would be a military crisis that only military leaders could solve.

The general was now completely awake. His olive green jacket was draped on the back of the chair. He got up and put it on. He tugged the hem to remove the wrinkles. He tugged it hard.

The bastard provocateur, he thought angrily. Chou Shin may have thought to confront the general and bully him into aborting his plan. That would not happen. In fact, Chou Shin would not set eyes on Tam Li until a frightened nation had surrendered its will to the military. Not only would a general become the effective leader of one billion Chinese, but Chou's antiquated Communist ideology would be buried at last and for all time. In a way, his arrival here was timely. Tam Li had planned to tell the prime minister that he was remaining in Zhuhai to watch the Taiwanese deployment in the strait, claiming it was more significant than usual. Now he could add to that the curious arrival of Director Chou, who was also supposed to be at the launch. The general would tell the prime minister that he was analyzing the data with the help of the Guoanbu.

Tam Li left the room with long, bold strides and entered a corridor that connected his office with the rest of the officers' compound. The morning light was coming over the strait in strong yellow splashes. The pale green carpet of the hallway looked like solid amber. The general did not notice the salutes of his command as he passed. His eyes were on an office ahead, the headquarters of the strategic planning officer, Colonel Hark. He entered without knocking. The tall, lean Hark was standing at an electronic table with four other officers. The men all turned and saluted smartly as the general entered. He returned the salute perfunctorily and stood beside the table. A map of the region was being projected from below. Electronic blips on top showed the position of every commercial plane and ship in the area.

"What is our status?" Tam Li demanded.

"The forward aerial strike force is thirty-five percent deployed," the colonel replied. "The naval task force is nearly twenty-five percent deployed. Everything is precisely on schedule."

"I want our forces boosted to fifty percent—full deployment within the hour," Tam Li ordered.

Hark regarded the general with open surprise. The other officers remained at attention.

"General, the Americans will see it on satellite," Hark pointed out. "They will suspect we are sending out more than a routine patrol."

"Thank you, Colonel. That had occurred to me."

"Sir, with respect, we all agreed that the main deployment should coincide with the situation at the launch—"

"Circumstances have changed significantly," Tam Li told him. "I want us to be seen."

There was a short silence. "May I ask why, sir?"

"Chou Shin is on the way to the base. I am going to

have him detained. If he suspects what we are doing, he will try to stop us. We need to maneuver events to a point where they cannot be stopped."

"Even if we are perceived as an aggressor?"

"Taiwan military vessels are in the water, and their warplanes in the skies," the general replied. "All of them are headed toward our shores. We need no other justification to field a defense force."

"Perhaps, sir. But we have never responded before in this situation. The attack on the rocket and Taiwan's opportunistic deployment was going to justify our own sudden and confrontational move—"

"Colonel, what is Directive Two forty-one?"

"'Taiwan is an integral part of China,'" the colonel replied.

"Directive Two forty-two?"

"'It is an inviolable mission of the entire Chinese people to reunify the motherland,'" recited Hark.

"And Directive Two forty-six?"

"'The sooner we settle the question of Taiwan, the better it is,'" the colonel declared.

"You understand the goal. With that in mind, what command would you issue if our ports and airfields were about to come under attack?" the general asked.

"I would simultaneously move and deploy our equipment, sir."

"Just so," Tam Li said. "We are under attack from ideological enemies at home. They may seek to confiscate our assets while they are in one place. We cannot allow that. Get our forces off the ground and out of the docks as soon as possible. They will not engage Taiwan. Not yet. Nothing else has changed. The rocket will be destroyed as planned. Our ships and planes will simply be closer to the enemy than we had planned. In a way, this helps us."

"How so?"

"Instead of hunting him down later, we will have already arrested the man who was responsible for the destruction of the rocket," Tam Li told him. "There is one thing more I want."

"Sir?"

"Have the white unit meet me in Hangar Three," he said.

FORTY-SIX

Zhuhai, China
Thursday, 8:02 A.M.

The standard Boeing 737-800 landed gently on the long military runway. The pilot reversed the engines and turned toward the terminal complex, a series of low-lying gray buildings at the hub of four radial airstrips. A number of aircraft were moving from hangars toward the different jet ways. There was no question about where to go: General Tam Li had dispatched an honor guard.

Chou Shin was not surprised. It had been necessary for them to circle the field before they were given clearance to land. Obviously, the general was doing something here he did not want others to know about. Chou had used his wireless laptop to track the general's actions as best as he could during the flight. According to on-site and satellite data collected by the Guoanbu, Taiwan had continued its limited deployment while Tam Li had accelerated his. That would have to be stopped, and quickly. The only way to do that was for Chou to witness the commander's activities firsthand and report them to the prime minister.

The intelligence director went to the front of the plane as it neared the building. The pilot did not so much finish taxiing as stop. There was no staircase or tunnel by which to exit.

Chou Shin waited until the engines had stopped. "Open the door," the director told his aide.

The young man bowed slightly, then turned and unlocked the cabin door. Chou stood in the oily heat of the open hatch.

"Who is in command here?" the director asked. He spoke softly to show that he was unconcerned and to make them come to him.

A lieutenant stepped up smartly. "I am in charge of these units."

"Have them bring us a stairwell," Chou said.

"Our orders are that you shall remain on the aircraft."

"Orders from whom?"

"The Security Detachment Office," the lieutenant replied. "The base is under a condition red alert. Your plane should not even have been permitted to land."

"Why was it, then?"

"The base commander has override authority," the lieutenant informed him.

"Your orders are treasonous," Chou informed him. "We will deploy the emergency exit equipment if we must, but I will leave this aircraft, and I will see base commander General Tam Li."

"Condition red dictates that we stop any member of your party who attempts to leave the aircraft."

"You would shoot the director of the Guoanbu?" Chou demanded.

"We would detain you by any means necessary."

Chou turned to the cockpit. The door was open. The pilots were still going through their postflight checklist. "Get me the minister of defense in Beijing," he said.

"Sir, we tried communicating with the tower when we

landed," the pilot informed him. "Our radio signals are being blocked."

Chou turned to his aide. "Cellular phones as well?"

The young man was holding his phone. He looked grim. "There are too many satellite dishes at the base. I cannot get a signal."

"Will the tower be able to block our Internet uplink?"

"That is very unlikely," the pilot answered. "Our airborne wireless operates on one point nine gigahertz, which is a privately used frequency. Unless the communications center knows exactly what that frequency is, they cannot block it. Not as long as we have direct line-of-sight access to the satellite."

"Thank you very much, Captain," the intelligence director said. He looked back through the door. He was perspiring slightly from the heat. Chou asked his aide for water. He did not want anyone to think he was afraid. As he drank, Chou was surprised to notice two men were approaching with a ladder.

"What are you doing?" Chou asked the lieutenant.

"You will close the door," the officer replied. "Otherwise, we are prepared to close it for you."

"We will close the door and leave," Chou decided suddenly. "You will see to our refueling."

"I will relay your request to the base commander."

"That was not a request," Chou informed him.

"I only take orders from the general," the lieutenant answered predictably.

Chou regarded him but said nothing. "Close the door," he told his aide.

The director of the Guoanbu returned to his seat. He opened his own laptop and began composing an E-mail to the prime minister's office. It would be marked *Top Priority, National Security*. The heading guaranteed that whoever received it would contact the prime minister immediately, wherever he was.

The pilot got on the public address system. "Director Chou, a fuel truck has been sent from the hangar."

That was a surprise. Obviously, Tam Li did not want them here. He would probably have the aircraft fueled as slowly as possible. He must believe that by the time Chou was in the air, it would be too late to stop him. It was curious that he was not concerned about E-mail. Perhaps he thought his signals would block it. Tam Li often acted with passion rather than sense.

Chou quickly composed his E-mail as the smell of jet fuel filled the cockpit. After several minutes the pilot came back on the speaker.

"Director Chou, please come to the cockpit," the captain said. "Something is happening outside."

Chou set his laptop aside and went to the front. He did not hurry. Panic was its own fuel. He stepped inside and looked out the window. He saw three fire trucks moving along the runway in their direction.

"Obviously, Captain, there is a fire somewhere," Chou said.

"If so, sir, there would be an alarm," the pilot replied.

The captain was correct.

"How has the refueling proceeded?" Chou asked.

The captain indicated a gauge. "It has not yet begun."

Chou felt foolish. Not just because he had overlooked the obvious but because he had underestimated General Tam Li.

"Captain, we need to take off," Chou said. "You have to get us to a commercial airstrip."

"Sir, the nearest fields are in Hong Kong or Canton, and we have barely enough fuel to reach either—"

"*Take off!*" Chou ordered.

"Yes, sir."

"If these trucks try to block us, go around them or over them, but get us out of here," he added.

The pilot and copilot immediately began preparing the

jet for power-up. Chou sat in the seat beside his aide. Both men buckled their seat belts. The plane rattled as the engines were started in tandem.

"Sir, why would the general give us fuel, then use fire trucks to close off the runway?" Chou's aide asked.

"I do not believe that is what he is doing," Chou said ominously. He cast a look out the window. The airmen were all watching the back of the aircraft. After a moment, they were given a signal to withdraw.

Chou undid his belt and jumped from his seat.

"Sir?" said the aide.

"The door!" Chou yelled. "Open it and deploy the emergency slide. We have to get out!"

The aide got up and went to the hatch. Chou stood behind him.

"Stop the engines," Chou told the pilots. "We're leaving—"

There was a whooshing sound from the back of the aircraft, like a gas range being ignited. Chou looked back. That was not far from the case. The windows in the center of the aircraft were suddenly filled with a smoky orange glow.

The orderly pulled open the hatch just as the dull light reached the forward section. The young man cried and stepped back as flames whipped over the foot of the doorway and into the cabin.

That was why the general was not worried about E-mailed messages, Chou thought. He knew they would never be sent.

Perhaps.

While the pilot jumped forward to close the hatch, Chou turned and rushed down the aisle. He reached his seat just as the aircraft lost all structural integrity. The fuel that had been set aflame below the aircraft ignited the fuel that remained in the tanks. The tires exploded first, dropping the aircraft to the tarmac a moment before it disintegrated. The fuselage blew open like a holiday firework. Instead of spraying the air with sparkling light, it threw shards of glass, metal, and quick-melted plastic in every direction. The wings were blown from the fuselage. Weighted down by the engines, one on each wing, they hit the asphalt and skidded several dozen yards from the sides. The tail section simply broke off and fell backwards, allowing a fist of flame to shoot from the back of the cabin.

Because the aircraft fuel tanks had been near empty, the blast was contained to the jet and the surrounding airfield. The three fire trucks that had already been en route arrived immediately after the explosion. Foam punched through the black smoke, hissing as it came into contact with fire and superheated metal. Within several minutes the flames had been extinguished. Men in fire-resistant white suits were beginning to move through the wreckage. They used back-mounted fire extinguishers to kill spot fires and search for survivors.

There were none.

There were not even remains that could be easily spotted, let alone identified.

General Tam Li was given an update about the spill and its aftermath. He thanked the fire captain.

Then he called the prime minister to inform him of the tragic crash.

FORTY-SEVEN

Xichang, China
Thursday, 8:55 A.M.

The prime minister was in a pleasantly detached mood as his plane neared Xichang. He had been reading for pleasure, not for work, which was unusual. But it had been an intense few days, and a search for the historical Wong Fei Hung was a welcome distraction. Tales of the nineteenth-century Chinese hero had been a favorite of Le's when he was a boy. The son of one of the Ten Tigers of Canton, Wong Fei Hung was a healer, a philosopher, a martial arts master, and a defender of justice. He was also the subject of over one hundred feature films and four times as many novels, which had obscured his real-life accomplishments. Le Kwan Po found the real man even more fascinating than the fictional one, living quietly as a peddler of herbal medicines while battling tirelessly for the rights of his fellow citizens. Married seven times—the last, to a teenage girl— Wong Fei Hung was obviously a man of considerable strength and stamina.

Anita was sitting beside her father, and Paul Hood was

sitting across the aisle. They were chatting amiably in English. Le Kwan Po was happy and surprised to see his daughter so relaxed. She had asked that Mr. Hood be seated across from her rather than in the section of the airplane reserved for dignitaries. That caused some indignant glances and awkward remarks from the European representatives, but Le ignored them. It was the privilege of a high-ranking official to be provocative. Besides, none of them had ever gone for a walk with his daughter.

Le had been tempted to ask what they were speaking about when the phone in his armrest beeped.

It was General Tam Li calling from Zhuhai. Chou Shin had been killed during an unannounced visit to the Zhuhai Air Base.

"I do not know why he was here," the general said. "We are trying to ascertain whether there were explosives on board."

Le Kwan Po's first thought was that Chou Shin may have been planning another unworthy act, such as a direct attack on Tam Li. It would have been a blow to the general's power base by hitting his eastern command hub.

It also would have been treason, Le thought. Chou Shin was many things, but he was not a traitor. The defense of China was as important to Communists as it was to the more progressive elements of government. Even so, there would have been no reason for the Guoanbu director to go there personally. *Unless it was to gain access to a place where others could not go.* Tam Li's office, for one.

"I had been preparing to leave for the launch, Mr. Prime Minister, but I want to be here for the investigation," Tam Li went on.

"I understand," Le replied. "Let me know what you discover."

"At once," the general assured him.

"And General?"

"Sir?"

"Has Taiwan begun its traditional coastal exercises?"

"They have," Tam Li replied.

"Then tell your bureau of information to inform the Defense Ministry that a government jet has crashed on the runway, nothing more," Le said. "Until your white team finds the director's remains and has confirmed his death, I do not want that information released."

"Yes, sir. May I ask why?"

"Taipei may see the death of our military intelligence chief as an invitation to expand their mischief," the prime minister replied.

"Of course."

"I will speak with you after the launch."

Le Kwan Po hung up. He turned to his left. Paul Hood was wearing a perplexed look. Anita regarded her father with open concern. Obviously, that was what had caused Hood's expression.

"What has happened?" Anita asked.

"Chou Shin has been killed in an explosion," he told her.

"One of his own design? An accident?"

"I do not know," Le said.

"Are you going to tell the gentleman?" she asked, indicating Hood with her eyes. She obviously did not want to say his name, which he would pick from the unfamiliar dialogue.

"American satellites will surely have seen the explosion," her father said. "I will have to tell him something." He could see that Anita wanted to suggest something. "Do you have any thoughts?"

"Tell him the truth," she said.

"Why?"

"He is an intelligence officer," she said. "He might be able to give us insight into the actions of another intelligence officer."

Le managed a small smile. "That is true. But that is not the insight we might need at this time."

"What do you mean?"

"Chou Shin and Tam Li were bitter rivals," the prime minister said. "It is the insight of a thwarted military officer we might need."

"I believe our guest may know someone like that as well," Anita said.

Le had to think for a moment. "The man whose company built the satellite?" he asked, once again avoiding any names.

Anita nodded.

"All right," her father said. "Let's have a chat with Mr. Hood. As quietly as possible, so the others do not hear."

Anita turned to Hood and said that her father wished to speak with him. Le took a moment to gather his thoughts.

He needed to find out why Chou Shin had gone to the base when he should have been flying to Xichang. It was unlikely that anyone at the Guoanbu knew. Chou Shin was a man who guarded his own activities as jealously as he kept secrets of state. Perhaps the intelligence director had contacted someone before leaving or while en route. The prime minister would have his assistant look into that.

Of more immediate concern, Le did not know whether Tam Li had simply decided to carry their feud to a new level. That was certainly a possibility. It was also the one that concerned him the most. Because if it were true, there was no telling where—or how—it might stop.

FORTY-EIGHT

Xichang, China
Thursday, 9:14 A.M.

Hood was not surprised by what Anita told him. He would not miss Chou Shin. The man was a hard-line ideologue who kept China anchored to its backward, isolationist past. Whose agents had helped to endanger his Op-Center field team in Botswana when they tracked a kidnapped priest.

But assassination, if that's what had happened, was not a policy that Paul Hood endorsed. It was the last and ultimately least effective resort of desperate megalomaniacs. If they did not have the support to accomplish what they wanted through legitimate means, murder was a short-term solution.

"Do you need help with something?" Hood asked the prime minister through his daughter.

"I am concerned about Tam Li," Le Kwan Po replied. "Your own friend the general might have some thoughts. Perhaps you have your own sources."

Ordinarily, Hood would be suspicious of a Chinese

leader who asked for help from American intelligence. Though the presidential envoy did not entirely trust the man, he believed in him. Le Kwan Po had been caught between two strong polar forces. One of them had just been eliminated. He was clearly looking to restabilize himself and perhaps his nation.

"I will call him when we land," Hood promised. He did not want to contact him while they were in flight. Rodgers was probably with the marines. The pilots might be able to track his call using the sophisticated electronics of the aircraft. He did not want to give them that opportunity. "In the interim there is someone else who might have some insights," he said.

Hood called Liz Gordon. The Op-Center psychologist had just gotten home and was feeding her cat.

"Paul Hood," she said flatly. "I didn't expect to hear from you again."

"Frankly, I didn't expect to be calling," he fired back.

As a rule, Hood had not been a booster of psychiatry or profiling. He still was not sure it deserved the validity and effort law enforcement gave it. Occasionally, however, it offered useful insights.

Gordon snickered. "Touché. What can I do for you?"

"Has Bob kept you abreast of the situation in China?"

"I read his summary before leaving," she said.

"There's been a new development," Hood said. "The nonmilitary individual was eliminated, apparently by his rival."

"The man who was hit in Charleston and Taipei struck back," she said.

"Right."

Hood knew that Liz would understand his shorthand. There were English-speakers on board the aircraft. The engines were loud but not that loud. Some of them might overhear.

"That doesn't surprise me," she said.

"Why?"

"Soldiers are not diplomats. They run out of words and patience faster than other people," Liz told him. "Where did this happen?"

"At a base in the east."

"Isn't this his rocket being launched?" Liz asked.

"Yes."

"Why isn't he there?"

"The big man says he is staying at home to oversee the investigation," Hood told her. "Perhaps he is concerned that the deceased succeeded in his alleged plot to booby-trap the mission."

"Why wouldn't he tell that to the PM?" she asked. "If he was responsible for this incident at the base, there is sure to be an inquiry. He will be a likely suspect. Information about a plot against the mission would give our man a reason for having acted the way he did."

She had a point.

"Do we even know why the deceased went there?" Liz asked.

"No."

"People tend to confront other people face-to-face for one of two reasons," Liz said. "Either they are flat-out nuts, or they have a virtuous cause and strength of numbers behind them. Was this man crazy?"

"Not at all," Hood said.

"Then he must have known something, or had something that he wanted to present to his rival. That's the information you should be looking for, information that may have been worth killing for."

"Mr. Hood!" Anita said urgently.

Hood looked over. She was pointing to her father's laptop. He nodded and held up a finger.

"Liz, this has been helpful. Thanks."

"You're welcome."

"Are you doing okay?" he added as an afterthought.

"Just peachy," she replied. "Go. We'll talk later."

"Thanks again," he said.

He folded away his cell phone as Anita typed a translation on the laptop. When she was finished, she handed the device to Hood. It was an incomplete E-mail from Guoanbu Director Chou. It had been sent around the time of the explosion. It read:

> I have come to Zhuhai to question Tam Li about a deployment being carried out under his command. It is a response to Taiwan's standard fielding of a non-aggressive military force for one of our launches. I believe the general plans to attack the enemy with overwhelming firepower. He is holding us on the tarmac, not permitting us to contact

FORTY-NINE

Xichang, China
Thursday, 10:22 A.M.

After landing at the airfield fifty kilometers south of the complex, Prime Minister Le Kwan Po had placed a call to the Ministry of National Defense. The minister confirmed that General Tam Li had reported organizing an appropriate "ready response" to the Taiwanese deployment. He had no information about Chou Shin's report of "overwhelming firepower."

"When was the last time you communicated with Tam Li?" the prime minister inquired.

"He called to inform me of the explosion," the minister replied.

"You have had no other reports of activity in the east?"

"None," the minister said.

Le was not surprised. Those reports would have originated at Zhuhai and been disseminated throughout the national defense system. The PLA was not equipped to spy on itself, and it did not have reciprocal arrangements with other nations. Still, someone was lying, either Chou Shin

or Tam Li. The prime minister could not imagine the intelligence director sending an E-mail claiming an attack was
being prepared unless he could have supported his claim.

"If there were an unusual deployment, and it were not
reported to you, how long would it take to get independent
corroboration?" the prime minister asked.

"Do you have reason to suspect that something is
wrong?" the minister asked urgently.

"I cannot go into that now," Le said.

"Mr. Prime Minister, if there is a threat to our national
defense—"

"I received an uncorroborated report of a possible
PLAAF buildup in Tam Li's command sector," Le said
quickly. He did not have time to debate with the stubborn
minister.

"A report from who?"

"Chou Shin, just before his death," the prime minister
answered impatiently.

"He was a patriot," the minister said. "Radar at the Nanjiang Military Region is piped to the Coordinated Air
Command in Beijing," the minister went on. "That tells us
at once how many aircraft are in the skies. At the moment
I see nothing unusual apart from the required patrols." He
added, "I would tell you, Mr. Prime Minister, if it were
otherwise."

"You are not someone I doubt," Le replied truthfully.

"Nor I, you," the minister told him. "But this information is not deeply useful to us."

"Why?"

"It would not take long to put several squadrons from
the Nanjiang bases into the air and over the strait," the minister said.

"Can you override Tam Li's authority?"

"Not until and unless he actually does something that
overreaches established protocol or expressed policy. So
far, he has acted in accordance with the rules of preemptive

engagement regarding Taiwan and air-lane security for a launch path."

"What does air-lane security entail?"

"PLAAF jets are scrambled to patrol well beyond the boundaries of the rocket's course," the minister said. "That prevents enemy aircraft from moving in and compromising rocket integrity."

"You mean firing a missile," Le said.

"Yes. The Russians and Americans have been known to observe our launches from high-altitude fighters."

"Our jets are already in the air?" Le asked.

"They are. A little premature but not alarmingly so."

Tam Li was doing everything according to schedule. He was not a fool. There was also a chance that he was not guilty.

Le thanked the minister and asked for updates if and when they became available. He sat back and looked out the tinted windows at the rustic countryside. It was possible that Chou Shin had been trying to frame the general. The intelligence director had been responsible for several explosions over the past few days. Perhaps he had gone to Zhuhai to attack the general's command post. The prime minister was willing to believe that Tam Li had struck directly at his foe, destroying the aircraft. The same could also be true of Chou Shin. His own explosives may have detonated prematurely.

Whatever the truth, there was nothing Le could do now but wait.

Wait, and hope that Paul Hood came up with something that might not be on the radar.

FIFTY

Xichang, China
Thursday, 10:28 A.M.

The Xichang Satellite Launch Center was one of three major launch sites in China. The other two were located in Jiuquan and Taiyuan. The Jiuquan site was built in 1968, one thousand miles from Beijing in the Gobi Desert. It was an old site but due to its geographical location was ideal for the launch of both manned and unmanned orbital missions. Taiyuan Satellite Launch Center was primarily a test site that was ideally situated for the launch of polar-orbiting spacecraft. It was the newest of the Chinese space centers, and began operations in 1988.

Xichang had been designed to put geosynchronous satellites into orbit, hardware that would remain in place over specific regions of China. A network of geosynchronous stations would create a relay system, making telecommunications and wireless technology available to all of the vast nation. Begun in 1978 and completed six years later, Xichang was built in the heart of an area populated with small farms. The facility was inaugurated inauspiciously with the disastrous launch of a satellite whose third stage failed to ignite. Several years of successful launches followed until the powerful Long March 2E booster exploded on takeoff in 1995. The debris killed six farmers and injured twenty-three others who were going about their business five miles downrange. The following year, a Long March 3B crashed in a hill just a mile from the launch pad, killing six and injuring fifty-seven. As recently as one year ago a powerful new Star Dragon 5 exploded upon liftoff, killing twelve technicians and destroying the pad. Very few of the local citizens relocated. They made too much money selling food, clothes, and other goods to the men stationed at the space center.

The failure of the Star Dragon 5 was one reason Beijing had invited international participation in the creation of the hardware. The old boosters were based on Russian designs. They were brutish rockets that could lift heavy payloads but had little finesse and sophistication. A great deal of time and money had gone into the reconstruction of the base. It was important that the hardware function properly. It was just as important that the invited dignitaries see the start of a successful new era in Chinese space activities. One way that Beijing hoped to raise money for future endeavors was by using their rockets to boost foreign payloads into space.

They could not afford a failure.

Mike Rodgers was very much aware of that. He was also aware of the fact that over four hundred people were going to be in the launch area, including five Americans. He did not want to see any of them vaporized. For that matter, an explosion would not do him any good. He was well within the fallout zone if the plutonium power source were attacked.

Rodgers had taken a commercial flight from Beijing to the Xichang Airport. He managed to sleep during the three-hour-plus flight. Studying maps and white papers was a key part of mission preparation. So was being rested. Since he would be on the outside, with the data available on his laptop, he opted for sleep.

The airport was small but modern. Rodgers took a taxi to the nearby Satellite Hotel which, as the name suggested, had been built primarily for visitors to the space center. He rented a car at the hotel, a reservation that had been made through the prime minister's office. Foreigners were not generally permitted to drive through the security-conscious area. He tucked himself into the compact cherry-red Xiali Bullet, one of the new generation of Chinese cars intended for domestic and international sales. Its pickup reminded him of one of the rickshaws that wove in and out of the streets of Beijing. Slow to build, once it reached the required speed, it hummed along nicely. Not that it mattered. Though a new freeway was being built through the region, it was not yet completed. Most of the hour-long drive took place on dirt roads, which cars had to share with bicycles and horses as well as herds of sheep and cows. At one point Rodgers had to wait for nearly twenty minutes while a bus driver and a woman argued in the middle of the road. From what he could gather based on the position of their vehicles, the woman's scooter had tried to pass the bus and ended up in a ditch. Every now and then she slapped the hood of the bus angrily, which was a greater insult than if she had struck the man. It was not the driver himself who had offended her but his ability. That was the equivalent of insulting his manhood.

The conflict ended when the bus driver simply drove off, leaving the woman shouting and cursing at his thick black exhaust.

After clearing that impediment, Rodgers checked in with the marines. They had gone ahead on the shuttle bus operated by the space center. They had flown in earlier with other specialists from Beijing. Throughout the mission the marines were going to stay in touch via text alert.

These were similar to cell phone text messages. The difference was that they were transmitted via wristwatch, as a crawling document. The wearer spoke his or her message, a chip in the watch transcribed it to text, and it was sent to every other wristwatch receiver in the network. The DoD was working on a heads-up display for eyeglasses, which would also display graphics images visible only to the wearer. Tiny but powerful antennae in the hinges would allow the wearer to intercept wireless data sent between stations. Rodgers's firm was bidding on the contract to develop the lens technology. By connecting to an international number, Rodgers's cell phone would be able to receive all the messages. His capacity to send was limited to text messages or sending a single tone to each of them. The watches would vibrate, and they would call him on their own cell phones. It was not a secure means of communication, but it might be the only one available to them in an emergency.

For now, all Rodgers needed to know was that they had gotten to the complex. He sent a tone. They were to respond by pushing their watch stem once. The numbers one through four would show up on Rodgers's cell phone, depending upon who had received. All four responded.

Not long after that, Rodgers received a call from Hood. The former director of Op-Center explained to his former number two what had happened in Zhuhai. Rodgers was surprised. He was also concerned.

"Do we know if our prime suspect blew himself up or was blown up?" Rodgers asked.

"I just got off the phone with Stephen Viens," Hood told him. "He said a routine satellite sweep of the region picked up the blast. He's having the photo analyzed now, but it looked like the explosion may have started with a fire under the aircraft. There was a tanker on the field, and the plane had apparently just been refueled."

"When did it land?"

"NORAD told Viens it was on the ground less than twenty minutes," Hood told him.

Since the homeland attacks of 2001, NORAD had been linked to every air traffic control system in the United States and, through relays and hacks, to virtually every ATCS in the world. If a plane diverged from its reported flight path for more than ten seconds, the United States Air Force went on intercept alert. That meant fighters were scrambled at once if the aircraft were over American airspace. If they were over foreign airspace, the information was immediately relayed to domestic and allied intelligence services. Flags had not been raised by Chou Shin's flight. But there was still a radar record of the trip from Beijing to Zhuhai.

"Chou Shin lands, does not get off the plane, and dies in the explosion twenty minutes later," said Rodgers. "If it wasn't a setup, it sounds as if Tam Li was willing to seize the moment. Neither man could simply eliminate the other without alienating their supporters in Beijing."

"It doesn't make sense, though," Hood said. "There will be an investigation. Interviews with eyewitnesses. If this was an assassination, Beijing will find out."

"Yes, if this is *just* an assassination," Rodgers said. "Obviously, this was something the general thought he could get away with. Why?"

"Because he expects the political situation in Beijing to be changing soon?" Hood speculated.

"That would be my guess," Rodgers said. He stopped while a herd of cattle crossed a muddy stretch of road. "We may have been looking at the wrong guy as a potential Xichang bomber."

"Why would Tam Li attack a project that would give him more prestige?" Hood asked. "What does it do for him?"

"It creates a power vacuum by killing the prime minister and several other high-ranking bureaucrats," Rodgers suggested. "And an explosion here would not be traced to him. He would not even be a suspect."

"That doesn't seem like enough," Hood said. "Too many key figures are missing. The president and vice president, the defense minister. The people who Tam Li would have to remove if he were planning a coup."

"Maybe he is working for the defense minister," Rodgers suggested as the cows finished their crossing. Spitting mud and drawing curses from the farmer, the Xiali started up again.

"Le Kwan Po just spoke with the defense minister," Hood told him. "The prime minister does not think he is involved in a plot."

"Is that based on evidence or hope?" Rodgers asked.

"Instinct," Hood answered. "That is what he told me when I asked the same question."

"How have those instincts been so far?"

"Untested," Hood replied.

"Helluva time to start," Rodgers said. "So let's assume we have a rogue general looking to blow up his own rocket and create a relatively small hole in the government. What does he gain?"

The men were silent for a moment.

"We may be chasing our own tails here," Hood said.

"That would make me very happy," Rodgers said. "But there is still a chance that Chou Shin set a countdown in motion, and his death may not change that. Whatever allies he has in a war against Tam Li might go ahead with it. They may not even know he's dead."

"True."

"And there's something else," Rodgers said. "There are two reasons to trigger an explosive."

"One of them I know. What's the other?" Hood asked.

"As a distraction," Rodgers replied.

"Are you referring to the attack on Chou Shin's plane?"

"No," Rodgers told him. "I'm talking about the rocket. What if there is a plot to blow it up, but it's Tam Li's operation? Something to make Beijing focus its attention here while he does something else."

"Such as?"

"I'm not sure," Rodgers said. "General Tam Li is supposed to be here. He is in Zhuhai. Why?"

"That is his command post. He told Le Kwan Po he was getting set to fly over when Chou Shin arrived."

"So he won't be coming."

"No," Hood said.

"Why would Chou Shin go all the way to the airfield when he and Tam Li would have seen each other here?"

"Not to reconcile, I'm guessing," Hood said.

"A confrontation would be more likely. Maybe the Guoanbu found out something, and Chou was going to investigate."

"Chou would not have gone there personally unless he was pretty sure of what he was going to find," Hood said.

"That's right. The question is, what did he find out?"

"I can ask the prime minister to check when we reach the space complex," Hood said.

"No. That doesn't leave us a lot of time," Rodgers said.

"The good news is we only need to focus on the space complex," Hood said. "If Tam Li is planning a diversionary strike and we can stop that, whatever else he has in mind may not come to pass."

"The material I looked at with the marine leader was tactics from the Guoanbu playbook," Rodgers said. "We have their MO from past operations, including intel from the Taipei police on the nightclub hit. I have nothing here on the PLA's covert military actions. Getting anything useful from G2 or Op-Center would take more time than we have."

"We may not need any of that," Hood said. "Get your

people into position. I'll call you in about a half hour, after I've had a chance to speak with the prime minister."

"What have you got in mind?" Rodgers asked.

"A low-tech remedy that may be exactly the one we need," Hood replied.

FIFTY-ONE

Xichang, China
Thursday, 10:31 A.M.

The procession to the space complex consisted of seven cars. The only limousine was the one used by the prime minister and his daughter. Everyone else was put in a clean but inelegant military vehicle.

That was what had given Hood his idea for intercepting a potential bomber.

The space center was shaped like a Y. The caravan drove in through the stem of the Y, then turned west. They drove past the low-lying Communication Center, past the Tracking Station, to the Technical Center. That was where the vehicles stopped and let them out. The launch pad was situated four kilometers to the north. The rocket was clearly visible as the guests stepped out. It stood gleaming white against the silver and black girders of the gantry. Smoke plumed from the three stages, dissipating quickly against the pure blue sky. Heat rising from the field between them caused the rocket to ripple slightly, like a mirage.

Xichang did not have a public relations organization.

Security personnel in severe, dark blue uniforms took charge of the visitors. There was one guard to each car-load. Interpreters who had traveled with them from Beijing translated the guards' instructions. Anita had joined them from her father's car. The prime minister himself did not emerge as the groups moved toward the Technical Center.

"There is a basement beneath the facility," Anita said for the benefit of the English-speaking group. "We will be observing the launch from there."

"I need to see your father," Hood said, sidling over to her.

"He will be out in a moment," she said. The prime minister's daughter was wearing an official face and talking in a very official voice. Hood liked the woman better when she was slightly uncertain, pressing him for information.

"I'll wait for him," Hood said.

"I think he would rather you go with—"

"Listen to me," Hood said. He leaned closer. "You're concerned about appearances. I'm worried about his life."

That got her attention.

"His life?"

"I will wait for him here," Hood said, leaning away.

"Then I will have to wait with you, to translate," she said. "What do I do about the other English-speaking guests?"

"They know what they are here to see," Hood replied. "They will manage without you for a while."

Anita looked concerned as she went off to tell the others she would join them downstairs. She returned just as her father stepped from his car.

"Do you have new information?" she asked Hood.

"Some."

The prime minister walked to where Hood was waiting. He looked from Anita to Hood.

"We have confirmed the destruction of the aircraft," Le said through his daughter.

"So have we," Hood told him.

"But you have more," Le said.

"A question. Is there any reason the general might have for wanting—or rather *needing*—to stay in Zhuhai?" Hood asked.

"I asked the defense minister a similar question," Le admitted. "He said there is nothing unusual going on in that region."

"Do you trust the minister?"

"I have no reason to distrust him."

"Excuse me. Is that an endorsement or diplomacy?"

"It is my answer," Le replied.

"Let's try this, then," Hood said with a trace of impatience. "Who will appoint Chou Shin's replacement?"

"The president," Le answered. "I was just conferring with him on that very subject. There is nothing in the appointment that benefits Tam Li. His replacement will be a Communist, not an ally to Tam Li." Le glanced toward the rocket. "I am beginning to wonder if this is about nothing more than the rivalry between the two men. With Chou Shin gone, perhaps this facility is no longer in danger. Perhaps it never was." He looked back at Hood. "You do not share that sense?"

"No, sir," Hood said. "Allow me one more question. Are there any men from Tam Li's command on the base?"

"Why?" the prime minister asked. "Do you now suspect that *he* may be planning an attack?"

"General Rodgers and I were wondering if an attack here might serve as a diversion that benefits Tam Li somehow," Hood said. He used Rodgers's title to remind the prime minister that there was a military voice in his reasoning.

"What could Tam Li gain by that?" Le asked.

"We don't know. But he is sitting on top of a fat arsenal. And an attack on the rocket might be the trigger he needs to launch it."

"Again, for what reason?" Le asked.

"Ambition?" Hood asked. "I don't know the man. But

we think the explosion at the airfield occurred beneath Chou's jet, not on it. That could be a singular incident. Or it could be the start of something larger." He looked at Anita. "A purge of government leaders, perhaps. More than a few are here now."

The translator's slightly angry expression suddenly grew more concerned. She finished translating and looked at her father. His own features were still neutral. He was, above all, a good politician.

"The guards are drawn from different branches of the military and rotated every six months," Le said. "I will find out who may have come from the Zhuhai command."

"Thank you," Hood said.

Le excused himself and went back to his car. Anita and Hood remained behind.

"Your concern is for the rocket," she said.

"And our lives," Hood told her.

"Why don't you leave the complex? We can search for the general's personnel, if there are any."

"I don't like the idea of running," Hood said.

"So you are staying to be manly?" she asked. "Like James Bond?"

He could not tell if she were kidding or not. "I am doing my job," he replied.

She smiled. "That is a very responsible answer. It is also very Chinese."

So, apparently, is megalomania and murder, Hood wanted to tell her. He refrained. The woman had her own definition of the Chinese character. It was about industry and honor, very much a reflection of how she saw her father. He would let her have that. He suspected that only events would rewrite her definitions.

Le returned. His expression bore a touch of gravity it had not possessed before.

"A unit was recently rotated in from Zhuhai," Le said. "I have asked that those individuals be brought to the Command and Control Center. I am going to meet them there now."

"Where were they stationed?" Hood asked.

"Originally, they were checking passes at the front gate."

"Originally?" Hood asked.

"Three weeks ago they were relocated at the request of the general himself," Le said. "He said this rocket was important to his base. He wanted to make sure the boosters were being watched by people he had trained and whom he trusted."

"I would like to go with you," Hood said.

"No. I will let you know what I find out. You can wait in the Technical Center if you wish. I will contact you there."

"Sir, we have less than ninety minutes to launch—"

"All the more reason for me to get to the command center," the prime minister said as he turned and left.

Hood started after him. "Anita, please ask him to wait."

"My father has told you what he plans to do," Anita said.

"Yes, but I have experience in this area—"

"Not here," she replied. "You don't even speak the language."

"I can read expressions, body language." Hood stopped. He looked back at the woman as Le got in the car. "Dammit, everything—*anything*—might help."

"If my father wants help, he will ask for it."

"When?" Hood asked. "After the rocket is destroyed?"

"My father knows what he is doing," Anita said. "He is an able man."

"But not infallible," Hood snapped. "He let the entire situation with the general and Chou Shin get away from him—"

"Mr. Hood, we are quite finished."

"No! You've stopped listening, which is not the same thing. The stakes are high here, Anita! This is not a time for ego."

"For once I agree with you, Mr. Hood. He told you where to wait, and I suggest you go there. Now, please excuse me. I, too, have a job to do." The woman strode toward the Technical Center.

Hood raised his hands in exasperation. But anger was not going to help, and he lowered them. He remained beside the wide asphalt road that ran through the complex. The cars were still parked by the side of the building. A guard at the door of the center watched Hood but did not move from his post.

The rising sun was hot, and Hood was perspiring. Only the slightest breeze moved across the field. Hood pulled his cell phone from the loop on his belt. He wanted to call Rodgers and tell him what he had learned about a squad from Zhuhai. At least he knew where the general's team had been. It would allow the marines to narrow their patrol zone.

Unfortunately, the communications at the complex interfered with the signal. He would have to find some other way to get this information to Rodgers.

Quickly.

FIFTY-TWO

Zhuhai, China
Thursday, 10:49 A.M.

Before leaving his post, one of the soldiers in the booster security detail sent an E-mail message to Zhuhai. It read:

Team recalled by PM.

It was not the kind of message the general wanted to receive. There was slightly more than an hour until launch. If the device he had planted were discovered and the rocket took off safely, the rationale for what he was planning to do next would evaporate. Without the explosion, Tam Li could never convince the surviving president that Taiwan had used the disaster—perhaps even caused it—to press a military advantage, and only the quick action of the general had thwarted a major strike against targets along China's eastern coastline.

It was dramatic action that would merit the general's appointment as the new minister of defense, or perhaps even as the prime minister. Since it was no longer necessary to attach suspicion to the late Chou Shin, Tam Li could concentrate on the purely military aspects of the action.

As long as the rocket blows up. Without that, he had nothing.

Tam Li sat alone in his office, staring out the window and thinking. He was not a man prone to displays of anger or frustration. He preferred to use his energies more effectively. Every problem had at least one solution, often more. It was simply a matter of finding the right one. The general had spoken with the white team officers when they came in from extinguishing the fire. They were loyal soldiers who understood why he had destroyed the aircraft. They were also well-paid members of Tam Li's black market gang. Explaining to Beijing what had happened on the airfield would not be a problem. Chou Shin's explosives-laden jet had blown up. The pulling of his rocket team was a greater concern, especially if the prime minister suspected an attack. A new security crew might find what had been done to the rocket.

The irony was that when they were called in, the Xichang team had been getting set to pull back and leave the space complex. They did not want to be within fifty miles of the facility when the plutonium core exploded. Tam Li could not count on them remaining silent as the countdown progressed. If they were still in the complex, chances were good they would die.

And then it occurred to him, a way to fix this situation. Tam Li would use the hide-in-plain-sight scenario.

He pressed the intercom on his telephone.

"Yes, General?"

"Get me the Xichang space center," he said. "I want to speak with the prime minister at once."

"Yes, sir."

Tam Li would tell the prime minister why he had assigned those men to the boosters, and why he must let them finish their job.

It was important, he would say, to protect them from the attack Chou Shin had been planning.

FIFTY-THREE

Xichang, China
Thursday, 11:00 A.M.

The voice on the loudspeaker was confident and proud.
"Launch minus sixty!"

Hood did not need a translator to know what he was
saying. The digital countdown clock on the wall had just
slipped under an hour. Not that he had a translator. Anita
had gone downstairs with the rest of the observers. Hood
had gone into the reception area as Le had suggested.
There was a guard seated behind a gunmetal desk. There
was no one else in the room. Hood had indicated to her that
he wanted to use the phone, but she shook her head. When
he tried to use it anyway, she rose and called someone's
name. The other guard entered. Hood backed off.

The launchpad was too far away, or he would have run
over and attempted to find the marines himself. He tried
his cell phone again. Then again. As the seconds slipped
away, the only option Hood seemed to have was getting a
ride to the gate to try to find Mike somewhere around the

perimeter. But even if he succeeded, that left very little time to actually locate a potential problem.

"Hood."

Hood turned to the desk. The woman was addressing him. She held the telephone toward him. Perhaps Rodgers had found him.

"Yes?" Hood said as he snatched the phone.

"Sir, this is Dr. Yuen, a fuel specialist on this project," he said. "I am translating for the prime minister. He says that he spoke with the general and is satisfied with the conversation."

"He is? What about the individuals he spoke with?"

Hood waited while the scientist translated. Either Tam Li was very convincing, or the prime minister was extremely gullible. In any case, there was one way to know for certain.

"The prime minister has allowed them to return to their duties."

"Ask him if he is sending men with them," Hood said. This was insane. The guy they were investigating vouches for himself, and Le accepts that?

Hood waited again.

"Mr. Hood, the prime minister is coming to the Technical Center," Dr. Yuen informed him. "He will be there in five minutes. He said he will talk to you there."

"Right," Hood said. "More time wasted."

"Sir, we invented rockets," the scientist said. "We were going through these trials centuries before your ancestors were born."

Hood did not respond. Built into that statement was the prerogative to venture and to fail. There was no way to argue with that kind of thinking.

Hood hung up. He needed to get in touch with Rodgers now. He smiled at the guard and reached for the keypad. The guard laid a hand across it.

"Le Kwan Po," Hood said with authority.

The woman replied with equal authority. She rose and did not remove her hand. She gestured toward a seat and then toward the stairs leading to the bunker. Obviously, those were the only options Hood had.

Hood held up an index finger. "One call. One. Please."

The guard shook her head and, pointing, repeated the options. Hood was about to pull her hand from the phone.

"Who do you wish to call?"

Hood turned at the familiar voice. Anita was standing at the top of the bunker staircase.

"I need to talk to an associate," Hood said. "Please."

"Apparently, my father was right."

"Excuse me?"

"He was afraid his decision might bother you," she said.

Hood walked toward her. "He was right about that, yes. I am not so sure he is right about the rest. I need to talk to someone for just a moment," Hood said calmly, evenly.

"Mr. Hood, I do not wish to be unreasonable, but we are here to witness a launch—"

"And I pray that is what I see," Hood told her. "I need to ask an associate just one question, Anita. We are desperately short of time, and you have nothing to lose. I promise, this will be brief."

Anita regarded him for a moment. "All right," she replied, then said something to the guard. The uniformed woman removed her hand from the keypad. She glared at Hood as she sat back down.

"One brief call," Anita cautioned him.

"Thank you," Hood said to them both.

He get an operator and gave him the number of Rodgers's cell phone. Because this phone was a land line, and because Rodgers was outside the base, Hood hoped the call would get through the satellite dish interference.

It did not. After a long, discouraging silence, Hood disconnected the call and stood there.

"Is there no answer?" Anita asked.

"No."

"I'm sorry," she said. "Let's go downstairs now—"

"Not yet," Hood said quickly. He punched in a second number. "I need to try again."

Anita was clearly unhappy, but she did not protest. Not with words, at least. Her expression said it all.

This time he did not call Mike Rodgers. He called someone else he hoped could help him.

FIFTY-FOUR

Washington, D.C.
Wednesday, 11:11 P.M.

Intelligence work and patience have a long history together. Whether it was breaking codes in World War II or reconnaissance against the Persians by the warriors of Sparta before the Battle of Thermopylae in 480 B.C., this was not work that could be rushed.

Bob Herbert weathered patience impatiently. That was both a strength and a curse. He looked for fresh leads while he waited for old searches to bring results. He had a problem, though, when those new leads took him nowhere. When every road he studied was a dead end. When there was simply not enough information to go off road, or enough lift to hoist him aloft so he could study a bigger picture.

It was then that Herbert felt trapped. And when he felt trapped, Bob Herbert kept hurling himself at the problem until his head hurt, until his heart raced, until he wanted to scream. Until he sat in his chair and wept from frustration and blamed his wheelchair and, by extension, the fact that the U.S. embassy had been bombed in Beirut and he was there at all. But most of all he blamed himself for choosing this life instead of opening a tavern in Mississippi and playing guitar on open-mike night and never worrying about anything that happened beyond the confines of the small Southern town where the air was muggy and close, and you were safe because absolutely no one came there who did not belong there.

Herbert had always imagined he would go back to Philadelphia, Mississippi, when he retired. He wished he could go now, but to do so meant to acknowledge defeat. Under those conditions his retirement would be a trap and not a release.

The intelligence chief sat behind his desk at Op-Center. He did not want to go home and be useless. It was better to stay here with the night crew and at least have the potential to do something. But that still did not make him feel like the hub of a wheel around which activity turned. He was helpless and he was desperate, and not just to prevent a possible explosion in Xichang. Motion defined him. Without it, he had no idea who or what he was.

It was worse because Rodgers and Hood were not there. They were always pitching ideas. Even if Rodgers was knocking them foul, he was still swinging the bat. It was action.

There had been virtually none of that since Viens had come to his office the day before. Herbert had asked for more information about the blips on the Pacific Rim. Unfortunately, when the photo recon officer compared current satellite images to past photographs, nothing stood out. The process was called ODA: overlay dissonance analysis. It was similar to what astronomers did when they compared celestial photographs from different nights. If something were out of place in the heavens—such as an asteroid approaching the earth—ODA let them know it. The process was a little more complex with intelligence work. Past military maneuvers were compared to current maneuvers, along with the responses of surrounding nations. Computers sounded an alarm if there were anything out of the ordinary. So far, the Pacific Rim activity had not caused anything like that. The NRO had picked up the explosion on the Zhuhai airstrip, and that obviously had a place in the overall picture. But no one knew how or why or when. Certainly no one knew whether it was somehow related to the launch.

However many times Herbert reviewed the existing data about troop movements or the explosions in Charleston, Durban, and Taipei, he could not extrapolate what might happen with the rocket. He did not see how they related.

And then Paul Hood called.

"Bob, I'm glad you're there," Hood said urgently. "I assume Mike has a way of staying in touch with his people?"

"By text alert," Herbert said. "They are all wearing—"

"I don't need to know that," Hood interrupted. "The uplinks here are messing with the cell phones. Can you get him a message?"

"Yes," Herbert replied. Because it was text rather than more sophisticated audio, the watches worked on a lower frequency that would not be affected by satellite communications.

"Tell him that Tam Li had a crew working on booster security."

"The fox watching the chickens?"

"Possibly. The team said they were returning to their posts," Hood went on. "If they do, great. If they try to leave the complex, we'll know why. Mike has got to stop them, make them talk."

"I'll tell him," Herbert said. "Do you have a description of the men?"

"No. I didn't meet with them."

"Do they speak English?"

"Doubtful," Hood said. "Mike can have them draw a diagram. In blood, if they have to."

"Got it," Herbert replied.

Hood clicked off, and Herbert swung over to his computer monitor. The thin, flat screen was attached to a boom on the left armrest of his wheelchair. Herbert accessed Rodgers's text address and quickly drafted a message. He then reduced it to as few words as possible.

Tam Li detail had access to boosters. May flee before ignition. Stop them and assess.

As Herbert typed, ideas began to form. A direction had been indicated. Tam Li blowing up the rocket—his own rocket, effectively—to solidify opposition to Chou Shin was a reason, but not strong enough. Besides, with the intelligence director dead, there would be no reason to continue that operation. However, there was a more compelling notion: it could be blamed on Taiwan as a counterstrike to the attack on their city. And who better to reply to such an attack than Tam Li, who was sitting across the strait with an army?

The scenario quickly acquired weight and detail. All it had taken was a phone call from someone with whom he had enjoyed an often hostile but very symbiotic relationship.

That was all.

But that was a lot.

FIFTY-FIVE

Xichang, China
Thursday, 11:20 A.M.

Mike Rodgers was sitting in his rental car in a field of high grasses roughly a quarter mile from the front gate of the space complex. The dark, asphalt road was to his left. It was a two-lane road that had simply been asphalted through the plain on a straight line from point A to point B. Cynically, Rodgers did not imagine that any environmental studies had been done to protect whatever wildlife may have lived upon, under, or in its way. There were several other cars parked in this area, along with motorbikes and even a horse. Obviously, a few hardy space buffs knew about the launch and were eager to witness it.

The amber grasses came nearly to the side window of the small car. They caused Rodgers's eyes to itch. He had taken off his sunglasses to rub them. He did not bother to put them back on. In a way, that was helpful. Rubbing his eyes and squinting into the bright daylight made it seem as though he had roused himself from a distant bed to get here in time for the launch. It added to the look of casual inattentiveness a spy tried to achieve. He slumped in his seat to enhance the sense of insouciance, just in case security guards were watching from inside the complex or from a quartet of helicopters that circled the perimeter of the space center. They had gone up at around the one-hour mark, probably to keep unauthorized planes from entering the Xichang airspace.

Rodgers reached for a bottle sitting beside him. It was a Chinese concession to American sensibilities, the sudden cultural need to suckle on an ever-present water bottle. Rodgers had bought it at the airport, not knowing how hot it might get out here. Unlike bottles in the United States, this one was made of glass. Someone somewhere in China probably had a lucrative recycling contract. For all Rodgers knew, the same guys who made the new bottles filled them with tap water. It tasted like it.

The text-message-capable cell phone sat beside him, plugged into the dashboard. Rodgers watched it for messages from his team.

It is not really your team, the former general reminded himself. They were on loan. He was out of the military business, downsized from the spy game. *Sure you are,* he thought. *That is why you are in the middle of a field in China waiting to hear from marines who are conducting emergency recon on a PLA rocket.* The irony was, all of that no longer defined a spy. It accurately described private enterprise in twenty-first century Asia.

Rodgers did not want to hear from the marines. He wanted everything to go as planned, and he was tired of his old life. It was not just the constant shuttling from one place to another but the sense of fighting a holding action instead of moving toward victory. For every overzealous general or corrupt politician he stopped, there was always another and another to fill his iron boots.

That was when his phone beeped. He looked down. There was a message. Rodgers input his code to retrieve it.

He sat up straight and was instantly in action mode. He glanced outside for just a moment, immediately reacquainting himself with the surroundings. That gave his brain a chance to process the details. Years of experience had made his subconscious mind a very powerful tool.

The message was not from the marines. It was from Bob Herbert. Rodgers read it quickly, then again. If he understood it correctly, some of Tam Li's people had been inside with access to the boosters. He was supposed to stop them if they tried to leave, find out what they knew.

Rodgers did not waste time responding, asking for further details. Herbert was good about packing everything he knew into small communiqués. The former general assumed the command center simply did not delay the launch because Tam Li's plan might be time sensitive.

Rodgers pulled his sunglasses on and looked toward the main gate. He knew from having studied the maps that even if the men exited one of the other gates, this was the only road from the complex. And chances were good that if anyone did come this way, it would be them. Though vehicles were continuing to arrive now and then, none was leaving the space center. Everyone who was inside either had a job to do or was watching the liftoff. He knew from experience that seeing a launch, any launch, was a thrill that did not get old.

Which was why the dark green vehicle immediately grabbed his attention. It looked like a van or minivan, and it disappeared into a small dip in the road about one mile away. When it reemerged, Rodgers could tell it was in a hurry. He looked to his left. The road was too wide to block, even if he parked sideways. The van would just swerve around him. If this were his quarry, Rodgers would have to find some other way of delaying them.

He had about thirty seconds before the van reached him. The retired general took a few of those moments to type a message into his cell phone. He considered his options as he typed. There were only two. One was to ram the oncoming van. Even though the compact might not actually stop the men, it would slow them. But if these were not Tam Li's men and Rodgers totaled his car—and possibly himself—he would have trouble mounting a second assault.

That left the chancier second plan. Rodgers finished the message but did not send it. He switched on the ignition and turned the car around so it was facing away from the complex. As he did, he removed his cell phone jack from the dashboard. He replaced the lighter, pushing it in hard. Then he uncapped the water bottle, pulled his handkerchief from his pocket, and stuffed it into the neck. He left a lot of fabric on top. He needed a big flame. The lighter popped out, and he touched it to the end of the handkerchief. It flared quickly. Leaving the car, Rodgers hurried through the high grass to the middle of the road. The speeding van was just seconds away. Rodgers held the flaming bottle high in his right hand, Mr. Statue of Liberty prepared to play a high stakes, high noon game of chicken with a gang of Chinese soldiers.

It was inelegant, but it felt right. The "Molotov cocktail" would not do much, but it did what he needed it to do: it got the attention of the men inside. He could see their surprised, worried faces as the van approached.

But they did not stop. They did not veer. They sped up. They intended to run him down before he could attack.

Rodgers hurled his little missile at the onrushing vehicle. He needed it to do just one thing, and it did. The flaming bottle hit the windshield hard, transforming it into a fragile webwork of glass. The concussion also extinguished the burning handkerchief with its own water. The men must have felt very lucky. The vehicle did not stop. As Rodgers jumped back toward the grasses, he could see someone in the passenger's seat trying to push the shattered glass outward.

He had learned what he needed to know. These soldiers

wanted to get away from the complex as quickly as possible.

Rodgers got back in his car and floored the gas pedal. Dirt and grass spat from the tires as he ripped his way to the road. Now he intended to catch the bastards and force them to stop.

As he gave chase, Rodgers hit Reply/cc to send the message he had typed. The same text was simultaneously sent to the marine team leader:

IDs confirmed. Am in pursuit. Boosters likely target.

FIFTY-SIX

Xichang, China
Thursday, 11:33 A.M.

Prime Minister Le Kwan Po felt anxious as he left the car and entered the Technical Center. On the short drive from the command center he had received word from the security office that one of the helicopters circling the complex spotted what appeared to be a chase along the main road from the complex. Military police from the space center had been dispatched on motorcycles, and the information had been radioed ahead to Xichang City. Several constables were driving out to intercept the two vehicles.

A call to the main gate revealed that no one had left by that route. The other gates were card-activated, with patrols on the inside but no checkpoints. Security cameras revealed that a dark green van had left nine minutes earlier. The card used for egress was a temporary pass issued to one of the security teams.

The unit Le Kwan Po had just spoken with.

The men reporting to General Tam Li.

The prime minister called the command center. The countdown was finally put on hold—a humiliating delay for the vaunted launch—and technicians were en route to the boosters to search for explosives. What worried Le was whether an explosive had been placed somewhere that would detonate regardless of the launch status. The result would be the same, a massive rain of radioactive dust across the complex.

The first thing Le had to do was find out what those renegade soldiers knew. The second thing was to get his daughter out of here. That was why he had not sent a helicopter to chase the soldiers. If they were used for anything, it would be an evacuation.

Paul Hood and Anita were waiting in the upstairs lobby of the Technical Center. Anita was conversing quietly but angrily with Hood, who was pacing in front of the security desk. Upon Le's arrival, his daughter stared at him for a long moment. She did not brighten as she typically did when he entered a room. No doubt she was surprised by the look of concern on his normally impassive face.

She did not ask what was wrong. She knew he would tell her when he was ready. He regarded Hood, who had stopped pacing.

"The soldiers I interviewed have fled," Le told Hood through Anita. "Someone is chasing them toward Xichang City. Would that be one of your associates?"

"Most likely," Hood replied.

"Is he equipped to stop them?"

"If you're asking whether he is armed, I do not believe so," Hood replied.

"The pursuit has been joined by agents from both the space center and the city," the prime minister informed him. "But that may not help us."

"Not enough time?" Hood asked.

"Scientists are on the way to the boosters. They know

the rocket, but they may not be able to find and defuse explosives."

Le noticed his daughter start when he said that. He was sorry she had to be here. He would get her out as soon as possible.

"I may be able to help," Hood told him.

"Please," Le said. He did not ask how. He did not at this moment care. His daughter would have to be evacuated in just a few minutes. There was not a lot of time to talk.

Hood made a call and spoke for several seconds. Anita discreetly translated his end of the conversation. Le's daughter was a thorough professional again. It was a sad irony that he had to be so frightened for her to be so proud of her. Like her mother, she was quite a woman.

Hood was talking to someone named Bob. He needed to meet the "team" as soon as possible. While Hood was still on the telephone, he turned to Le.

"I need a landmark by the boosters," Hood said.

Le shook his head helplessly.

"Sir?" said the guard.

"Go ahead," Le told her.

"There is a large holding clamp on the northeast corner of the pad," she said. "I have been there. It is painted red, and it is very easy to see."

The prime minister nodded once. Anita translated for Hood. The American finished his conversation, hung up, then turned to Le.

"I am going to meet some people there, people who have been briefed by Mike Rodgers," Hood said. "I will meet them alone."

There was no time to debate this. Le nodded. He indicated for Anita to go with him to his car and explain to the driver.

"You leave him and come back here immediately," her father said.

"I will," she promised.

When Anita and Hood were gone, the prime minister went to the telephone. He asked the guard to excuse him. The young woman rose, bowed, and stepped outside. The prime minister did not want her to know that he intended to evacuate his daughter. This girl was also someone's daughter, and he intended to stay with her. But Anita was neither a soldier nor a politician. She would be ferried to safety.

The space center operator connected Le with the director of security. He told the former PLA officer that he wanted to know as soon as Hood and his personnel had reached the launch pad. Then he wanted one of the helicopters flown to the Technical Center and placed at his disposal.

"I am sorry, sir, but we cannot do that."

"What are you talking about? This is the prime min—"

"I know who you are, sir," the director interrupted. "But we will be using the helicopters ourselves."

"For what?" Le demanded.

"To evacuate, once we have eliminated the American and any of his allies for General Tam Li."

FIFTY-SEVEN

Xichang, China
Thursday, 11:40 A.M.

The only thing going faster than the van was Mike Rodgers's mind. He needed to figure out a way to slow the soldiers' flight.

At least the broken window was keeping them within range. It could not be easy to see through the cracked glass, and diamondlike particles were shooting every which way around the van. Pieces were certainly flying at the driver as well. Part of that was likely being caused by the passenger, who was trying to kick it out. Every few seconds Rodgers could see large slabs of fractured windshield tumble onto the hood and over the side.

His attack had hurt them, but it had not stopped them. He needed to do something else. He thought about calling Bob Herbert and asking for a missile strike on the road ahead, something from Taiwan, South Korea, or Submarine Group 7 based in Yokosuka, Japan. He dismissed that idea as provocative, and not just to the PLA. Tam Li would see it coming. They might inadvertently give him an excuse to do whatever he was planning to do. It would be a shame to save the rocket and lose the war. Besides, he did not know if such a strike could be launched before the van reached Xichang City. Rodgers could also ask Herbert for a satellite look at the road ahead. There might be someplace where he could cut through the grasses and shave time from the run.

And then fate gave him a hand.

One of the smaller sections of glass and part of the windshield frame pinwheeled around the driver's side and dropped under the van. As the van rolled over the glass and metal, the rear left tire blew, sending the vehicle into a swerving forward slide. The flapping shards of the tire dropped away, and the bare rim spat sparks in all directions. The driver was able to regain control of the vehicle, but he could not maintain his speed.

Rodgers closed the gap quickly. Conscious of the fact that these men could have firearms, he remained directly behind them. Eventually they would have to stop and either commandeer his car to complete their getaway or let him know what had been done to the rocket. If they attacked, Rodgers would run the nearest man down and try to get his weapon. It was not an ideal plan, but it was something. Besides, they were less than three miles from the space center. If the rocket blew up, they were well within the red zone for radiation poisoning.

The van slowed, and Rodgers slowed with it. He did not want to be right on top of it. That would not leave him with any room to maneuver. As he drew to within two car lengths, he heard sounds coming from behind. Rodgers glanced in his rearview mirror as three men on motorcycles whipped into view. They were all wearing uniforms. From his reading, he recognized them as Xichang space center security. What he did not know was whose side they were on.

If they were the enemy, he was in a lot of trouble. He

would have to move around the van and use them as a shield while he tried to get away.

Rodgers's phone beeped. It was the marine team leader sending him a text message.

> Security team en route to help you. Need bomb location. We expect armed resistance.

Tam Li must have additional allies at the complex, men who no doubt had an exit strategy or else were willing to die for their commander. That suggested something new to Rodgers. People did not surrender their lives simply to help a man gain power. They died to support an idea. Tam Li must have a vision for China that appealed to these men and probably to others like them. Usually, the vision of military men resulted in death on a staggering scale.

The van struggled for another quarter of a mile or so before stopping. Rodgers stopped behind it, and the men on the motorcycles stopped in a row behind him. Obviously, these men had not been briefed. One of them was on the radio. The other two drew firearms from their holsters. They were hunkered low behind their handlebars as they waited for instructions.

There was no time for this. Rodgers opened the door but did not immediately get out. He waited to make sure, first, that the security men did not fire. They did not. Slowly, he swung his legs from the car and emerged with his hands up, his back to the security team. He was watching the van from behind his open door. He could see a face in the side mirror. What he needed to do was get from his car to the other car and beat that face until it gave him the information he needed. At least now there was someone who could translate for him.

Rodgers lowered his hands and turned. He indicated, by gestures, that he was going to the other car.

The security guard who had been on the radio said something. One of the other guards fired a round. Rodgers dropped to the road. The other rear tire exploded with a loud wheeze. The guard said something else. Translated, it probably meant, *"Now they are definitely not going anywhere."*

They also did not return fire. Perhaps they were waiting for Rodgers or the guards to make themselves better targets. The soldiers probably did not want to damage the car or motorcycles.

Suddenly there were new sounds, a low whine from the direction of the city. Through the noontime haze Rodgers saw several police cars approaching, their top lights flashing.

Now the men in the van pointed automatic weapons out three windows and opened fire. Rodgers jumped back into the car, which was still running. He left the driver's side door open and threw open the passenger's side door to give the security guards a little added protection. The guards returned fire as they moved behind the open doors, driving the soldiers back into the van. There were two guards on the passenger's side and one on the driver's side.

This was not going to get them the information they needed.

Lying with his feet on the passenger's side, Rodgers swung back behind the wheel. He sat very low and put the car in drive, steering it slowly toward the van, the guards firing around the sides of the open door, the pops of each round nearly drowned by the clang of the bullets striking metal. When the rental car touched the rear bumper of the van, Rodgers asked to borrow one of the guns. The innermost guard on the driver's side was not at a good angle to hit the van. He gladly surrendered his weapon. Rodgers fired a burst through his own windshield to smash it, then sat back and pushed the window out with his foot. Tucking the gun into his belt, he climbed through it onto the hood of the car, and from there to the roof of the van. He moved quietly, on his knuckles and the balls of his feet. He stopped above the cab. He knew that if he fired through the roof he might kill one or more of the men. He also knew that the survivors would fire back. Instead, he motioned for the security guard on the driver's side to stop firing. Drawing his gun, Rodgers crouched on the edge of the driver's side but facing the passenger's side. He waited until the driver poked his hand out to return fire. Then he jumped down, landing on his feet and facing the driver. That was only one gunman he had to worry about. The others would not fire for fear of hitting the man at the wheel.

Rodgers slammed the man's extended arm against the side of the car and pointed his automatic at the man's head.

"Drop it!"

The soldier probably had no idea what Rodgers was saying. But he released the weapon, and the others ceased firing. Perhaps they were looking to get a shot at Rodgers. Fortunately, the side of the van afforded him a slight degree of cover.

The security guards shouted something. Rodgers heard a series of thumps as the other weapons fell. He edged forward toward the window. He did not release the man's arm but twisted it, holding the palm. The move was known as a *kodogash*. The pain in the victim's wrist guaranteed that he would move where Rodgers wanted him to go. And right now, Rodgers wanted him to remain a shield.

Rodgers looked into the window. The men had their hands raised defensively. There were no weapons. He used the gun to motion for the men on the passenger's side to get out. They did, arms lifted higher now. The security guards moved from behind the doors of Rodgers's car. The former general released the driver and gestured for him to get out the other side. The frightened man scooted out just as the police arrived. Rodgers tucked the gun back into his belt and walked toward the back of the van. He went through a pile of papers on the passenger's seat of his car. He pulled out a set of blueprints and grabbed his cell phone. He opened the large document on the hood of the car and motioned for the security guards to bring one of the men over. The man was pulled roughly toward the red Xiali.

Rodgers pointed at the diagram. "Boom!" he shouted, throwing his fingers outward to simulate a blast. Then he ran a hand palm-up over the blueprint. "That's universal for 'Tell me what the hell I want to know, or I'll slap you silly.'"

The security guard obviously understood. He said something to his captive, who muttered something back and pointed a trembling finger at the diagram.

"Shit," Rodgers said and got on his phone.

FIFTY-EIGHT

Xichang, China
Thursday, 11:49 A.M.

Hood reached the holding clamp before the marines arrived. The clamp was one of two huge, inverted L-shaped structures that held the rocket in place as the boosters fired. Ignition typically occurred four to six seconds before liftoff. When the two powerful engines had built to maximum thrust, the clamps were drawn back so the rocket could lift off. The clamps were about the size of a full-sized semi, bent at the rig and slung over flanges on the bottom of the boosters. In front of him were stacked pipes that carried coolant to the launchpad. They were heavily insulated with a ceramic thermal coating to keep the contents from boiling and exploding during the launch. To the left was an equipment rack the size of a cottage. It was set well back from the raised launchpad and contained various monitors, cameras, and other recording devices. There were also several emergency generators there, used to keep the rocket functioning in case of a power failure during the postignition moments of the countdown. That was not a time when mission control wanted to have a dead, flaming rocket on their hands.

The entire area was protected by a massive blast shield. That would keep the equipment box and generators from being immolated during launch, but it would not protect a person from the heat or smoke it generated.

The marines showed up about a minute later. They were dressed in lab coats and coming from several different directions. A moment after that, the car that had brought Hood returned. Hood was shocked to see Anita get out. She was waving to him and shouting.

"More of Tam Li's men are coming!" she cried. "My father just warned us about it—"

As she spoke, the helicopters that had been circling the perimeter converged overhead.

"Get away!" Hood yelled, motioning her back. "We'll deal with this!"

Anita hesitated.

"Go!" he shouted. This was something else he did not need to worry about. Not now.

Anita got back in the car, but she did not leave. The driver pulled up beside the large equipment bay.

Hood looked back at the marines. He pointed up and shouted, "Bad guys!"

The marine leader nodded and directed his people to stay back, under cover. They took up positions behind large wheels that controlled the flow of coolant to the rocket. A system of hoses was designed to keep the booster and its mechanisms from being affected by the intense heat of ignition. The external hoses were released at launch. The remaining liquid raced through the rocket, turning to steam and being vented as the rocket rose.

Hood crouched beside the clamp as the marine leader continued running toward him. A slight overhang of metal from the clamp afforded Hood some protection overhead. Huge fuel lines stacked along the pad protected him in front. Fortunately, the helicopter could not come much lower. Between the pipes and the transformer there was not enough room to accommodate the rotor radius.

As he waited for the marine to move confidently along the coolant pipes, Hood felt a flash of anger—at himself. This was not the trade Hood was supposed to be practicing. This was not like a natural disaster or terrorist attack where bystanders pitched in. Hood had put himself in this position. Twice before he had been in situations like this, once in the Middle East where an Op-Center team was missing, and once when he rescued his daughter from UN hostage-takers. In both cases he had strong personal reasons for being there. Not now. He was a bureaucrat, not a soldier. He should be back at the White House drinking coffee in an air-conditioned office with CNN reporting on what other crazy damn souls were doing.

This was stupid. Worse than that, it was irresponsible. His presence could be a burden to the process, a distraction to the marines. It had already drawn Anita here, risking her life.

The marine arrived, ready to work.

Kick yourself later, Hood told himself. Right or wrong, he was here in the thick of this.

"Do you have weapons?" Hood asked.

"Yes, sir," the marine said as he threw off his lab coat. He pulled an M-9 semiautomatic from a holster under his left armpit. "It doesn't have the kind of reach they've got up there. We need them a lot closer before it'll do any damage. But, sir, we have worse problems."

"How can it be worse?"

"I just heard from General Rodgers. The bomb is in here, sir." The marine rapped his knuckles on the clamp.

Hood swore.

"Exactly, sir," the marine said.

Bullets pinged above them. The marine pushed Hood down slightly. Hood felt his age under the kid's firm hands.

"Does Rodgers know anything else?" Hood asked.

"Nothing helpful," the marine went on. "According to what the general gleaned from his prisoner—and this makes sense—the explosive has a double-jeopardy trigger. It blows either when the clamp lifts or when the timer hits zero. If the bomb detonates, the clamp will most likely be destroyed, the rocket will fall over, and the fuel will be ignited by the fire from the bomb."

"Same result."

"Yes, sir.'

"In nine minutes?" Hood said, glancing at his watch.

"My timer gives us seven, sir," the young man replied with unflappable Marine-bred directness. "The problem is, sir, even if we had the tools, I do not know that we can get to the device in time. Cutting through the clamp will take longer than we have. General Rodgers said he is standing by to help, as are Chinese security forces. Unfortunately, the men with the guns are all on Tam Li's side."

"Of course they are," Hood said bitterly.

They built the goddamn bomb into the clamp, Hood thought. It was smart and devious and well-planned.

Gunfire chattered from the helicopters. The gunmen were not at a good angle to hit Hood or the marine. In addition to the overhang, the gantry and various pipes impeded their view. He found himself wondering which would be the better way to die: shot or incinerated. There was something surreal about the calm with which he asked himself that question.

"Cutting through them," Hood muttered, repeating what the marine had said.

"Sir?"

Hood glanced behind him. The rocket loomed, the boosters almost overhead. Each opening was the diameter of a good-sized swimming pool. "What if we could actually do that?"

"How, sir?"

"I watched all the Gemini and Apollo missions as a kid. Sometimes those rockets would flame and not take off. What if we did that?"

"Turn on the boosters and melt our way through?"

"Right. We can ignite the thrusters without lifting the clamps, give them a good frying, then shut the rocket down."

"If we weaken them, the rocket would fall over anyway," the marine pointed out.

"That in itself probably would not cause the plutonium cell to be destroyed," Hood suggested.

"True. And the heat might be enough to slag the bomb," the Marine said.

"That's what I am hoping," Hood said.

"Sir, it is a chance."

"Alert General Rodgers and have him pass that along to the launch crew," Hood said. "Then help me figure a way to get us out of here."

The marine input the text message to Rodgers. He was poised and focused as bullets chewed at the concrete several feet away, spitting splinters at the two men. He was an inspiration to Hood, who was squatting to the man's left, slightly behind him. Hood had not noticed until now that the marine had positioned himself almost directly between the helicopter and Hood.

"General Rodgers is phoning the information to one of the English-speaking scientists here," the marine said.

Hood nodded. His legs were beginning to cramp, but he dared not move. Not until he had to. He looked to his right at Anita's car, which was still near the heavily reinforced equipment shed about three hundred yards behind them. He could not understand why she was just sitting there. He waved for her to go. The windows were darkly tinted, and he could not tell whether she had seen him.

The marine's wristwatch flashed. He read the incoming message.

"The Chinese agree with the plan and are undertaking an expedited countdown," the young man said.

"Which means we have to get the hell out of here," Hood said.

"Affirmative, sir. They're lighting them up in three minutes."

Hood was looking ahead, trying to figure out how to get from their position to anywhere else. There was nothing that did not cross exposed spaces. The choppers were moving lower and converging. Their shots were coming at a different angle but still falling short of the spot below the clamp.

"Do you think they know what mission control is planning?" the marine asked.

"Doubtful. They would have been cut from the comm loop as soon as they showed their hand."

Either way, it was not good for Hood, his partner, or Anita. In two minutes they would be under cryogenic propellant that was fired to a temperature of five thousand degrees.

Hood was scared now. He was aware of each breath, every heartbeat, all the perspiration that was running from his temples and armpits. He wanted it all to continue. He did not want this complex symphony of the taken-for-granted to end.

"Thoughts?" Hood asked.

"Only one, sir. The car."

"Forget it. I am not going to ask the prime minister's daughter to drive through the gunfire—"

"I've just watched the vehicle take multiple hits, sir," the marine told him. "I think it's armored."

Son of a bitch. Hood glanced at the black sedan. The marine was right. Of course the vehicle was heavily protected. That was the car that traveled with the Chinese prime minister.

Suddenly, the sedan revved its engine and sped toward

them. Anita must have heard from her father what was being planned. Hood was certain that the prime minister had told her to leave. Hood also did not doubt that she was going to try to give them a way out.

Hood watched anxiously as bullets flashed off the roof and hood. They dented the metal but did not go through it. White scrapes appeared on the windows as gunfire skidded across the dark surfaces. One of the choppers moved in lower. It evidently intended to try to pick off the men when they tried to get into the car.

Behind them, steam began hissing from vents in the rocket as coolant was pumped through thick capillaries in the metal skin.

The car stopped about twenty feet beyond the clamp, at a point where the coolant pipes turned away from the launchpad. The passenger's side was facing the two men. The door opened.

"Come on!" Anita yelled.

The marine rose and peered over the topmost coolant pipe. He looked out and began typing a text message.

"We have to run for it," Hood said.

"You'll never clear that open space," the marine told him. "Give me another few seconds."

"These idiots may hit the rocket," Hood said. "They're shooting wild—"

"They won't. The fireball would catch them, too."

The kid was right. The chopper descended and fired more carefully on their position. Hood felt foolish as the men dropped back behind the pipes. The marine had a grasp of the obvious that Hood had somehow lost or misplaced. That was the problem with having a head too full of experience. Information was something you kicked around behind a desk. In the field, it obscured instinct and wisdom.

Fortunately, Hood did not dwell on his failings. The clang of the bullets on the metal was unnerving. The marine finished typing his message, then sent it to the other members of his team.

Suddenly they heard the drumbeat of coordinated fire from the other side of the sedan.

"Are the choppers within range?" Hood asked.

"No. They won't be able to get any lower."

"Then what are your guys firing at?" Hood asked.

"Just be ready to follow me," the marine said as he moved into a crouching position facing the car.

Hood turned and looked over the marine's shoulder. He looked past the sedan at the blast shield where it had been parked a minute before. Flashes were sparking off the transformer—one bullet after another in the same spot. Finally one of them punched through the gas tank and another followed it through. The hot shells ignited the fuel and caused a small blast that sent smoky plumes of dark smoke rolling upward.

"Follow me," the marine said.

The young man rose, his shoulders hunched low, and moved to the edge of the pipes. Hood followed him. They stopped just a few feet from the car. As the smoke continued to blanket the area, the marine put his left arm around Hood's shoulders. He pulled him close, shielding Hood with his own body.

"On my word we run for the car," the marine told him.

The gunfire thinned as the smoke obscured the launchpad. Hood felt himself being ushered forward, even as the marine shouted, *"Now!"*

The two ran toward the car. Bullets pierced the thick cloud as they crossed the open space between their makeshift sanctuary and the car. It was only six or seven yards, but each step seemed like a long flight of stairs. Smoke and fear took Hood's breath away as they ran ahead. As the smoke thickened, the driver beeped his horn to give them a beacon. Hood could hear the delicate whiz of gunfire and the jazzlike beat it produced as it struck metal and pavement. When they reached the car, Hood was shoved forward onto the leather seat. He scrambled across to make room for the marine. The young man literally dove in after him.

"Go!" the marine shouted as he turned and pulled the door shut.

"Is there anyone else we need to pick up?" Anita asked.

"No," the marine replied. "I told my coworkers to head for the command bunker once we were rescued."

Hood looked at the young man as the car sped off. "Are you all right?"

"Intact, sir," the marine said.

Anita turned and regarded the young man. "You are not a scientist," she declared.

The marine put the gun in its holster. He did not answer. He looked out the window at the retreating launchpad.

"Who are you?" Anita demanded.

Hood responded. "He's just a man who may have helped save your space complex and your father's government." Hood smiled. "Speaking of saving, thanks for pulling us out of there."

Anita looked at Hood. Gunfire continued to hit the car. Depending on the angle, the shots rang like a bell or sounded like a cat scratching. The sedan left the asphalt and began racing across the field that separated the launchpad from the Technical Center. The rutted ground caused the car to bump and rattle. The high, rigid grasses sounded like steel wool along the chassis. But all of the sounds, all thought and lingering questions, vanished when the booster lit up. It was about three quarters of a mile behind them. Hood heard a deep blast, then felt the car tremble. Everything from the license plates to the seat belts rattled, like teeth. The vehicle was literally bumped forward, skidding slightly as a shock wave hit the car. The invisible fist rolled over the roof and rattled the grasses in front of them. The air itself was distorted as the hot wind blew through.

Hood and the marine turned. The helicopters went into retreat as opaque, lumpy waves of gray-and-white smoke spilled from the bottom of the rocket. The rocket towered above the flat countryside, stark against the distant mountains. It was quickly obscured as thick clouds crawled in all directions. The smoke all but smothered the red orange flames that flashed deep within. A second wave of air rushed toward them, superheated gas from the postignition burn. The air in the car quickly grew very hot. The smell of melting rubber filled the interior as the seams around the windows softened.

"What is the time frame?" Anita asked anxiously.

"You mean, when do we know if we've succeeded?" Hood asked.

"We are twenty seconds from what should have been liftoff," the marine answered. He was looking at the digital numbers on his watch.

Hood was impressed that he was professional enough to do that. Though he realized, of course, that they would know soon enough how things were going. If the clamp blew up, they had failed.

It occurred to Hood that these could be the last moments of his life. Even if the clamp were destroyed, and the bomb with it, the rocket could still fall over. If it did, the size of the explosion would depend upon how much fuel remained in the tanks. Dying was bad enough. Dying, knowing that Tam Li had succeeded, even without the explosion, would be worse. Even if the prime minister moved to have him arrested, there were powerful elements in the government that would back the general, men who wanted a final showdown with Taiwan.

The clamps and most of the rocket were entirely obscured by the thickening exhaust. The rumbling roar was all around as the engines strained to carry their payload aloft.

"The first-stage rockets only have another fifteen seconds of burn in them," the marine said. "They're going to shut off at approximately the moment the bomb would probably go off."

"Probably?" Anita said.

"The bomber does not benefit if it explodes after the rocket has lifted off," the marine informed her.

Hood was only half-listening to the exchange. Once again, he was impressed with the marine's clear-headed reasoning and the pertinent facts he had picked up during his tenure. Though it also made Hood sad. Unlike Op-Center's late Striker force, this man had enjoyed some prep time before going on his mission, as well as time to reconnoiter on the ground. That made a great deal of difference.

"Five seconds," the marine announced, looking at his wristwatch.

The smoke was now black and gray. More than the fuel was burning. The pipes they had been hiding behind were probably gone. There was a small red-and-yellow flash from the area of the transformer. The intense heat must have destroyed everything behind the blast shield.

The car continued to bounce across the field. It was sweltering and extremely stuffy inside, but they did not dare open the windows. Though the helicopters appeared to have left, the car would still afford them some protection from any shrapnel that might come flying off the rocket.

The marine lowered his wrist. "Zero," he said.

A moment later the rumbling stopped. The only sounds were the thumping of the car as it raced across the final stretch of the field. The smoke dissipated slowly, and the rocket was visible wherever the sunlight found its white skin.

"Oh, shit," Hood said.

It was an involuntary remark, uttered as he watched flames claw at the base of the rocket. The bomb had not exploded. They had apparently succeeded in melting the device. But smoke was curling from behind every plate and rivet as fire crawled up the depleted booster. Whatever was under the exterior skin was burning: tubing, electronics, everything flammable.

It was making its way to the second stage.

A stage that was fueled.

FIFTY-NINE

Xichang, China
Thursday, 12:02 P.M.

"Purge the second-stage fuel!"

Prime Minister Le Kwan Po was sitting at a communications console in a private room of the Technical Center. He had declined an offer to be evacuated. He wanted to see this through. And his daughter was still out there.

Five crews were quickly mobilized. Through a headset, he was listening to the conversation taking place at the command center. The discussion was between the mission director and the chief of launch operations. Because of the expedited countdown, technicians had not been able to fully drain the fuel from the upper stage before the hoses were burned. The director's command was unequivocal, but the CLO had reservations. A color monitor in the console showed the burning rocket. A pair of technicians were sitting on either side of the prime minister. One of them was on the telephone with an observation tower near the front gate.

"Sir, there is very little fuel in there. If we release it, we will feed the fire, and we risk a complete vehicular melt-down," the CLO said.

"The plutonium core will likely survive the heat," the director said. "It may not survive an explosion if the flames get that high."

"With respect, I do not see much difference between 'likely' and 'may,'" the CLO pointed out. "And with the fuel on the ground, we will have a terrible fire to try to contain."

"We can contain a fire easier than fallout," the director said. "Dump the fuel now before the fire climbs any higher."

"Yes, sir," the CLO said.

Le Kwan Po removed his headset but continued to watch the screen. "Where is my daughter's car?" he asked the technician.

"Safe," he replied. "It is just leaving the field."

"Thank you," the prime minister said.

Anita and the others were safe for now, at least. The prime minister watched as what looked like steaming water poured from four spouts in the midsection of the rocket. One of the technicians explained that the mixture was composed of liquid oxygen and kerosene. The downpour hit the rising flames with a flourish, drawing sheets of flame from the smoke below. They rose on all sides like an orchestral crescendo, wrapping the rocket in a blanket of fire. The camera operator zoomed in on the payload, a gumdrop-shaped container perched atop the second stage. The flames did not yet reach that high, though ugly black smoke from the spilling fuel curled around it, driven by small air currents.

"We're losing her!" one of the technicians barked.

Le Kwan Po watched as the top of the rocket began to list. The camera pulled back as the sixty-meter-high rocket pivoted unsteadily on its base, moving away from the gantry like a baby taking a first step. Apparently, both of the restraining clamps had been destroyed. Then the rocket began to fall toward the left, away from the support tower and into the unbroken wall of flame. Though the fuel tanks were nearly empty, spillage picked up on the lower side as the rocket tilted. The fires sizzled and flashed higher. In moments, the nuclear payload would fall into the inferno.

Le Kwan Po could feel the tension of the other men as they watched the cataclysmic ballet.

As the rocket vanished in the mound of coal-black smoke, a bright, white explosion flashed from somewhere inside.

"What was that?" one of the technicians asked. "The payload should not have exploded that way."

"Could it have been the bomb?" the other man asked.

Le Kwan Po said nothing. There was nothing to say. The men watched as the mountain of black smoke took on a pale, ashen color at the base. Long gray tendrils crawled through the gantry and up from the fallen rocket. The smoke thinned quickly, and the fires subsided considerably. The camera moved in. The rocket itself was still obscured by smoke and fire. Except for the skeletal gantry and a charred blast wall, the surrounding structures were devastated.

"The coolant tank is gone," one of the technicians said. There was joy in his voice. "That was what caused the flare. A blast of steam."

"Are we all right?" Le Kwan Po asked.

"I think so, sir," the technician replied tentatively. He peered closely at the monitor. "The coolant has a thirty-seven percent water content. It is designed to evaporate so the rocket does not have to carry it aloft. It appears the water has doused whatever fires it touched."

"There is no oil in the fuel mixture?"

"No, sir," the technician replied. "Only hydrogen and oxygen."

The gentle winds in the launch area caused the smoke

to thin. The wreckage of the rocket was visible now, lying in puddles of fire and debris. The first stage was lying across the launchpad. The second stage and payload were separated from the first and from each other. They were spread across the asphalt. The payload section appeared to be intact.

The Americans had done a formidable job.

Le Kwan Po thanked the technicians for their hospitality, then left the bunker. He went up the concrete stairs to the main room. The guard had been watching the event with binoculars through the open doorway. She turned.

"I am happy to say that your daughter has returned safely," she said. "May I ask if the operation was a success?"

"It is strange to call the destruction of our rocket a success, but I believe you can say that," the prime minister said.

The guard smiled for the first time, then returned to her desk. Le Kwan Po walked into the once-bright noon, which was now clouding over with smoke. Sirens screamed in the distance as the space center fire department rushed to the blaze. He saw all that in just a moment. Everything vanished as he saw his daughter step from the car. Anita ran forward and embraced her father.

"I think you were five or six," her father said.

"Five or six?"

"The last time you ran to me," Le told her. There was a catch in his voice and tears on his cheek.

Anita smiled warmly. "You should be pleased you raised such a self-sufficient daughter."

"I am more than pleased," he said. "I am proud. Very, very proud."

Le broke the embrace as Paul Hood and another man walked by. They had walked well out of the way to give the prime minister and his daughter privacy. There would be time enough for that later. Right now he wanted to talk to the men.

"Mr. Hood," he said, speaking directly to the American in broken English.

"Sir?" Hood said. He stopped.

Le Kwan Po motioned for his daughter to interpret. "I want to thank you and your associates for everything you did out there."

"Sir, we got very lucky out there," Hood said.

"Men make their own luck," the prime minister replied.

"Perhaps," Hood said. "But it looked to me like the coolant did a lot of the heavy lifting."

"The pipes were weakened because Mr. Hood and his friend hid there, and Tam Li's men were shooting at them," Anita said.

"You see?" Le told her. "Nothing is entirely the work of chance."

Anita translated for Hood while Le regarded his Asian companion. He was a young man, dirty and slick with perspiration, but with eyes full of purpose. He was looking at his cell phone.

"I would like to meet this other hero," the prime minister said to Hood.

"He is one of Mike Rodgers's associates," Hood said.

The young man looked up as the prime minister offered his hand. "Thank you for the work you did today."

"I am glad I could help, sir," the marine replied in Chinese.

"May I ask your name?"

"It is Kim." The young man smiled.

"You are not Chinese," the prime minister said. "Korean?"

"No, sir," the marine replied. "American." He held up his phone. "Sir, I've just received word that some of my associates were slightly injured by gunfire from the helicopters. I would like to see them."

"My driver will take you," Le Kwan Po said. "And thank you again."

"It was an honor to meet you, sir," the young man answered.

While Anita finished translating for Hood, Le turned. The dignitaries who had come to watch a launch were beginning to file from the basement observation area. They asked questions in several different languages, and Anita went to see what she could do to calm the group. Several of them pointed at her father. At his expression in particular. They seemed mystified by the fact that the prime minister had the hint of a smile on his face.

Le walked toward the bunker quickly but without urgency. He excused himself from answering questions with a polite wave. He had to telephone the president and the minister of defense. He had to let the former know what had happened. He wanted the latter to make sure that any other aspects of Tam Li's plans were stopped, and the general was brought to swift justice. Both men would already have been briefed through channels, but he wanted to give them his perspective. That report would be his political trophy for seeing this through.

He entered the communications room and asked the two technicians to excuse him. They left without question, shutting the door behind them. The prime minister sat and placed the first call.

The failure of their communications satellite was a setback. But compared to what the nation had gained, it was worth the price. They had stopped a general from a scheme they had yet to ascertain. More importantly, they had done so by forging an international union among longtime adversaries. In so doing, they had moved a step closer to peace.

That was important to a prime minister. But it was enough to make any father smile.

SIXTY

Zhuhai, China
Thursday, 12:18 P.M.

With regret but also with resolve, General Tam Li sent the stand down code to his forces. All it took was a password entered into his computer and a typed command sent to both air and sea command at the base. The officers in charge relayed the message to their assets in the field and to the other bases from which planes and ships had departed.

Tam Li had learned of the failure of the bomb from his airborne group commander. The general had not anticipated much of a risk if the security team were captured when they left the space center. He thought it would be too late to get to the bomb. He was mistaken. Before leaving the complex, the airborne team leader said that the rocket boosters had been ignited prematurely and apparently melted through to the bomb, preventing it from exploding.

It was a very clever maneuver, desperate but effective.

The general shut down his computer and rose. He looked out the window at the sea. This was supposed to have been his moment of ascension. Instead of rising to the sun like the planes he had recalled, he had fallen to earth. It was not in the best interest of the nation to proceed with the attack on the Taiwanese military. Not now. Without the sabotage of the rocket, he would not convince Beijing that Taiwan had been seeking to take advantage of Chou Shin's treasonous act.

If any of his security team confessed, he would not convince Beijing that Chou Shin had been responsible for this attack. That was the reason for using Chou's bomb-maker instead of their own. Tam Li did not just want to defeat his foe—he wanted to blame him. Everything had depended upon the events happening one after the other, until Beijing was in so deep militarily that there was just one way out: to crush Taiwan. With that little financial engine out of the way, and Tam Li in a new position of authority, he would have been able to turn China into the strongest, most fertile financial power in the region. Even Japan, with its deepening debt, would not have been able to compete. Some of those profits would have gone to modernizing and expanding the military. Some would have gone to Tam Li and his associates. With its vast workforce and resources, China would have become the world's greatest superpower in Tam Li's lifetime. Unlike the plans of other conquerors, there would have been a minimal amount of strife and bloodshed.

The vision had been so clear, the end so clearly attainable. The plan itself had been clean and perfect.

Now it was dead.

Tam Li found that fact difficult to process. It had been in the works for over a year. It had occupied his thoughts constantly as he maneuvered the strife with Chou Shin, planted his personnel at the space center, felt success come nearer and nearer. His peripheral vision caught sight of the firearms in a display case. These were the guns he had carried throughout his career. He thought of using one now to avoid the inquiries and eventual trial. He decided against it, not from cowardice but for principle. He still believed that China was destined to dominate the globe. His people had been using explosives when the rest of the world was still fighting each other with spears and boiling oil. China would seize that advantage again.

But not today. And not with General Tam Li leading the assault.

He did not turn from the window but continued to look outward. Toward the future. He stood there even when there was a harsh knock at the door. The door was unlocked. After a minute the men entered. They stepped behind the general and asked him to come with them.

Tam Li turned. One of the three men standing in the sharp sunlight was a vice admiral, his own handpicked chief of base security. A half hour before, this small, gray-haired man had been an ally.

"The prime minister has asked to see you," the vice admiral said.

"Only me?"

"Yes," the vice admiral replied.

The naval officer's expression was stern save for his sad, guarded eyes. The vice admiral knew it was within Tam Li's power to stop the investigation by taking the blame for all the misdeeds. He could also boot the responsibility back down the chain of command and take others with him.

Tam Li smiled. "There is no reason for him to see anyone else, is there?" the general asked.

"I would not know," the vice admiral replied.

"Who will be running operations here?" Tam Li asked.

"Officially, that is no longer your concern. You have been relieved."

"Unofficially?" Tam Li pressed. He did not move.

The vice admiral's unhappy expression showed that he understood the choice. He could be stubborn and risk being named by the general. Or he could bend the rules of de-

tention and tell the general what he wanted to know. In so
doing, he would lose face in the eyes of the two security
officers.

"Come with us, General," the vice admiral replied.

Tam Li was pleased. The vice admiral still had a backbone. He was willing to risk his future to preserve his credibility as a commander. Perhaps he knew that the general
would not seek to bring him down. Through the vice admiral at least the idea of Chinese supremacy would remain
alive. If he would not undertake another operation like this
one, he might inspire someone under him to try.

Tam Li left between the two security officers, the vice
admiral leading the way through hallways the general once
commanded. The general stood with his shoulders back,
beaten but undefeated. No one saluted as he was walked
through the compound to a waiting helicopter. Most of
them probably had no idea what had happened. Perhaps
they thought this was about Chou Shin's airplane or some
other high-level machination. Whatever they thought, the
staff was doing what most people do in a time of crisis.
They stayed clear of the event.

Mao had learned that successful revolutionaries have
unyielding allies. Defeated revolutionaries have unyielding
quarantine. This was not the kind of fallout Tam Li had expected, but he would take the heat. He would stand trial
and describe what he had done and why. In a land of over a
billion souls, someone would hear.

Someone would continue what he had begun.

Or rather what someone else had begun, he thought,
smiling with pride. Those bold and curious ancients who,
like him, had used explosives to announce a Chinese presence on the world stage.

SIXTY-ONE

Beijing, China
Friday, 10:00 A.M.

The state-run newspapers and telecasts said very little about the loss of the Chinese rocket. They reported that there had been an accident at Xichang involving "foreign-built technology" but offered little elaboration.

It was typical of China, Hood thought. Every failure was easy to hide and absorb because every step forward was tentative, uncertain, almost apologetic. Even if Tam Li had succeeded in getting his confrontation with Taiwan, even if he had enjoyed a personal bump in power, he might not have gotten the coup he apparently sought. After centuries of war and upheaval, the giant nation had become entropic. Change would be slow and prompted by outside economic investment, the spread of technology to the remote farms and mountains, the glacial improvement in education and the quality of life. China probably would not change dramatically in Hood's lifetime.

Hood wondered if that was also true of Anita.

The prime minister's daughter had come to the embassy

to see him off. She had been there before, at official receptions, but never without her father. Hood saw her in the downstairs library. Anita was standing in the center of the room. She was dressed conservatively in a black skirt and white blouse. She turned when he entered. The big, open smile on her face surprised him.

"Well, that's nice to see," Hood said.

"What is?"

"Your smile," he replied.

"Oh," she said self-consciously as she frowned her way into a more neutral expression. "Is this better?"

"You didn't have to do that. I liked it," Hood said. He motioned toward the high walls lined with leather-bound volumes and even occasional scrolls tucked in cylindrical cases. "This is obviously your idea of heaven."

"If I believed in heaven, it would be," she said.

She was looking directly at Hood when she said that. He wondered if he had just made a big foot-in-mouth faux pas. This woman did risk incineration to save him, after all.

"Did you sleep well?" she asked.

"Like Rip Van Winkle," he replied as he reached her side.

"I'm glad to hear that."

"You?"

"The same," she said. "My father is sorry he could not be here."

"I am sure today will be a busy day," Hood said.

"He barely slept last night," Anita said. "But it was a good insomnia, if there can be such a thing. He was more energized than I have seen him in a long time."

"I assume there will be a trial," Hood said.

"There will be hearings, but I suspect they will be private. My father does not want to give Tam Li a forum."

"Understandable," Hood said.

"Do you think so?" Anita asked. "I would have expected you to be an advocate for free speech."

"I don't think a government official should be allowed to justify the lies he told and the murders he authorized to send his nation into a reckless and lawless war," Hood said.

"I am glad to see that we agree," Anita said.

"If we had the time, we would probably find we agree on a great deal," Hood told her.

"By the way, my father asked me to tell you that he attempted to thank General Rodgers and your other associates yesterday," Anita said. "But they seem to have disappeared."

"Mike left right away on a Lufthansa flight," Hood told her. "He called and told me they had insurance matters to discuss immediately back in the States."

"I see. And the others? The young men and women?"

"I suppose they went back to work."

"At the space complex?" she asked.

"I don't know," Hood replied. "I did not have time to speak with them."

Unlike the other night, Anita let the interrogation rest. She had obviously realized there was more to be gained by long-term trust than short-term pressure. She did a little turn around the library. "I like that story very much," she said.

"Which one?" Hood asked.

"*Rip Van Winkle*. I like all of Washington Irving, in fact. Now there is an author who captured the real American. Not jingoistic, militaristic ideologues."

"What is your definition of 'the real American'?" Hood asked.

"The tough but good-hearted innocent," she said. "You are that, I think."

"Is that a good thing?" Hood asked. He was not sure that it had been a compliment, entirely.

"It is very good. Innocence is a clean slate," she replied. "It is open and receptive to outside ideas. The toughness makes it discretionary. It only allows ideas that are enriching."

"There is one place where the author may have captured something more universal than that," Hood said.

Anita's smile returned. "Waking up from a long slumber and expecting the world to be the same," she said.

Hood had been formulating an answer more or less along those lines. Her smart and self-aware response stopped his thought process dead. There was nothing he could add to that except an impressed little smile.

"China has indeed been internally focused for many, many years," she said. "But we do not expect the world to stay still. We expect to learn from the mistakes of others. My father taught me that all of civilization is still relatively young, composed of creatures who are closer to the caves than to the heavens. He believes that if we move too quickly we risk making catastrophic errors. He is correct. Look at what happened yesterday. Our rush to embrace the technology of other nations, to gain scientific parity, nearly resulted in disaster."

Hood's smile broadened. "I was not alluding to China," he said.

Anita was still for a moment, and then her pretty face flushed. Now she was the speechless one.

"I'm sorry," Hood said. "I did not mean to embarrass you."

"I believe you did," she said, still flustered.

"Absolutely not," he assured her. "You heard the thunder. You heard the sound of little men playing duckpins, but you did not rise with uncertainty or confusion. You jumped up. You saved my life."

The woman relaxed somewhat. "I thought you meant—"

"That you are a bearded old man with sore knees?"

"That I am living in a political, academic, and cultural cocoon." She smiled.

"Anita, the chances are very good I would never even have used all those words in one sentence."

"You're being modest, which is one of the things I've come to admire about you," Anita said. "Though you were very wrong about one thing. It was ninepins."

"Excuse me?"

"The little men in *Rip Van Winkle* were playing ninepins, not duckpins," Anita informed him.

Hood smiled as modest a smile as he could muster. "I have a suggestion. When you can get away for a week or so, why don't you come to America. We can take a drive to the Hudson Valley where Washington Irving wrote, see if there are pins of any kind lying around in the countryside."

"I would like that," she said.

"I promise there will be fewer fireworks," Hood said.

"Why? Fireworks can be nice," she said.

"Then you should come to America on the Fourth of July," Hood said.

"I was not alluding to pyrotechnics," Anita said over her shoulder as she walked toward the door.

Now it was Hood's turn to blush. He did not follow her out but waited. He would not have known what to say after that. Which was almost certainly what the woman had intended.

Hood did not feel too bad, however. Anita did say the ideal American was innocent.

He glanced at his watch and realized he was late. There was a car waiting to take him to the airport. Like Rodgers, Hood would be flying commercial.

That was one good thing about a government job. It was a bureaucracy. Unlike private industry, accountability did not have to be immediate. Which was a good thing. Because right now, a comfortable seat and a few mindless DVDs sounded like a great idea before tackling his mission report for the president.

SIXTY-TWO

Washington, D.C.
Friday, 10:22 A.M.

The phone call from General Raleigh Carew was not unexpected. His message, however, was not at all what General Carrie had anticipated. She suspected it would not be good when the chairman of the Joint Chiefs of Staff called on her private, secure cell phone rather than on the office phone. Op-Center would have no record of the call being received.

"He won," Chairman Carew said unhappily. "But that is not what bothers me the most."

By "he," General Carrie assumed Carew meant Paul Hood and, by extension, the president.

"He defused this situation with the help of one of your people and with your field team," the chairman went on. "He assembled an ad hoc intelligence group that, in fact, was simply his old team burning through overhead provided by others. Do you understand what I am saying?"

"Not entirely," Carrie admitted.

"The president has a personal crisis management czar

now," Carew said. "This individual has no staff and, if we can control the funding, he will never have much of one. So what did he do? He successfully, I would say brilliantly, outsourced this mission. He cannibalized from you, from Unexus, and from the bloody damn Chinese."

"Mr. Chairman, with respect, I think you are overreacting to a singular situation," Carrie said. "Our marines were on site in Xichang, positioned to act independently if they had to. General Rodgers sent them to help Paul Hood, who was already at ground zero for the attack—"

"According to the report I just read from Paul Hood, your man Bob Herbert relayed the SOS to Mike Rodgers."

"He did that, yes," Carrie agreed. "Are you saying we should have left Hood out there without backup?"

"The mission should have come first," Carew said.

"I'm sorry, but I believe it did. I read the same report, Mr. Chairman. We appear to have stopped an attack against Taiwan."

"That is speculation."

"Taipei reported that radar had picked up an unusually high level of PLA activity in the region."

"Which was terminated by Zhuhai command," Carew said. "We don't know what they were planning. That is what intelligence is for, Morgan. And right now we have lost four sources for that. Your undercover marines were sent to China as floaters. Their specific mission in this instance was to protect a satellite from being destroyed. The intelligence Mr. Herbert possessed should have gone to the team leader so he could determine a course of action. It should not have gone to Paul Hood."

Carew practically spat the name. Carrie understood now why he had not said it before.

"The marines and Hood were in the same place," Carrie said. "And it was General Rodgers who obtained the intelligence from a Chinese source."

"You are missing my point," Carew said sternly. "The

marines were drawn into a mission that was designed and executed by Paul Hood. Mr. Hood was replaced because he has never followed a playbook. He ran Op-Center based on cronyism, on questionable international interests and alliances, and used civilian attitudes on military operations. His approach caused dozens of military casualties."

"I am not a fan of Mr. Hood," Carrie said. "But in fairness, he also defused numerous international crises."

"Mike Rodgers did that. Colonel Brett August did that. Lieutenant Colonel Charlie Squires did that. They were the men in the field, improvising their way through situations in which Hood had placed them. Our boys signed on to protect the United States of America. Instead, they have given their lives to protect India, Japan, and Russia. We are not the intelligence police of the world, Morgan."

She could not disagree with that assessment. Years before Homeland Security was given the job of defusing domestic crises, that had been the chartered task of Op-Center—the National Crisis Management Center.

"Hood did his reckless seat-of-the-pants thing again in Xichang," Carew said. "No one was consulted, no one gave him any parameters. And he dragged your people into it. The press and the president look at the gains. They crow about how we saved lives, created an international bond. I look at the debits. I don't care about the rocket, I don't give a damn about the prime minister, and I am not concerned about what would have been a very short pissing match in the Taiwan Strait. In fact, I might have gone along with it."

"An air and sea battle that we would have been committed to be part of?" Carrie said.

"It would not have lasted long enough for us to do much," Carew said. "I've read the file on General Tam Li. He was a progressive, a black market capitalist. He got rid of Chou Shin, a hard-line Communist who was no friend of ours. He apparently blew up a boat in Charleston and a nightclub in Taipei. Maybe Tam Li should have become the next prime minister. He sounds like someone we could have dealt with."

General Carrie was trying to figure out where Carew was going. A rant like this did not come without a price.

"The lost political landscape is not for me to say," the chairman went on. "I am sure that Chinese security forces are reviewing tapes of the Xichang facility, looking to ID the team. What concerns me is that four highly trained intelligence operatives will have to be withdrawn."

Carrie did not know how to respond. She saw his point. The team had been compromised looking out for Chinese interests involving a satellite built by a largely European conglomerate. The gain for the United States was peripheral and hazy.

"Here's the bottom line," Carew went on, his tone a little softer now. "My vision for Op-Center is to make it larger and more effective. You know that, and I know you share that vision. Otherwise you would still be at G2. But I cannot get you the budget you need when your team makes someone else look good. Not when this man, Paul Hood, gives new meaning to the term Op—'one person.' I want Op-Center to have a good relationship with the other intelligence organizations as long as it does not compromise your mission or your charter, which is to defuse crises that affect this nation."

"I understand," Carrie replied.

"This is not about me, and it is not about you. It is about the uniforms we wear and the unique bond that gives us to the nation they represent."

"I understand that, too."

"I would like to see Mr. Herbert dismissed," Carew said.

Carrie was surprised by the request. "Mr. Chairman, I believe I can make him understand—"

"That's the point, isn't it?" Carew said. "You can't afford to have people there who require convincing. I've already spoken with the new topkick at G2. You can take whoever you want as an interim intelligence director while you search for a permanent replacement."

Carrie believed the chairman was overreacting. But she shared his vision for Op-Center and, while she could refuse to dismiss Herbert, there was something to be gained by making an object lesson of the intelligence chief. The NCMC could not tolerate loose cannons. They could not accommodate those with divided loyalties.

The general promised to take care of it and hung up. She called Liz Gordon first to tell her what was going to happen and to ask her advice on handling Herbert. The psychologist had known him for many years and had written nearly a dozen psych profiles of the man. In situations where post-traumatic stress could apply—the loss of his wife and his legs in Beirut—a yearly overview was mandatory.

"I think he's ready to move on, frankly," Liz said. "But that doesn't mean this will go down easy. Do you have to dismiss him?"

"I do," Carrie said. "Any advice?"

"He's gonna be Bob Herbert," Liz said.

"Meaning?"

"Expect him to be very bitter and sarcastic, but don't offer to help him find anything," she said. "Herbert does not like to feel disabled in any way."

"All right."

"Also, may I come to see you when you're finished?"

"Of course," Carrie said. "Make it eleven."

Liz thanked her, and Carrie hung up. She asked Bugs to have Herbert come to see her. She had already decided that he would not be escorted out by security guards. It would not be that kind of dismissal.

Bob Herbert arrived looking more rested than he had

since Carrie's arrival at Op-Center. The two had spoken only briefly after the mission was completed, and Herbert had seemed pleased with the way it worked out. She asked him to shut the door behind him.

"One-on-one before lunch," Herbert said. "That isn't good for me."

"What makes you say that?"

"There's nothing happening abroad; I've read all the intelligence briefings. So it's a local matter," Herbert said. "Things percolate through the D.C. political system at night, decisions get made in the dark, and those encyclicals are handed down early in the morning. For top officials, that means shortly after ten." He looked at his watch. "It's half-past ten now. Obviously, whatever this is, it could not wait." Herbert looked at Carrie. "Also, Paul Hood called me at home. The president is happy, but the Joint Chiefs are upset with how this played out, especially the exposure of the field ops. Someone has to be scapegoated for that."

Carrie was impressed by Herbert's comprehensive analysis. It gave her second thoughts about what she had to do.

"I am not happy with the way priorities were established by your office, nor with the overall evolution of the mission in China," Carrie said.

"Should we have let the rocket blow up and a Taiwanese force be annihilated while we collected intel?" Herbert asked.

"The mission parameters were about the payload, which was lost," she pointed out. "The situation in Taiwan is speculative and secondhand. Moreover, a team that had been seconded to Op-Center was exposed."

"That's not so bad," Herbert said. "We usually kill our field units."

She did not reply to that.

"When do you want my resignation?"

"That won't be necessary," she said.

Herbert seemed surprised for the first time. "What do you mean? Are you firing me?"

"Very reluctantly," she said.

"You're fucking *firing* me?" he exclaimed. "I take the fall for the marines so you don't have to?"

"You take the fall for the marines because you were the middleman between them and the orders of outsiders," Carrie said. "You acted unilaterally without considering the long-term effect on Op-Center."

"If I had not acted, the team would have been fried, along with two of our distinguished alumni!" Herbert shouted.

"That was not your decision to make," Carrie said.

"Like hell!"

"If you'd like, I can show you the job description," she said evenly. "The director of intelligence does not give orders unless they apply directly to the collecting of information. Since neither General Rodgers nor Mr. Hood was authorized to command the team, you should have gone to Mr. Plummer or myself."

"I don't believe this."

"I am not happy about it either, but I cannot have rogue directors working under me."

"Okay. I won't do it again."

"I know," she said firmly.

Herbert got the message. "Screw you, ma'am," he said, then turned and opened the door. He stopped. "If you send security, I'll piss on them," he warned without turning around.

"We would not want that to be your final act here," she said. "You can leave at your leisure."

"I'll be gone by lunchtime," Herbert said and wheeled himself through the door.

General Carrie was sorry the conversation had taken the turns it did, but there was no way to prevent that. The dismissal was humiliating, but Herbert would get another position. And Op-Center would be on notice that there was a chain of command that had to be followed.

She punched on the intercom. "Bugs, have Darrell come in and get me General Selby at G2. Tell Lowell Coffey I'll want to see him in an hour. Also, please get Liz on the phone."

"Yes, ma'am."

The first thing Carrie needed to do was replace Bob Herbert and have Darrell McCaskey ready to interface with the new person. She assumed McCaskey would stay on. Unlike Herbert, the former FBI agent was a career team player. As for Coffey, she wanted to make sure there was nothing Op-Center needed to do legally in regard to Bob Herbert. She wanted it understood that his dismissal was due to a serious infraction of policy and not his disability. She did not think he would pursue that route, but angry men often behaved unpredictably.

Bugs beeped. "Liz Gordon is on line two."

"Thank you," Carrie said as she scooped up the phone and punched the button. "Liz, can we postpone our chat till later?"

"Of course. How did it go?"

"Pretty much as you said. He's not happy."

"He holds on to grudges, but they're part of what fuels him," Liz admitted.

"Was there something you needed to talk about quickly?" Carrie asked.

Liz hesitated. "No." She added, "Not quickly."

"Okay. Then we'll get together in the afternoon, if that's all right."

"Sure."

There was something oddly reserved in the psychologist's answers. She was usually very outspoken. But General Carrie could not worry about that now. She had a command to run.

She had a responsibility that was greater than the moment and the people moving through it. Chairman Carew was right. There was a nation to keep secure.

Nothing was more important than that.

SIXTY-THREE

Washington, D.C.
Friday, 10:43 A.M.

Liz Gordon sat alone in her office. The door was shut, and air hummed from the vent overhead, from the back of her computer.

The machines were breathing easier than she was.

What the hell is going on? she asked herself.

She knew the answer, of course. General Carrie had grabbed her attention and teased her imagination. Liz would miss Bob Herbert. He was a fascinating man and a valued coworker. But Carrie's decisive action against his bad judgment had done more than impress her. It had encouraged and emboldened her.

It was schoolgirl stupid, but she had a crush on the woman. The question was what to do about it.

Liz had wanted to meet with the general to discuss counseling for staffers about the fallout of the firing. But Liz had really wanted to meet with the general so she could take another physical and emotional core sample on herself. To see if she could work with Carrie without being distracted by her. To see if perhaps Carrie found her intriguing or maybe more.

Perhaps it was just as well the meeting was delayed. That gave Liz a little more time to collect herself.

Into what? A more composed exterior? Her insides would be the same: roiling and eager, frightened and hopeful.

She thought back to Martha Mackall. It had been different with the late political liaison. Liz had liked the woman, but there was no chemistry. Martha was pushy, not strong. She was out for herself. The good of the organization did not matter to her. It mattered deeply to Morgan Carrie.

She said the name again in her head. It was a strong name. It went with her strong character.

It was not just her style of leadership that had won Liz Gordon, it was her attentiveness. Liz had spent the better part of two decades looking into people's eyes to see what they were about. The people who had nothing to hide looked directly at you. The people with something to share did so with words and with unflinching commitment. That came through the eyes.

During the limited time they had been together, General Carrie always looked at her flush, square, and bold. Liz did not think it was simply because Carrie had the confidence of a three-star general. Liz believed that all women shared a bond that transcended the practical needs of the moment. The notion of unimpeachable sisterhood was a myth. But the desire and capacity to love was strong. Especially among female soldiers who are forced to break the rules of traditional gender roles and behavior. In times of war they must be as aggressive as men. In times of peace, they work harder to recover their gentler humanity.

Being decisive at the helm of the NCMC was like being at war. General Carrie would also need downtime to reflect on that. A husband, even a caring and devoted one, could not understand that in quite the same way as a woman.

He could not. Another woman would not need the reclamation process explained to her. Especially if that woman were in the trenches as well.

Of course, not every woman understood that she required the attention. Sometimes she had to be educated. Therein lay the delicacy of the situation. Liz did not know what General Carrie knew or understood or sensed.

But she would.

The psychologist tried to concentrate on work as her heart throbbed anxiously in her throat. She made a list of the people who had worked closely with Bob Herbert, who would be hardest hit by his firing. Darrell McCaskey, of course. But the man was a professional and would roll with it. Lowell Coffey—who did not get along with the intelligence chief but respected him—and Ron Plummer, who found Herbert sharp but abrasive. Their main concerns would not be about Herbert but about how to avoid his fate. How to make sure Op-Center ran smoothly and efficiently during the transition. That was surely the result Carrie was after.

Liz had to be careful she did not upset that goal, or she could be dismissed herself.

It was exciting and frightening, uplifting and unnerving. For the first time in a long time there was optimism in the psychologist's racing heart and a powerful sense of belonging.

Life was good.

SIXTY-FOUR

Washington, D.C.
Friday, 3:48 P.M.

"Life sucks," Herbert said into his glass.

Bob Herbert and Mike Rodgers were sitting at a small rectangular table in Off the Record when Paul Hood arrived. The tavern was located just below street level at the elegant Hay-Adams Hotel, a short distance across Lafayette Park from the White House. Hood walked over, enjoying the warm, clear late afternoon. It was remarkable how clean the air was compared to Beijing and even Xichang. Or maybe he was just happy to be back and intact. It was probably a lot of both. On the way he phoned the kids to see how they were doing. He also phoned Gloria Lynch-Hunt to make sure they still had a date for tomorrow night.

The kids were fine. The date was on.

Life was good.

After an unsteady start, Hood was actually fairly alert. The new executive crisis management adviser had slept until eleven. Yawning but alert, he went to his office at the White House where he had a brief meeting with President

Debenport. Since Hood had already filed an overview report he had written on the plane—the Ben Affleck movie was not one he had been wanting to see—the Oval Office meeting was primarily a chance for the commander in chief to congratulate him. Even Chief of Staff Lorraine Sanders was complimentary.

It was easy to be gracious in victory, and Hood smiled a great deal. The big smiles also helped him to cover up the lingering yawns.

Chairman of the Joint Chiefs of Staff Raleigh Carew came by and offered a big handshake and a tight expression. He had come to see the president, not Hood. That marked the end of the Oval Office meeting.

Hood had intended to call the kids and go through his voice mail messages, then head to his new office. Even though his assistants would not be starting until Monday, he wanted to get a feel for the place. He was feeling good about his new position and wanted to be a participant in the process instead of a passenger. But then Bob Herbert called, asking to meet him at Off the Record. Herbert did not say what it was about, and Hood agreed to stop by.

Hood had not known that Rodgers was going to be there. He joined the men at the dimly lit table well away from the bar. It was strange to be together like this for the first time in months. It used to be a daily occurrence, usually strained by outside events or their own mismatched personalities. But it did not feel wrong. Whatever their differences, they had been through wars together. They had survived.

Bob Herbert made his comment about life and then fell silent. Herbert was often gloomy, so his pronouncement was not a surprise. What he said next, however, was very unexpected.

The Mississippi native looked up. "I got shit-canned, Paul."

"What?"

"The general fired me."

Hood was stunned. "No notice?"

"None."

"Why?" Hood asked.

"For helping you guys," Herbert said.

"I can't believe that," Hood said.

"I can," Rodgers told him.

Hood regarded him.

"There's a general in charge of Op-Center now," Rodgers said. "Officers run things very differently than civilians. Bob went outside the chain of command. The general made an example of him."

Rodgers's tone was cold. Perhaps it was Hood's imagination, but there seemed to be implicit criticism of the way he had run the NCMC.

"Do you agree with that?" Hood asked him.

"In theory, yes," Rodgers said. "In practice, I would have given the individual a warning."

"Gentlemen, can we not discuss whether my execution was an overreaction?" Herbert asked.

"Sorry," Rodgers said.

"That's okay," Herbert said as he drained his glass. "What happened is not important. What matters is that I'll know better next time. I won't answer any ads that say, 'Results matter less than the process.'"

Hood and Rodgers were silent.

The waiter came over. Herbert asked for a refill, and Hood ordered a cola.

"Pope Paul," Herbert muttered. "Did you know we used to call you that?"

"Yeah," Hood said.

"We all thought you were righteous and clean, above corruption." Herbert nodded. "You did a good job setting a moral tone. That's rare in government."

Rodgers raised his beer. Hood acknowledged with a nod.

"So. Any thoughts about what is next?" Hood asked.

"Defection? Maybe Prime Minister Le Kwan Po will give me a job."

"Don't joke about that," Rodgers said, looking around.

"Why? Is the military running the bar now?" Herbert asked.

Rodgers did not answer. Hood felt a chill. The drinks arrived, and Herbert sat back in his chair.

"No, Paul. I do not know what is next. I guess I'll hit my network and try to find a job. Probably in private industry."

"The regimentation is worse there," Rodgers said. "Especially if there are stockholders. Why don't you start your own think tank?"

"Ah, a consultancy," Herbert said. "The face-saving fallback of the fired."

"It doesn't have to be," Hood told him. "You have an impressive CV. You could attract other independent thinkers. I would be able to bring you in on some of my projects."

"Face-saving and a mercy fuck," Herbert said. "Thanks for the offer, but that's not what I need, guys."

"What do you need?" Hood asked.

"For that bitch in green to put me back where I belong, where I've served hard and well and loyally," Herbert replied.

The others were silent. They could not disagree with Herbert's ambition or the sentiment.

"If you want, I'll talk to the president," Hood said.

"You couldn't save your own ass from getting removed," Rodgers said.

"That was different—"

"Shit, I'm sorry," Herbert said. "I shouldn't have asked you here. I'm gonna be pissing fire for a while."

"That's nothing new," Hood said.

Rodgers smiled. Even Herbert chuckled.

For a moment, it was the old days again. Three men in stark disagreement but in concert about one thing: that

their unwieldy, cranky, dissimilar, and theoretically un-
workable parts somehow produced something unique and
important.

*The same could be said for Adams, Jefferson, and
Franklin,* Hood thought in a rare moment of uncritical indulgence. People could not have been much more different
than the New England attorney, the Middle Atlantic diplomat, and the Southern farmer who had created a new nation.

The reference to the past got them talking about old
times, about people who had come and gone, about missions and challenges, about victories and losses. Differences notwithstanding, they all had a lot to be proud of.

Hood took a long, mental drink of the moment. It would
probably never get any better than this. But how many men
were fortunate enough to have had this at all?

The hours passed. When it was time to go, there were
handshakes all around and a strong sense of camaraderie.

As well as a big, big question mark about when and
even if their paths might intercept again.

As he crossed the park, a line from a movie flashed
through Hood's mind. He could not remember which film
it was. He had watched it with the kids one rainy afternoon
years ago. A young woman was leaving her father to be
with her fiancé in some remote place. As the train approached, the woman wept, "God only knows when we
will see each other again."

And her father replied with a catch in his voice, "Then
we will leave it in His hands."

Hood felt the same as he walked toward the White
House and the future.